THE
MITFORD
VANISHING

JESSICA FELLOWES

THE MITFORD VANISHING

MINOTAUR
BOOKS
NEW YORK

Published in the United States by Minotaur Books, an imprint of St. Martin's Publishing Group

THE MITFORD VANISHING. Copyright © 2021 by Jessica Fellowes. All rights reserved. Printed in the United States of America. For information, address St. Martin's Publishing Group, 120 Broadway, New York, NY 10271.

www.minotaurbooks.com

The Library of Congress has cataloged the hardcover edition as follows:

Names: Fellowes, Jessica, author.
Title: The Mitford vanishing / Jessica Fellowes.
Description: First U.S. Edition. | New York : Minotaur Books, 2022. |
    Series: The Mitford murders ; 5 | First published in the United States
    by Minotaur Books, an imprint of St. Martin's in 2021.
Identifiers: LCCN 2021048552 | ISBN 9781250819208 (hardcover) |
    ISBN 9781250819215 (ebook)
Subjects: GSAFD: Mystery fiction.
Classification: LCC PR6106.E398 M5933 2022 | DDC 823/.92—dc23
LC record available at https://lccn.loc.gov/2021048552

ISBN 978-1-250-84872-7 (trade paperback)

Our books may be purchased in bulk for promotional, educational, or business use. Please contact your local bookseller or the Macmillan Corporate and Premium Sales Department at 1-800-221-7945, extension 5442, or by email at MacmillanSpecialMarkets@macmillan.com.

Originally published in Great Britain by Sphere, an imprint of Little, Brown Book Group, a Hachette UK company

First Minotaur Books Trade Paperback Edition: 2022

10 9 8 7 6 5 4 3 2 1

FOR CLARE

THE
MITFORD
VANISHING

PROLOGUE

~~~~~~~

The sun, so hot earlier in the day, had lowered, and a damp chill crept into the shadows where she was standing. She thought about the games of her childhood: the music stopping and everyone freezing, hardly daring to breathe in case the laughter that threatened to burst out made you move, and lose.

But she'd never lost a game as serious as this one.

She was crouching, her back to a brick wall, her knees pulled in as close as she could bear, almost willing herself to be hidden by the jumble of packages and ropes that were stacked around her. The sweat on her back began to cool and she shivered, but not from the dropping temperature. She had to resist closing her eyes and force herself to keep looking, reminding herself that, just because she could see them, it didn't mean they could see her.

She had run, fast, to the docks. Although it was approaching night-time, the place was busy, the air thick with shouts and commands in French, sometimes Spanish, occasionally English. Vast ships filled the narrow waterways that led out to the sea, their cargo stacked high, wooden totems of boxes and crates. She wondered whether they contained the contents of a person's life, packed and ready to be sent away over the ocean to somewhere brand-new where no one could lay claim to them or tell them what to do. With a desire so sharp she could have cut packing string with it, she wished she could fold herself into a box and nail it shut, be posted to a land more foreign and strange than this.

A man's shout. English.

Instinctively, she put her hand over her mouth to prevent herself from crying out. He mustn't find her here.

One, two. She stretched and stood, paused and then ran, faster than she'd ever run before, her heart beating in the base of her throat. She ran to stay alive.

PART ONE

CHAPTER ONE

The note from Nancy Mitford was delivered by a young boy in short trousers, which made Louisa laugh. Anyone would think it was Dickensian London, but this was 1937 and there were telephones and telegrams. Nancy had always been curiously old-fashioned, for all her love of cocktails and Chanel; Louisa rather loved her for it. The envelope was thick white paper and in the top left-hand corner was *By Hand* in black ink, underlined. The card inside had 'Mrs Peter Rodd' and Nancy's Maida Vale address embossed on it, but the first thing Louisa noticed was that the note had been scrawled – in haste, perhaps. Nancy's handwriting was usually easy to read, but not here. Louisa squinted and held the card a little closer.

Decca missing. M & F frantic. Police hopeless.
Please come to Rutland Gate. Urgently. N x

A summons from Nancy was not an altogether unusual thing, but the last time it had happened Louisa had ended up on a liner in the Mediterranean with Lady Redesdale, Nancy's mother, and Nancy's sisters, Diana and Unity, and they had become embroiled in a murder and the murkier side of British government. Admittedly, it hadn't *all* been Nancy's fault. Louisa looked down at the floor, where her baby girl, Maisie, almost a year old, was lying on the rag rug, happily gurgling at the woollen rabbit she held. Today was Louisa's final day at home before she joined her husband, Guy Sullivan, at work. From tomorrow, Maisie was going to be looked after by her grandmother, Guy's ma, who only lived around the corner. Old Mrs Sullivan had muttered her misgivings but Louisa and Guy had stood firm, and when she understood that it was either her or someone else looking after her granddaughter, she had agreed to do it. Now it looked as if Louisa was going to have to ask her mother-in-law to start a day early.

Louisa knew that Nancy was aware of Cannon & Sullivan, the private detective agency she and Guy had established six months previously. They rented a minuscule office space above a betting shop in Hammersmith, with two desks, a filing cabinet and a telephone. In fact, a few months before, when Nancy had sweetly said she'd like to meet Maisie, Louisa suggested they have tea in the office, knowing it would tickle her old friend. They had known each other almost twenty years now, meeting when Louisa had gone to work in the nursery of the Mitford household. In 1919, Louisa had been a bedraggled, frightened young girl escaping London, and Nancy had only just emerged from the schoolroom herself. In many ways, in spite of their differences, they had embarked on early adulthood almost side by side. Their relationship had its complications, but now – married and a mother – Louisa felt she had at last thrown off the shackles of servitude the Mitfords used to invoke in her. Which was why she questioned her hasty response to Nancy's request. Did she want to go, or did she *have* to go? Rutland Gate meant Lord and Lady Redesdale, her former employers – and not people given to thinking of former servants as anything but.

And yet.

Decca, the sisters' nickname for Jessica, the second to last youngest of the seven siblings, was nineteen years old, and Louisa had a hunch that the situation had to be more serious than her spending one night too many with a friend.

Not to mention that this could be Louisa's first official piece of work for Cannon & Sullivan.

Louisa picked her daughter up from the floor, held her warm, dumpling body close and kissed her smudge of a nose. 'Let's go and see Granny, shall we? Your mother has got to go to work.'

CHAPTER TWO

❧

With Maisie safely and happily ensconced in her grand-mother's arms, Louisa took the two buses necessary to get from Hammersmith to Rutland Gate. She considered telephoning ahead but, if circumstances truly were as Nancy described in her note, then she was bound to be with her parents at their London residence. Nor would any of them leave the house so long as news might reach them there. Louisa picked up a newspaper to read on the bus but, as she flicked through, she could see no headlines about Decca; either she hadn't been missing very long or they had managed to keep it quiet.

When Louisa first worked for the Mitfords, they had been living in a very pretty house in Oxfordshire, Asthall Manor, which had since been sold, much to everyone's regret. Lord Redesdale built a new house, Swinbrook, which Nancy insisted on calling Swine Brook; it was generally agreed to be too cold and too severe, and the family had sold it a few months before, stranding them, so Nancy claimed, in London. Even Nanny Blor, who'd looked after them all since Nancy was six, had moved to Rutland Gate. The thought of Blor made Louisa smile – she'd have liked her for her own Maisie. Not that she could entertain that idea for a second. It had been hard enough persuading Mrs Sullivan that she, Louisa, was going to work with Guy, let alone that she might employ someone to live in the house and look after Maisie while she did so.

Louisa jumped off the bus outside the Albert Hall and walked the last stretch fast. It was bitterly cold, with a wind that snapped at her ankles like a terrier. The house, with its stacked seven storeys, fronted out onto a small cul-de-sac, close to the wide green spaces of Kensington Gardens and Hyde Park. Louisa walked up the steps and knocked firmly. She was not arriving as a servant today.

It was a maid who opened the door, however. A young girl in a blue-and-white toile de Jouy dress with plain linen apron, the uniform that Lady Redesdale favoured for her staff. Louisa walked into the hall, relieved to feel its warmth, and took off her hat, fluffing her hair a little. 'Would you tell Mrs Rodd that Mrs Sullivan is here?'

'Yes, ma'am.' The maid ducked out of view for a minute or two before she came back. 'I'm to take you through, ma'am. Follow me, please.'

Louisa had never worked in this house. Even when she had stayed there the night before her wedding to Guy, it had been in the former coach house attached at the back. But she had visited Nancy and her mother there a few times before so was reasonably familiar with it. She expected to be taken into the library but was instead led up to the first floor where the drawing room was situated, a rather larger room. Louisa soon realised why the meeting was taking place there: it seemed that almost the entire

9

family was present. Nancy ran up to Louisa and kissed her on both cheeks with even more effusiveness than usual.

'Oh, darling, I'm so pleased to see you. As you can see, we're all in bits.'

Louisa looked around to see the evidence of this. Lady Redesdale perched on a narrow armchair by the fire, dressed in a plain skirt and twinset in navy, her face drawn and pale; she did not stand but acknowledged Louisa with a nod. Lord Redesdale was leaning on the mantelpiece, one hand in his pocket, looking rather older than Louisa remembered. His long, lean figure was dressed as elegantly as always, but his face was gaunt and his hair now the steel grey of a pan scrubber. He gave a grunt that could be loosely interpreted as a greeting. Louisa did not blame either of them for their abruptness: they were not people given to changing their view of the world, and former servants becoming equals in their drawing room was a bridge too far. Tom Mitford, their only son in a family of six daughters, was smoking a cigarette in a chair by the window. He turned and gave Louisa a 'Hi', his hand in the air, before he resumed his position, gazing listlessly at the street.

Debo came up too, just behind Nancy. The youngest of them all, she was in that sweet phase between being a girl and a woman, a touch plump and uncertain. She gave Louisa a kiss and grabbed one of her hands for a squeeze before dropping it quickly. 'It's so lovely to see you. I just wish . . .' Debo trailed off miserably and went to sit back down.

'I'm sorry to turn up unannounced, as it were,' said Louisa, 'but I got your note this morning, and it said it was urgent—'

'You sent her a note?' Lord Redesdale looked accusingly at his eldest daughter.

'Yes, I had to. We're at our wits' end, aren't we?' Nancy gestured to Louisa to sit down, so she pulled out a small wooden chair that had been hidden against the wall. Lord Redesdale flinched as the former nursery maid took a seat. Lady Redesdale barely acknowledged the action in the room; the cup of tea she held on her lap was half-drunk and grey. Nancy sat down on the sofa beside Debo.

'As you can see, most of the family has gathered here. Pam's in France with Derek in newlywed bliss, Unity is in Munich, although on her way back. And Diana is—' She hesitated and glanced at her parents before stage-whispering, 'Well, she's with the Ogre. We won't say any more about that.'

Louisa knew from Nancy that Diana, now divorced from Bryan Guinness, was living in sin with Sir Oswald Mosley. Which was presumably why her name was *verboten*.

'You said that Miss Jessica is missing.'

'Yes, she—' Nancy broke off. 'You're writing this down?'

'I don't want to get any of the facts wrong.'

'You really are a private detective?' asked Debo. 'Farve said it sounded like something out of one of Nancy's books.'

'Not that he would know,' said Nancy.

Lord Redesdale chose not to rise to this tease, but lit his pipe instead.

'Yes, Miss Deborah,' Louisa replied, trying to hold her nerve. She didn't want to tell them that this was the first assignment she had decided to take on. 'Mr Sullivan and I, we've set up our own agency.'

'He's left the police?' Tom had swivelled around. 'Why? He seemed to be doing rather well, from what I saw.'

Tom's work as a junior barrister on a case that Guy had

brought to the Old Bailey almost two years before had made them near colleagues at the time. But it was that very case that had led to Guy's resignation from the police force he had so proudly joined more than fifteen years earlier. Louisa and Guy no longer had blind faith in their government or its institutions. It was a destabilising feeling, one that had taken a while to get used to. When the king had abdicated the year before, he was no more than another falling domino to them, while the rest of the country reeled.

'It seemed like the right thing to do,' Louisa replied as briskly as possible, not wanting to get derailed by Tom. 'May I ask what the police response has been so far?'

'None,' growled Lord Redesdale. 'She's a grown woman, they say, knowing nothing of what an imbecile she is. This leaves her perfectly at liberty to do as she likes, according to the schoolboy who passed himself off as a constable.'

'Miss Jessica is nineteen years old now, yes? What has been the cause for concern, exactly? Can you tell me what happened, ideally from the moment you last saw your daughter?'

Lord Redesdale straightened up at this, but when he turned towards Louisa she saw the bewilderment and sadness in his face. 'I suppose you're our best hope at present.'

'I promise you that Mr Sullivan and I will do everything we can. In fact, if it reassures you, why don't we telephone the office and ask him to join us at this meeting? It would only take him half an hour to get here.' Louisa didn't like to admit that this was probably more for her reassurance than theirs, but she knew equally well that Lord Redesdale would prefer to talk to a man. He was of the Edwardian era; it wasn't his fault.

'Yes, yes, I think I would like that. Dear, what do you think?'

Lord Redesdale bent down and touched his wife lightly on the knee. She started at his gesture and looked up at him, her eyes red with worry.

'It's all my fault, isn't it? I knew she was unhappy. I just couldn't fathom why.'

'Let us bring Mr Sullivan in, then.'

Nancy stood. 'Follow me, Lou-Lou. I'll take you to the telephone. It's just in the hall downstairs.'

CHAPTER THREE

✦

When the telephone call came through to the office of Cannon & Sullivan, Guy was under the desk looking for a pencil he'd dropped. In his haste to catch the 'phone before it stopped ringing, he banged his head and knocked his glasses off. Not for the first time, he swore at the juxtaposition of his height and the smallness of his office.

When Guy resigned from Scotland Yard in the late summer of 1935, he knew it was what he had to do. But that hadn't prepared him for the grief he felt at leaving the career that had been his guiding force since he was a young man. Unable to fight in the war, thanks to his extreme short-sightedness, signing up to the police had been his way of serving his country and proving to his family that he had both a sense of duty and moral courage with the best of them. Promoted from the transport police to the London Metropolitan Force, his appointment as a detective inspector for Scotland Yard had been his proudest hour, and as he had looked down the track ahead of him, Guy had been reassured by the linear progression offered by his chosen career: further promotions with corresponding rises in salary and respect from his juniors, culminating in a handsomely pensioned retirement. Guy also liked to think he had a talent for the job, enjoying good working relationships with both his peers and his seniors, as well as solving the odd murder or two.

All of that had been shattered within minutes of Louisa confessing to him what she had known to be the hidden undercurrents of an investigation he had led and taken to the Old Bailey across two years. A secret that his most senior officers and the government had forced his wife to keep from him. Louisa always had a natural inclination to cynical suspicion – or at least a critical questioning of the country's finest institutions – but Guy knew that even she felt cast adrift by this revelation of their underhand methods. She too had given up her plans to become a court stenographer, unable to work for what presently felt like 'the wrong side'.

Still, they had each other, and that counted for a lot. In those uncertain months in the winter of 1935 they clung together even more closely, watching with joy as the bump in Louisa's belly grew. Guy knew that alone, he would have floundered, afraid and full of trepidation, but Louisa and the promise of their child rooted him and gave him strength. Together they planned the beginnings of their own private detective agency, one in which they would work as a partnership. Money was tight – both of them worked a series of odd jobs to raise the initial capital – but Louisa was nothing if not capable, never too proud to do whatever was necessary. Guy had watched with awe as each challenge seemed to set off more waves of efficiency and inventiveness in his wife, and she kept them both buoyed.

A few weeks before Maisie arrived, they moved into a two-up, two-down house a few streets away from his mother. They were ready to begin a life – even at their advanced ages of thirty-six and thirty-eight – as a family with their own business.

One year on, Guy was ready for Louisa to join him, physical space notwithstanding. Although he knew he loved Maisie with all his heart, and he loved them being a trio, he also missed spending time with his wife. He had waited so long to be with her that he still couldn't get enough of her. He had planned to spend his last day alone in the office tidying up and making it as welcoming as he could. He was even contemplating a trip to Peter Jones's china department – he'd been getting by with a cracked cup for himself, offering his only decent cup and saucer to clients.

Clients. There weren't quite enough of those, either. Guy had placed ads in the *Kensington Post* and *The Times* – 'Experience in all confidential work' and 'All cases undertaken' – but even his Scotland Yard history wasn't bringing in the jobs he'd hoped for. He'd handled one or two blackmail cases, but the vast majority of enquiries were from wives wanting their husbands to be followed for suspected infidelity, or husbands needing a 'co-respondent' in a divorce case. It had been rather depressing. It wasn't quite that a murder or a missing person would be cheering, exactly, but he felt that his capabilities were not being tested. He was almost beginning to worry that he might forget how to conduct an investigation. He hoped not only that he and Louisa would enjoy working together but also that her female presence would attract more – or, at least, different sorts of – cases. It was a modern world now, a world in which women worked and traffic clogged the streets of London, quite unrecognisable to the world he had grown up in, with King Edward VII on the throne and the sound of horses' hooves clip-clopping as they pulled carriages. There had been no telephones, no radios, no aeroplanes – even electricity had been a novelty. Now there was so much information, noise and new-fangled inventions everywhere, Guy sometimes wondered how a man could ever rest. These had been his thoughts as he had dropped his pencil, and then the telephone had rung.

CHAPTER FOUR

⁓

After Louisa had telephoned Guy, as she had predicted, he arrived at Rutland Gate with haste. While they were waiting for him, the maid brought a tray with a fresh pot of tea for everyone. Guy entered the drawing room with an air of professionalism and gravitas that made Louisa proud. She knew it was going to be difficult to prove herself his equal in the business – not because she was a woman but because he had a career as a detective inspector behind him. On the other hand, Louisa's childhood had exposed her to criminality, even if on a mostly minor level, before her subsequent involvement in one or two murder investigations ... She knew she could make a decent contribution. She was excited by that idea. But right now she was concerned for Decca. For several reasons, she would not have hoped for her first assignment to involve the Mitfords.

Guy politely refused the offer of tea and remained standing while he acknowledged the greetings from each member of the family. Pulling out his notebook, he flicked to a clean page and asked the question almost exactly as Louisa had. When had they last seen Miss Jessica, and what had happened?

'She told me she was going to stay with friends of hers – the Paget twins – in Dieppe,' said Lady Redesdale, who had recovered herself a little with sweetened tea. 'She showed me their letter of invitation a few weeks before, which asked her to join them in a house their aunt had taken. The suggestion was that they would do a motor tour to amusing places nearby, which was very clever. It meant I shouldn't expect to be able to get hold of her easily.'

'Did you have the address where she was staying?'

'Yes, 22 rue Gambetta.'

'Did you write to her there?'

'Immediately, so that the letter should arrive when she did. She obviously received it as she wrote back, mentioning details I had put in the letter to her.'

'Right. We'll return to that in a moment. For now, could you tell me about when she left?'

Lord Redesdale answered, his impatience barely contained. 'It was Sunday the seventh of February. Lady Redesdale and I took her in a taxi to the station. We paid her train fare – a return ticket to Dieppe. We even made sure that she was comfortable and told her to enjoy herself, goddammit!'

'She was travelling alone?'

'Yes. It was the thin end of the wedge, I can tell you, but I had been persuaded.'

Louisa and Nancy exchanged a glance at this. Louisa remembered that Jessica's three eldest sisters – Nancy, Pamela and Diana – had not been allowed to go anywhere unchaperoned until they were married. Diana had not travelled alone on a train until she was twenty-three years old and the mother of two boys. It seemed that by the time he had reached his youngest daughters – Unity, Jessica and Deborah – Lord Redesdale had been worn down.

'After you left her on the train, did you watch it depart?'

'We waved her off, until the train was out of sight,' said Lord Redesdale.

'Did you happen to notice if anyone else joined that particular carriage after you had left her?' Guy barely looked up as he kept writing. Louisa wondered if he was a touch nervous among so many Mitfords. They were quite overwhelming as an entirety.

'No, I don't think so. I don't know. Perhaps someone did? There were several people getting on and off the train.'

'No one you recognised?'

'No.' Lord Redesdale's face was morose.

'And it was not long after she left that you heard from her?'

'Yes.' Lady Redesdale picked up the sorry tale while her husband glowered into the fireplace. 'I was here, packing and preparing for our trip. When she returned, we were due to go on a cruise with Debo. We've cancelled it now, of course. Since then I've received some postcards from Decca, and a letter.'

She showed Louisa and Guy the post she had received: perhaps the only suspicious thing about the letters was how bland Jessica's descriptions were. 'The cathedral is lovely,' she wrote in one, among general remarks about the weather. She said she would not be home before 21st February.

Guy inspected the stamps on the cards and envelopes. 'Only the first letter is from Dieppe,' he remarked. 'The others are from Compiègne and Rouen, it seems.'

'Yes, supposedly sent from different stops on the motor tour.

But I sensed that something wasn't right,' said Lady Redesdale, 'and cabled the twins' mother in Austria. The address had been given in the original letter, the invitation Decca had shown me.'

'Do you have that letter?' asked Guy.

'No, Decca kept it as it was hers. I made a note of the address when she showed it to me.'

'What did the cable say?'

'*Do you know where Decca is?* I also wrote to the twins' aunt in London. I know her slightly. The forged invitation said that the mother's house in London had been let, but I supposed that that was also an untruth. I was right.'

'You got a reply?'

'Yes, very quickly. As we know now, Decca's story had been a complete invention. She wasn't with the twins in France. They were in Austria with their mother, completely unaware that she had dragged them into this lie.'

'Did the Pagets say if they knew where she was?'

'I suggested the mother ask her daughters, but received the message that they knew nothing of any of it.'

'Is there any chance they could be concealing her from you?'

'I suppose there is, but why would she do such a thing? Why would she hide from me?' There was anguish in her voice. Louisa had never seen Lady Redesdale look this grey, with shadows under her eyes that told of several sleepless nights. This woman had certainly weathered enough shocks in the two decades that they had known each other, but she had nearly always managed to keep Louisa – or anyone else – from knowing what she truly felt about anything. Not now.

'She finally ran away,' said Nancy, 'as she'd been threatening to do for years. We can't say we weren't warned.'

'Miss Jessica opened a Running Away account when she was twelve years old,' Louisa explained to Guy. 'Every time she was given money for her birthday or Christmas, that's where it would go.'

'How much was in there?' Guy's pencil was poised.

'About fifty pounds,' said Debo, who had been sitting on the green silk armoire, listening to every word. 'She showed me her bank book not long ago.'

Guy couldn't help it: he gave a low whistle. 'That's three months' salary for a policeman,' he said. 'She could get quite far on that.'

'I'm not sure that's what one might call a helpful remark,' Nancy quipped.

'It's worse than that,' said Lady Redesdale. 'I gave her thirty pounds as an advance on her dress allowance for the cruise.'

'Thirty pounds!' exclaimed Lord Redesdale, and resumed his stand-off with the fire. Then he muttered, 'I gave her ten pounds when we said goodbye.'

Guy wrote down the impressive sum: ninety pounds.

'What cruise?' asked Louisa. She thought of the last liner they had been on; it was surprising that they were going on another, given past events.

'I came up with the plan before Christmas, to cheer Decca up because she had been rather unhappy. We were going to go with Debo and a friend of theirs, next month, although I admit that none of the conversations we had about our plans ever seemed to make her any happier.'

'Do you think she's gone to Russia? Farve says she's a Bolshevik.' Debo's blue peepers were wide and her eyebrows had the thin, arched look that was fashionable.

At this, Lady Redesdale slumped back in her chair and stared, glassy-eyed, at the fire.

'Be quiet, Nine,' said Nancy.

'I wish you wouldn't always call me that. I'm sixteen.'

'You've still got the brain of a nine-year-old, as you have just demonstrated.'

'What was the date of the last correspondence you had from Miss Jessica?' asked Louisa.

Lady Redesdale looked at the stamps. 'It appears to have been posted on Friday 12th February, but I received it on Monday.'

'And that was the reply to the letter you sent her, to the address in Dieppe?'

Lady Redesdale nodded.

'Today is the 19th, so that was a week ago. And there's been no word of her since then.'

'No.'

'But we can at least confirm that she must have been in Dieppe on the 12th February. If she was there from the morning of the 8th, that's at least five days she was in the town. She must have been staying somewhere,' said Louisa.

'Have you telephoned any of her friends, to see if they know anything?' asked Guy.

'What friends?' said Nancy harshly. 'She was stuck out in Swine Brook until not long ago. There's no one there. She didn't go to school, and her only friend is Unity, who is in Munich. Don't you see? It's deadly being a Mitford girl. All we all ever longed for was to get out.'

'That's not true,' said Debo. 'I love being at home. I even miss Swinbrook.'

'You're the exception that proves the rule,' said Nancy, but she spoke more gently. There were sixteen years between the two of them, the oldest and the youngest, and so many dramas over the years. It must have been hard for them to remember they were sisters when Nancy had left the nursery almost before Debo was out of nappies.

'Lady Blanche Hozier lives in Dieppe, doesn't she?' said Louisa. 'We all stayed there one summer, I remember, not too long after I first came to work for you.'

'Who is Lady Blanche?' asked Guy.

'My aunt,' replied Lord Redesdale. 'She died in 1925.'

'Yes, but Nellie is in Dieppe,' said Nancy.

'Nellie?' Guy was trying to keep up with his notes but, as usual with the Mitfords, it was difficult to ascertain what was necessary information and what was needless teasing.

'Nellie Romilly,' Nancy explained. 'Lady Blanche's daughter. She's as mad as a box of frogs. One couldn't put it past her to be part of Decca's hare-brained scheme.'

'I take it her address is not 22 rue Gambetta?'

'No. And if Decca wanted to go and stay there, surely she would have told us. We're not banned from seeing Nellie.' Nancy picked up a cigarette box and took one out but didn't light it.

'No, but we've never met Nellie's boys, have we?' Tom, who had been quiet throughout, stood as he said this. 'Rather too Red for you, aren't they, Farve?'

Lord Redesdale barely acknowledged this statement, but turned to Guy. 'I hardly think you need a run-down of all my batty cousins and their offspring. We'll be here until next Tuesday if you do.'

'No, sir,' said Guy, 'but I think perhaps if there is a relative in the last place that Miss Jessica was known to be, we ought to contact them in case they have heard anything. Sometimes a process of elimination is the only way to begin. It would be helpful if you could give me Mrs Romilly's address and telephone number, if she has one. In the meantime, I'd like to confirm some of the facts of Miss Jessica's appearance and so on.'

Lady Redesdale nodded but remained in her listless position by the fire, loosely holding the letters and cards her daughter had sent. 'What if something has happened to poor Decca?' she said, looking up at her husband. 'What if I have driven her away into the hands of white slavers because I didn't see how unhappy my own daughter was?'

Lord Redesdale looked at his wife. 'We don't know that. Try not to think that.'

Louisa had never heard them so tender with each other. It was almost as if they had forgotten that she, or anyone else, was in the room.

CHAPTER FIVE

~~~~~

Nancy stood. 'Would you both come with me?'

'Of course,' said Louisa. With a wave of farewell, she and Guy followed Nancy out of the drawing room and down the stairs to the library. Nancy gestured for them both to take a seat. The room felt cold – there was no fire – but there was a lightness to the air somehow, after the intensity of the conversation they had just had.

'I apologise for being so abrupt, but I don't think the poor Old Humans can cope with any more conversation today. They've been utterly miserable since they discovered Decca's pack of lies.'

'When was that exactly?' asked Louisa.

'Two days ago, after Muv received the reply from the Paget twins' mother in Austria. We spent twenty-four hours in a spin before contacting the police. And then I wrote to you this morning. We didn't know what else to do.'

'Can you give me a description of Miss Jessica?' said Guy. 'I'm not certain I've seen her since our wedding, and she may have changed.'

'She's pretty, I suppose, but she wears terribly plain dresses. It's the Bolshie in her.'

'I was thinking more hair colour, height, that sort of thing . . .'

'Oh, yes. She's a little shorter than me, I think that would make her around five foot three, with dark hair and blue eyes, like an Irish faery. She's pale, too.'

'Could I have a photograph of her? In case we need to show it to anyone.'

Nancy looked around the room and picked up a small silver frame. 'Here.'

'Thank you. Perhaps not in the frame.'

Louisa removed the backing and took the photograph out. It showed Jessica standing with her sheep, Miranda. It was a couple of years old but it would do to help with identifying her.

'Do you know what she was wearing when she took the train?'

'Yes, Muv and I discussed that already. How drear her outfit was, given she was off to stay with the twins in France, and how much more chic they were bound to be. Brown shoes, brown woollen stockings, a tweed skirt, pale yellow shirt, tweed jacket – a cast-off of Diana's, not matching the skirt – and a hideous cape thing for a coat, with a red scarf and brown beret. She'll have had a pair of gloves too.'

'Do you know what she carried with her?'

'She took a suitcase with enough clothes for a week or so. Nanny Blor has been wailing that she only has two pairs of knickers with her and they are too small. I imagine there were a few shirts, stockings, perhaps one evening dress, but she left behind her Worth dress.'

'Anything of value?'

'No jewels. Only the money from her Running Away account.

27

I don't think she even has a wristwatch. Why, do you think she might sell things?'

'Sometimes we can trace a person by items they've sold at pawn shops,' said Guy.

'Yes, I see.'

'Mrs Rodd, do you mind if I ask you frankly – what do you suspect your sister has done?'

Nancy patted her hair, which was still dark and thick. Louisa knew the two of them looked older than when they first met, but Nancy had kept a good figure and she dressed well: she had lost none of her charm. 'It's rather as I said upstairs. Decca has been wanting to run away for a long time, and now she's finally done it. I understand that. What I don't understand is why she feels the need to put our parents through the wringer. I know I've done some awful things to Muv in my time, even if I felt she deserved it. But this is terrible. It's as if Decca were dead. Look—' She indicated three vases of varying heights standing on a low table, each one filled with flowers. 'People have started to send these. They must expect the worst. I think the relics do, too. I can't stand it for them, especially Farve. I don't think he'll ever forgive Decca either.'

Louisa and Guy exchanged a glance. She turned to Nancy. 'Do you think there's a boy involved? There has to be a reason she's kept all this secret.'

'I agree she's hiding something more than her whereabouts, but I can't imagine it's a boy. It's impossible for a Mitford girl to meet a boy, let alone plot to run away. I mean, she's barely out and she loathed the entire charade – the dance cards and the mothers chatting about which partners were the most eligible. We all detest it, obviously, but Decca seemed particularly pained by it.'

'Why?'

'Oh, you know, her politics, or so she says. I think it's just a reason for a tease.'

'What do you mean?' asked Guy. He was not so well schooled in the Mitford tradition of teasing.

'Unity and Diana are sworn fascists. The only way Decca can be noticed is to do something completely different. So naturally she has become a Communist.'

'Don't you think she means it?' asked Louisa.

'Well, she might a bit. Not enough to swear off Worth dresses altogether, I notice. But Muv told me she's been raging lately that she's being forced to live a life of luxury that is provided by "the very people" that are enabling the Spanish war. It's not as if Farve has been supplying arms to the Nationalists, is it?'

'Does she know any Communists?' Louisa thought Nancy could have undermined Decca; she'd always seemed to her a very sincere girl. And it was possibly quite tricky to be a revolutionary while stuck in Rutland Gate.

'I doubt it. I think the nearest she's ever got is a poster of Trotsky on her wall. She pinned it up next to Unity's poster of Hitler.'

'Thank you,' said Guy. 'We've got enough to get started, I think. Can you give us Mrs Romilly's address?'

'Yes. I'll have to find it, but it won't take me long. Shall I telephone it to you, at your office? I've got the number now.'

'If you would. And perhaps you could ask your mother to keep thinking back over the last few weeks, in case there's any clue there at all, some minor detail that seemed insignificant at the time.'

'Of course,' said Nancy. She took Louisa's hand and clutched it briefly. 'Darling Lou-Lou, you're always there for us. We do appreciate it, you know. Even if we are completely hopeless at showing it.'

This moved Louisa. Emotions were running high for all of them. 'I do know, but thank you for saying it.'

With a silent farewell, she and Guy showed themselves out through the front door and back out into the biting cold, where the noise of the traffic was loud after the muffled quiet inside the house.

'Is Maisie with Ma?' Guy asked.

'Yes, a day early, but neither of them seemed to mind too much.' Louisa smiled at her husband. She'd always loved the sight of him in his trilby hat and long navy coat, his glasses glinting in the wintry sunshine.

'Then we had better get to work.'

CHAPTER SIX

B ack in the office, Louisa looked around. She'd been in there before many times, but today she was seeing it with different eyes. It was no longer the place her husband worked; it was her office, too. The lettering etched into the glass door front said *Cannon & Sullivan*, a heartening reminder that she belonged there. There had been some debate as to the name. Initially, there had been an assumption that it would be Sullivan & Sullivan but Louisa soon realised that, although she had been very proud and happy to take Guy's name as his wife, she wanted to be 'Cannon' for her work. She was not a young girl who had moved from her father's house to her husband's, after all; she had been Louisa Cannon for thirty-four years. Equally, she didn't want Guy to lose face in front of his mother and brothers. Her final persuasive argument was that there could be times when it would be helpful if a client didn't realise they were married. So Cannon & Sullivan it was.

There were two windows that looked out onto the busy road and a row of shops and offices opposite; sunshine struggled to find a way in. One desk dominated the middle of the room, which Guy was using. It had a few papers on it, a pot of pencils, an empty, unwashed cup without its saucer, and a telephone. A small table on the side had a camping gas stove with a kettle, spoons, tins of tea and coffee, a bottle of milk. Against the other wall there was a table with a typewriter and a stack of blank paper: Louisa's desk. She put her coat on the back of the chair – she would buy hooks for Guy to nail up – and sat down, turning the chair around to face into the room. Guy did the same by his desk.

'Here we are,' she said. She felt a quickening of her heartbeat, not so much from nerves as from a sense of occasion. This was a new beginning and all she wanted was to be up to it: not to let Guy down.

'Yes, here we are. I'm sorry it's a bit of a mess. I intended to make it more welcoming for you.' He straightened up some papers as he said this, as if completing a job he'd started.

'It's perfectly fine. I'll buy some flowers later.'

'Flowers, yes. I hadn't thought of those.'

'So. Where do we start?'

Guy pulled out his notebook and laid it out flat. 'We've got a nineteen-year-old woman who has always wanted to run away from home, in France. We know from her correspondence that she is most likely alive and well.'

'Do we know that?'

'I'd say the probability is high. I don't think it's a kidnapping. She left for France, she invented a story for her parents about where she was going and who she was staying with, and there's been no ransom demand.'

'Yes,' conceded Louisa. 'If we believe she is deliberately hiding her whereabouts from her family, then we need to find out why.'

'Most missing persons don't want to be found,' said Guy.

'Are you saying you don't think this is a case we should take on?'

'I'm saying I don't know if there *is* a case. The chances are, we'll find her and she won't want to come home. That she's perfectly safe and very happy to be away from that coven of Mitfords. I can't say I'd blame her either.'

'I know they're not an easy—'

'I think Lord and Lady Redesdale are hiding something from us,' interrupted Guy.

'What?'

'Well, why are they so worried? And why haven't they asked Lord Redesdale's cousin, the one who lives in Dieppe, if Miss Jessica is with her? The most obvious place to start, surely? I don't think they're telling us the full story. There's nothing inherently dangerous about a young woman being in France—'

'*Alone* in France.'

'You say that, but she's almost certainly with someone. We have to ask: who is she with? Why do they want her found by us before anyone else finds her?'

'They said they tried the police but the police won't help.'

'We don't know that. I'd be surprised if the police won't investigate. But you and I know what some of those commissioners are like. They can't resist the opportunity to suck up to a peer of the realm. They'd help if they were asked. I don't think they have been asked.'

Louisa contemplated this. She heard an angry car horn outside, and a low rumble in her stomach reminded her she was hungry; she'd become used to eating like clockwork lately, feeding herself and Maisie.

'You think Lord and Lady Redesdale suspect their daughter

of being with someone or a group of people that they wouldn't want the police to know about?'

'The police or the public, generally. If the police know about it, the public soon will.'

'I don't know, Guy. I still think that's a stretch. What sort of person could that be?'

He leaned back in his chair and crossed his legs at the ankles, looking absurdly long for the room, like a snake in a cage. 'A Russian Bolshevik?' he said. 'That's our only lead so far, given Miss Deborah's comments.'

'Nancy said she didn't think Miss Jessica had very many friends and certainly hadn't met any Communists.'

'That's what Nancy says. She's a married woman now, isn't she? She hasn't lived with her sister for some time. And if we know one thing about those girls, it's that they are well practised in deceiving the rest of their family.'

This was true. Whether it was Nancy slipping out of a debutante dance to go to a nightclub or Diana hiding her affair with Sir Oswald Mosley, they were all women who knew how to keep secrets.

'What do we do first?'

Guy brought his feet up, sat straight and looked at her, saying nothing as he smiled. Louisa touched her face, self-conscious. 'What? Why are you smiling at me?'

'Because you don't know how nice it is for me to have you here, to ask what *we* are going to do next.'

'I'm not sure how helpful I can be. I've realised, now I'm here, that I don't know what to do.'

'You will. And we're in this together, aren't we? I'm not expecting you to have all the answers. It's about two being better than one.' He gave another big grin. 'That's what I've always tried to persuade you of, isn't it?'

'Get on with you.' Louisa laughed. 'We need to concentrate. Come on. What's Jessica's secret? If it's that she's with Communists in France, how do we find that out?'

'Perhaps the question is, why would she go to France to meet Communists? I didn't know the French were that way inclined.'

'They threw their royalty off the throne, didn't they?' said Louisa, but she didn't want to joke; she wanted to get some answers. 'We must concentrate. Whatever we might think, it's clear that the family are worried about her. She needs to be found. Is there, I don't know, some sort of Communist centre in London we could ask?'

'There's probably a headquarters. We can look in the phone books, in the library. It's only around the corner.'

'Yes,' said Louisa. 'I can't help feeling that would intimidate her. I think we need something less official, somehow, like a café where Bolsheviks drink endless cups of black coffee. They might be able to tell us what's happening in France. It's a long shot, but it's all we've got at the moment.'

'It's imaginative thinking,' said Guy. 'I like it. I know of one in Soho—'

He was interrupted by the sound of the telephone ringing, answered it, gave a few brief replies to the person at the other end, and noted something down on the pad on his desk.

'Who was that?' asked Louisa.

'Nancy. She's given me Mrs Romilly's address and telephone number, but said that Lord Redesdale had insisted on telephoning her first. She hasn't heard from Jessica, or seen her in Dieppe.'

Louisa began to tidy the paper on the desk. 'Do you believe her? Mrs Romilly, I mean?'

'We have no reason not to,' said Guy. 'I think we'll assume that's the truth, or we'll never move forward. As I said before, it's as much about elimination as anything else at this stage.'

'Yes. We can cross the Romillys off the list.'

CHAPTER SEVEN

~~~~~

Louisa and Guy arranged to meet at Piccadilly station later, as he had various appointments that afternoon. Louisa remained behind for a moment, content to sit and consider the possibilities around Jessica's absence. She was soon so lost in thought that she almost didn't notice the woman standing in the doorway, hesitantly knocking on the open door.

'Excuse me? Are you one of Cannon and Sullivan?'

Louisa stood, she wasn't sure why. To gain a height advantage, perhaps. The woman before her was as tall as a man, wearing wide trousers and a white shirt beneath a coat that gave no hint of feminine curves. Her short hair was swept back and her face was free of cosmetics, so definite in its features that it could have been hewn out of marble. The effect was striking, if unusual.

'Hello, yes, I'm Louisa Cannon. How can I help?'

'My name is Julia Attwood. I don't know if you *can* help, but—' Her distress was palpable.

'Please, sit down. I'm sorry, I was miles away when you came in.' Louisa sat back in her seat and Julia took the chair opposite.

'It's my sister, Petunia Attwood. She's been missing for three weeks, at least.' She had what sounded like an acquired London accent, or perhaps one that was a touch posher than the one she had been born into.

'I assume you have told the police?'

'Yes, she's registered as missing with the Latchmere Road police station in Battersea. But they say she's a grown woman and she could have left for reasons of her own, that perhaps she didn't want me to know.'

'It's true – they don't tend to look for missing people unless they're children,' said Louisa. 'But what makes you think there's more to it? Why are you concerned?'

'It's instinct as much as anything,' said Julia. 'She never missed a day's work before, has rarely even been ill. And although we weren't in close contact all the time, this is the longest we've gone without speaking to each other.'

'Is there anywhere you can think of that she might have gone?'

'Well, yes.' She stopped and opened her bag. 'Do you mind if I smoke? I'm sorry, it's very upsetting, you see. I know I shouldn't, but I can never seem to stop.'

Louisa pulled an ashtray out of a drawer, bought especially for clients, and put it before Julia. She lit a cigarette with a heavy gold lighter.

'I think she might be in Spain.'

'Why?'

'The last time I saw her was at Christmas. It was just the two of us – we're all we've got when it comes to family. It was something she said then. I wasn't really listening; I took it as no more than a light-hearted piece of wishful thinking. She told me that someone in the office had gone to the war over there.'

'And it sounded as if she wanted to go too?'

'Not exactly. It was more a tone of romance. As if she envied the person's sense of purpose. That was how I read it, but I might have been wrong. In any case, I dismissed the thought because I never thought she'd have the courage to do something like that. Again, perhaps I was mistaken. But I saw an article in the paper yesterday about men and women who are going there, to fight in the war, and it reminded me of what she'd said and I thought . . .' She put her cigarette out and exhaled the last of the smoke above Louisa's head, where it spiralled and dissipated in the light.

'Can you tell me more about your sister? Do you have a photograph of her?'

Julia brought out two photographs from her inside pocket and laid them flat on the table. One showed a woman standing shyly beside a tree, her hands clasped before her. She had a half-smile and was looking up into the branches. Her hair was dark, her dress was plain, and she had a more conventional appearance of prettiness than her sister. The other picture showed Julia and Petunia together, at Christmas judging by the paper crowns they wore, their arms around each other's shoulders, laughing.

'We spent Christmas together, at her flat.'

'Did you notice anything unusual about her mood then?'

'No,' said Julia. 'You can see how happy she looks there. We had a good day. Neither of us are married, neither of us have children. I doubt I ever will.'

She paused, waiting for Louisa's acknowledgement, which she gave.

'But Petunia always wanted a family of her own. She's forty-two now. Strangely enough, I had a hope that, because it is too late, she had at last come to a peaceful acceptance of the fact.'

'What is her work?'

'She's a secretary in the claims department of Lee Worth, an insurance company. But she was officially on holiday when she . . .' Julia didn't repeat the fateful word again. 'It's why I'm not exactly certain when she went missing.'

'Does she live alone?'

'Yes, in a block of flats which are mostly occupied by single women. I think she was friendly with a few of them, but for one reason or another no one noticed she had been missing. She was due back at work on the 8th of February and she didn't show up. That sent up a red flag because she was a conscientious worker. After she didn't come in the following day, the woman who sits next to her in the office went round to her flat and noticed that no post had been collected in some time, and she asked a neighbour if they had seen her. She reported back to their boss, who had my telephone number as an emergency contact.'

'Your sister didn't have a telephone in her flat?'

Julia shook her head.

'Any boyfriend that you knew of?'

'No. There was someone, a few years ago, but it petered out. I think she discovered he was seeing other women, and not too discreetly.'

Louisa asked Julia for the address of the flat, which was in Clapham, and of Lee Worth Insurance, which was in Victoria.

'Have you been into the flat?' Louisa asked.

'Yes, I had the spare keys. I couldn't see anything out of place.'

'Did it look as if she might have left deliberately?'

'It was tidy, as it usually is. I couldn't see her bag.'

'Did she have a passport?'

Julia held her hands up. 'I don't know. She might have done.

She went to France the year before last so I assume she had one, although I don't think you have to have one if you go to Paris just for the weekend, do you? I didn't look for it. I—' Her composure broke. 'I'm sorry. I couldn't bear to be in her flat for long without her there, not knowing where she is. No one will help, and I don't know what to do. She's not stupid, not at all, but she's too trusting ... That is, she's so kind and hard-working, she only sees the good in people.'

Louisa handed Julia a tissue from the box on the desk. Guy had anticipated the need for it with clients.

'We can begin enquiries. There is a cost, I'm afraid.'

Julia blew her nose. 'Yes, of course. I don't have terribly much but I just want to know she's alive and well ...' She trailed off, her hopelessness all too apparent.

'I will do everything I can to help you find her, I promise you,' said Louisa.

They discussed the terms, and Louisa kept the photographs. Even without knowing Petunia, Louisa felt the poignancy of her picture at Christmas: her smile when her future had looked certain and safe.

CHAPTER EIGHT

O n the spur of the moment, Louisa decided to head to
Latchmere Road police station. It wouldn't take her long
to get there and she'd still be in time to meet Guy. At the very
least, she could verify whether Julia Attwood had told her the
truth. Guy had warned her that there were plenty of people out
there who found it amusing to waste the time of investigators,
creating drama where there was none. (She knew something of
that from the Mitfords, too.)

Latchmere Road was only a little way south of the river, not
terribly far from Chelsea, where Louisa had grown up, yet there
was an undeniable difference in atmosphere on the other side
of the bridge. Not necessarily better or worse – although Louisa
knew there were greater areas of poverty the further south one
went – but tangibly different. The vast power station's chimneys
belched smoke, the streets felt wider, with fewer cars, and the tall
red-brick flats that lined the road were a more impressive sight
than the rows of terraced houses in Louisa's neighbourhood.
When she got off the bus, she walked along for a few minutes,

pausing to enjoy the pleasant sight of a teacher corralling several young pupils into the corner entrance of the park.

At the station, Louisa went up to the front desk, which was manned by a constable who looked worryingly young: the first sign, she knew, that she was feeling her age.

Louisa explained that she was looking for a Miss Petunia Attwood, a woman of forty-two years old who had been missing for some three weeks. Her disappearance had been reported to this station. Could she check if she was on the missing persons list?

'Yes, madam,' said the constable. Louisa felt her hair go grey at the word – when had she stopped being 'miss'? He reached under his desk and pulled out a worn-looking ledger book before flicking through the pages. 'Here we are.'

He showed her the entry, written in black ink only the week before: her name, her age, last known address, date presumed missing, and the name of the person who had reported her, Julia. Under 'identifying marks' was written 'none'.

'I find that hard to believe,' said Louisa, pointing to the spot. 'Everyone has an identifying mark of some kind, don't they?'

The constable closed the book. 'I expect the officer didn't ask – they don't always bother.'

'Why not?'

He had a kind face, and Louisa was reminded of her own husband when she had first met him. 'Because they're not going to be looking for her. This book – it's a formality, something to make them feel better when they report their missing relatives. There's not much we can do, you see? We haven't got the manpower.'

Louisa looked around her. The station was small, as they

usually were. She knew, from Guy's days with the Metropolitan Police, that there would be a few rooms off the one she was in. A couple of cells, an interview room, a room with two or three desks and filing cabinets. She could hear a telephone ringing in the distance, someone shouting a name. It was true, there wasn't much in the way of manpower in one local police station. She also knew there wasn't much in the way of willingness when it came to a missing middle-aged woman who had no political power or clout. On the one hand, there were the Mitfords, deliberately hiding the fact that their daughter had run away because of the attention her disappearance would attract: from newspapers, from the police, from politicians and from the man on the omnibus. Jessica Mitford's absence from the world, when it became known, would spark headlines all over the country. Yet when Petunia Attwood vanished, a woman who was a diligent worker, a good citizen, it didn't matter how loudly *her* sister shouted; no one would hear.

All at once Louisa understood Guy much better than she ever had. She saw how one might be pleased to have found work, a case for them to investigate, while the pleasure could only be bittersweet when it came at the cost of someone else's distress. She could only hope she had the chance to put that right and prove to Guy that she could find Petunia Attwood.

CHAPTER NINE

B efore Louisa could start her investigation into Petunia, there was still the small matter of the missing Miss Jessica to resolve. She and Guy met outside Piccadilly station and walked the short distance to Soho – not a part of town that Louisa had been to for some time. The last time had been with Nancy and Pamela, sneaking into the 43 nightclub on Gerrard Street, sleazy then and no less so now, even in the light of a cold day, with half the establishments closed until evening. The few people who were walking around all had their collars up and their hats pulled down low, as if to make sure no one recognised them. Guy stopped and asked one or two men for directions, and within a few minutes they found themselves outside a small café with a dark red awning. Its door was closed and a sign hung on the inside, visible through the glass. It was printed with symbols Louisa didn't recognise.

'What's that?' She pointed.

Guy shrugged. 'Something in Russian, I suppose.'

He pushed the door, and a faint bell sounded. Inside the café was busy – it was late afternoon, and Louisa's stomach was feeling hollow after her busy day – but there was an empty table to one side, squeezed in between others. They pushed their way to it and sat down. There was a heavy fog of cigarette smoke in the air, and a smell of cooking that was as unfamiliar to them as the symbols – a mixture of fish and vegetables and something else they couldn't identify. All around them, diners were drinking either tea poured out of elaborate silver teapots or what could only be vodka, constantly refilled in little painted tumblers. A young woman with thick black hair tied back came to the table and said something unintelligible to them.

'I'm so sorry,' said Louisa. 'We don't speak Russian. Do you speak English?'

The woman rolled her eyes. 'Lunch? You want?'

'Yes, please. Is there a menu—'

Before Louisa had stopped talking the waitress had disappeared through a curtain, releasing a fresh puff of steam and the aroma of boiled cabbage. Guy and Louisa looked at each other, bemused, but not for long: two bowls were put down in front of them, with red soup and thick slabs of black bread balancing on the edge. Louisa bent her head a little and inhaled: her mouth started watering immediately. Quickly, the two of them ate, saying little, revelling in the strangeness and delight of being somewhere completely different, together.

Sated only minutes later, Guy leaned back and wiped his mouth with the heavily starched napkin. 'I've never had anything like that before. Delicious.'

One of the two men sitting at the table beside them looked across and laughed. 'Your first borscht?' he asked, with a strong Russian accent.

Guy and Louisa nodded, somewhat awestruck.

'What brings you here?' the man asked, then shook his head. 'Forgive me. I'm Pieter Groskop. This is my colleague, Ivan.'

Ivan gave a brief nod but clearly did not wish to be interrupted from his own food.

'We're looking for someone,' said Guy. 'We don't think she is here, in this restaurant, but she has expressed an interest in your country's politics ...' He tailed off. Pieter was regarding him seriously.

'This person, she is a comrade?'

'We don't know how seriously,' interjected Louisa. 'We believe she's gone to France and we thought there might be a connection between that and her politics.'

Pieter turned to Ivan and said something to him in Russian. Ivan shrugged and replied very briefly.

'We do have many comrades in France, but those who wish to fight for the cause may travel to Spain.'

An alarm bell rang in Louisa's mind – *Petunia* – but she kept her face still.

'Of course, the Spanish civil war,' said Guy. 'It's fascists versus Communists over there, isn't it?'

Pieter looked grave. 'In a manner of speaking. It is very brutal, this war – I hope your friend is not there, for her sake.'

Louisa touched Guy on the arm. 'I can't see Miss Jessica off to fight a war. Is there anywhere in London where people of your—' She hesitated. Why did naming someone's political loyalties seem intrusively personal, somehow?

'My?' Pieter regarded her, a shot of vodka halfway to his mouth.

'Political persuasion?'

47

'I am Russian, my friend. First and foremost. We are thinkers, philosophers. You have never been to my beautiful country?'

'No, I'm sorry.'

'You should be sorry. We have everything there. But I must be here.' He drained his drink.

'Is there anywhere else you go, to think and be philosophical?'

Pieter laughed at this and had another brief exchange with Ivan, who also chuckled and gave Louisa a friendly glance.

'Perhaps you mock but no, I think you are sincere?'

'I am,' said Louisa, feeling quite cut adrift in this conversation, while basking in the novelty of it at the same time. It was like being on holiday.

'We go to church, we sit in each other's rooms, we read.' He thought for a moment. 'There is a bookshop on Lincoln Street, not far from here. Some of your own countrymen – writers and thinkers – meet there. Perhaps your friend knows it.'

'I'm not certain I'd call my friend a great thinker,' said Louisa, feeling disloyal. She reminded herself that Jessica had frequently expressed a desire to be educated at school when she was younger – perhaps there was a brain there that had been frustrated by the series of governesses Lady Redesdale had installed in the nursery.

'Thank you,' she continued. 'You have been so helpful.'

'It was my pleasure,' Pieter said charmingly. 'Good luck in finding your friend.'

Guy summoned the waitress and they paid their bill, a very modest sum, and set off for Lincoln Street.

CHAPTER TEN

～～

Lincoln Street was a narrow alley off Leicester Square, and the bookshop itself looked as if it had been wedged in between the buildings on either side. The Victorian windows with their thick plate glass were grimy but, when Louisa and Guy went through the door, there was a reassuring warmth and the always comforting smell of old books. The shelves were crammed with volumes of all kinds, old and new, leather-bound and paperback, with no apparent system in place. Louisa looked up at the ceiling and was surprised to see it completely papered in pen-and-ink portraits.

'Poets,' said a man close to her.

'I'm sorry?'

'The drawings up there,' said the man, hands jammed into his trouser pockets, shirt sleeves rolled up to the elbows. Louisa could see that the edge of his collar had been badly darned. 'They're of different poets. All done by an Italian I know. Delightful, aren't they?'

'Yes,' said Louisa, uncertain where to take the conversation next.

'Anyway, I won't interrupt. Please, look around.' He disappeared around a set of shelves.

Guy had been caught in the doorway, allowing someone out first, and he came up to her now, just glimpsing the man's retreat. 'Who was that?'

'I don't know.' She looked at some of the book titles: *In Defence of Trotskyism, The Age of Revolution, What Is To Be Done?* 'It's certainly a radical bookshop. I'm not sure what we're doing here, really.'

'Nor me,' admitted Guy. 'But as we said, we've not got much to go on yet. Let's just ask a few questions here, then we can get home to Maisie.'

They weaved through the narrow gaps between shelves. There were a few customers in the shop too, mostly quite oddly dressed, or perhaps they were bohemian: long silk scarves with printed patterns, elaborately coloured shirts, jewellery that looked home-made. It wasn't Louisa's style but she admired the originality of it: these people weren't reading magazines that told them how to dress. At the back was the shop till. The man in rolled-up shirt sleeves was sitting on a stool beside it, leafing through a pamphlet. He looked up as Louisa and Guy approached.

'Hello, what can I do for you? Are you looking for something that is not a portrait of a poet?' His voice was gentle and low, but not serious.

'What?' Guy was confused.

'It's the prints on the ceiling,' explained Louisa. 'I was looking at them when I came in. They're all original drawings, by an Italian artist.'

'I see,' said Guy, his head tilted up, although he didn't sound as if he were any the wiser.

'We're not looking for a book,' Louisa said to the man. 'We're looking for a person.'

'Any particular person?' The smile did not quite show itself, but it was definitely there.

'Miss Jessica Mitford.'

He thought for a moment. 'No, I'm afraid that doesn't ring any bells. Is that her real name?'

'Yes,' said Louisa. 'Why do you ask?'

'We have quite a few people that come through here in search of another way of life – they sometimes like to hide themselves behind another name. I'm Donald Oliver, by the way. And it is my real name, yes.' This time, the smile broke through. He was probably in his early forties, and there was a warmth to him that Louisa could not help but find agreeable.

'I'm Louisa Sullivan and this is my husband, Guy. We're private detectives.'

'A husband and wife team,' said Donald. 'That's rather wonderful. When did this Miss Jessica go missing?'

'She left for France on 7th February but she never arrived at the place she was supposed to be at. That is, she told her parents a false story about her intentions.'

'Young, I suppose?'

'Nineteen years old,' said Guy.

'And what made you think she might be here?'

'We didn't necessarily think she would be, but she has expressed an interest in Communism, and we wondered if that might hold the key to her disappearance. Someone in the Russian café near here suggested we try this shop.'

'Ah, yes, our Russian comrades. They often come by. I like their conversation. I am very sympathetic.'

'Is it your shop?' asked Louisa.

'Yes, it is. For my sins,' said Donald. 'Which are considerable, I'm afraid. Well, as I say, I'm very sorry I can't help you today, but do you have a card? I can certainly telephone you if I do hear anything. Jessica Mitford, wasn't it? As I repeat it, I wonder, *do* I know someone of that name?'

'You might have heard of her sisters. They're quite often in the papers.'

'Are they? What for?' Donald leaned towards Louisa and cupped a hand around his ear. 'Go on, give us the gossip.'

Louisa laughed. 'Nothing that's not been printed. But Nancy is a novelist, Diana left her husband for Sir Oswald Mosley, and Unity is a friend of Hitler's.'

'Quite the collection of siblings: a novelist, a fascist, a Nazi and a Communist.' Donald pretended to whistle. 'The only wonder is how this latest one hopes to stay under the radar. I do know something of them, I think. But not Miss Jessica, not personally.'

'We knew it was a long shot. We'd better go now. Thank you for your time,' said Louisa. She nudged Guy and he patted his pocket, bringing out a small white card: *Cannon & Sullivan, Private Detective Agency, Hammersmith 6834.*

'Thank you,' said Donald and opened the shop till, putting the card inside. Louisa could see there wasn't much money in there. 'I'll be in touch if I have reason to be.'

They said goodbye and turned to leave, Guy walking ahead of Louisa as he always did, in order to hold open the door for her. She couldn't be absolutely sure but, as she left, she thought she heard Donald speaking as if on the telephone, asking for a message to be sent to 'Esmond'. She stopped a second too late and didn't catch the rest. Esmond. She knew she had heard that name before – but where? Could there be a link, if Donald had picked up the telephone the second they had left him?

Louisa took Guy's arm as they stepped out onto the pavement. She was probably overthinking things, as she often did. Besides, they needed to hurry now or Maisie would be bawling.

CHAPTER ELEVEN

The following morning Guy headed off to the office first, while Louisa got Maisie up and breakfasted before dropping her round at Mrs Sullivan's. She felt frustrated by the lack of ideas in their search for Jessica, and decided to go for a walk to clear her head. It wasn't long before she hit Exhibition Road, near the museums. Her father had brought her to these when she was a girl: each museum was vast and packed tightly with extraordinary objects, whether dinosaur bones or molluscs, a Russian queen's wedding dress or a life-sized model of Stephenson's Rocket. It did her good to think of these things again – a world beyond the Mitfords, a reminder that our time on Earth is but a speck in the universe.

There was a stiff breeze, and Louisa pulled the lapels of her coat tighter around her throat. She was feeling slightly discombobulated by the events of the day before. Then she remembered Petunia Attwood. Louisa stopped by the railing of the Natural History Museum, the museum's gargoyles staring down upon her, and pulled out her notebook. South Kensington tube was only a minute's walk away; from there she could easily get to Victoria and ask a few questions at the office where Petunia had worked.

Lee Worth was a grey brick three-storey office between a legal practice and a bank, part of a long line of uniform buildings close to Victoria station. Its name was painted on a white strip along the front, above a row of windows that could have done with a wash. Louisa rang the bell by the heavy wooden door, which was opened by a young man in a suit that showed too much of his socks. A receptionist sat behind a large oak desk that looked suitably impressive, with a green-leather top, but only one open book and a pen visible. She was sitting there quite still, and said nothing until Louisa had reached the desk.

'Good morning. How may I help you?'

Louisa started to speak when the telephone on the desk rang. The receptionist held up her hand, palm out. 'Excuse me a minute. I have to take this call.'

Louisa stood and waited. The desk was situated in a large hall with a black-and-white tiled floor, and she could hear the clack of typewriters beyond, in rooms that led off it on the ground floor. There was a generous staircase that presumably led up to the offices of the rather grander members of the Lee Worth staff.

'Yes?' The receptionist had put the telephone down. From what she'd overheard, Louisa suspected it had been the receptionist's mother at the end of the line.

Louisa smiled at her warmly. She would need a favour. 'Hello. I'm looking for the manager of the Claims Department.'

'There are four. Do you have a name?'

'No,' said Louisa. She'd have to try another tack. 'I have some confidential information about Miss Petunia Attwood and I need to talk to her manager.'

The receptionist shrugged. 'She works here. Not seen her for a while.' She leaned forward and Louisa could smell the sugary mint of a sweet she must have been sucking on earlier. 'Has she had the sack?'

'No,' said Louisa. 'If you could help me with my request, please.'

'I know which one it is. You don't have an appointment, then?' She'd leaned back, all hope of a gossipy chat gone. Unhelpfulness resumed.

'I don't, and I don't know his name, as you've guessed. But if you can help me find him, I won't take up much of his time. Could you please tell whoever needs to know that my name is Louisa Cannon, and I have been hired by Julia Attwood with regards to her sister? I'll wait for as long as it takes.'

Louisa went and sat down on a chair to the side of the desk. She knew the receptionist's interest was piqued.

The answer came back: Mr Cornish would see her immediately.

The directions were simple to follow. Louisa walked along the corridor to the left, past two large rooms that held several typists and further closed doors with brass plaques on them.

At Mr Cornish's door, Louisa knocked and heard him call her in. He stood briefly as she entered, but soon sat back down again. There was a large pile of papers on his desk and several very sharp pencils lined up neatly. Mr Cornish adjusted his pale blue tie. His specs were the same as Guy's, she noticed: thick lenses and a round wire frame.

'Miss Cannon. I gather you are here about Miss Attwood? May I enquire your connection?'

Louisa explained.

He raised his eyebrows and fiddled with his tie again. 'You're a private detective, are you? I must say, you don't much look like one.'

'That is precisely the point,' said Louisa.

'A-ha, yes. I do see that. I do.' He pushed the pencils into a straighter line. 'Well, it is very puzzling, I must say. Miss Attwood is a good worker, reliable. It was Miss Piper who went to her home to try to establish why she hadn't returned to the office at the start of the year.'

'I don't want to take up too much of your time, but I need to ask some questions, if I may?' Louisa held her pencil, poised.

'Yes, yes, of course. Go ahead.' He leaned back stiffly.

'Can you confirm how long Miss Attwood worked here?'

'Yes. I checked her employment records when we first were concerned about her not turning up at work. It's unblemished. She began in May 1928. She was a general secretary to begin with and has since been promoted twice. She is currently in the claims department, as a typist, one of three.'

'Did she have any unexplained illnesses in the past? Or any other absences?'

'No,' said Mr Cornish. 'I'm sure she must have taken a day off sick here and there, but nothing untoward.'

'How long have you been her manager?'

'About six years. I've been at Lee Worth for twenty-one years altogether. Man and boy.' He tried a chuckle as if he had made a joke, but failed.

'Did she take her holiday days generally?'

'Yes – sometimes one had to nudge her to take them all before the year ran out, but I believe she did. She always volunteered to do holiday cover over the Christmas period and would generally take time off at the end of January instead.'

'So the last time you saw her was when?'

'Friday 29th January, before her week off. We close at half past five, so I imagine she went home then. I can't say I specifically remember seeing Miss Attwood on that day, but she is in the register as having been in work.'

'And you say there was no blemish at all on her working record?'

'None,' said Mr Cornish.

'May I speak to Miss Piper? The colleague you mentioned?'

Mr Cornish rubbed his nose with his fist. 'Oh, ah. Yes, that's possible. I'll have her brought in here.'

'I'd rather talk to her alone. You understand? Sometimes people say things more easily.'

Mr Cornish gave a tight nod. 'Absolutely. Come with me.'

CHAPTER TWELVE

‎᠆᠆᠆᠆᠆

Louisa waited in the corridor while Mr Cornish went into another office and came out a minute or two later with a middle-aged woman in a fusty floral dress and brown laced shoes that needed a polish.

Louisa held out her hand. 'Miss Piper, I'm sorry to interrupt your work. But might I talk to you for a few minutes? It's about Miss Attwood.'

Miss Piper looked to Mr Cornish for approval.

'Take your time, ladies. You can use my office. I've got an errand,' he said, backing off in the direction of the building's entrance.

In Mr Cornish's office, they sat down in the two chairs in front of his desk and turned towards each other.

'I'd like to see if there are any clues in her movements or her mood in the weeks leading up to her disappearance that might help me to establish where she is.'

In a series of brief answers, Miss Piper confirmed that she had worked alongside Miss Attwood for four years, and they frequently took their lunch together. Occasionally, they had met up at the weekends to go to the cinema or for a walk around the park. She said that they never met in the evenings after work: often Petunia would stay in the office later or would say she had commitments to charity work.

'Did you notice any change in Miss Attwood in the weeks before she went missing?'

'No.'

'She came to work as usual? You had lunch together as much as before?'

'Yes. She was a reliable co-worker. The other women in the office are younger than us. I don't have anything in common with them.'

'Did you notice any difference in her mood – even a small one?'

Miss Piper considered this. 'I have thought about this a lot. I've wondered if there was a sign I should have spotted. But if anything, I thought she was happier than usual. I think I must have put it down to it being the start of a new year because that's when ...'

'That's when what?'

Miss Piper smoothed out her skirt. 'The two of us don't have much family. Christmas isn't usually particularly jolly. It's a relief when it's over.'

'Yes, of course,' said Louisa sympathetically. 'I gather Miss Attwood spent it with her sister this year.'

Miss Piper nodded. Louisa was afraid she was holding back tears. She moved the conversation on.

'I know that Miss Attwood was a very conscientious worker—'

'Yes, she was.'

'But was there ever any trouble at work at all?' Louisa dropped her voice a touch. 'There are more men than women in this office, I can see. Sometimes that can cause difficulties ...'

'No, there wasn't trouble on that score. No more than the usual.' Miss Piper looked briefly out of the window, which faced out onto the road. A bus rumbled past. 'There was *something*, but I'm not supposed to talk about it. I promised her at the time.'

'It could be important. You never know. Sometimes it doesn't appear that way.'

'I don't want Mr Cornish to know I told you either. They – the bosses – they said there was no evidence, and so we weren't to say anything that could harm the business. They said they'd dealt with it.' She was picking at her dress – a tiny thread that Louisa couldn't see.

'Please, Miss Piper. I want to find out what happened to your friend.'

She took a breath and said it in a single gulp. 'She reported Mr Plum – Bernard Plum. She thought he might be taking money from some of our customers. Elderly women.'

'When did she report him?'

'I don't know exactly. Just after Christmas, I think.'

'Did Mr Cornish know about this?'

Miss Piper nodded. 'Yes, but those of us in the claims department were told to be quiet about it. They didn't want to risk anything getting out. Bad press, you know. Nothing was proven. Eventually, they said they'd investigate it.'

'Do you think they have?'

'Possibly. The likes of us don't get told.'

'And Mr Plum? Is he still here?'

'No. He was suspended – I don't know much more than that.'

Louisa looked at her notebook. She hoped she'd be able to read her own writing later. 'What is he like, Mr Plum?'

Miss Piper couldn't keep her hands from fidgeting. In spite of her stout figure, she reminded Louisa of a nervous child. 'I didn't work with him. Miss Attwood used to do the majority of his secretarial work.'

'What was his reputation in the office?'

'I don't know. He'd been here about five years, I think, as a claims clerk, but there are a few of them. They work in a separate office and we don't have much to do with them, though we do their typing. I think there was mention sometimes of him losing his temper if things weren't done the way he'd asked. But he's not the only one. And he was popular with the other men here. They go out for luncheon together, or to the pub after work. They're not occasions any of the girls are welcome to join.' She stood up. 'I've got to get back to work. Please don't tell Mr Cornish I told you.'

Louisa promised. 'I'll make sure you hear of any developments. It was good of you to talk to me. Thank you, Miss Piper.'

They shook hands and parted.

Louisa was sitting in the chair by the desk when Mr Cornish returned, a crumb of whatever he'd been eating lodged in the corner of his mouth. He didn't notice Louisa at first and jumped slightly when he did. 'You're still here,' he said, somewhat pointlessly.

'Yes, there was something I forgot to ask you, that Miss Attwood's sister mentioned.'

He gave her a quizzical but amenable look as he shuffled round to his chair behind the desk.

'It may not be anything at all, but I gather that Miss Attwood made a complaint about one of the managers here, Bernard Plum.'

'Ah, well, yes,' said Mr Cornish, not meeting Louisa's eyes but busying himself with the papers on his desk. 'A minor thing, but it has been resolved.'

'Forgive me, but since it happened so close to Miss Attwood's disappearance, and appears to have been a matter of conflict, it's important that we rule him out.'

Mr Cornish's shoulders slumped and he put his hands in his lap, giving up the papers for the moment. 'I appreciate that this is important, but I really do have to get back to work. I've been as accommodating as possible.'

'What was the complaint, Mr Cornish?'

'I talked to Mr Plum about the matter, but . . . it's rather embarrassing. It's not the sort of thing I'm terribly comfortable talking about, and it is confidential.'

Louisa kept her gaze steady.

'Fine, fine. It seems that Miss Attwood was . . . well, she had something of a . . . personal fondness for Mr Plum. He was deeply embarrassed by it all – he's a married man. Naturally, he had to reject her advances. I'm afraid her complaint was nothing more than spiteful retaliation. It pains me to say it, but there you are. She wasn't the first secretary to fall for her boss, and I'm awfully sorry but she almost certainly won't be the last.'

'She wasn't the first to have a "personal fondness" for Mr Plum?'

'Not Mr Plum specifically, but we are a company with capable men in charge, and young girls working for them. It's something that happens.'

'May I talk to Mr Plum?' Hopefully she could flush out the information from him without having to disclose that she already knew from Miss Piper.

It was like taking sweets from Maisie, as it turned out.

'Ah.' Mr Cornish gave an embarrassed cough. 'He's been suspended from work and I'm afraid I don't know where he is.'

'Because of the allegations, which you said were untrue?'

'Miss Attwood claimed that Mr Plum might be skimming some cream off the top, you might say. A serious allegation, and as she made the complaint formally, there is a procedure that needs to take place. But she named no names and gave few details. As I said, I don't think there was any basis in fact.'

'Does Mr Plum have an unblemished record at this company, like Miss Attwood?'

Mr Cornish stood up. 'I'm terribly sorry, but I'm going to have to ask you to leave now. I've helped you as much as I can. I do hope you find Miss Attwood, and please let us know the moment you do. The company only wishes her well.'

With these words, Mr Cornish firmly steered her towards the door and out into the corridor. The last thing she heard was a click as he turned the lock.

CHAPTER THIRTEEN

⁓

B ack at the Cannon & Sullivan office, Louisa sat down at her desk with a cup of tea, a pencil and a piece of paper. First, she added to her notes of the morning by jotting down her impressions of Mr Cornish and Miss Piper. They seemed to be telling the truth. The puzzle was Bernard Plum: could he be a clue to Petunia's disappearance? Louisa considered the options: that the two of them being out of contact was a coincidence; that they had run away together – to Spain? – and Petunia, embarrassed at having changed her mind about him, had decided not to tell anyone; that there had been a row, possibly fatal. The second seemed the most likely, but she couldn't take it any further at the moment.

More pressing was the need to find Jessica. Again, Louisa wrote down everything she knew about her disappearance so far: that she had forged a letter from the Paget twins to say that she was invited to stay with them and their aunt in a house they had taken in Dieppe, from where they would motor to various places.

The Paget twins, their aunt and their mother had all confirmed that this was a lie.

But Jessica *had* sent a letter and postcards from Dieppe and places nearby. So she was in France, and clearly had the means to move around. Either she was with someone who was driving a car, or she was taking trains or hitching lifts. Louisa could not imagine that Jessica, for all her long-held determination to run away, would have the courage to get herself to different places in France without someone beside her to help.

Louisa thought about the girl she had known. When she was little, Jessica had been rather sweet, adopting a lamb, Miranda, that had gone with her almost everywhere she went; Lord Redesdale had only drawn the line at Miranda attending church on Sunday mornings. She'd always been single-minded when she wanted something – although this was a trait that all the sisters shared – and she was clever, too. Jessica and Unity spoke in a secret language, Boudledidge, which made them close, even as they fiercely defended their opposing political views. Nancy had been right when she'd said that it could be difficult to be a Mitford girl. There were different versions of what made life hard, of course, and Louisa's own childhood would not have seemed attractive to many, with both parents working long hours and her uncle Stephen forcing her into committing criminal acts. But it had been secure, in its own way, and she had enjoyed her schooling and had good friends in the neighbourhood where she grew up. Going out to work at fourteen meant she kept busy. She might have been tired, often frustrated, and determined to do better eventually, but she had never been bored. Nancy and her younger sisters chafed at the bits that their parents pulled on to rein them in. They had not been brought up with any expectation of a career; their success would be measured by the success of the men they married. No one could have foreseen the changes the world would go through in the aftermath of the Great War and the Spanish flu. Now, women were not just encouraged to work; many had no choice if they wanted to eat, and there were fewer men available to marry. Even so, many of the older generation could not understand the need for suffrage. There was a gulf of misunderstanding between parents and their children. Perhaps it had ever been thus, but Louisa wondered if this was at the heart of Jessica's disappearance.

In sum, what Jessica most likely wanted, that she felt she could not tell her parents about, was to fall in love and marry someone – it was this that would give her the independence she so badly sought. If such a someone was connected to her politics in some way, it could heighten the drama considerably, which she would also enjoy. In a flash, it came to Louisa: her parents would not know the truth, and Nancy was insistent that Jessica had no close friends to confide in, but the daughters did talk to the servants in the house. Louisa knew this, after all, from personal experience. She needed to speak to Nanny Blor and any young maids working at the house.

CHAPTER FOURTEEN

Having telephoned ahead, Louisa was back on the doorstep of 26 Rutland Gate not long after Lord Redesdale had finished his elevenses. This time, however, Louisa deliberately knocked at the back door. She had no need to see any of the family, although Nancy was aware of what was happening; she wanted to talk to the servants. Prepared this time for her official day of work as co-founder of Cannon & Sullivan, Louisa carried her own notebook and pencil in her coat pocket. She reached inside and felt for them, as reassuring as smooth pebbles on a beach.

The door was opened by the same maid who had let Louisa in the day before.

'Oh, miss,' she said, surprise on her face. 'I'm so sorry – didn't no one let you in at the front? I didn't hear the knock.'

'I didn't go to the front. It's you I'd like to talk to, if that's all right?'

The maid looked behind her, checking if anyone was in earshot. 'Have they found out about me going out to see Bert? It was only that one—'

Louisa kept her amusement in check. Lord Redesdale was

clearly still trying to impose his Edwardian values on the young maids but, she was quite pleased to realise, mostly in vain.

'No, it's not about that. May I come in?'

The maid stepped back. Louisa followed her through the short corridor and into the kitchen. There was a cook in there, not the same one Louisa had known at Asthall Manor; she acknowledged Louisa's presence but continued to prepare lunch. Another young maid was washing up the breakfast things.

'Is the servants' hall through here?' asked Louisa, walking through the doorway, the maid keeping up behind her. It was a decent-sized room, made for a larger staff than the Redesdales kept, with a dining table and dresser, plus two armchairs by the fireplace. Louisa pulled out a chair and sat down, then put her notebook on the table. The maid stood in the doorway, silent, watching Louisa's every move.

'I know you have work to do, so I won't keep you long. Is Nanny Blor upstairs in the nursery, do you know?'

'Yes, miss, she is. Shall I fetch her?'

'No – that is, not yet. Thank you.' Louisa paused, took a breath. 'I'm sorry, I haven't introduced myself. I'm Louisa Sullivan. I used to work for the family, as a nursery maid, then lady's maid. I was Louisa Cannon then.'

'Yes, I've heard of you. The girls have talked about you. And Nanny Blor.'

'What's your name?'

'Annie Mullins.'

'And how old are you?'

'Eighteen, miss.'

'Don't be nervous, Annie. I'm here because I'm trying to find Miss Jessica.'

'They don't know where she is, do they?' Annie was fiddling with a duster she had pulled out of her apron pocket.

'No. Lord and Lady Redesdale are understandably very worried. I wondered if you knew anything? Or any of the other maids here?'

'I don't know anything, miss.'

'Who are the other servants?'

'There's Mrs East, the cook. She don't talk to nobody, really. She doesn't live in, she goes home at night. And there's Milly, she's only a tweeny. She lives out, too, with her family.'

'That leaves you and Nanny Blor as the only live-in servants now?'

'Yes, miss.'

Times had changed, thought Louisa. Well, she knew that. What she hadn't known was how much her former employers had been forced to change with them.

'Did you work at Swinbrook?'

'Yes, for about six months, and then they offered me to come here with them. I'd never been to London before, so I was happy to do it.'

'So you knew Miss Jessica?'

'A bit. She's nice, you know? She talks to us, not like we're anything below her.'

Louisa looked at her notebook, which was still blank. It hadn't seemed right to put anything down of Annie's conversation. She knew that she needed to keep Annie comfortable, keep her talking. Guy had told her often enough that witnesses didn't know what they knew; you had to make sure they told you everything they could think of because the golden nugget was probably buried beneath several layers of useless, dry detail.

'Did you notice any change in her in the weeks before she left?'

Annie looked up at the ceiling. She was doing Louisa the courtesy of trying to remember. 'No, not really.' She stopped and stared at her hands, holding the cloth. 'Except, maybe . . .'

'What?'

'When we were in Swinbrook, she used to come and find me quite a lot. We'd chat – not about anything special, just this and that. She'd ask me if I had a sweetheart, and she'd talk about how she'd like one.'

'Did she ever say that there was anyone she liked particularly?'

'No – she used to moan that she had no chance of meeting anyone, or not anyone she'd want to meet. She didn't like the parties she went to last summer. I used to tell her she didn't know what side her bread was buttered when she told me what they were like – all those lovely dresses and royalty at every corner. It was funny. She used to say that she wanted my life, the freedom, she called it, to go out and meet people on my days off. But I've never had a dress like the ones Miss Jessica has, I've never been to the palace and met the king and queen, and I can't see that I ever will.'

'Stranger things have happened,' said Louisa, 'but I know what you mean. I used to feel the same.'

'And you don't now?'

'No, I'm older. I'm married and I have a baby girl – those things make me happy, not dresses and parties. But I remember wanting to see the world the way they did.'

'Yes, that's it. I wonder sometimes what it's like to have their eyes.' Annie gave an embarrassed smile and stuffed the duster back in her apron pocket. She made as if to go.

'Wait, Annie. Can you think a little more for me? You said that Jessica changed from how she was at Swinbrook?'

'Well, her mood changed, and I couldn't see why. She was always bad-tempered at Swinbrook, and even after we'd all left that house and come to London, she was still fed up a lot. And that was when she'd find me. I think I cheered her up. Then in the few weeks before she left, she was happy. She wasn't fighting with her ladyship, not like before. And she didn't come to see me as much.'

'So something brought about a change in her mood, not long before she left. But you don't know what it was?'

'No. There was only one thing she did different for a week or so before she went to France. Every morning at ten o'clock, she made a telephone call.'

'Do you know whom she was calling?'

'Whom!' Annie laughed. 'You ain't been below stairs for a while, have you? No, I don't know.' Then her posture changed: she straightened and her eyes widened. 'She got one call – I'd forgotten 'til now. I think it was the day before she left. I took it, someone asked for her. A man.'

'Did he give his name?'

'Robert, I think. Robert Bannon or Sandon or something like that. I'm sorry, miss. I can't remember exactly.'

'Would you have written it down at all?'

'Yes, miss. On the notepad by the telephone in the hall.'

'Thank you so much, Annie. You've been such a help. You can go back to work now.'

'Thanks, miss.' She turned to go, then looked back. 'It was nice to talk to you.'

It was, thought Louisa. And now she had a clue.

CHAPTER FIFTEEN

⁓

Louisa had two brief conversations with the cook and the tweeny maid but it was clear that, although they were sympathetic, they did not know Jessica to talk to. After she had been shown upstairs, Louisa made a diversion to the telephone in the hall and found the notepad beside it. She looked through a few pages and there it was: Robert Brandon, 4.30 p.m., 6 February. The day before Jessica had departed for France.

After a quick check with Lady Redesdale – she had never heard the name Robert Brandon, she hadn't realised Jessica was making telephone calls daily at the same time – Louisa left the house and found a telephone box.

First, she looked in the telephone book for a Robert Brandon listed in London. There were three. Louisa telephoned each one: the first answered the telephone and was clearly a very old man; the second was answered by a maid who said he was out at work at the bank. Louisa discounted these for the time being. The third said: 'If you're another of those Commies, I'm going to come and knock your block off!'

'What?' said Louisa, momentarily taken aback.

'Why are you calling?'

'I'm looking for Miss Jessica Mitford. She knows a Robert Brandon and I wondered if it was you.'

'I don't know who that woman is. Is she a Commie?'

Reluctantly, unsure of what she was getting into, Louisa said that she was.

'Someone with the same name as me has written a Commie book and it's causing me no end of aggravation. I don't know why they get it into their heads – they call me up asking me to come and give a talk. I don't know—'

Louisa cut him off, thanked him and ended the call.

So that was clue number two.

Next, Louisa made a call to Guy. After they had agreed everything between them, she got the bus back to Soho.

At the door to the bookshop on Lincoln Street, Louisa pushed back her shoulders and headed in, full of determination and righteousness. So she was somewhat disarmed when she found Donald sitting by the till, leafing through another book, hardly looking up. 'I thought you might be back.'

'Why did you?'

He put the book down and put his hands on his knees. 'Just had that sense. I think perhaps I recognised another intuitive person.'

'So you do know Miss Jessica Mitford.'

'No – as I said yesterday, I might have read her name in the papers but no more than that.'

'Do you know Robert Brandon?'

Donald rubbed his knees a little. He was wearing brown

corduroys, well worn. 'He's a Communist writer, and we have his books here.'

'Is he a famous writer?' Louisa adjusted to the warmth of the shop, which came more from the stacks of books than any heater but was better than the sharp cold outside.

Donald gave a small laugh. 'There's no such thing as a famous Communist writer, but he is well known in those circles, you could say. A hero to some.'

'Can you tell me anything about him?'

'Well, let's see. He lives in Abergavenny, he has barely any money because he gives away almost everything he receives, and he is vegetarian. Oh, and he's seventy-two years old.'

Louisa's shoulders dropped. 'So he hasn't run away with Miss Jessica, then.'

'I'd say the chances were slim.'

'A Robert Brandon telephoned Miss Jessica the afternoon before she left. I thought it might be a clue.' Louisa watched Donald fiddle with the various accoutrements he had around his till; there was something nervous in his movements. Why would he be nervous? What was he hiding? 'After we left you yesterday, I thought I heard you make a telephone call. A message for Esmond somebody.'

Donald's hand stopped briefly, and he looked up. 'Perhaps. What of it?'

'It struck me as strange at the time, that's all. That the moment we left, you would make a call. I thought there might be a connection.'

'No, there wasn't.'

'Hmm.' Louisa looked around again at the piles of books, disordered and dusty. She could hear one or two people shuffling about. It wasn't a hive of activity. It wasn't apparent that Donald was a man with urgent matters to attend to: who could have needed such a message? 'Where might I find Robert Brandon's books?'

As if he had lost interest in the conversation, Donald didn't look at Louisa as he replied, but continued to shuffle papers around. 'We have a few, but they're scattered across different sections. You might find one or two in the shelves on the left down there. He wrote a biography of Lenin.'

'Thank you,' said Louisa, feeling rather peremptorily dismissed. She found the Lenin book and flicked through it, but there was nothing inside to yield any further information. She didn't know what she was looking for, but she didn't want to leave the shop and abandon all hope of finding a link to Jessica's disappearance. Louisa scanned the shelves, half out of curiosity, half idly looking for another Robert Brandon book. There were three or four more, some no thicker than pamphlets, a rudimentary printing with no illustrations, the large text on the front declaring A *Treatise on Marx* or *Class Struggle and the Industrial Revolution*. She was about to give up and leave when she spotted one in a box on the floor, beneath a handwritten sign: *Second Hand*. There was a red hardback – Brandon's book on the class struggle. Louisa took it and opened it. There, on the flyleaf, was what she had been looking for, handwritten in black ink: *Esmond Romilly, Wellington, 1932.*

CHAPTER SIXTEEN

~~~~

Louisa closed the book and returned to the till, where Donald had remained. She waited for him to finish dealing with a customer then handed the book to him.

'I'd like to buy this, please. It was in your second-hand box.'

Donald gave her a friendly smile. 'Of course. It's five pence.'

She handed the money over while he put the book in a paper bag. 'Do you remember who gave you that book?'

'No. We get given quite a few, usually when people need to raise funds. I give them what I can in exchange for a box of books.'

Louisa took the package. 'I was interested in this one because it belonged to Esmond Romilly.'

Donald exhaled and put his hands on his knees. 'Ah.'

'Why did you deny knowing Esmond Romilly?'

'I didn't do that, strictly speaking.'

'I asked you if you had sent a message to an Esmond yesterday.'

'Well, yes. I am guilty of omission.'

'Mr Oliver, this isn't a game. Miss Jessica Mitford is missing and her family are very worried about her. Esmond Romilly is a cousin of hers. Nobody was aware that the two of them knew each other. But a Robert Brandon telephoned Miss Jessica the day before she left for France. I think Mr Romilly used that name as a code.'

'You might be right.' Donald wasn't smiling, but Louisa could tell that he was being level with her.

'Do you know Mr Romilly? Do you know anything of his plans? Did he ever mention Miss Jessica to you?'

Donald held out a hand. 'Hang on a mo with all those questions. Yes, I know Mr Romilly. He's a very impressive young man. He's spent some time in here, and he gave me a box of his books a while ago, before he went to Spain.'

'He went to Spain? When was that?'

Donald stood up. 'I think we're in for a long conversation, and I could do with a cup of tea. What about you? I can hang the closed sign up for half an hour, while we go across the road.'

'Yes, that would be good.'

A short while later they were sitting opposite each other in a café with the requisite steamed-up windows and short-tempered waitress, teas before them. Donald spooned three sugars into his. 'I can't seem to give it up,' he said light-heartedly.

'Mr Romilly,' was Louisa's only reply. 'As much as you know, please.'

'Yes, but keep your voice down. Police spies are always listening in.'

'Are they?' Louisa almost looked behind her to check.

Donald leaned in. 'The Establishment doesn't like Communists. It's up to us to stay one step ahead.' Whether he had reassured himself that there were no official eavesdroppers, Louisa didn't know, but Donald continued to talk, slightly louder than before. 'I'm not a bosom buddy of his, but I'll tell you what I know.' He gave his drink a final stir and clattered the teaspoon noisily on the saucer. 'He's still young, not yet twenty, and I've known him for about four years, I'd say. He's clever, and charming. I think sometimes his passion gets misread for a bad temper, but I've not seen a bad side to him.'

'Miss Jessica will be used to that. With her father.' It was indiscreet of her, she knew, but there was a warmth to Donald that somehow invited confidences.

'He was rather badly behaved at school. Then again, he was at Wellington, which couldn't have been less suited to his personality. I was there too, albeit a long time ago, but it meant I found it easy to sympathise with his frustrations. He and his brother made it into the papers because they started a magazine which they sold to boys in public schools all around the country.'

'What was in the magazine?'

'Nothing to please the headmasters, that was for certain. There was poetry and some good-humoured stuff. I liked it. But too much politics of the wrong sort, so far as the school was concerned. It got him booted out. That was when he came here for a while, to get himself started in London. His mother lives in France, so far as I know. I don't get the impression she has much to do with him.'

'No,' agreed Louisa. 'She has a reputation for being not quite all there. What did he do in London?'

'Oh, the usual red-blooded-young-man sort of thing. Went to political demonstrations, did various jobs. He sold silk stockings at one point, then I think he got a fairly decent commission selling ads for *World*. You can't accuse him of being workshy. Then he went to Spain last year. I had supper with him on his last night in London but haven't seen him since then. I don't mind admitting that I was worried about him.'

'Why?'

'Because although he's sharp and educated, he's impulsive. I knew he'd head for the action. Have you read anything about the war that's going on there?'

'No, I haven't.'

'Do you know who is fighting the war?'

Embarrassed, Louisa shook her head. She had seen mention of it in the newspaper, but it had looked to her like something that was happening far away, irrelevant to her daily life, which at the time was almost completely consumed by the novelty of motherhood. Now it seemed as if everyone was dashing over there.

'In short, Spain has a left-wing government, the Popular Front. Last summer saw a revolt led by the Nationalists in a military coup of sorts. General Franco is their leader, and he's said to be particularly ruthless.'

'The Nationalists are right-wing?'

'Very much so. The problem is that various factions and band-wagons have joined either side. Anarchists and Communists supporting the republicans – that is, the government. Fascists and monarchists clubbing together with the Nationalists. It's messy. Civilians are getting caught in the crossfire, there isn't enough money to properly arm or defend either side, and there are too many people going out there who simply want a fight. Esmond knows how to look after himself, so I believed he would probably survive. But it would be dangerous nonetheless.'

'Did he come back?'

'Yes. He joined a battalion of men – fifteen Englishmen and others from France, Germany, Italy, Poland and elsewhere. An International Brigade. Only he and one other of his fellow countrymen survived. Even then, he only returned to England when he got dysentery. That was at the start of this year.'

'You didn't see him, then.'

'No, but we've been in touch through the occasional letter. The last was only a few weeks ago and he wrote that he had recovered well.'

'He never mentioned Jessica Mitford?'

'No. That part is true. I have heard of her, but not because of him.'

Louisa slumped in her chair. 'I couldn't say that she is definitely with him, then.'

Donald looked at her sympathetically. 'No, but it seems likely, doesn't it? They're cousins, and she is sympathetic to the cause. Esmond is a young man, good-looking in his own way.'

'Is he?'

'He's a little on the short side, and he has red hair. But he's zealous and ambitious. That all adds up.'

'Yes, I can see he might be her type.' Then Louisa remembered the question she hadn't asked yet. 'Why were you telephoning Esmond yesterday? Where did you telephone to?'

'I didn't telephone him directly. I was sending a message.'

Louisa said nothing but looked at him. Donald returned the stare but his shoulders dropped. 'Fine. I wanted him to know that people were looking for him. You never know who it might be and, whatever your story was yesterday, I didn't know that I could trust you. But I can't be certain that my message got to him. I telephoned his brother, Giles, who is at their father's house in Herefordshire. He told me that he doesn't know where Esmond is. After his spell in hospital, he went to recuperate at someone's house. A godmother, I think, but I don't know. His brother suspects that Esmond is returning to Spain, via France.'

Louisa absorbed this information. 'Why do you trust me now?'

Donald shrugged. 'I don't know. Instinct. I'm a soft touch.' He pulled some coins out of his pocket and put them on the table. 'Looks to me as if you've got a trip to France coming up.'

'Maybe.' Her mind was whirring. What about Maisie? Could she really leave her and go haring off after two impetuous young people, possibly caught up in a nasty civil war? There was an outside chance that it could lead her to solve the disappearance of Petunia Attwood, but she wasn't hopeful. Yet the reminder of who she was, the excitement that she knew she chased, had her heart beating faster than it had in a long time.

CHAPTER SEVENTEEN

While Louisa was at Lincoln Street, Guy had been on the telephone to ferry lines asking for passenger lists on 7th February, but since he was no longer a policeman they were refusing to hand over any names. He had tried Customs at Folkestone, but with the same result. He was considering contacting the French police when Louisa came into the office.

'I know who Jessica is with,' she said. He noticed that her cheeks were flushed, from the cold air outside, and once again marvelled at the pleasure of having her interrupt him in the office.

'Who?'

'Esmond Romilly.'

'Romilly. Her cousin?'

'Yes – do you remember Nancy said something about Lord Redesdale's aunt's sons being "too red" for them to meet? I should have picked up on that. They're called Esmond and Giles, which I knew but I'd forgotten.'

'Tell me how you found out.'

Louisa told him how she had stumbled across Esmond's name in the flyleaf of a book by the Communist author. She showed Guy the slim hardback.

'Hmm. But does that prove anything?'

'No, but Donald Oliver, the man who owns the bookshop, knows Mr Romilly well. Mr Oliver told me that he's already been to Spain to fight in the war over there. We know his mother lives in Dieppe. It's only logical, isn't it?'

'Logic isn't evidence,' said Guy. 'But you've done a great job here. I mean that. We don't know if they know each other, do we? Her parents and sisters don't seem to think Miss Jessica knows him, or they would have mentioned it.'

'Yes, but that's not to say she doesn't. I think we have to go to France to find them.'

Guy pinched his nose, knocking his glasses slightly. 'France is a big place, Lou.'

'Dieppe, then. We can start there. We know the French police won't help us. The police here aren't doing anything – or at least, even if they might, it seems Lord and Lady Redesdale don't want them involved. It's down to us. Mr Oliver told me a little about this war. It sounds frightening. I know Decca is nineteen, but she's naive. If this cousin has persuaded her to go there with him, she probably doesn't know what she's let herself in for. She needs to be brought home and we're the only ones who can do it.'

'What about Maisie?'

'I've thought about that. We don't need to be gone for more than a few days, but I know it could be too much for your mother. So I've telephoned Mary.'

'As in Mary and Harry?' Harry was one of Guy's oldest

friends – a jazz musician who had married Mary Moon, a policewoman Guy had worked with when he first joined the Metropolitan Police.

'Yes. They've got two little ones of their own, and they know what to do. Maisie would be very happy there and I know we can trust them to look after her properly. We'll get paid to find Miss Jessica, so I can pay them out of expenses. It needn't be much but it would help them.'

'I see you've worked this all out, then.'

'Don't laugh at me. But yes, I have.'

'I'm not laughing *at* you, my darling. *With* you. For being so efficient, and determined. None of which is a surprise to me.' He threw his hands up in the air. 'Right. We'd better find our passports and go and talk to Lord Redesdale. If we're going to do this, we should do it as quickly as possible. The longer we leave it, the further away they'll get.'

By seven o'clock that night, Guy and Louisa were at Victoria station, waiting to depart on the same train that Miss Jessica – and, they presumed, Mr Esmond Romilly – had taken eleven days before. In Guy's pocket was a letter from Lord Redesdale on headed notepaper to say that they were authorised by him to make enquiries as to where his daughter was. That had been Louisa's idea – she thought it might help them with any necessary authorities. Lord Redesdale and his wife had confirmed that they hadn't seen Mr Romilly at the train station when they said goodbye to Jessica, and that they had no knowledge of the two of them meeting. They said they would conduct their own enquiries to find out when this might have happened, although Louisa doubted Lord Redesdale would be able to do anything sensibly. He had been apoplectic at the notion that his 'under-age' daughter might have run off with a man. Louisa would have telephoned Nancy to discuss it with her, but she needed every minute she could snatch to pack their cases and take Maisie over to Harry and Mary's house. She had given Maisie a long cuddle goodbye and kissed her several times on her soft, warm face, but reassured herself that her daughter wouldn't realise too much what was happening, and they would be reunited in just a few days. In the meantime, Louisa knew Maisie would be safe and well looked after in Mary's house, which was cosy with children's toys and their happy noises. Walking away with Guy, she came close to turning back but took his arm instead, reassured as always by his confident strides.

CHAPTER EIGHTEEN

In the early hours of the morning, Louisa and Guy disembarked, somewhat groggily, at Dieppe. The crossing from Newhaven had been rough and, though they had booked a cabin, the constant swell and the sound of people groaning all around them had not made for a good night's sleep. The thought of the mission they had undertaken, now with a significant chance of finding Decca, spurred them on. Neither Louisa nor Guy said it explicitly, but they knew that with all the publicity the Mitfords tended to generate, finding Decca could be good for their business. Only if, however, they were successful. If they failed, it could spell the end of Cannon & Sullivan.

And they had to be quick. The longer someone was missing, the graver the danger they could be in. Lord Redesdale and his wife had not been able to furnish any further details about Esmond Romilly. It seemed as if that branch of the family had been cut from their mind. Lady Redesdale admitted that she had read newspaper articles about him, and was grateful that her girls did not know him or his brother. What they knew of him – his rebelliousness, recklessness, eagerness to go into battle and the short temper that Donald Oliver had referred to – did not ease their concerns. Jessica may have gone with him willingly, but it was also highly likely that her determination to get away would lead her into jeopardy if they did not find her quickly. Louisa changed the hour on her watch and was momentarily stilled by the ticking of the second hand. Each movement counted.

Not long after Louisa had first started to work for the Mitfords, they had taken a summer excursion to Dieppe. It had been the first time Louisa had left England, and she could still recall her delight at how different everything had seemed. Even today, with the slate-grey sky overhead and a thick scarf wrapped around her neck, she remembered breathing in those first lungfuls of salty, warm air, wondering if the seagulls cawed in a French accent. The entire Mitford family and Louisa had stayed in a rented villa close to Lady Blanche Hozier's house. She had been known to all as Aunt Natty. Now, as they walked, Louisa told Guy about Lady Blanche's reputation for gambling and enjoying a string of lovers. Her four children had had two different fathers, and there was much tragedy between them. The youngest daughter had died of typhoid fever and her only son Bill had quite suddenly taken his own life not long after the Mitfords had arrived in Dieppe that year. The rumour was that he had gambling debts he could not repay – a story made worse by the fact that Nancy and Louisa overheard Lady Redesdale refusing to lend him money only weeks before.

Of the two remaining daughters, Clementine was married to Winston Churchill, a prominent politician, and Nellie, mother of Esmond, still lived in Dieppe, in her mother's former house. Bill had been her twin. It had been more than fifteen years since

Louisa had been there but, as she walked through the seaside town, she thought she could remember where Lady Blanche's house was. They had packed lightly, only expecting to stay a night or two, and decided to carry their bags with them rather than lose more time finding somewhere to stay.

'Bit bleak, isn't it?' remarked Guy. There were few other people to be seen on the street and several shops looked permanently closed.

'It is out of season. But yes, you're right, it's run-down. It was a fashionable town at the end of the last century, but not any more.'

'Why would Miss Jessica want to come here?'

'She probably didn't. I mean, we don't think they'll have stayed here, do we?'

'No, that's true. Let's hope this Nellie Romilly has some answers for us.' They walked past a hotel with a *Fermé* sign in the window.

'And let's hope we can find somewhere to stay.'

'There'll be a room somewhere, even if the hotels are closed.'

They walked briskly for a few minutes more. Louisa was beginning to doubt that she had led them down the right road when the villa that the Mitfords had taken all those years ago came into view. 'I know where to go,' she said triumphantly, and a few minutes later, when she saw the sign for rue du Faubourg de la Barre, she knew she was right.

Rue du Faubourg was a long road in the centre of the town, with the usual assortment of buildings in the French style: some red brick with elaborate window frames and balconies, some plain plaster with painted shutters. Nellie's house was narrow and unprepossessing, with dirty net curtains at the windows. It seemed almost to lean onto the building next to it, as if it had been added as an afterthought. Louisa stood to the side, while Guy knocked three times.

There was no stirring within. It was nine o'clock in the morning and they hadn't even had a cup of tea – if they could find one in France. Louisa remembered the buttery croissants they had had every morning that long-ago summer.

'Perhaps she's not here,' said Guy.

'Lord Redesdale telephoned her here only a day or so ago. She must be. Knock again.'

Guy knocked again. This time, for good measure, he peered through the letterbox. 'I think I can hear someone moving,' he said, his voice muffled, then he stood up quickly. 'She's coming.'

CHAPTER NINETEEN

There was the sound of bolts being drawn, and then the door opened. A woman with thick dark eyebrows and pale skin stood in the doorway, a woollen cardigan wrapped around her, at least two sizes too big. 'Who are you?' she demanded.

'Mrs Romilly, please forgive us for arriving unannounced like this,' said Louisa. 'I'm Louisa and this is my husband, Guy Sullivan. We're looking for Miss Jessica Mitford. I believe you spoke recently to Lord Redesdale, your cousin?'

'I already told him that I don't know anything about his daughter. Why should I? I haven't laid eyes on the girl for years. I've nothing against her, but my cousin is a frightful snob. I'm not inclined to worry on his behalf when he's certainly never worried on mine.' She moved to close the door but Guy stepped forward.

'We've reason to believe she's with your son, Esmond.'

Nellie pulled the cardigan around her long cotton nightdress. 'Why would you think that? They've never met.'

'We think they have. He has never mentioned her to you, then?'

'Didn't I just say that?'

If Esmond did have a quick temper, Louisa could make a good guess as to which parent he had inherited it from.

'We haven't much to go on but, the day before she departed for France, Jessica received a telephone message from a Mr Robert Brandon . . .' Louisa waited to see if the name provoked a reaction, but Nellie remained impassive. 'I believe your son used to own some books by an author of the same name, which he sold to a bookshop in London.'

'The Lincoln Street bookshop?'

'Yes,' said Louisa, surprised that this was the detail to elicit a response. 'Do you know it?'

'It's the bane of my life. Esmond has been in that wretched place far too much. He fooled me into thinking it was respectable. The owner is an Old Wellingtonian, but the place is stuffed with poets and Bolsheviks. The poor boy has been deluded into thinking he's one of them. Well, I must admit, you're cleverer than you look. It is exactly the sort of trick he'd use – a code name to leave a message.' She gave a sigh. 'I suppose you had better come in, though I don't know what use I can be to you.'

Reluctantly, Nellie walked off down the hall. Guy and Louisa followed. The house was filthy, with piles of newspapers and empty glasses much in evidence. The walls were covered in an Edwardian wallpaper that was peeling at the edges. 'I haven't quite got to tidying up yet this morning,' Nellie said airily. 'I didn't have a very successful night at the casino.'

She took them into the kitchen and gestured for them to sit down at the wooden table, sloppily collecting the dirty plates that were on there. 'I'm not sure what I can offer you. I think I might have some tea somewhere . . .'

'Thank you but there's no need,' said Guy. He wanted to get out of there as soon as possible. 'If you could sit with us, so that we may ask you a few questions?'

Nellie took a chair, a little away from them. Her skin had the grey pallor of someone who enjoys a nightcap too often.

'When was the last time you heard from your son?'

'Oh, I don't know.' Nellie looked around her vaguely, as if the answer might be pinned up on the wall.

Louisa spoke next, more gently than Guy. She didn't blame him: his training as a policeman meant he was better prepared to tackle criminals than confused mothers. It was perhaps one example of where she could contribute to their enterprise. This heartened her. 'Can you think for us? Perhaps a letter, or a telephone call? We know he returned to England with dysentery at the end of last year.'

'Yes, you're right. He had a short stay at the King's Hospital in London. I spoke to him on the telephone then. I would have gone to see him, but I was needed here. Besides, I think his father might have tried to visit . . . ' She trailed off. 'Perhaps not.'

'Do you know where he went from there?'

'Probably to stay with Dorothy Allhusen, his godmother. She's half in love with him, the poor dear. He doesn't need all that mothering; I brought my boys up that way. But she insists.'

Guy wrote the name down, while Louisa continued with the questions. 'Is it likely that your son would have been in touch with her recently, to tell her where he was?'

'Yes, I suppose so.'

'Could you give us a telephone number and address for her?'

Silently, Nellie tore a strip off the top of a newspaper that was on the floor, took a stray pencil from the table and scribbled the details down before giving it to Louisa. 'Are you going to be here much longer? I have got things to do, you know.'

A skinny black cat came into the kitchen at that moment, and padded over to an empty bowl on the floor.

'Only one or two more. It's important, you see. We think they might be on their way to Spain, to the war. Do you think Esmond would return? In spite of having got so ill there?'

'Oh, yes. But I don't know about him being with Jessica. I asked him if he had a sweetheart – a mother likes to know that sort of thing – but he told me he was in no position to fall in love as he cannot support a wife. I quite agree. He's in constant debt, simply doesn't seem to have a clue about how to look after himself. But he insisted on leaving school and going to work.' She gave a dramatic sigh. Louisa half-expected Nellie to hold the back of her hand to her forehead. 'He's always lived in complete defiance of law and order. If they are in Spain, I do hope they're in the north. There's no fighting there.'

'I see.'

'I'd help you, my dear. But my son doesn't tell me much of what's going on in his life and he would never listen to any instruction from me. So, you see, it's quite hopeless. I'm sure he's perfectly all right and if Jessica is with him, which I hope she's not, he would probably keep her decently looked after.' She gave a sudden burst of laughter. 'I suppose cousin David must be going quite loopy at the thought of his precious daughter with my son!'

'If Esmond was on his way to Spain, do you know what route he might take?'

'I think when he went before he took a ship from Bayonne. That would be my best guess.'

94

Guy spoke. 'Do you have a photograph of your son that we could borrow? It would help.'

Nellie went over to a dresser and rifled through a drawer or two before pulling out a square photograph. It showed a young man with thick dark hair and the same eyebrows as his mother, looking intently into the camera. 'And now, you'll have to excuse me but I really must be getting on.' She stood and indicated in the direction of the hall.

Louisa and Guy stood. 'Of course, Mrs Romilly. Thank you so much for your time,' said Guy. 'We will let you know as soon as we hear anything.'

'Hmm. I wouldn't bother. You can see yourselves out, can't you?'

CHAPTER TWENTY

B ack out on the street, they were silent until Louisa led them to a nearby café that she remembered.

'Thank goodness it's still here,' she said as the waitress brought them *chocolat chaud* in bowls, with baguettes and pats of butter. They tucked in. When their stomachs felt half full, they began to debate their next move.

'We'll have to talk to Dorothy Allhusen,' said Guy. 'Did she give you a telephone number?'

Louisa took the scrap of paper out of her pocket and looked at it. 'Yes. I'm not sure if that's a 1 or a 7, but we'll give both a try.' She put it away again. 'Do you think we have to go to Bayonne?'

'I don't think we should both go,' said Guy. 'It could take a while and—'

'If you're thinking about Maisie, I don't think you should worry. I'll telephone Mary in a minute, but I know she'll be happy there. We've only been away a night. How far away is Bayonne anyway?'

'It's on the border with Spain, so quite far. And we don't yet know if she's even there. We'll have to find out more. Before we do that, let's check the address she gave her mother.'

'The false one?'

'It was false in that she wasn't staying there, but it was a real address, wasn't it? Lady Redesdale's letter got there, and presumably Miss Jessica has been seen because she collected that letter and replied.'

'All right, we'll go there.' Louisa paused and took another slow sip of the hot chocolate – one of the most delicious things she had tasted in a long time. 'She didn't seem as if she was the most affectionate of mothers, did she?'

'No, she did not.'

'I can't help but wonder what that does to a person.'

'Neither of us was smothered in kisses,' Guy pointed out.

'Perhaps not – that wasn't the way of our parents' generation. But at least we knew they cared.'

Guy shrugged, unwilling to speculate. He preferred the hard facts of a case, and that meant they needed to get to rue Gambetta as soon as possible.

With the help of the waitress and another diner, who spoke good English, Louisa and Guy found rue Gambetta without trouble. It was only ten minutes' walk away. It was a narrow street with squat red-brick houses built cheek to cheek. They knocked on the door of number 22, and it was opened quickly by an old woman with white hair. She looked at them suspiciously.

'*Bonjour, madame*,' began Louisa, aware that she had started in a way in which she could not go on. 'Do you speak English?'

'Eh?'

'English. Do you speak English?' She spoke slowly.

The woman shook her head and plodded away, leaving her

door open. They stood there waiting, unsure, until a man in his twenties arrived.

'Allo?'

This time Guy spoke, with better luck: the man spoke English, if only a little. Guy showed him the photographs of Edmond and Jessica.

'Yes – this man, he take a letter. He said it was an *erreur*.'

'When was this?'

'Six or seven days ago, I think.'

Louisa showed him the picture of Jessica again. 'And did you see this woman, too?' she asked.

He peered at it more closely. 'I don't know. Maybe.'

'Did they tell you where they were going next?'

'*Non*.'

His mother called from the house and he called back. 'I have to go.' Guy and Louisa thanked him and walked away.

'That's something, at least,' said Guy. 'Mr Romilly and Miss Mitford must be together.'

'That man didn't recognise the photograph of her.'

'No, but surely Mr Romilly wouldn't have collected the letter for her otherwise?'

'Yes,' said Louisa. 'I'd just prefer to know for certain that they are travelling together.'

'Maybe. More to the point, they were here a week ago. We don't know where they are now.' Guy put his arm around his wife's shoulders. 'We're doing well, I promise you. It can be a laborious process sometimes, putting the pieces together. But we'll start to see the whole picture soon. I think we should find a hotel that has a telephone. Then we can talk to Mary to see how Maisie is, as well as call Dorothy Allhusen.'

'And Lord and Lady Redesdale, in case they've heard from Miss Jessica.'

'Good thinking.' He gave her another squeeze.

'Why are we doing this, Guy?'

'What do you mean?'

Louisa hesitated. Perhaps she was being dramatic. And then she thought: no, I've got to talk honestly to Guy. 'It's just that we're a whole country away from our daughter, freezing cold, and chasing after the Mitfords again. Am I going to be tied to them my whole life?'

Guy laughed. 'No, you're not. You haven't been. There's plenty you've done without them. But this is different. They need you – and me. We're solving a case, and if we find Miss Jessica it will put Cannon and Sullivan on the map. Don't worry. We'll make those telephone calls and find out about Bayonne. I'm sure we've turned a corner now.'

The street they were on ran parallel to the sea. Louisa was reminded of one of the first times she had met Guy and realised what a good man he was. They had eaten hot, salty chips in Brighton, overlooking a rough sea, the very one she could see today; the sound of the waves crashing onto the beach had been somehow at once disturbing and comforting. Louisa knew it was her headstrong determination that had taken her from the hard years of her childhood to a life that was completely different to those of her parents. But she also knew that Guy's calm – he was the port in her storm – kept them steady. She held on to him and they walked on.

CHAPTER TWENTY-ONE

⁓

Most of the hotels along the seafront were shut but, with the help of one or two passers-by, they found one open. The owner was willing to let them use the telephone for a fee. She even brought them a pot of strong coffee. Louisa could not afford more than a very brief telephone call with Mary, but it was enough to confirm that Maisie was her usual happy self and had been playing with Mary's two children, had eaten up everything put before her, and had slept through the night. 'I think Mary's doing a better job than I am,' Louisa said when she hung up, but she was pleased.

Lady Redesdale listened in silence to the news that her daughter was definitely with Esmond Romilly. After a minute she said in a strained voice, 'I shall have to tell Lord Redesdale. It's not going to go well. Are you *absolutely* certain?'

Louisa said yes, she was. Everything pointed to it – not least the man who had seen them together. But there was one piece of good news: another postcard had arrived from Jessica, sent from Le Mans. Clearly she was still unaware that she had been rumbled.

'We've looked it up on the map,' said Lady Redesdale, 'and it's only a few hours' drive from Dieppe. I thought that meant perhaps she was on a driving tour, that she might have told us a half-truth. But if you're right and she is heading towards Spain, then it would indicate that she's on her way south.'

'When was it posted?'

There was a rustle while Lady Redesdale looked at the card again. 'The fifteenth.'

'Monday.' That meant they could be at Bayonne already, thought Louisa, or even beyond. The receptionist had kindly rung the local train station for them and confirmed that it would take two nights to reach Bayonne by train. 'Does she say anything to indicate where she is?'

'No. The usual lines about pretty flowers and delicious food. She does sound jolly, at least. I was grateful for that, but now I know she's with that fearful cousin of hers ... ' She was quiet again.

Louisa waited a moment or two. 'Lady Redesdale? Are you there?'

'Of course I'm here,' she snapped. 'Louisa, we can't have anybody find out about this. Do you understand?'

'Perfectly.'

'It could be very embarrassing for Mr Churchill.'

'Pardon?'

'Mr Churchill is our cousin – and Mr Romilly's. There's already been too much in the newspapers about Mr Romilly and his antics at school. The last thing we need is Decca in the papers too, connected with him. It could ruin Debo's chances at her season. We need Decca brought home – quickly. Without any fuss.'

'Yes, I see,' said Louisa. 'We will do our best.'

'If you would,' said Lady Redesdale, and hung up.

Seething, Louisa replaced the handset and returned to the table in the foyer where they had temporarily set themselves up. The coffee was still warm but it was far stronger than she was used to and she left half her cup. After a few minutes, Guy came back. He had been on the telephone to Dorothy Allhusen.

'She chewed my ear off,' he said, sitting down. 'She's a fan of young Mr Romilly. Told me his mother has been *in absentia* most of his life, and she became his guardian after he got sent to a remand home and Mrs Romilly told the court she couldn't control him.'

'Goodness.' Louisa started to wonder if perhaps Lord and Lady Redesdale might have a point about their daughter getting too close to Esmond.

'It seems that she had Esmond to stay with her at the start of this year, as part of his recuperation from dysentery, and it was at his suggestion, apparently, that Jessica was invited down to her house for the weekend.'

'So they met in England before all this happened?'

'Seems so.'

'Why didn't Lord and Lady Redesdale know this?'

'Well, they might have known she was staying with "Aunt Dorothy" – that's what Miss Jessica calls her – but not that she met Esmond there.'

'Did she notice the two of them ...?'

'Getting friendly? She says not. But they did sit next to each other at the first dinner, and she said they might easily have managed to walk around the garden together.'

'They had plenty of time to plot, in other words.'

'Exactly.'

Louisa relayed her conversation with Lady Redesdale. 'It's infuriating. Why can she not credit us with discretion? She's still treating me like a gossiping kitchen servant.'

'She's a frightened mother,' said Guy. 'And she's probably afraid of her husband's response to the news.'

Louisa decided not to press the point. There was no time to complain. They had a job to do and they still hadn't done it. 'I think I should talk to Mr Oliver at the bookshop. He might know someone who could point us in the right direction towards Spain.'

'Someone who might have been to the war there, you mean?'

'Perhaps, yes.'

Guy downed the last of his cup, grimacing at its bitterness. 'Louisa. I don't want you coming to Spain, if that's where I've got to go.'

'What? Why not?'

'Because it's dangerous. There's a *war*. We can't risk it. For Maisie's sake.'

'I wouldn't endanger myself. And why would it be any better for you to be at risk?'

'Believe me, I'm not planning on putting myself in the firing line either. But it's safer for a man.'

'I don't see that it is.' Louisa could feel frustration building in her chest. 'A man is more likely to be a target than a woman. And don't forget, Miss Jessica knows me. If we have to persuade her to return home, I think she'll listen to me.'

'We don't know that. And civilians are getting caught in the crossfire. I don't think we can say that women are less of a target. And Miss Jessica knows me, too. I might not have a woman's touch when it comes to persuasion, but she will know that she can trust me.'

'Guy—' She knew she was losing. She and Guy rarely fought, but when he was sure of his side he could be as obstinate as . . . well, as a Mitford. That was saying something. 'Fine. But I'll come with you as near as I can. Then I can wait for you.'

'Lou—'

'No. That's my compromise. I'll stay safe, but this way we'll be together, we can still work on this together. That's what we said we'd do, isn't it? When we started our agency. Maisie is fine. At worst, we'll only be a week or so.'

Guy nodded. 'All right. Then let's get going. We can buy some food to take with us and catch a train this afternoon.'

'I'll telephone the Lincoln Street bookshop while you get the food. I saw what looked like a grocer's further along the road, left out of the hotel.'

When Louisa rang the Lincoln Street number recorded in her notebook, she was unprepared for the conversation that was to follow.

'How extraordinary that you should call. A letter from Esmond arrived this morning – with no address on it, before you ask. He wanted to let me know that he's on his way back to Spain.' Donald's voice crackled down the line.

'Did he say where he is now, or that he's with Jessica Mitford?'

'He doesn't mention her precisely, but he wrote that he was very happy. No, he didn't say where he was. But he said that he thinks someone is following him.'

'He must mean us.'

'That's just it – I don't think he does mean you.' There was another crackle of static on the line that swallowed his next words. All she heard was ' . . . they want to settle the score.'

'Settle the score for what?'

'What was that? I can't hear you.'

'Mr Oliver? Can you hear me now?'

More static, so loud it was a struggle to keep the handset to her ear. And then she heard: ' . . . be careful, in case they're following you to find him.'

'What? Mr Oliver, do you mean someone's here, in Dieppe?'

But Louisa was talking into a void. Mr Oliver had rung off.

CHAPTER TWENTY-TWO

'That settles it. You're not coming with me to Bayonne,' said Guy.

'What?'

'It's too risky, this business of Spanish men on the trail of Miss Jessica and Mr Romilly—'

'Not Spanish men. A man. And we don't know if he's on the trail, or even if he's Spanish. It's just a suspicion—'

'A suspicion that is clearly worrying Mr Romilly.'

Louisa sat on her case. She had brought their things outside, having settled the bill for their coffee and the telephone, and waited for Guy to return with the food. If they were to make the first afternoon train, they didn't have much time to spare.

Guy held her close. 'My darling. Don't you see? You mean everything to me. Please, go home to Maisie. I will go to Bayonne, and if this man is hoping I will lead him to Mr Romilly, I will be able to throw him off course much more easily on my own.'

'It feels as if I'm being cowardly, or weak.'

'You're not. You're protecting Maisie. We'll stay in touch. Go to the office every day, then I can telephone you. You can keep talking to Lord and Lady Redesdale, even Donald Oliver. There might be more to find out; we had to leave in such a hurry. And the likelihood is that Miss Jessica and Mr Romilly are no more than sweethearts on the run from their parents. There's no need for two of us to bring them home.'

Louisa nodded, and kissed her husband. She was disappointed but she knew he was right. 'At least you have plenty of food to yourself,' she said, raising a smile.

'Yes,' said Guy, letting go of her and picking up the paper bag. He looked inside it. 'Bread, cheese, apples. I even bought two slices of peach tart. Would you like one of them?'

'No, don't worry. I can find something for myself. I've got time to spare now I have to wait for the ferry back. It won't be until the early morning, so I'll stay in the hotel.'

'Perhaps I should stay with you? I could go to Bayonne tomorrow.'

She briefly wondered if this was the right moment to tell Guy about Petunia, so he could look for her too, but felt herself resist: her pride might lead to a fall, but she so wanted to find her and show Guy that she could do it alone. Besides, there was nothing to indicate that Petunia was in Spain, or anywhere near there.

'No. It's best if you go now. You've said it yourself – the quicker the better or they'll get further away. Or married.'

'Yes, that's a point. That really would be the end of Lord Redesdale, wouldn't it?' When they kissed, she felt the bump of his glasses. It made her heart ache. It was funny. All those years of being by herself, resisting him, wanting to make her own way in the world – as she had thought of it then – and now they would be separated for a week? It was hard to stand.

She handed him his case and watched him walk away before she turned back into the hotel to book herself in for the night.

The following evening, after the long journey home – the hours on the ferry had seemed interminable once she had finished her book – Louisa called in at Mary and Harry's place. Maisie was in bed, fast asleep, and Louisa did not like to wake her, so she gave her a gentle kiss on each of her fat cheeks instead. She asked if Mary and Harry might keep Maisie with them for a few more days, as it would allow her to go to the office and continue the investigation. Knowing how happy Maisie was there made it all much easier, and she knew that Mary was grateful for the extra money. Even so, being in her house without her husband or her child felt lonely and she slept fitfully, grateful when the clock struck six and she could get up. It was pitch black and deathly quiet – the only sound she could hear was her own breathing. On a Sunday at this time there were no cars on the road. It felt as if she were the only person awake in the whole of London. She would have put the radio on, a present from her in-laws, but programmes wouldn't start for at least three hours. Louisa regretted not having Maisie with her. She would go into the office, wait for a telephone call from Guy, then telephone Lord and Lady Redesdale. After that, she'd pick up Maisie. Of all people, Mary would understand. Mrs Sullivan could look after her granddaughter this week as they had originally planned. Guy would go to Bayonne, find Jessica and Esmond, and bring them back home. It had been a flurry of excitement, but she was pretty certain that it would soon be over.

CHAPTER TWENTY-THREE

It was not long since dawn had broken. The half-light seemed to throw an invisibility cloak over everything as Louisa turned the corner into Glenthorne Road. There were outlines and shapes but nothing in the way of colour – it reminded her of a news reel at the cinema. There were hardly any cars and no other people. This made it all the more surprising that it was not until she had almost reached the blue door at the side of the betting shop that led up to their office that she saw the man leaning against it, smoking a cigarette. She gave herself the small nudge that all women do when they are alone and a strange man hoves into view: a bracing of the shoulders, a silent reminder that there's probably nothing to worry about. Men in the grip of gambling were often to be found by the betting shop door, waiting for the shop to open, a desperation and a hopefulness they knew was misplaced writ large on their pallid faces.

This man didn't look desperate, or flat broke. His shoes were shiny and his coat looked thick and warm, if a touch too big for him. As she got closer, he flicked his cigarette to the kerb.

'Are you from Cannon and Sullivan?' he asked.

Guy had already prepared her for this scenario.

'Who's asking?'

'Tony Little.' He put his hand out and she shook it briefly. 'I'm from the *Daily News*.'

'You're out very early, and on a Sunday.'

'No rest for the wicked.' He let out a rough smoker's laugh. She couldn't tell his age. She wasn't afraid of him, but there was a seediness about his manner that made her want to get away from him.

'A little bird tells me you're looking for the honourable Miss Mitford.'

'I don't know what you're talking about and I can't help you, I'm afraid, Mr Little. If you'll excuse me, I need to get past.'

She moved to reach past and put her key in the lock, but he stepped to the side and blocked her. 'And from what I hear, she's more of a "dishonourable", if you get my drift.' His tone was threatening.

Louisa stood still. 'No, sir. I do not get your meaning.'

'She's on the run with a young man, ain't she?'

'I don't know where you got your information from, but it's wrong. Good day, Mr Little.' This time Louisa pushed past and he let her go, a smirk on his face. She slammed the door behind her and ran up the stairs into her office, her hands shaking, fumbling at the second lock. How the hell had he got wind of Jessica going missing? And how could he know anything about her being with a man? He hadn't mentioned Esmond's name, which was something to be grateful for – hopefully that was because he didn't know it. The question was, who had leaked the information? The Mitfords would blame her and Guy, she was sure of it.

Louisa thought about who knew Jessica was missing. All of the Mitfords, of course. Which was a considerable number of people alone. And most of them seemed not to mind their names appearing in the papers – in fact, they had been known to actively encourage it. But Nancy would surely not jeopardise their investigation? Louisa was certain that she wanted Jessica to be found as quickly and discreetly as possible. Pamela, newly married, was unlikely to have said anything, if she was even in England. Diana might have done, if only to divert the attention that was usually on her, but would she run the risk of reporters crawling all over the family? Unity was travelling back from Munich. She might have been a candidate, given that she and Jessica sat on opposing sides of the political fence, but they were still good friends. Deborah was too young and innocent to have done it. Louisa discounted Jessica's parents immediately.

Which left Donald Oliver, Nellie Romilly, and maybe the mysterious man who was apparently following Esmond. Nellie was too mad. Donald didn't seem the type, somehow, with his paranoia of tapped phones. So who was the man that had worried Esmond?

First, she needed to reassure the Mitfords that it wasn't her. Because if she knew one thing, it was that Mr Little would have already paid a call to Rutland Gate.

Sitting down, Louisa checked her watch: half past eight. Lord Redesdale had breakfast at eight o'clock every day of the week. It was early to telephone, but she had better get it over with.

At that moment, the telephone rang. Deep in thought, Louisa jumped so violently at the sound that she knocked her shins against the desk. When she picked up the handset, she was unable to stop her yell of pain.

The operator must have switched Guy onto the line as fast as possible.

'Louisa? What's going on? Are you all right?'

'Sorry, yes. I'm fine. I got a shock and banged my shin. How did you know I'd be here this early?'

'I didn't.' Guy's voice was clear – she could never get over how close someone could sound on the telephone. 'I've arrived in Bayonne and I thought I'd try you on the off-chance before I go and find some breakfast.'

'I couldn't sleep, so I came in. Maisie is still with Mary and Harry, but I'm missing her. I'll try and collect her later.' She told Guy she'd been to see them on her way home the night before.

'Give her a kiss from me.'

'I will.'

There was a pause, then the pips.

'Has something happened?' said Guy. 'You sound funny.'

'Nothing, really. A journalist was at the door when I got here, that's all. He knew Jessica was missing. I'm worried Lord and Lady Redesdale will think we leaked it.'

'That's all we need. Who do you think did it?'

'I don't know, but I'll try to find out. What about you? What are going to do in Bayonne now you're there? And was there any sign of that man on the train?'

Guy started to answer but the pips started going more loudly.

'You need more money, Guy.'

'I haven't got any more,' he said. 'I'll try you again lat—'

That was it. The line went dead.

CHAPTER TWENTY-FOUR

A ware that the seedy journalist knew where she was, and since she'd had the luck to talk to Guy on the telephone, Louisa saw no reason to stay in the office. She came out cautiously, checking there was no sign of Mr Little. There wasn't, but she decided to walk for ten minutes to a further bus stop, just in case. There were so few people around, even at this slightly later hour of the morning, that it would be too difficult for him to follow her. Satisfied she was in the clear, she waited at the stop and caught the first bus to Rutland Gate. She could only hope that Lord and Lady Redesdale weren't too disturbed to have a visitor on a Sunday morning, but she couldn't leave it too much longer or they would be in church.

As it turned out, there was no chance of that.

Louisa was taken aback when the front door was opened by Nancy, who looked up and down the road before letting her in.

'We've had news,' Nancy said breathily. 'I had to check there were no reporters outside.'

'I've had one,' said Louisa. 'A Tony Little.'

'I don't know what their names are. Horrid men in Mackintoshes. Come up, we'll tell you what's happened. I'm not sure if it's good news, but Decca is alive and well.'

'That's definitely good to hear. I've got some news for you, too. I got back from France last night.'

Nancy was hurrying up the stairs ahead of Louisa, her skirt narrow, her heels high. She never could resist the allure of chic clothes, even in a crisis.

'Yes, we want to hear all about it.'

Louisa led her into the drawing room she had been in only a few days before. Only this time, she was unable to disguise her shock at Lord Redesdale's appearance. He seemed to have aged a decade in a week, his hair dishevelled, dark shadows beneath his eyes. His wife looked grey with exhaustion too. As before, Tom and Deborah were there, sitting in the same places as before. Unity was present, acknowledging Louisa with a nod. There was a heavy silence in the room. If this was the mood, Louisa could only guess that what had happened to Jessica was a fate worse than death.

'Louisa is only just back from Dieppe,' Nancy announced to the room. She turned to Louisa. 'Does that mean Mr Sullivan is still there?'

'Yes, he's arrived in Bayonne. We believe Jessica may be there. But as I said, we don't think she's alone—'

'We know,' said Lord Redesdale, his voice hoarse. 'It was worse than we thought. She's with a *most* disreputable young man.'

Louisa tried to wave away the irritation she felt at this. She and Guy had gone to Dieppe and the discovery they had made was – what? Old news?

'Can you tell me how you discovered this?' she asked. Formality would keep her professional.

'A friend of theirs came and told us,' said Nancy. 'Poor bugger, he was the one tasked with confronting the Old Human.'

'Language,' said Lady Redesdale faintly, without taking her eyes off the fire.

Nancy had gone to sit beside her mother, leaving Louisa to stand awkwardly, her hands longing to slide into her coat pockets.

'Sorry, Muv,' she said, more gently this time. 'It makes me want to spit with fury. Where's their courage? Why couldn't they tell you themselves?'

There was no answer to this.

'A friend of theirs?' Louisa prompted.

'Yes,' said Tom. He had come to stand by the mantelpiece with his father. 'We don't know the chap, but it seems he had met Decca coincidentally once or twice during her season. And obviously he knows Esmond. Peter Nevile's his name.'

Lord Redesdale shook his head again at the name.

Tom gave him a worried glance, then carried on. 'He told us they're staying in a cheap hotel in Bayonne and that by now they will be married.'

'Married?' Louisa said it without thinking. 'She's only nineteen.'

'Yes, quite. He is only eighteen. I don't see how they could be married, as they're minors, even in the eyes of French law. So we can only hope that they haven't managed to do the deal.'

'A cheap hotel,' Lady Redesdale repeated, barely audible. 'Together.'

'It's a rock and a hard place, isn't it?' said Unity. 'Either they're married or living in sin.'

'Be quiet,' said Nancy. She turned to Louisa. 'She's back

from Munich and her new friend has infected her with a most revolting type of confidence.'

'I forbid you to say anything against Herr—'

'You'll forbid no such thing.' Lord Redesdale had briefly returned to life.

'Do you have an address for the hotel? Mr Sullivan can go there and find them.'

'Do you really think he can? And bring them home?' Deborah this time. She looked so young and pink-faced among the rest of them, like a new tulip flowering at the end of spring.

'He'll try his very best,' said Louisa. She knew that bit was true. She was less certain, however, in the face of what was clearly a thought-out plan by Jessica and Esmond, that they would willingly troop home behind Guy. 'Did Mr Nevile say anything of their plans in Bayonne?'

'No, not beyond the hotel they were in,' said Nancy. 'There was such a hoo-ha after he delivered the news, he rather took shelter and scarpered. We were simply going to write to them at the Hôtel le Pont Neuf and beg them to return.'

Louisa hesitated. But she had to tell them all she knew. 'The thing is, we believe that they may be on their way to Spain.'

'Spain?' said Lord Redesdale, as if naming a particularly rotten specimen of nations.

'Yes. You see, there's a war on—'

'I know there's a war on!' he roared. 'What the hell do you think my daughter wants to do there?'

Louisa resisted the temptation to check her hat was still on her head after that blasting. 'I believe she may be accompanying Mr Romilly, who has been there before.'

Lord Redesdale's head was in his hands.

116

'But what would she do there? She can't go into battle. She's got nothing with her but the sort of clothes one takes for a motor holiday,' said Lady Redesdale.

'I don't know,' said Louisa. 'Mr Sullivan was going to find out as much as possible. Bayonne is a popular last stop before people go further on.'

'They'll run out of money soon enough,' said Nancy. 'That'll bring them home.'

'They can't get to Spain without a visa for work,' said Tom. 'It's possible they've arranged something. It's been two weeks since they left. They could have got the visa in that time.'

'In which case, the Spanish embassy may know something,' said Louisa.

Lord Redesdale looked up at his wife. 'We're going to have to bring in the big guns.'

'Winston,' she said, with a sigh.

CHAPTER TWENTY-FIVE

⌒

Arriving in Bayonne had been something of a revelation for Guy. From the station, he crossed a bridge over a river and walked into what he assumed was the town centre. It felt more intensely French than Dieppe, with vast churches and tall buildings lined up along wide streets, shutters painted and thrown open, all the better to let in the brisk sea air. Along the lower half of the road were rows of shops and cafés, all shut, their awnings rolled back. Unlike the deserted seaside town he and Louisa had arrived in, Bayonne was busy, but not with prosperity. Groups of exhausted-looking dark-haired families clustered on benches, neither talking nor smiling, but for a few children, inventing games with sticks and pebbles. What appeared to be their worldly possessions were tied in bundles at their feet, and they wore layers of jumpers, coats and scarves.

Refugees.

He had had two fairly sleepless nights on the train, more or less sitting upright for the entirety of the long journey, but he did not feel tired. Now that he had arrived and believed himself to be closer to Jessica and Esmond, he was determined to prove that this was a case he could solve. The problem was that he spoke neither French nor Spanish, and did not have a clue where to begin in this large town, whose doors were closed.

The churches, however, were open. Guy decided that was as good a place to start as any, and walked into the one on the square in which he had been standing, contemplating his next move. It was a square construction of yellow stone and would not have looked out of place in the English countryside: it had arches over the wooden doors and a vast medieval rose carved on the front. What appeared to be a few congregants from a service that was over were trickling out. Inside, the stone arches above him were high enough to suggest they almost reached the heavens, and the bright southern light made the stained-glass windows glow above the crucified Jesus. Guy rarely went to church, and it gave him the shivers.

A man wearing a white collar and a black buttoned-down robe was standing by a pew, talking and shaking hands with the last of the attendees: three extremely elderly women who almost mimicked his appearance with their very white hair and solid black clothes, which revealed nothing of their true shape or personality. Eventually, with small bows of the head and mutterings, they departed and the priest, having noticed Guy waiting, gave him a friendly nod.

'Hello. Do you speak English?' asked Guy, walking towards him.

'Yes, I am proficient,' said the priest. 'Religious education is good, eh?'

Guy put out his hand and introduced himself. 'Forgive me for a little business on a Sunday, but I'm here looking for two people and I'm not certain where to start.'

'Are they from England too?' The priest indicated a pew. 'Please, let us sit together.'

Guy shuffled sideways into the pew and sat down, catching a strong scent of incense as he did so. 'Yes, and they are well known over there, which is why I am making a discreet investigation into their whereabouts. I'm a private detective, a former policeman.'

'I see,' said the priest. 'People do seek refuge in my church and we always welcome them, but I have not had an Englishman walk through my doors for some weeks.'

'Oh.' Guy's disappointment must have shown.

'However, I do know where they tend to go. There is a hotel not too far from here. The Hôtel le Pont Neuf. It is cheap and popular with the foreign volunteers, you might say. Can you tell me anything of them? In case I have heard?'

Guy showed the priest the photographs of Esmond and Jessica, gave him their names and ages, and explained why he believed they were in Bayonne.

The priest closed his eyes briefly. 'I will pray for them,' he said. 'I do not wish for them to be on their way to Spain. It is very hard there now. You will have seen the many people who have fled the war, trying to find a place here, where there is none. There is so little we can do. I am not Jesus, able to turn water into wine, or one loaf of bread into many.'

'Is the situation really so bad?'

'Yes. It depends, of course, on exactly where they are situated. But food is scarce, the streets are piled with rubbish, and there are many badly organised factions armed with guns they do not know how to use properly. If you find them, you must tell them to go no further.'

'That's my intention,' said Guy. 'But Mr Romilly has been there already. It's my belief that he will be eager to return to the fray. He's a young man with something to prove, from what I've heard.'

The priest tutted and shook his head. 'Go to the le Pont, tell them Father Basset sent you. I'm afraid it won't get you a free room, but they may be more inclined to show you the guest book. My prayers go with you.'

Guy thanked him and left quickly, not wanting to breathe in any more of the heavy incense.

CHAPTER TWENTY-SIX

Winston Churchill may no longer have been in the Cabinet, but it seemed he still had friends in high places. Before the bell had rung for luncheon, the Foreign Office had been in touch with the consul in Bayonne, but was told it would be the following morning, Monday, before a definite answer could be given.

Louisa had remained with the family while the calls were being made, but did not stay for the roast beef. Instead, she went to collect Maisie from Mary's, scooping her deliciously warm, happy baby into her arms with gratitude and relief.

'She was as good as gold,' said Mary. 'We'll be sorry to see her go. Especially the girls – they loved having her.'

'Like a living doll.' Louisa smiled. 'Sometimes I feel the same. Thank you so much for looking after her so well.'

'Any time.'

'Be careful, I might hold you to it.'

With Maisie waving goodbye, Louisa hauled her out – how could one tiny person need so many things? – and decided to take a taxi home. She would put it on her expenses – since, after all, she would not have needed to have Maisie stay with them if she weren't looking for Jessica. Now that the family were sure she was in Bayonne with Esmond, she was at least safe. Lord and Lady Redesdale may not have been exactly ecstatic at the news of the marriage, but better that than the alternative.

If only the alternative were not such a close threat.

When Louisa got home, there was a telegram from Guy, asking her to telephone him as soon as she could at the Hôtel le Pont Neuf – the hotel where Jessica and Esmond were staying. She hoped it was not coincidence, and she could not help but be delighted at the thought that her husband had managed to get to them faster than the powers of the Foreign Office.

With coins in her purse, and Maisie on her hip, Louisa went to the telephone box that was only two streets away. She had to wait a few minutes – Sunday was a popular day for those who had moved away from home to talk to their families – but the sight of Maisie seemed to hurry the person along. Juggling baby, telephone number and coins, Louisa called through to the international operator. She wouldn't have long.

CHAPTER TWENTY-SEVEN

⁓

The priest had given directions that were easy to follow, and after a short walk, Guy saw the Hôtel le Pont Neuf. Its white plaster was chipped and its awning was faded, but it was at least open, with the promise of answers and coffee within.

Guy walked through the front door into what he assumed must be the reception area. It was no more than an open hall with a strong smell of unwashed bodies and a harassed young woman behind a desk. Crammed onto a few chairs and sitting on the floor were more of the by now familiar figures he had seen in the town. Their air was one of desolation. And this wasn't even Spain.

Guy walked up to the desk and greeted the receptionist. She had her hair pulled back neatly and wore a thin shirt that showed dark patches under the arms. She replied in a stream of fast French that he knew he had no hope of understanding.

'I'm so sorry, but do you speak English?'

Her only reply was another incomprehensible burst that sounded angry. Today was not a good day for her.

A young man approached the desk and stood by Guy. 'I can translate for you,' he said. He had a three-day beard and noticeably long eyelashes. Shyly, he held out his hand. 'If you can give me some centimes?'

'Of course,' said Guy, digging his hand into his pocket. 'Thank you.' He handed over the coins and the man put them quickly into his pocket.

'My name is Guy Sullivan. Please could you ask this lady if she can help me find two people I am looking for? It is possible that they are staying here.'

'Hello, Mr Sullivan, I am Ivo Fernandez,' he replied charmingly. He then turned to the receptionist and translated. Her reply was a Gallic shrug before she returned to her paperwork. Ivo smiled at Guy. 'I think you understand what that means.'

'Could you please tell her that Father Basset sent me. I am a private investigator looking for Jessica Mitford and Esmond Romilly.'

Ivo translated. With a dramatic sigh, she pulled out the guest book and put it in front of Guy. She spoke. Ivo told Guy that she didn't know, she couldn't remember every person that dragged themselves in through the door, but if Father Basset sent him then he was welcome to look. Guy thanked her and opened the book. It was simple enough to follow, with dates of arrival in the left column and departure on the right, the names of the guests and their home address in the middle. Guy didn't have to turn back many pages before he found what he needed.

14 Février   *Mr et Mme Esmond Romilly,*   *18 Février*
45 rue de Faubourg, Dieppe

But that was not what he wanted to see. They were married, and they were no longer there. Guy closed the book and handed it back. Was there a telephone he could use? There was.

'Mr Fernandez, I need to make a telephone call and then stay here to wait for an answer. Can I buy a bowl of soup here? And perhaps one for you, too?'

'Thank you, that would be—' He searched for the phrase. 'A relief for my stomach and my soul.'

Having sent the telegram to Louisa with the hotel's telephone number, Guy and Ivo took a table in the hotel's small but functional restaurant, ordering two bowls of the daily soup – potato – and bread, which arrived quickly. Ivo gulped down half the bowl before looking up, then laughing. 'Forgive me, Mr Sullivan. I was hungry.'

'So I see. Would you like another?'

He gave an embarrassed nod. Guy waved it away before ordering his new companion a second helping.

'You haven't heard of Jessica Mitford or Esmond Romilly, I suppose?'

'No,' said Ivo. 'I'm sorry.'

'What is your story?' asked Guy. 'Where have you come from?'

'My family lived in a small village close to Madrid. When the war began, we were afraid but the fighting did not come near. Until it did. At the end of last year, we were forced to flee our homes. My brothers, my sisters, my cousins – we all left. My mother and my father decided to stay. They said they were too old to move.'

'Do you know how they are now?'

Ivo's head dropped. 'No. I have been travelling since

December. It took me a long time to get to Bilbao, then I had to wait to get on a boat. There are many, many of us. I have lost contact with my family almost completely. My parents, they have no telephone and the post is almost gone. I am afraid for them.'

Guy was moved. 'I'm so sorry. I didn't know how bad it was.'

'It is very, very bad.' Ivo looked up at Guy with the dignity of a statesman. 'I am young, only nineteen. I will be well. I am educated, my family once had money. But there are many children who are frightened, old people who cannot leave. There is barely any food, constant shelling, no medicine. Our own government does not care or cannot do anything, and no other government will help us.'

'Where are you going to go from here?'

'I don't know. Part of me wants to fight, to save my country. Another part wants to save myself, to stay alive. What good can I do anyone if I am dead?'

Guy remembered his own conflicted feelings about the Great War. He had been unable to fight, failing the medical test thanks to his extreme short-sightedness, but his brothers had gone and one had been killed. For a long time Guy had been frustrated by his inability to fight for his country – it was one of the reasons he had gone into the police – but the more years that went by, the more he realised he had been favoured by good fortune. So many had died, and those who had survived had been left with terrible mental scars, if not actual physical disabilities.

'Tell me. If you were Esmond Romilly, this man I am looking for, where do you think you would be? I know he has been in the war, fighting in the International Brigades. He is with his wife now, and I think they are trying to get back there. Where would they go?'

127

Ivo considered. 'If you know they were here, it was probably because they were trying to get a boat to Bilbao. It's the only way, unless you cross the Pyrenees, which is perilous. If he has his wife, you may be lucky; he may not be fighting. Is he an educated man?'

Guy said he was.

'Then perhaps he is working as a news reporter? There seem to be a few ambitious Englishmen who do that, and it is one way to get a visa. Americans too. Journalists who call themselves heroes.' He gave a hollow laugh. 'They do not know the meaning of the word.'

Bilbao. Guy could feel himself being pushed further towards a scene of great despair, but he was powerless to resist.

CHAPTER TWENTY-EIGHT

On Monday morning, Louisa was back at Rutland Gate. There was news to share on both sides.

'Let's go for a walk,' said Nancy, greeting Louisa at the door. 'I think I'll go mad if I'm stuck inside with the grieving humans any longer, and they're not in any shape to receive company.'

They crossed the road and went into Kensington Gardens, heading by silent mutual agreement to the Albert Memorial. Louisa knew it was one of Nancy's favourite routes, a familiar one from when she was a very young girl and the family had lived close by in a different house, before moving to Asthall Manor. The sun shone a little more brightly today, giving Albert's golden pate a definite glow, though it was still cold. Green shoots were poking through the flowerbeds, and the snowdrops were almost over. When Louisa knew spring wasn't far away, she always felt cheered.

'I spoke to Guy yesterday. He arrived in Bayonne and found the hotel where they had been staying. I'm afraid they had checked in as Mr and Mrs Esmond Romilly.'

'So it's true, then,' said Nancy. 'The stupid little girl. She doesn't see how society will shut her out. Or if she does, she doesn't think she cares. But she will. A respectable marriage is still what matters the most about a woman, even in 1937.'

'Yes, I suppose you're right. But perhaps they are very in love?'

'Don't be naive. It's lust. She's barely come up close to a man, then Esmond shows up in all his red-blooded glory – and I mean Red. She won't know how to resist. The exact same thing happened with Diana and Sir Ogre, I'm sure of it.'

'Mrs Guinness was married before,' said Louisa, careful to use the correct name for Diana. Nancy, for all her cynicism about her class, could be a stickler for formality.

'Yes, but she didn't fancy him, she just thought he seemed very sweet. And he was a means to leaving home. Don't you see? That's all the Mitford girls want, no matter what people say.'

'And what is it that you want?' Louisa longed to ask but didn't dare. However long Louisa had known Nancy, there was always an impenetrable wall between them, and Nancy never let Louisa know what she was really thinking.

'Guy says the likelihood is that they will already have moved on to Bilbao. At least, that's where ships go from Bayonne.'

'That's what we think too,' said Nancy. 'I'll explain in a minute. Go on with what Guy told you.'

'He says he will do his best to follow them, but he needs to find a ship that will take him, and he needs a visa. We don't know if they'll still be in Bilbao, of course. They could have left by now.' Louisa waited a moment while Nancy acknowledged someone she knew walking past. 'I wouldn't want to tell Lord and Lady Redesdale this, but Guy said he spoke with a young man, a Spanish refugee. He says it's pretty desperate out there. It could be dangerous for Miss Jessica.'

'You mean Mrs Romilly.'

'Oh, sorry—'

'I'm teasing. We don't know it for *absolute* certain, do we? There's a shred of hope.' She straightened her face.

'There's something else,' said Louisa. 'Esmond has written to a friend of his, a man who owns a bookshop. He didn't reveal much of where he was, other than that he was on his way to Spain, but he said that he thought someone was following him.'

'In a sinister way?'

'Our line wasn't good, but he seemed to think that whoever it was wanted to "settle a score". That was why Guy sent me back to London and stayed in France alone, in case we were being followed as a way of getting to Esmond.'

'But who knows that you are on Esmond's trail?'

'Not many, that's true.'

'Nevertheless, it's worrying.' Nancy briefly watched a young boy run across the grass, his uniformed nanny in hot pursuit. 'I don't know how brave Decca is. I can't see her out on the frontline. She's never shot so much as a rabbit at home. Never went out with the hounds.'

'I really do think it's more serious than that. From what we hear, in Spain there's next to no food, no medicine. Thousands of people have been forced out of their homes.'

'War. I can't bear to think of it. She's only a few years younger than us, but she remembers nothing of the Great War. We do.'

Louisa agreed. She had been young while it was happening, but she'd read the lists of the dead in the newspapers, had heard the neighbours crying when the telegrams arrived. For years afterwards, there had been blind and maimed soldiers begging in the streets.

'What was your news?'

'Muv got a hysterical letter from Nellie Romilly this morning. It seems Esmond wrote to her about the same sort of time as Peter Nevile was dispatched to Rutland Gate. Seven pages of her madness, how thrilled she is to have Decca as a daughter-in-law but how her son has no hope of supporting a wife, how defiant he has always been. She finished it by saying she hoped "the children" were in northern Spain, where there was no fighting. You can imagine how that went down. I don't think I've seen Farve read something with less enthusiasm since my last book came out.'

Louisa put her arm through Nancy's and gave her a squeeze. 'We'd better go back to the house. Has there been word from the Foreign Office yet?'

'Yes, the consul in Bayonne confirmed that they were in Spain. So the next thing is a message to the consul in Bilbao. Winston says he has persuaded Anthony Eden—'

'The Foreign Secretary?'

'That's the one. He's going to personally cable the consul there, to ask him to find her and send her home. Not that a consul will have any luck with either of those two. But we've got one more trick up our sleeve. Farve's solicitors are going to cable Esmond that Jessica is a ward of court and if he marries her he is liable to imprisonment.'

'Is that true?'

Nancy shrugged. 'That's not the point. Farve is determined to stop them and he doesn't much mind what is said. If they *are* already married, I doubt he'll send his son-in-law to prison.'

They had reached the edge of the park and were about to cross the road back to Rutland Gate when they saw a newspaper seller pushing along his cart of newspapers. Bundles of the *Daily Express*, tied up with string. Nancy stopped and jerked Louisa's arm.

'Oh God. Look.'

The headline was all too clear: large and splashed across the front page: PEER'S DAUGHTER 'ELOPES' TO SPAIN

Daily News

PEER'S DAUGHTER 'ELOPES' TO SPAIN

Staff Reporter

Private detectives are searching for the Hon. Deborah Vivien Mitford, seventeen-year-old daughter of Lord and Lady Redesdale, who is believed to have gone to Spain in an attempt to marry her eighteen-year-old cousin, Esmond Romilly, nephew of Mr Churchill.

Romilly, recently fighting on the Madrid barricades in the International Brigade, is believed to be making for Bilbao, government stronghold now cut off by insurgent troops.

Miss Mitford was believed by her parents to be staying in Dieppe, where Colonel and Mrs Romilly have a house. Last week a messenger brought them a letter dated from Bayonne, on the France–Spain border, stating that she might attempt to marry Romilly in Spain.

Lord Redesdale made every possible attempt to intercept his daughter and bring her home. His solicitors are seeking the aid of Scotland Yard, the Foreign Office, the Consular Service and the Spanish embassy. When they realised their daughter was not in Dieppe, the family hired the services of a private detective agency, Cannon & Sullivan, as they believed the French police would not aid them in their search.

They found that the girl had not visited Colonel or Mrs Romilly. They did not know she had fled from Dieppe.

Miss Mitford has a British passport. It should not be difficult for her to pass the French and Spanish frontier guards and through the insurgent and government lines into Spain.

"If I knew where my daughter was," Lord Redesdale said last night, "I would go to Spain at once or get somebody else to go and bring her home. We think she may be in Bilbao."

All British consular posts in Spain and near the border have been given a description of the girl. Spanish embassy officials have advised Lord Redesdale that they will do all they can to trace her.

Miss Mitford's family fear the couple may attempt to make a Communist marriage. Such a ceremony would need no previous notification or any residential qualifications.

The Spanish embassy have advised the family that such a marriage would be illegal. Spanish law demands thirty-two days' notice.

Miss Mitford is the youngest of Lord Redesdale's six daughters. She is already well known in society.

Three years ago Esmond Romilly ran away from Wellington College, where he was educated with his brother. It was stated then that he was under the influence of a group of London Communists. He went to Spain and joined the government forces in the early days of the war.

CHAPTER TWENTY-NINE

Nancy bought ten copies of the newspaper – 'it's ten fewer people reading it around here' – and carted them back to the house. They had got as far as the turning into Rutland Gate when they saw a gaggle of at least six reporters standing around on the pavement opposite number 26.

'Blast,' said Nancy. 'That's gone and done it. The Old Humans are going to go to pieces.' Her bravado faded for the briefest second. 'That bloody Decca. Why did she have to do things in this way? It's all right for her, holed up God knows where with her lover. We're the ones who have to face all this. I could kill her.' She marched towards the house, head held high. 'Keep close, Lou. Don't make any response, don't answer any of their idiot questions.'

Louisa eyed the men warily. They were of varying ages but were all in a similar state of disrepair, in worn-out shoes, cheap dark coats, hats pushed back on their heads. Some of them almost seemed to be acting the part of intrepid reporter with pencils tucked behind their ears, notebooks sticking out of their pockets, cameras hanging from their neck. Others stood languidly, bored already, smoking cigarettes and barely even looking at the door. But as soon as Nancy approached the steps, they came alive like an octopus spotting prey and moved fast across the road, shouting out questions or statements designed to provoke.

'What does Herr Hitler think of the Communist in the family?'

'Are they living in sin?'

'How can the Hon. Miss Deborah get married underage? She's only seventeen! Has Lord Redesdale given permission?'

'To a *Bolshie*?'

'Does this mean she won't be a debutante?'

Nancy, running up the steps, came to a halt, almost sending Louisa flying backwards. She turned around. 'Miss Deborah?'

There was a chorus of 'Where is she?' and 'When is she coming home?'

'It's not Miss Deborah that's gone missing,' said Nancy, unthinkingly.

'Shhh!' Louisa gave her a shove. 'Let's get inside, quick.'

They ran in and slammed the door behind them, then Nancy dropped all the papers on the floor bar one and they read the front page.

'They think it's Debo that's missing,' said Nancy. 'I'm not sure if that's better or worse. Someone is leaking information, but it's not coming from either of us, is it?'

'No. If it came from any of us, they wouldn't have got the wrong daughter.'

'Exactly. It must be something to do with that horrible little man that was waiting for you at your office. He's scented something.'

'Even so, he must have got it from somewhere. I'll try and do some digging.'

They headed up the stairs to find out how the news had been received by Lord and Lady Redesdale.

Not well, it seemed.

In fact, the shouting could be heard from the floor below. Nancy walked ahead slowly. Louisa was hoping it would have died down before they opened the door, but there was no chance. Lord Redesdale was in full flow. Even their appearance in the drawing room did not staunch his anger.

Nancy walked around her father, like someone dodging a Catherine wheel on the lawn, and took Louisa off to the side. 'Now is not the time, Lou. We'll have to wait for the storm to pass. Even Nine's waterworks have burst.'

Louisa took this to mean that Deborah was in floods of tears.

'I had better get back to the office, in any case. I've got an idea or two to try, to find out who leaked it.'

'If you can, but we need to find Decca more urgently. Will you telephone me as soon as you hear anything from Mr Sullivan?'

'Of course.'

With Lord Redesdale's fierce threats to horsewhip the editor of the *Daily Express* still ringing in her ears, Louisa departed Rutland Gate.

CHAPTER THIRTY

With the help of Ivo, Guy obtained the address of the British consulate in Bayonne from the hotel's receptionist. With Jessica and Esmond on their way to Spain, Guy was sure they must have gone there for their visas. At the very least, he would find out about ships going to Bilbao and try to see if he could obtain a visa for his own passage. Guy tried to imagine himself in Spain, but found it difficult. As much as he relished solving a case, this was beginning to feel more like chasing naughty children lost in the park. If he did find them, he wasn't at all sure he'd have the means to persuade them home. Everything here was different, and exotic for it. He could see that Jessica Mitford, who had been plotting most of her life to escape from home, would be nothing but enthralled by the promise of adventure. She was not, after all, the only one. The more Guy looked, the more he could see groups of American and British men clustered in cafés plotting their journey to Spain, almost matching in numbers the groups of Spanish refugees who had fled.

On the train, Guy's antennae hadn't twitched. He hadn't

seen anyone following him. And now, in Bayonne, everything was unfamiliar. He couldn't be certain whether or not there was anyone behind him behaving suspiciously, insofar as almost everyone was.

When Guy reached the consul, there was a desultory queue that snaked out of the building and along the road. He joined the end, and it was only a minute or two before someone else arrived and they struck up a conversation. It was something that felt familiarly British, at least. His name was Keith, and he was hoping to get a visa.

'But there haven't been any ships heading out to Bilbao for five weeks now,' said Keith. 'Danger of mines, apparently.'

'Have you been here as long as that?'

'Nah. Only a week or so. It's not that bad. The hotels are cheap, the food is OK. And there's plenty of company. I've met all sorts. It's more interesting than writing reports on the village jumble sale.'

'Which is what you were doing back home?'

Keith nodded. His jacket and trousers had clearly done him good service, and his shoes needed a decent polish, but he was otherwise clean-shaven and his nails were clean. 'I'm hoping to get a bit of work for the *News Chronicle*, but there's a few of us after the same thing.'

'Can you get a visa without a job promised?'

Keith rubbed his chin. 'It's not easy. I did it before but they're clamping down now. Making it harder. But I'm not in a rush. I'm standing here mostly because it's something to do.'

More people joined the queue. The weather was warmer than England, though Guy found he always longed for the sunshine and then when it came it was too hot for him. He pulled at his shirt collar, which was beginning to feel a little tight. He had left his case at the hotel; a small one, as he hadn't brought much with him. He would need to buy a couple of new shirts if this was going to go on any longer, or he'd start looking like an anarchic fighter himself. 'You've been here before, did you say?'

'Last year, for a few weeks. I heard the fighting had started, word got around. I'm not a Commie but I won't stand for fascists either. They're a real danger and people don't seem to realise. Hitler, Mussolini and now this lively lot, the Nationalists. It's not something we want in Blighty, that's for certain.'

'No one wants another war in England,' said Guy.

'Of course not. But Hitler does. You betcha. Those coves who think they can negotiate peace with him and keep their freedoms. It's not language he understands. Look at that army he's building. He says it's just a matter of national pride? Don't make me laugh.'

Guy found himself listening to this more seriously than anything he'd heard on the radio. It had all seemed like so much noise, too far away to worry about, even with the things Louisa had told him about Diana and Unity. That had seemed like the fickle adventures of the upper classes, nothing that could turn into real war. Not after last time, not when so many people in government were doing all they could to prevent it. But in this foreign country, with the tangible sight of refugees and mission-ary soldiers – in the end, that's what they were – all around him, it felt palpably close. Perhaps what Jessica and Esmond were doing was necessary – admirable, even.

'What are people doing if the ships aren't sailing to Bilbao from here, then?'

'You can travel a bit further south, St Jean de Luz, and catch

141

a ship from the port there. There's all sorts of cargo ships. It's a messy business with the refugees and stowaways, and plenty of captains aren't keen on these extra bodies in the hold. If you've got a visa, they can't refuse, and some of them are in support of the anti-fascists, of course. But, as I say, it's not easy. You've got to have a bit of mettle.' He paused. 'You haven't got a smoke, have you?'

'Sorry, no.'

'Fair enough.' The queue shuffled further forward. 'If people don't fancy trying to boat it, and if they haven't got a visa, then they might cross the Pyrenees. Not a route I'd recommend. Pretty treacherous if you don't know what you're doing, or don't have the right kit with you. But it can be done. You could pay a guide, I suppose.'

'I don't think I'll be doing that,' said Guy.

'No. There was a couple who left here a week or so ago. Everyone thought they were mad to do it, but they were determined.'

'Who were they?'

'I don't know. Didn't see them myself. It was just a bit of gossip among us, if you like. Young, I heard. They'd have to be, going on a foolhardy mission like that. There was talk last night that they've been trapped in a snowstorm.'

'A man and a woman?'

'Yeah.' Keith started to look out into the street, bored with the conversation and the queue. 'Just married, or about to be. Strange sort of honeymoon, don't you think? Crossing a mountain range to go and fight in someone else's war. But I can kind of understand. Trying to do the same, ain't I? And a girl beside me would make it a lot more pleasurable. Eh?' He gave Guy a playful nudge.

'Do you know anyone who might have more details on this couple? Who might have talked to them before they left?'

Keith looked Guy up and down. 'Might do. What's in it for me?'

'I'll cross your palm with silver, if that's what it takes,' said Guy.

'Nice one, matey. Let's go then. I'll take you now.'

CHAPTER THIRTY-ONE

❧

I n the office, Louisa left a message for Guy at the hotel in
Bayonne asking him to call her. The telephone bill was going
to be extortionate. Lord Redesdale was not a man known for
throwing his money around – the family had always claimed
hard times, if not quite penury. Lady Redesdale sold eggs laid
by her hens to pay the governesses' wages. Louisa hoped they
would honour the agreement to pay all expenses in the search
for Decca. Now that information – and misinformation – was
flying around from various places, Louisa worried that it would
dilute the work that she and Guy were doing. Particularly Guy.
She couldn't help worrying about him in Bayonne, even though
he was capable and a good detective. But he couldn't speak
French, and ... perhaps she had to admit she was less worried
than missing him. Since they had married and had Maisie,
they had barely spent a night apart. She didn't relish the idea of
going home and having supper without him, or getting into bed
without his strong body to curl up against. If Decca had started
to have that experience with another man, she might find him

difficult to leave behind, too. Guy was going to have a task on his hands to bring her back.

As she was thinking this, the telephone rang.

'Guy?'

'Louisa, I can't talk for long, the money will run out.'

'There's news?'

'I think so. I keep hoping not but—'

There was a pause. Louisa could hear someone shouting an incomprehensible foreign phrase in the background, the distant metallic clatter of a busy street.

'But what, Guy?'

'There's reports of a young couple having gone into the Pyrenees.'

'Why would they do that?'

'It's one way of crossing into Spain, rather than waiting for a boat. But it's dangerous.'

'Do you think it's them?'

'I can't confirm it. It's a young man and woman – the age fits. I haven't managed to talk to a witness, show them photographs.'

'What do we do?'

'I don't know. I can't follow them there. There's simply no way of knowing what route they took, and I would be days behind them.'

'Should I tell the Mitfords?'

The pips started.

'Not yet. I'll try to find out more.'

'The Foreign Office is involved now, they might know something.'

'Just wait. One more day.'

'Please be careful, Guy. I love you.' But he had been cut off.

What if it wasn't Jessica and Esmond but Petunia and Bernard? Louisa knew she wouldn't be able to involve the Foreign Office in the case of Petunia Attwood, but she felt guilty that she had pushed the missing woman to the back of her mind. She resolved to get back on the case promptly and, if she had to involve Guy, of course she would do that.

CHAPTER THIRTY-TWO

A short walk later, Guy was in a run-down café in a Bayonne backstreet. Keith greeted several people before sitting down beside a man hunched over a cup of coffee and a French newspaper. Guy took the chair opposite and started to introduce himself, but Keith silenced him with a wave of his hand.

'Comrade,' said Keith, 'mind if we join you?'

The man barely looked up, shrugged.

Keith gave Guy a wink, then spoke again to the man, his voice low. 'This chap here, he's wanting to get to Spain too. He's on our side.'

The man gave Guy a brief glance. His black hair was neatly slicked back but he looked as if he hadn't shaved for a few days. His expression seemed determinedly neutral.

'The young couple that were crossing the Pyrenees – do you know if they managed it?'

'Maybe,' replied the comrade in an accent that Guy thought might be Italian. 'The hut keeper left them to get some supplies, but he couldn't get back after the weather changed. The snow is deep there now. He says there's enough food to last them a day or two. They'll be safe.'

'Do you know their names?'

'Why should I tell you if I do?'

Keith leaned back, put his hands up as if in surrender. 'He wants to find them and he's willing to pay for the information.'

'Maybe so, but it's not easy. Everyone is looking for someone here. But we are each one of us alone. Or we would like to be.' He turned a page of his newspaper.

'Their names are Jessica Mitford and Esmond Romilly,' said Guy boldly. 'Have you heard of them?' He stopped himself and held his hand out. 'Sorry, I didn't introduce myself. I'm Guy Sullivan.'

The man didn't take his hand. 'I am Luc. I do not know the other name but Romilly, yes, I know of him. He was in the International Brigades. I heard he was a brave fighter.'

'Do you know if they are the couple said to be stuck in the hut?'

'No,' said Luc. 'I do not know. But that man, he is a survivor. If they are there, they will live. Why does he want to take a woman with him to Spain?'

'I believe they are newly married,' Guy replied. 'Or hoping to be soon.'

'Then they are reckless.' He turned another page.

'This hut keeper, would he be here?'

'No – the story came from Barèges, a distance from here. It would take three or four days to walk it.'

Guy felt deflated. It was one step forward, four steps back with this case. Everywhere he looked, there were so many layers of caution and subterfuge that it was almost impossible to get a straight answer about any aspect of it.

'Keith,' said Guy with determination. 'Thank you for your help, but I think I'm going to have to stick with the official route. I'll give the consul another try.'

'As you will,' said Keith. 'If you need me again, you can look for me here. Best cooked eggs in town, even if the frogs don't know how to fry bacon.'

Guy handed him some money and said goodbye.

CHAPTER THIRTY-THREE

⁓

Feeling helpless, Louisa busied herself with Maisie. She knew Guy was right: there was little to gain in telling the Mitfords that their daughter could be walking across a mountain range wearing clothes more suited to a genteel motor around the north of France. There would only be needless worry if it turned out it wasn't them.

But she couldn't stop turning over the possibility in her mind. If they were in the mountains and there was any risk of avalanche or bad weather, if no one was out there trying to find them, they could get stuck somewhere and never be seen again. Unable to ask Guy how he had got this piece of flimsy information, or what had led him to take it seriously, she was almost angry that he had told her. The Mitfords might not be worrying, but she was.

The following morning, having had yet another sleepless night and finally dropped off into a fitful dream, she was woken minutes later by Maisie. It was still dark outside. 'It's back to Granny's for you,' she said, kissing her gurgling baby. Louisa envied her daughter's state of blissful ignorance.

An hour later, she was in her office, staring at the *Daily Mirror*.

Fears that a young couple snowed up in a mountain hut in the Pyrenees may be a Baron's eloping daughter, the Hon. Jessica Mitford, and her eighteen-year-old cousin, Mr Esmond Romilly, nephew of Mr Winston Churchill, are to be investigated.

Saying that she was going to spend a holiday in France, Miss Freeman-Mitford, aged nineteen, daughter of Lord Redesdale, eloped, and at a secret rendezvous at Bayonne met her fiancé, who has been serving with the International Brigades in Madrid.

The two stranded in the hut, reports Reuter, are trapped amid snow eight feet deep. When the couple arrived at the hut yesterday morning, they asked the hut keeper for a meal. The keeper replied that he was going down to Barèges to fetch supplies, but there was enough food in the hut for twenty-four hours. He then went away on his errand, and on his return found it impossible to go on because of the snowstorm.

The article was short, but said more than enough. Lord and Lady Redesdale were going to read about it within minutes, if they hadn't already.

How could Reuters possibly have discovered this at the same time that she did? She knew there was no chance Guy had told a journalist. His honour and decency were written through him like words through a stick of rock. But the coincidence of timing was worrying. If it hadn't been him, then it was someone close to him – very close.

CHAPTER THIRTY-FOUR

Louisa telephoned Rutland Gate, and Nancy asked her to come by. 'Lord and Lady Redesdale are better off when they can report to you. This wretched article. How does anyone know these things? The police still aren't involved, which seems madness when the Foreign Office has put wheels in motion. But most of all, Farve keeps getting sidestepped by reporters and saying things to them, which is never going to improve matters. Please come, Lou. You're the only one among us who knows how to keep their head.'

Which Louisa could only agree with when she arrived at the house.

The newspaper article, unsurprisingly, had not eased tensions. 'We can't understand it. The consul in Bayonne has told us that Decca and Esmond are in Spain, by which they presume Bilbao. It's the port to which all the boats travel from Bayonne and St Jean de Luz, you see.'

This was intoned to Louisa, rather to her surprise, by Peter Rodd, Nancy's husband. Louisa had met him before, but she was aware that he and his in-laws were only cautiously on good terms. This wasn't because he was unsuitable particularly, even if there was nothing in his family or career background that could mark him out as a man of success. It was more that he was the dullest man they had ever met. Louisa could only assume that Nancy saw a side of him that no one else did. Or she was blinded by his good looks. What everyone else saw was a pedantic know-it-all who professed himself an expert on any subject that was mentioned. The fact that Nancy largely kept him away from the family suggested to Louisa that she was either protecting him or protecting herself from their sideways glances.

Anyhow, now the crisis was fully on, it was clear that Peter had decided that what the family really and truly needed above all else was his help.

'I see,' said Louisa. 'Guy is in Bayonne. He heard reports of a couple travelling to Spain via the Pyrenees and was going to find out what he could about who they were.'

'It won't be them,' said Peter.

Louisa decided that this was, after all, her and Guy's investigation, and it behoved her to ask the necessary questions. 'How do you know that?'

'They don't have the right clothes with them,' said Lady Redesdale.

They might have bought clothes, thought Louisa. But she could see that there was no point in pushing the theory, given that she had no evidence herself that they were up a mountain.

'What have the Foreign Office said to this?'

'Mr Eden has agreed to allow someone from the family to travel aboard a naval destroyer from Bayonne which is soon to leave for the port of Bermeo.' Peter had taken up position in front of the mantelpiece, legs splayed, hands in a prayer position beneath his chin. 'Bermeo is thirty miles from Bilbao. The destroyer is travelling there in order to remove British subjects and refugees trapped by the fighting.'

Since she had been rushed into the room, and Peter had immediately delivered his lecture, Louisa had been slow to realise that Tom, Diana and Unity were all present too, sitting together on the sofa. Lord and Lady Redesdale were sitting further away from the fire than usual, on the least comfortable chairs in the room. As Peter spoke, there was a chorus of interruptions from the siblings on the sofa. Eventually, Tom's voice won. 'Look here, I say we leave Decca and Esmond out there. It's where they want to be. What good will it do to bring them home? If they're married, the damage is done, so far as we're concerned.'

'You can't seriously propose allowing your sister to stay out there fighting alongside Communists?' Peter spat out the C-word as if he had identified a particularly filthy rodent in his kitchen.

'Not darling Decca,' said Diana in her silky voice. 'She won't be *fighting* with anyone. I bet you anything right this minute the two of them are tucked up cosily having tea with freedom fighters, listening to their ideas. She'll be lapping it up, but she won't actually want to *do* anything.'

'There's no need to sound so pleased about it all,' snapped Nancy.

'Why would I be pleased?'

'She's taken the heat off you and Sir Oswald. But I wouldn't rest for too long. The papers are only too quick to mention her Nazi-sympathising sisters.'

Diana said nothing to that.

Louisa felt as if she were standing in the middle of a civil war herself.

'Perhaps I should go out to Bilbao,' said Unity in the silence.

Everyone turned to look at her.

'I mean it. I am perfectly capable. I've just scrammed back from Munich. Decca would listen to me.'

This was cogitated by all the persons present.

'Esmond would not listen to you,' said Tom at last. 'He thinks we're all Nazi lovers. But you actually are one. You'd probably send him shooting further off into the distance, and he'd take Decca with him.'

'I'd like to get over there and horsewhip that fellow,' said Lord Redesdale with feeling.

Peter coughed. 'I think the sensible solution is for Nancy and I to go out there.'

Nancy looked up at her husband. Louisa could see the conflict on her face: she didn't know he was going to say this; she wasn't going to disagree with him in public.

'David—' Peter began. Lord Redesdale's jaw twitched. It was perfectly proper for his son-in-law to address him by his first name but it was, perhaps, an unpleasant reminder of their familial proximity. 'If you could see your way to providing the expenses, we can leave this afternoon and catch a train to Paris, and then travel on to Bayonne to meet the consul. It will take us a few days but we can then make the necessary arrangements to board the destroyer and find Jessica. I'm sure she won't refuse and, of course, I have enough legal knowledge to rebut any potential barriers that she may put up.'

Lord Redesdale and his wife exchanged a look. Weariness

seemed to overcome him, and he sat down. He waved a hand in Peter's direction. 'Yes. Do what you must.'

Louisa risked a small cough. 'Mr Sullivan is out there – in Bayonne, that is. He is in place, as it were, to make any arrangements for Mr and Mrs Rodd, as necessary.'

'Yes, that's a good idea,' said Peter pompously. 'I'm afraid Mr Sullivan would not be able to persuade my sister-in-law to return, which is why we must make the journey. It is not an easy undertaking but one which we—' He cast a glance in Nancy's direction, waiting for her nod of agreement. 'One which we are willing to do for the sake of the family.'

Louisa confirmed that she would be in touch with them in order to co-ordinate with Guy, then she left.

It was a relief.

CHAPTER THIRTY-FIVE

ೋ

Louisa had only been back in the office for five minutes when the telephone rang. As she picked it up, she had a sixth sense that this was going to be important.

'There you are,' said a breathless woman's voice. 'I've been trying to get hold of you all morning.'

'Who is this?'

'Sorry, it's me – Julia Attwood. The police telephoned me at nine o'clock and they said—' Her breath caught, and Louisa waited in silence. 'They said they've got Petunia's body.'

Louisa felt goose pimples rise all over her body. Guilt. In all the drama of the search for Decca, she had forgotten the missing Petunia. If she hadn't, would Julia's sister still be alive?

'I know it's stupid,' continued Julia, her voice still unsteady, 'but they've asked me to go down and identify her, and I don't want to go alone. Could you come with me?'

'Of course,' said Louisa quickly, wanting to atone. She took down the address and, having not even taken her coat off, left immediately.

Julia was waiting outside the mortuary when Louisa arrived, her collar up against the sharp breeze that had whipped up. Drifts of litter had washed up against the kerb – a page of newspaper that looked as if it had been used to wrap chips, an empty paper bag, cigarette stubs – and the banished sunlight gave the day an aura of gloom.

'I'm so sorry,' said Louisa as she drew closer. Julia didn't seem able to speak. She nodded in reply, then headed in through the double doors. Inside, they were greeted by a sombre receptionist who asked them to sit down. She left the room briefly and a man came in, wearing an ill-fitting suit. This was unsurprising when one took in his height; he practically had to stoop to go through the doorway. But he was young and there was an awkwardness to his gait that made him seem friendly in spite of his pressed lips and solemn expression.

'Is one of you Miss Julia Attwood?' he asked.

'That's me,' said Julia, standing.

'DI Morgan.' He put out his hand and Julia shook it.

'I've been assigned to this case. I believe you reported your sister as missing a few weeks ago?'

'Yes.'

He looked at Louisa. 'And you are?'

Louisa introduced herself, leaving out the part about being a private detective for the moment. Julia confirmed that anything he had to say could be said in front of both of them.

DI Morgan started to rifle through the pages of a notebook. Louisa saw him flush.

'We found your sister's body in the early hours of this morning on Duffield Street.'

'On the street?'

'Yes – or rather, just a little off it, behind some large bins.'

'You mean she was found in an alleyway?' clarified Louisa.

'Oh my God,' said Julia. 'What ... how could she have got there?'

'She appears to have been attacked there, and left for dead.'

Julia was unable to reply.

'Miss Attwood, before I ask you to identify the body, I should warn you that the face has been very badly damaged.'

Julia remained standing but Louisa saw her face go very pale, so she stepped closer to her and took her arm.

'I'd still like to see her, please,' Julia said, her voice as quiet as a child in church.

DI Morgan walked out, and the two of them followed him along a corridor until he knocked on a closed door. Inside, a mortuary assistant in a white coat ushered them in silently. A body was already laid upon a table, covered in a white sheet. Close by on another table were laid what Louisa assumed were the clothes and personal items found with the body. Julia went over and picked up a navy duffel coat. 'This is hers,' she said. Then her gaze fell on a gold powder compact, in the shape of a pearl shell, with *Petunia Attwood* inscribed on the front. Grief seemed to strike then in its most vicious form, as if it had physically winded her.

Before Louisa could stop him, the mortuary assistant started to turn down the sheet, revealing a head on which blood had so coated and dried on clumps of hair that it was impossible to tell its colour. Louisa looked away as soon as she saw the face, nausea rising in her throat. Nothing was left of Petunia that anyone who had known her could claim as hers. Before the sheet could be pulled back any further, Julia cried out: 'Please, don't.'

After a nod from DI Morgan, the assistant covered her up again.

'I have to ask, Miss Attwood, if your sister had any identifying marks we could use to verify her appearance?'

Julia, her shoulders shaking, her head in her hands, said no. Louisa put her arm around her and started to pull her towards the door. 'I think that's all she can manage,' she said to the detective. Before they could reach the door, Julia ran out, her hand clamped to her mouth, and Louisa knew she was going to be sick.

She turned back to DI Morgan. 'Do you know who did this?'

'No,' he admitted. 'I don't know what you can tell Miss Attwood, but the street where her sister was found is ... well, it's not a good one. We've had two women beaten and left for dead there in the last year. Many more are attacked but don't bother telling us about it.'

'Prostitutes?'

He gave a short nod.

'I don't believe Miss Attwood—'

He cut her off. 'Families never want to believe it. But those women don't always tell their families; they keep it a secret. It's just a way to earn a bit of money to them.'

'Was there any evidence found at all? She must have been attacked with a weapon – did you find it?'

'No, and I'll be honest with you, though I'm sorry to say it. I don't think we'll find whoever did it. They could be strangers to the area, they could have been in a car and they could be any-where by now. We've been through this before. No one round there will say if they saw anything. No one will talk to the police.'

Moments later, out in the fresh air they so sorely needed,

Louisa walked away with Julia. She would find a café nearby, somewhere they could sit quietly and drink hot, sweet tea. She felt both horribly appalled and angered by what had happened. Such violence could only have been visited on that poor woman by someone with strength. It had to be a man. The police might have already given up, but Louisa knew where to start looking for Petunia's killer.

CHAPTER THIRTY-SIX

﹏

As soon as she was able, Louisa decided that the next step was to visit the sulky receptionist at Lee Worth.

'Hello, I'd like an appointment with Bernard Plum.' Of course, he wouldn't be there but she had to pretend otherwise or she wouldn't get the information she needed.

'Will he know who you are?' She barely looked up from the magazine she'd been flipping through.

Louisa regarded her red lips and off-the-peg dress. 'What is your name?'

'Eliza Martin.'

'Miss Martin, I am not inviting your commentary. I'm here on an investigation. Now, if you would, an appointment with Mr Plum.'

'Mr Plum is not here.' Eliza gave Louisa a wide smile: the pleasure was all hers.

'When will he be back?'

'I couldn't say.'

Wouldn't, or couldn't? Either way, Eliza was determined to

be an obstacle in Louisa's path. Louisa looked down at the desk. As before, there wasn't much to see. But there was a wastepaper basket visible, and what she saw there gave Louisa an idea.

'I see you've bought a pair of Diamond Point stockings,' said Louisa.

Eliza glanced at the discarded packet then back at Louisa, confused. 'Yes.'

'Marvellous, aren't they?' Louisa went on, as if harmlessly gossiping. 'I think I prefer rayon to silk, with that little stretch in them.'

'Yes, I suppose so,' Eliza replied.

Louisa leaned forward and whispered, 'I gather the company frowns on relationships between its employees. Hadn't you better be more discreet?'

'What?'

'Come along. You and I both know there's only one reason you've bought a fresh pair of stockings on the way into work this morning.' Louisa straightened up again. 'Now, about that small favour that I wanted. Mr Plum, where is he?'

'He's suspended. At home.' Miss Martin hesitated. 'I suppose you want his address?' She pulled out a large address book from another drawer and wrote down Bernard Plum's home address before handing it to Louisa. 'I'll get in trouble for this if anyone finds out.'

'No one will.' Louisa did up the buttons on her coat and thanked Miss Martin politely, as if they had just a completed a business transaction. In a way, she thought, they had.

On the bus, Louisa looked at her notes. Julia Attwood had last seen her sister on Christmas Day, so she couldn't be of any help with what had happened in the subsequent weeks. After that she had returned to work, and her neighbours would have seen her around. But what of her movements in the first week of February? Louisa knew it was possible that someone at the building where she lived might have seen her since then, although of the neighbours who had been asked, none had said as much to either Julia or Miss Piper. A gas bill sent to Petunia on 2nd February had been left unopened in the building's foyer, which meant she must have been away from her home since then, if not before.

Louisa considered Petunia, trying hard to think of her as she had been alive, not as that distressing, disfigured sight on the mortuary slab. The photographs she had of her were not of a beauty, nor had she borne her sister's unconventional strong looks. If Miss Piper and Petunia were confidantes, had they gravitated to each other because they had things in common or because they were the only women of a certain age in their workplace? Miss Piper's fustiness had a bossy quality and Louisa could imagine her making disapproving sniffs if Petunia wore a dress that might be considered too racy, or discussed a haircut that was a touch *outré*. It might sound insignificant to others, but these kind of things could knock a person's confidence.

Most of all, Petunia's life had the sallow air of loneliness about it. With almost no family and only sporadic contact with her sister, her social life seemed to revolve around work and occasional forays with Miss Piper to the cinema or the park. Louisa wondered what sort of books Petunia read: romance or detective novels? Did she listen to the radio? Did she wish she had a lover? She had, according to Julia, spent a long time wishing for a husband and children, and might recently have reached a peace with the diminished likelihood of her own family. But this was only Julia's guess; it might not be true.

The business with Bernard Plum seemed unsatisfactory, too. According to Mr Cornish, he claimed that Petunia was in love with him, or that she favoured him in some way. This attention was, apparently, so unwanted and distasteful that he had rejected her advances to such a degree she had reported him for serious professional misconduct. Was this in Petunia Attwood's nature? A baseless retaliation, one that could lead to him losing his job? Louisa felt that it didn't fit. It would have been too risky for her.

A *fatal* risk?

Louisa couldn't help feeling that Petunia's accusation was, surely, easy for Mr Plum or any of his cohorts at Lee Worth to prove wrong. If Mr Cornish thought that her pointed finger was a pathetic attempt by a spurned woman to exact revenge, why had they suspended him?

On the other hand, she had been an employee with nine faultless years' work at Lee Worth. Mr Plum had worked there for five years but had been accused of fraud. Petunia's accusation may have carried enough weight to ensure his suspension, if not an immediate sacking.

The picture painted was of a lonely, possibly embittered, woman and a man, whether wrongly accused or not, who had feared for his livelihood. The search for Mr Plum, at least, would not be a long one: only a few more stops to go.

CHAPTER THIRTY-SEVEN

❧

As Guy walked towards the consul, deflated, he became aware of running footsteps behind him. Instinctively, he turned and saw Luc, the rather curt man whom Keith had introduced him to only moments before.

'*Monsieur*,' he called. 'Forgive me, I did not want to say anything in front of Keith.' He pronounced the name with a hiss between his teeth.

'Why not?' asked Guy.

'Because one never knows about anyone. I am careful. But if you are willing, I think I know the man and woman you are looking for, and if you have—' He made here the international sign for money, rubbing his fingers and thumb together. 'Even a little. I can take you to them.'

Guy sighed. His police training did not yield easily to handing over money in exchange for information.

'Fine.' He handed over a note – generous enough, he hoped. It was.

'Follow me,' said Luc. They walked fast, along streets that

became increasingly narrow and cooler, away from the glare of the sun. Past cafés outside which the now familiar groups of refugees huddled, several of them around one small table, sometimes with only two or three cups of coffee between them. Mothers who looked tired, their hair greasy, holding on to children whose eyes lacked the spark of shiny expectation that Guy saw in Maisie. There was a permanent smell of cooking, but not one to make you hungry; the scent reminded Guy more of overcooked vegetables or stringy meat. He was used to poverty, of course. As a policeman, you could never avoid it. And his own upbringing had been modest, with many families in his street reduced to hard circumstances if a father lost his job. As a child he had played with others who had no shoes, or who were forced to wear hand-me-downs that were the wrong size entirely. Yet there was something in the air here that chilled him to the bone: it reeked of hopelessness and fear. He had never before understood politics, why the ordinary man or woman should be concerned with the business of government. Guy had always been content to believe that those in power were there because they knew more and were better able to make the difficult decisions necessary to run a country successfully. Today he understood that this could be wrong. Everywhere he had travelled, he had seen only disparity alongside apathy. He felt a surge of sympathy for Decca and Esmond: at least they were trying to create change.

At last, they stopped before the front door of a house that boasted no fripperies, only faded blue shutters that looked as if they might be about to creak off their hinges. Guy happened to turn and look behind him as they arrived, and he noticed what seemed like a fast shadow retreating. Had someone been following them? He was inclined to retrace his steps and look but Luc tugged his sleeve.

'Here,' he said. 'Knock on this door and they will be here.'

With that, he was gone.

Guy knocked on the door and waited. After a minute or two there was the sound of shuffling, then the sound of locks unbolting.

'Hello?'

The door opened. A young man stood there, wincing at the light that had come into his dingy hallway. 'What is it?'

The man was well-spoken and blond: he was not Esmond.

'I'm so sorry to bother you,' said Guy. 'I was told that a young couple were here who recently got caught in a snowstorm in a hut on the Pyrenees.'

'Yes, that was me,' said the man. 'Bloody idiotic of us, but we're fine. Are you from the papers?'

'No,' said Guy, disappointment sinking through him. 'I thought you might be someone else, someone I'm looking for.'

'Oh? It's only me and Mrs Nickerson here, I'm afraid.'

Guy asked a few more questions, to be absolutely sure. But there was no Decca, no Esmond. Only him, and his hope of succeeding retreating ever further.

CHAPTER THIRTY-EIGHT

Louisa had taken the bus from Lee Worth in Victoria to Battersea, which lay just south of the river. She disembarked not long after they had passed the startling sight of the recently built power station with its vast chimneys and plumes of smoke that puffed white vapour, like man-made clouds, across the cold blue sky. Grateful that she had remembered to bring an A-Z with her, Louisa looked up Bernard Plum's address in the index: 34 Rowditch Lane. It was close enough to the railway lines to hear the whistle and rumble of the trains. The houses were neatly lined up, like a child's drawing, with front gardens laid out before each one in varying degrees of verdure. Mr Plum's house had no flowers in the front, but there were white net curtains at the windows and a red front door with a polished brass knocker. Louisa made a bet with herself that Mrs Plum didn't go out to work.

A flutter in her stomach, Louisa knocked three times. It wasn't long before she heard someone drawing back a bolt and the door was opened a couple of inches, the chain kept on the latch. She saw a narrow nose and blue eyes peep through the gap.

'Mrs Plum?'

The eyes continued to look at her.

'My name is Louisa Cannon. I'm sorry to intrude. I wondered if I might speak to your husband?'

The eyes withdrew for half a second, then came back. 'He's not in.'

'Will he be returning soon?'

'No.' The door started to close, but Louisa put her foot out. It didn't jam hard; there wasn't much strength in Mrs Plum's push.

'I've come from Lee Worth. I just need to ask him some questions about—' About what? Louisa hadn't thought this through. Who was she to turn up at Bernard Plum's house and insist on asking him questions? Still, now she was here . . .

'What? About what?'

Louisa thought quickly. She couldn't say it was a murder investigation – she knew the police should be doing that.

'Miss Petunia Attwood. She worked with Mr Plum and I'm investigating her disappearance. I need to know if he saw or heard her say anything out of the ordinary, something that might give us a clue as to where she is.'

'I don't know anything about that.'

The door closed. Louisa feared the worst, but then she heard the faint clink of the chain and the door was opened again, wider this time. The woman holding the door had brown hair tied back, wisps framing her face, which was pretty but tired, free of any make-up. Her dress was simple and well worn, with a navy cardigan buttoned up over the top.

'I don't know that name,' she said. She gave a quick glance at the house opposite. 'But you had better come in.'

'Thank you.' Louisa stepped over the threshold into

the narrow hall, following Mrs Plum into the front room. Everything was as neat as a pin, as her mother would have said, but there were very few personal effects. Only one picture hung on the wall, of a clipper ship on a stormy sea; there were no framed photographs, no flowers, not even a rug on the carpet. The colours of the sofa and the walls reminded Louisa of how Guy's mother liked to take her tea – strong and milky. The two women stood awkwardly in the middle of the room for a moment until Mrs Plum sat, or perched, on an armchair and gestured to the sofa.

There was silence, so Louisa decided she had better lead the conversation. 'Mrs Plum, please forgive this intrusion. But I wouldn't be here if it wasn't important.'

'Did you say you had come from Lee Worth?'

'Yes.' Louisa knew she was fudging this, allowing Mrs Plum to believe that she had been sent by Mr Plum's place of work. But it might prompt more information, so she was going to let it go for now.

There was a nod, and Mrs Plum gazed out of the window. 'Did they tell you what had happened?'

'I know that Miss Attwood made an accusation against your husband, which has led to his suspension while they investigate. There is no conclusion on his guilt or otherwise at this stage.'

'Hmm.' The lips were pressed thinly together. 'You know what they accused him of, then?'

'Perhaps I had better not say.'

'I'd really rather you did.'

There was no way of knowing which was the right direction to turn in. 'I don't know the full details. It was to do with pro-fessional misconduct of some kind.'

171

'Not an affair?' Mrs Plum was still looking at the window, rather than Louisa. Tears had sprung in her eyes but not yet spilled over.

'No,' said Louisa, 'not so far as I am aware.' Was she right, or was she wrong? Either way, she didn't feel it was her place to tell this poor woman what Mr Cornish's dim view of the situation had been. Even if Mr Plum had done nothing, no wife wanted to hear about another woman favouring their husband.

On a small table by the side of the sofa, Louisa noticed one thing: an ashtray, completely clean. There was no smell of smoke in the air, only the faintest whiff of wood polish. If Mr Plum was a smoker, he hadn't smoked in the house that day.

'When did you last see your husband, Mrs Plum?'

Mrs Plum gave a choked sob, then gulped it down. 'Almost a month ago. I don't know where he is. I didn't know he would go, and I don't know when he'll be back.'

'You haven't heard from him in that time?'

A vigorous shake of the head. Mrs Plum brought out a scrunched handkerchief to blow her nose.

'Have you reported him as missing?'

'No. He's done it before, and he always comes back. But I didn't know about this Miss Attwood. He hasn't done that before.'

'There's no suggestion that the two of them—'

'No. No, no.'

Louisa stopped talking. She waited for Mrs Plum to speak first, to gather herself together. She felt as if an intimacy had been shared between them, but uncomfortably so.

Mrs Plum took a deep breath. 'I'm sorry, I can't remember your name.'

'Louisa Cannon. Please, call me Louisa.'

'I'm Janice. And you're looking for my husband? His boss has asked you to find him?'

'Well, no. I'm looking for Petunia Attwood, a secretary at Lee Worth. The search took me first to her workplace – I wanted to see if there was any clue as to why she would disappear without telling anyone where she was going. I was told that she had a good record of employment, and there was nothing to suggest she might suddenly want to leave. The only thing that had happened of note was that she had made a complaint against your husband. That was why I wanted to talk to him, to see what he might know. To eliminate him from our enquiries.'

'I see. So you haven't been sent by Lee Worth?'

Louisa had to admit it. 'I have just come from their offices, but they don't know that I'm here. They don't know he's missing; since he has been suspended from his employment, temporarily, they were not expecting to see him in the office anyway. The connection has been made by me, not by them.'

'I understand,' said Mrs Plum thoughtfully. 'In that case, I can talk to you. I'll tell you what I know.'

CHAPTER THIRTY-NINE

Mrs Plum offered to fetch them a cup of tea, which Louisa gratefully accepted. It had been a long day on her feet, even without having Maisie to look after, and at the thought of her she felt a tug in her chest. She knew she was doing what she wanted to do, but it was nonetheless an adjustment to be without her child all day. It was lonely, too; there were few women she could talk to who would understand. The other mothers on their street were much younger than she was or, if the same age, had older children who helped look after the babies.

There were no signs of children in this house. Mrs Plum looked to be in her forties, so either they were long grown up and gone or they had never been.

When Mrs Plum returned with a tray of tea and a plate of biscuits, a formality settled over them. There was a silence that Louisa felt couldn't be displaced by the usual pleasantries about milk and sugar, the mildness of the weather. Louisa needed to break the ice. Whether Mr Plum's absence was connected with Petunia's, she didn't know, but it seemed likely. Mrs Plum had to know something that would be of use, whether she knew it or not.

'Mrs Plum, I think you should know that I'm a private investigator.'

'Oh.' She seemed taken aback.

'Yes, I work with my husband, a former policeman, Guy Sullivan. I call myself Louisa Cannon because that was my name for so long, it's hard to let go.' She added, as if sharing a secret, 'I didn't marry until I was thirty-one years old.'

'I was twenty-two when I married Bernard.'

'Have you always lived here?'

Mrs Plum smiled, something Louisa hadn't seen yet. It transformed her face, like petals opening. 'No, we've been here ten years but before that we travelled all over. France, Spain, Germany. We even went to Holland for a few months. We were rarely in the same place for long. Bernard's an adventurer. A pirate, he used to call himself. He's got a scar from his collar-bone to his left shoulder and told me different stories about how he'd got it.' She gave a dry laugh. 'I used to think it was exciting.'

'But not any more?'

'Do you have children?'

'One, Maisie. She's not much more than a year old.'

'We never had any. Bernard didn't want them, said they would stop our adventures. And then I didn't want them because . . .'

Louisa didn't know whether to push her to finish the sentence. It was private, probably irrelevant to her purposes. But she also sensed that Mrs Plum had had no one to talk to for a long time.

'For a long time, I wasn't sure that I wanted a child,' said Louisa. 'People assume that every woman wants them but—'

'Yes. Exactly that. Everyone would assume, and Bernard would say that we didn't do things like other people. I don't think I really knew what I thought. Anyway.' A briskness returned to her tone. 'It's too late now.'

Louisa was in danger of losing Mrs Plum again. 'Do you think your husband will return soon? You said he's done this before.'

'Yes – sometimes it's a few days, sometimes longer. It's not often been as long as this.'

'And in that time, you don't hear from him at all?'

'No.' She gave a half-laugh. 'He says it keeps me on my toes, not to know.'

Louisa thought again about how clean the house was. She wondered if Mrs Plum had been told by her husband to keep it spotless, ready for his return at any moment. A way of controlling her even in his absence.

'Does he ever tell you where he's been?'

She shook her head. 'Not really. I pick up clues in a way. Foreign money in his pockets.'

'Do you wish you were with him?'

'No. I've had my fill of travelling. I want to be in one place. I want—' She stopped, looked away. 'I want to be somewhere where I have a chance of making a friend or two.'

The sadness in her voice almost made Louisa cry. She'd become more liable to weeping since Maisie was born, but she had always found loneliness in others to be unbearably poignant: the one thing everyone is most afraid of.

'Would you like me to help you find your husband?'

'No. Yes. I think so. Oh dear, I'm so sorry.'

'There's no need to apologise. I've turned up unexpectedly, it's a lot to take on. You can think about it. But perhaps you could answer some questions for me? In case there is a link with Miss Attwood.'

Mrs Plum swallowed something that had threatened to become a sob. 'Yes, if I can.'

'What happened the last time you saw him?'

'We had supper together, fish pie and peas. He complained that I had cooked it too often. I washed up while he listened to the radio, and then I went to bed. I usually go before him and I'm not aware of when he joins me. But at some point in the night, he left.'

'You woke in the morning and he had gone?'

'Yes. I could see that he had taken the suitcase – it's not a big one. And he had packed some clothes, his toothbrush and shaving things.'

'Did he take a passport?'

'I don't know. Possibly. I never knew where he kept it.'

'What date was it?'

'February fourth.'

The day that Petunia had been due back in the office and had not shown up.

'The last time he went away, did you have any idea where he'd been?'

'Spain, I thought. And France. There were francs and pesetas in his pockets. We'd travelled there together at the start of our marriage, and we were happy there.'

Spain, and France. Two places much on Louisa's mind. And Petunia's too, perhaps.

'Is he political, your husband?'

Mrs Plum seemed to struggle with the answer. 'If it suits his purpose to be political, then yes.'

'How do you mean?'

'My husband likes to win games. It doesn't mean he is a winner, you understand. It's just that I think he doesn't see things in terms of right or wrong; he sees things in terms of whether he's winning or losing.'

Louisa took this in. 'Forgive me, but do you want your husband to come home?'

Mrs Plum's voice dropped to a whisper. 'I don't know that I do. I'm afraid, sometimes, of him coming back.' She closed her eyes. 'Forgive me. Please don't repeat what I've said – not to anyone. I shouldn't have said it. I'm so sorry.'

CHAPTER FORTY

L eaving Mrs Plum's house, Louisa felt terribly affected by the woman's bleak existence. A marriage that had once promised adventure, but now she was alone in a house empty of any sign of joyfulness. On the spur of the moment, Louisa decided to go to the Lincoln Street bookshop. She had a few hours until she needed to be home for Maisie, and there was something about the atmosphere in the shop that was oddly comforting. Also, she could ask Donald if he had heard again from Esmond.

When she arrived, she saw immediately, pleasingly, that things were as they had been before. The occasional scruffy customer, the books piled in assorted stacks, Donald sitting by the till, his hair mussed, his trousers worn at the knees. He was engrossed in a book and didn't even look up until she said hello.

'Mrs Sullivan. What a pleasure to see you.'

'You too, Mr Oliver.' His warmth made her smile. 'Do you have a moment?'

'Of course. I'm afraid I can't offer much in the way of sustenance. The wretched camping stove we used to make tea broke last week and I haven't yet got the funds to replace it. A glass of water, perhaps?'

'I don't need anything, but thank you. I was wondering if you had heard again from Esmond Romilly?'

'Ah, yes, well . . .' He peered around but nobody seemed to be close enough to hear. 'There has been some news on that front. But I think you will have heard it, too?'

'The marriage?'

'Yes. I don't know if it's definite, but certainly the intention is there.'

'That's how we see it too. They may not have married yet, as they are minors, but they're living as husband and wife.'

'He's a naughty boy, that one.' Donald chuckled. 'Are you sure you don't want to perch? There's a stool here.' He pulled it out and Louisa sat down.

'Where did you hear the news?' she asked.

'I have my sources.' He tapped the side of his nose.

'Mr Oliver—'

'Please, call me Donald. We don't stand to attention in here.'

'Donald, you said before that Mr Romilly was worried that someone was trying to follow him. Have you heard any more about that?'

'No, not as such.'

Louisa waited patiently. They both knew that Oliver's comment neither answered nor closed down her question.

'I mean, I think there are a few people who would like to find him.'

'Why?'

Donald held up his hands. 'Who knows? He's a well-known character in this part of the world. There are Communists who think he could be useful for their cause, and fascists who would like to get rid of him. And then he was on the frontline. I don't think we can fully understand how dangerous and nasty it got out there. Things happen in wars that don't translate to life outside it. Some men take it badly.'

'But you don't know anyone specifically? You don't have a name?'

'No, no. Now, I must root around here. I'm sure someone bought me a packet of biscuits ...'

'Don't change the subject.' Louisa felt quite cross. 'We know Mr Romilly and Miss Mitford are heading to Spain. He'll need a visa to get in.'

Donald looked admonished. 'Yes, I don't think it's a secret to say that the *News Chronicle* gave him an advance to report on the war. The advance would have enabled the visa.'

'Did Mr Romilly tell you that?'

'No, I heard it elsewhere.'

'Where?'

'Mrs Sullivan.' Donald looked at her, not unkindly, 'I do understand you are doing your job, and you'll have to forgive me for not answering you directly, but I am taken into the confidence of all kinds of people, some of whom are doing work that the government doesn't like very much. I can't go bandying about everything I hear. I have to keep my counsel.'

Now it was Louisa's turn to feel small. She realised that Lincoln Street bookshop was, in its own way, the pond of Communist life in London, and Donald was the biggest fish in it. But she felt she was getting closer to the cause of trouble: stories were getting leaked to the newspapers and Esmond had a job as a reporter.

The connection was surely obvious.

CHAPTER FORTY-ONE

❧

The following morning, Louisa met Julia Attwood outside Baker Street station, having received a brief message asking her to be there at ten o'clock. 'Miss Attwood, I'm so sorry to say that I'm not any further along in finding—'

'No, no,' said Julia, 'that's not it. The thing is, I've been thinking a lot about Petunia, and I don't think that was her body.'

The day was brisk and cool. Julia was walking fast in the manner of a chic headmistress, a scarlet silk scarf threatening to float away from her neck.

'You don't?'

'None of it makes sense. I know she wouldn't have been a street-walker. She didn't have much money, that's true, but she had enough.'

'She might have just taken a wrong turning.'

'I thought about that but I don't think that fits, either. Why would someone be so badly beaten for simply being in the wrong place? Anyway, I had an idea, and I wanted you with me. It's not far.'

Puzzled, but compelled to go along with it, Louisa almost trotted to keep up until they arrived at what looked like a townhouse with a door freshly painted in black gloss paint and a gleaming brass letterbox. There was a list of four names and bells at the side, each one showing a different doctor's name. They were here to see Dr James. When they went through into the doctor's office, Louisa was pleasantly surprised to see a woman sitting behind the large desk. Plumes of purplish smoke were thinning out above Dr James's head, and there was a distinct smell of cigar smoke.

'Sorry, Miss Attwood,' she said, flapping her hands, 'the man before you insisted on smoking through his appointment. I suppose it helps them take bad news. Do take a pew. And who do we have here?' She turned her gaze on Louisa, serious but friendly. She looked more like a farmer's wife than a doctor, with ruddy cheeks and a tweed skirt.

'This is Miss Cannon,' said Julia as they sat. 'I'll explain in a moment why she is here with me. Dr James, I've got rather awful news, but we're hoping you will be able to help.'

'Oh?'

'It's Petunia – she's missing. She's been missing for a while and the police told me they had found her body.'

'I'm so sorry.'

'Don't be. I'm certain the body they've found is not hers. She was found wearing a coat that looked like one Petunia owns, but her face was unrecognisable. She was found with Petunia's powder compact on her, so the police have decided it was her. Because I was in shock, I agreed with them.'

'Go on.'

'Miss Cannon is a private detective. I asked her to help me

find Petunia, now I want her to help me prove this one way or another. It occurred to me that you might know if Petunia had any identifying marks on her body, so that we might return to the police and ask them to check the body again.'

'I see,' said the doctor. She had leaned her elbows on the desk, and she bowed her head before standing up and going to a filing cabinet in the corner. She pulled out the middle drawer and rifled through a few files before pulling one out, then she sat back down and opened it on her desk.

'I'm in a difficult position, you must understand,' she began. 'Naturally, my patients' files are confidential. That's how I work; I know not all doctors are the same. But I don't agree with the way a lot of my colleagues work. I never talk to a husband about a wife's diagnosis or treatment without her consent, for example.'

'I know,' said Julia. 'That's why Mother was so keen that we should see you.'

Dr James acknowledged the compliment. 'And although I'm wrestling with this slightly, perhaps I should tell you.' She went quiet again and Louisa resisted the temptation to grab the file. 'She has no moles or scars that I'm aware of – nothing I could be certain of enough for you to take to the police. But there is something else that would help you in this matter. The difficulty is that Petunia wanted no one to know about it, and on this point she was very certain.'

'Please, Dr James,' said Julia. 'I need to know if my sister is alive or dead.'

'Knowing whether or not this body belongs to her does not decide that,' the doctor reminded her. 'Your sister has been missing for some time, you said.'

'I know. But where there's hope . . .'

'Yes, I do see that. She had breast cancer. A serious case, and very advanced. The only possible cure I could offer her was a double mastectomy, but she refused it.'

Julia cried out and covered her face with her hands. Dr James waited sympathetically for her to recover.

'Do you mean to say she is dying?'

'It's impossible to know with cases like this, when the patient refuses an operation. But yes. I am so sorry to have to be the one to tell you, and to tell you now.'

'No, it's not your fault. I'm glad you told me. When did she discover this?'

'Not so long ago; she came to see me in January. It wasn't a tricky diagnosis; I could feel the lumps quite distinctly. I had worried about the fact that she hadn't been back to see me recently, but people deal with these things in their own way. I cannot compel them to accept treatment if they don't want it.'

'Forgive me,' said Louisa, 'but if I'm right in understanding what you're saying, you've told us this because it means we can use this information to establish whether or not the body in the morgue is Miss Petunia or not?'

'Exactly.'

Louisa turned and placed her hand on Julia's arm. 'Let me go to the police alone. I can do this for you. If you give me a letter of permission, I'll talk to them. I think you should go home and rest after this upsetting news.'

Sniffing, Julia nodded. Dr James gave Julia a piece of paper and a pen to write the note. Thanking them both, Louisa headed to the morgue.

CHAPTER FORTY-TWO

The discovery of the body, and the suspicion that it didn't belong to Petunia, alongside the search for Decca and Esmond, was becoming increasingly difficult for Louisa to manage alone. She needed her husband.

On the telephone, Louisa told him about the Attwoods and he listened, as he always did, with sympathy and patience. 'What do you think I should do?' she asked at the end.

'You're doing everything that can be done,' Guy reassured her. 'You've talked to her place of work, you've established a reasonable suspect, you've spoken to the suspect's wife, and you've taken the doctor's evidence to the police. I think you should rest now. There's no more to ask for the moment. It's a serious case and it's probably right that we're not involved any more.'

'Thank you,' said Louisa, taking the compliment but feeling a lurch of disappointment. She had wanted to solve the case for Julia. And besides, if Petunia wasn't dead, just missing, they could still look for her, couldn't they?

But for the moment she would have to leave it. Guy was in

France and he had only one case on his mind. Which was as it should be. With Deborah having been mistakenly named in the papers as the missing daughter, all sorts had been worming out of holes, claiming to have found her, even though the name had since been corrected. There had been numerous calls to the office and one nasty letter that claimed to recall a detailed conversation with a distressed Deborah, on her way to throw herself off a bridge. The writer signed off 'yours sorrowfully'. Louisa wanted to burn it but Guy had already told her it was necessary to hold on to all of these reports, however false, in case they later turned out to be a clue if any genuine threats were discovered.

And this was only what Louisa had had to cope with. The situation at Rutland Gate was appalling. There was now a more or less permanent throng of reporters on the pavement outside, accosting anyone who left or went near the house, whether Lord Redesdale or the postman. The family effectively being held hostage in their house added to the tension of Jessica and Esmond's elopement. All semblance of normal life had gone, Louisa told Guy. 'It makes me angry with Jessica. I don't think she thought this through at all. Poor Miss Deborah – through no fault of her own, she can't go out and see a friend, let alone go to a dance or do any of the nice things she should be doing. Lord and Lady Redesdale have aged a decade with worry. It's selfish.'

'It is,' agreed Guy. 'But I think she's been propelled by a force more powerful than we understood.'

'Love?'

'Politics. Now that I'm out here, seeing it all in action, it's exciting. I didn't think I'd ever say that, but it's not like at home. You see why it matters.' He paused for breath. 'It frightens me a little bit, Louisa. It feels as if it's coming in our direction. To England, I mean.'

'I don't think English people are made like that.'

'That depends who you talk to.' Guy told her about Keith, a man who seemed to see a frontline as an opportunity for adventure. A man who found Britain small-minded and boring, lacking a leader who could offer a bright future. 'He says our Prime Minister is being cowed into negotiations for peace with Hitler, that we have to go to war to have peace on our own terms.'

'Don't you start going down this road, Guy.'

'I won't. It's food for thought, that's all.'

'We haven't got much time to talk. What did you find out from the British consul?'

'He was reluctant at first, but when I showed him the letter from Lord Redesdale, he was more forthcoming. He said the British ambassador is in Bilbao, in a temporary embassy. He's not best pleased about this situation, apparently.'

'I bet.'

'There's a real crisis there. English people who have been living in Spain and now desperately want to be rescued by the Royal Navy are banging on his door daily. And then there's no food – the continuing deprivations of war. On top of that, he's got two young people who are under the protection of the Foreign Secretary for no real reason anyone can fathom. As I understand it, he's offered them space on a British destroyer, one that's evacuating women and children refugees. We believe that Miss Jessica has agreed to be on it, but that she'll only go as far as St Jean de Luz.'

'Where Mr and Mrs Rodd are headed. It's as far as they can go because they haven't got Spanish visas.'

'Who?'

'Nancy and her husband, Peter. He's been quite determined to be the one who brings them home. I think he sees it as a way of gaining favour with his lordship.'

'The only way anyone can gain favour with his lordship is to be a salmon at the end of his line.'

'Ha, yes. True enough. The thing is, no one holds out much hope for Mr Rodd's powers of persuasion. You need to be there.'

'I want to be there. I want to see this through to the end.'

'Let's hope it is the end. I want you home, Guy. And so does Maisie.'

'I want to be home, too. Please give our daughter kisses from me. It won't be long, I promise.'

The pips sounded and the line went dead.

CHAPTER FORTY-THREE

The next steps were not easy, with Louisa and Julia working together and separately to persuade the police and
coroner to reinvestigate the identity of the body they held in
the morgue, using the notes from Dr James. After several days,
they were invited in to talk to DI Morgan at the police station
in Latchmere Road, Battersea.

Standing outside the station, Louisa noticed that Julia looked
paler than usual. Her anxiety about her sister must have caused
sleepless nights. Now they would find out whether or not
Petunia was incontrovertibly dead, or if there was a glimmer of
hope that she was still alive.

'This almost feels worse than when I was called the first time,'
said Julia. 'Then, the shock was too much to absorb. Now I know
how much I miss her and have been grieving. I almost can't bear
to discover the answer one way or another. If she is alive, she
is not only missing but seriously ill with—' She couldn't bring
herself to say 'the big C', the only way anyone ever referred to

cancer. Why, Louisa could not fathom, but the disease always came with the stigma of shame.

'I know.' Louisa squeezed Julia's arm, as intimate a touch as she knew Julia would allow. There was a dignity to Julia's bearing that never deserted her, even in her deepest grief. 'Let's go in and face it together.'

Inside, when they had given their names, they were quickly shown to the usual soulless police room and left waiting a few minutes for DI Morgan to come in. Even when you were not the accused, the rooms bore a chilling threat, with their sparse furniture and faded paintwork. There was only one high window, with bars across it.

DI Morgan entered, carrying a large bag and a file, his head ducking under the door frame.

'Miss Attwood and Miss Cannon, thank you for coming in.' He placed the bag carefully on the table. 'I'll get to the point.'

'Please,' said Julia.

'Our coroner has reviewed the case. Given the notes from Miss Petunia Attwood's doctor indicating an advanced case of . . .' – he paused and opened the file, as if needing to read from it, but Louisa knew he was avoiding their eyes – 'of, er, invasive ductal breast cancer, it has been conclusively established that the body of the deceased held in our mortuary is definitely . . .'

He looked up at them. Julia reached out for Louisa's hand. Louisa gripped Julia's firmly in return.

'*Not* that of your sister, Miss Attwood.'

'Not my sister. It's not Petunia?'

DI Morgan shook his head. 'No. We're very sorry for the

distress this must have caused you, but we had strong reason to believe otherwise, as you know. Which is why I would like to discuss with you the contents of this bag.'

Julia nodded, still overcome. Tears ran freely down her face and she gave tiny gasps of relief, but Louisa knew that she would not be feeling straightforwardly happy. There were hard questions remaining that needed to be answered.

'We need now, urgently, to try and establish the identity of the deceased. As you know, we contacted you because there were items about the deceased's person that indicated you were the closest relative.' He reached into the bag and pulled out some small items: the powder compact, the cigarette packet and matches.

'Does this compact belong to your sister?'

Julia picked it up. 'I saw this before, and yes, it is hers.'

'Did she smoke?'

'No,' said Julia. 'I should have said something about that before, but I wasn't thinking straight. And I suppose it's something that she might have taken up recently, though I'd be surprised. I've always smoked and she's never asked me for a cigarette.' She stopped and thought. 'There's something else. She always wore a gold chain with a heart on it – it belonged to my mother. But it's not here. And you didn't find her handbag, did you?'

'No,' said DI Morgan. 'These items could easily have been stolen, however.' Then he pulled a coat from the bag. 'Do you recognise this coat?'

Julia pulled it towards her. It was an inexpensive navy wool coat from the Army & Navy Stores, practical and utilitarian. It looked as if one or two of the buttons had been stitched back on, and the hem was beginning to fray. Louisa automatically pulled the coat towards her, feeling the coarseness of the material as she ran her fingertips along the edges.

'Yes, I saw this before too. This is my sister's, I'm sure of it.'

DI Morgan had reached into the bag again, presumably to pull out the remainder of whatever the deceased woman had been wearing, when Louisa felt something small and stiff in the hem of the coat.

'Wait,' said Louisa. She flipped the coat over and felt along the stitching where the lining met the hem, but it was machine-sewn and there were no gaps. Then she looked at the pocket lining, and found a hole in one corner. With Julia and DI Morgan watching her with bemusement and intrigue, Louisa widened the hole until she could fit her hand through it, then felt inside the coat. 'Ah. Got it.'

She pulled it out. In her hand was a rectangular white card with a name and address on it:

BERNARD PLUM ESQ.,

Claims Clerk

Lee Worth Insurance,
Victoria Road, London

Daily Mirror

CONSUL CHASES
PEER'S DAUGHTER

The British consul at Bilbao is to sail for Bermeo –
twenty miles from the consulate – today, states Reuter,
to get in touch with the Hon. Jessica Lucy Mitford,
nineteen-year-old daughter of Lord Redesdale, and her
eighteen-year-old cousin, Mr Esmond Romilly, nephew
of Mr Winston Churchill. Mr Stephenson, the consul,
has, it is understood, been asked to persuade the couple
to return home. He will sail in a destroyer if the weather
is calm enough to call at Bermeo, which is harbourless.
The Spanish government consul at Bayonne says that Mr
Romilly told him they would get married at Bilbao. British
United Press states that Mr Romilly and Miss Mitford,
while stopping at a Bilbao hotel, denied that they had
been married.

CHAPTER FORTY-FOUR

～～～

G uy arrived at St Jean de Luz after a long, uncomfortable car journey – he was not used to the idiosyncrasies of French drivers – and was deposited on the pavement outside the hotel close to the port. He had been given the hotel's name by Lord Redesdale, who sent a telegram with the details to his hotel in Bayonne. Guy knew this was where Nancy and Peter were staying, having arrived a day or so before. With a destroyer full of evacuees due to arrive, the modest seaside town was busier than usual for early March. There were parked cars jammed up against the pavement, nose to bumper, and a general feeling of hubbub, more jolly than in Bayonne. At the front desk of the Hôtel de Mer he was relieved to discover that the receptionist spoke good English. On hearing his name, she gave a friendly exclamation. 'Monsieur Sullivan, I have a note for you.'

Guy opened it.

Dear Guy

We are in Room 14. As soon as you arrive, please ask the desk to call up and we will come down to meet you in the salon at the back of the hotel. We are dining in our room for all meals, will explain.

Nancy

Guy did as instructed, asked if the receptionist could store his case for the moment – he wondered when he would ever be able to take a long, hot bath again – and followed the directions to the salon. Self-consciousness at the thought of meeting Nancy and her husband started to set in, but he had at least managed to buy a clean shirt in Bayonne, which he had put on that morning. The sharp bends on the route down had made him sweat but, with luck, not too badly.

The salon offered little in the way of comfort, with its dark walls and hard-backed armchairs paired with tables that looked too small to fit more than one cup and saucer. Guy took a seat in the far corner after dragging a third chair there. There were a few magazines in a rack but they were French with no illustrations, so he couldn't even pretend to read them. Thankfully, he wasn't made to wait long.

'Mr Sullivan, thank goodness you're here.' Nancy's cut-glass English tones were a culture shock after so many days away. She came across the room almost at a run, dressed beautifully in an oyster-grey woollen skirt and jacket. Behind her lumbered Peter, an awkward figure in spite of his lean frame. Guy just caught his mutter of 'We would have been perfectly all right by ourselves, you know' as he came up and gave Guy a watery handshake.

They sat down and Nancy found a bell, which she rang. A young maid came through and Nancy ordered tea in perfect French. In between, there was the usual chatter about their journeys and the difference in weather this far south in France. The tea arrived and was poured.

'Before we get down to business, I've got a letter for you from Louisa.'

She handed it over. Guy went to put it in his jacket pocket, but Nancy put her hand gently on his arm. 'She said you need to read it straightaway.'

'Right. Will you forgive me a moment then?' Guy opened it, his heart quickening. They had never exchanged many letters, because theirs had not been a conventional courtship. He treasured moments like this. Inside there was just a single page in Louisa's neat writing, with two photographs. In the letter, after she had assured him how much she was missing him, Louisa described the case she had decided to take on.

I'm writing this in a rush because Nancy is waiting for it, so I can't put all the details down. We've had confirmation that the body that was found is not Petunia Attwood's. She's still missing, and so is Bernard Plum. If she's alive, we can't discount the possibility that they have run off together. His wife says the last time he went away, it was to France and Spain (and from what I can gather, it's not a happy marriage). Miss Attwood's sister says she was talking about the civil war and was interested in it. It's possible she thought it sounded romantic. As you are on the spot, can you ask around?

197

Guy read it with pride. He loved his wife, her confidence and her daring. He put the photographs and the letter in his pocket. 'Sorry about that.'

Peter gave a tut of impatience and looked at his watch. 'It's not very long now until the destroyer is due to arrive. We ought to be making tracks. I need to identify the best point at which we can view Jessica as she exits the ship.'

Nancy gave a sage nod of agreement. 'Absolutely, darling. We will go, in just one minute. You see, Mr Sullivan, it seems that there are rather a lot of people here . . .'

'Yes, I got that sense when I arrived.'

'Some of them are various good people waiting to collect the evacuees and take them off somewhere. But I'm afraid a ghastly number of them are reporters. That's why we had to dine in our room. They were sitting next to us in the hotel restaurant, writing in their notepads every time we took a mouthful.'

'I can see that wouldn't have been very comfortable.'

Peter made a noise at this, a loud 'ha!' Nancy flicked her gaze at him. 'The thing is, one can't tell them simply to naff off. They'll make more trouble. And I'm sure Esmond is only doing this for the publicity. He's bound to love it. What I'm saying is, if you could escort us to where we're meeting the destroyer, we'd be most terribly grateful.'

'You'd like me to make sure the reporters don't come near you?'

'If you would, you'd be such a darling. Wouldn't he, Peter?'

Peter did not respond to this, but he must have acquiesced to his wife's demand, for he stood up and urged the two of them to go with him, at haste, or they would miss the arrival of 'the prodigal daughter'.

*

Nancy hadn't been wrong about the press interest. The sun was high, warmer than any of them had felt for several months back home in England. Guy could feel his shirt sticking to his back under his jacket, as much from the sight of the crowds as the temperature. Reporters with cameras around their necks were jostling by the gangplank, and a flank of others surrounded them, half of them looking as if they didn't fully understand what the fuss was all about. The destroyer had docked but the gangplank had not yet been laid down, so Guy was able to lead Nancy and Esmond to the correct place in the nick of time. An official from the port was there to greet them, a task he completed with brevity. The atmosphere was sombre. When the first few people emerged from the ship, Guy understood why. This was no 'welcome home' for holidaymakers disembarking a transatlantic liner. Instead of comfort and luxury, there was monotone grey paint on everything, and lines of Royal Navy seamen were positioned on the narrow seam of deck between the torpedo mounts and a low railing. The first to come off the warship, accompanied by officers, were women and children, wearing expressions of both exhaustion and relief. They carried little luggage, for they had not been able to plan for their journeys but only managed a hurried escape. As they came onshore, they were herded to a makeshift entry point where, presumably, they would be divided among the charities that had come to offer them refuge. It made the appearance of Jessica and Esmond look somewhat less than heroic – frivolous, even. Jessica was smiling, dressed in a dark coat with co-ordinating hat, a white scarf stylishly tied around her neck. But as she stepped onto land, Guy didn't know what made her flinch more: the flashbulbs popping or the sight of Nancy and Peter waiting for her on the dock.

Esmond strode to the top of the gangplank and, on seeing the gathered crowds, raised a fist in salute.

Peter rushed forward and pulled his arm down. 'Stop that,' he hissed.

'I won't be told what to do by a Nazi,' Esmond hissed back.

Nancy ignored them and rushed to Jessica, shielding her as much as possible with her arm. 'Come with us, quickly, darling,' she urged, and signalled to Guy that he should clear the path ahead of them back to the hotel, which was, thankfully, only a five-minute walk away.

CHAPTER FORTY-FIVE

Between the port and the hotel, none of them said a word as they pushed, grim-faced, through the people and reporters shouting out their names. Guy led the way, while the two couples held on to each other behind, Jessica and Esmond effectively sandwiched between Guy and Mr and Mrs Rodd. At last, feeling hot and nervous, Guy held open the front door of the hotel and ushered them through. One reporter made an attempt to sneak in with them, but was easily pushed back. The receptionist came and locked the door. 'For the moment,' he said with an apologetic shrug. 'I cannot do it for long. We have other guests.'

'We don't want special treatment,' said Esmond. 'You can unlock the door.'

'Leave the door locked,' Peter retaliated immediately.

'I think perhaps we should all go through to the salon at the back.' Guy gestured to the hall. 'We won't be disturbed there.'

Again, acquiescent in silence, the four of them followed him through to the dark, uncomfortable room. It was, at least, cool and quiet. Chairs were arranged around a table. When they sat down, Guy found that Esmond had come to sit with him, leaving Jessica with Peter and Nancy at the other end of the table. She looked across at him pleadingly but Esmond shook his head. He pulled out a packet of loose tobacco and papers and said to Guy, almost as an aside, 'I'm leaving them to it. I can't talk to that sister.' He started to roll a cigarette. 'I can't talk to any of them, in fact.'

Guy decided not to enter into this, not least because the conversation between Nancy and Jessica – Peter was, mercifully, quiet – was growing louder.

'What *are* you doing here, Naunce? It's lovely to see you but a complete surprise, do admit.'

'Come to bring you home, of course.'

'We won't be coming back to England, if that's what you think.' Jessica removed her hat calmly and put it on the empty chair beside her. 'But we can have a nice time before you return. Are you staying at this hotel? Perhaps they have a room to spare?' She spoke as if arranging a pleasant weekend by the sea.

'Two rooms, you mean,' said Nancy.

'We're married in every way apart from the eyes of a law we don't recognise.' Jessica's dark curls were flattened but she was very pretty, with big eyes and high cheekbones, now flushed. 'We've been living as husband and wife since we left London. You can't tell us to do things differently just because you've decided to pitch up.'

'I can when I'm paying,' said Nancy. She was keeping her cool, but barely.

'You're paying?' scoffed Jessica. 'You mean the Old Human is. Well, anyway, we may not even stay here; we had other plans.'

Nancy didn't need to reply to this. She rang the bell and a waitress came in quickly enough for Guy to suspect she had been listening at the door. They ordered tea, with bread and cheese for Esmond.

'We're famished,' said Jessica.

'I take it you'll let me settle this bill, then?'

'Don't bring everything back to money.' Jessica leaned towards her sister. 'We don't care for it – there's no point in using it for blackmail.'

Nancy looked as if she was going to reply, but held her tongue. 'I'm going to return to London tomorrow by train – to Paris first and then on. You will come back with me.'

'I won't be doing that,' said her sister, displaying her own mettle. 'Nor will Esmond. We only left Spain because we were forced—'

'Forced?'

'We met the British ambassador in Bilbao. Frightful stuffed shirt called Sir Henry Chilton. He told us that the Basque government was relying on the Royal Navy to evacuate the refugees, women and children, because the battle lines are moving closer to the coast. He told us that unless I boarded the ship, the British government would refuse all further co-operation in the evacuation programme, and he would tell the press exactly why. It would have been on our heads, which is very unfair but typical of a capitalist bully—'

'I don't think you understand how worried we all were. Winston had to put pressure on Anthony Eden. One only has a certain number of favours, and we have had to use ours up on *you*.'

Esmond turned around. 'It was a bluff, I know it.'

'I very much doubt it,' said Peter. No one responded.

'We might have lost our Spanish visas if we didn't comply. That's the only reason we came here.' Esmond stubbed out his cigarette. He had presence, there was no denying that. But he seemed very young. He was only eighteen and, from what Guy could see, he barely needed to shave yet. He was shorter than Jessica and wiry, a coiled spring of tension and strength.

'Enough of all that. I'm so thrilled to see you,' said Jessica, light and sunshine in her voice. A young woman in love. 'We've had the most terrific adventures, I've been dying to tell you—'

Guy was astonished. Didn't she feel guilty? Didn't she realise what she had done?

Peter cut her off. 'We haven't come all this way, and nor has Mr Sullivan – who, incidentally, has been searching for you for weeks – to hear about the fun you've been having.'

Tears smarted in Jessica's eyes. She turned to Guy. 'I'm sorry, Mr Sullivan. I didn't realise.'

Guy shook his head. 'No matter.'

'It isn't "no matter",' said Nancy vehemently. 'Lou-Lou had to leave Maisie behind so she and Guy could go tearing to France. We thought you were stuck in the Pyrenees at one point. There are hordes of reporters on the doorstep at Rutland Gate at all hours. Muv and Farve look a thousand years old; they've barely slept and won't take anything except weak tea. The papers mistakenly named Debo as the one who had run off, and now her reputation is utterly compromised—'

'Why compromised?'

'Because the *Daily Mirror* said she'd eloped and now what will people think of her when it comes to her deb season?'

'Oh, that,' said Decca. 'That's all a horror. I've saved her from it – she should be grateful.'

'No, you have not!' Nancy's voice was raised in real anger. 'Stop being so selfish!'

'I am not being selfish! I've given up everything to fight against fascism!'

'You've given up everything to be with a man. But let me assure you, you have given up *everything*. If you don't return and do things properly, you will find that society will make things beastly for you.'

'I couldn't give a fig about society, and nor could Esmond!'

'Society certainly won't give a fig about you—'

And on it went, for some time.

When it became clear that the argument between Nancy and Jessica wasn't going to allow any interjections from anyone else, Peter came and sat with Guy and Esmond. Someone had brought in tea, bread and cheese, and retreated quickly. Guy was longing to pour a cup but the tray was on Nancy's table.

'I say, old chap,' Peter began congenially. 'I know it's a bit early, but would you like a stiffener? I could do with a brandy myself after all that.'

Esmond said nothing, merely gave a shrug. He was watching Jessica intently, as if willing her to say the right words.

Peter followed Esmond's eyeline, gave an awkward cough and tried again. 'No, no, you're quite right. Bit early.'

Guy shuffled in his chair. He longed not to be there.

'What I mean to say is, Esmond . . .'

Esmond turned around at this.

'I mean to say, I rather think that if Decca comes home with us, her father might be persuaded to give her an allowance. I'm sure I could talk him around—'

'A bribe, do you mean?' Esmond's bright blue eyes narrowed.

'No, no, heavens, one wouldn't call it that,' spluttered Peter. 'I simply mean, if you need a helping hand, I'm sure you could both do with some cash in the old back pocket. Couldn't we all?' He made an embarrassing attempt at a laugh. 'So long as Decca comes back with us. Give it some time and things will be seen differently. You are both frightfully young—'

'We're old enough to know our own minds. And you've got another think coming if you think I'm going to take any money from that Nazi baron.'

Esmond stood up. 'Now, don't be hasty—'

It was no good.

'Decca, get up. They're of no use to us. Come on, we're going. We've got things to do.'

Decca half stood, reaching for her hat. 'Do we?'

'Yes, we do.' The emphasis left no doubt.

Decca put her arm through his. 'Just tell me where to go.' They walked to the door. Nancy and Peter sat in shocked silence. Only as she was about to leave did Decca stop. 'I'm sorry, darling,' she said. 'But this is my decision. I'm with Esmond now, we're together and nothing can pull us apart. Send my love to Nanny Blor, would you? Tell her not to worry.'

The door closed quietly behind them.

CHAPTER FORTY-SIX

'Sorry, Mrs Rodd, but I've got to go after them,' said Guy, standing quickly as the door shut.

'Is there any point?' said Nancy. She looked exhausted. Defeated, even. He'd never seen her like that.

'I don't know, but I've got to try. Your father has hired me to do a job, and I need to try to complete it.'

'I really think that if Mrs Rodd and I couldn't do it, you—' Peter started pompously, but Guy cut him off.

'Sorry, sir, not a moment to lose.'

Guy ran out of the door and to the front desk. As he had suspected, the two of them had left their cases with the receptionist and were now picking them up. Jessica was crying.

'Beg pardon,' Guy began.

Esmond turned, like a boxer in a corner. 'Look, we've said our—'

Guy held up his hands. 'I come in peace. Can we at least talk? Why don't we go to a café nearby? I can buy us some coffee. Something to eat.'

In the heat of the row, the bread and cheese had been barely touched.

'Who are you?'

'Guy Sullivan, I—'

'He's married to Louisa, remember? She was our nursery maid when I was very little. I've known her forever and Guy was a policeman but now he's a private detective. Es, darling, please let's go and sit with him. I'm miserable and hungry after this morning.'

Esmond acquiesced and the three of them, with Jessica and Esmond carrying their battered cases, walked a few minutes to a café. The streets were quieter now the refugees had been met and, presumably, sent on their way, though Guy suspected most would get no further than Bayonne. The reporters hadn't stayed at the hotel either, thankfully, likely because they had gone elsewhere to wire through their stories and photographs.

Seated, with coffee and bread before them, the three began to talk. Esmond was much more open with Guy than he had been with Nancy and Peter, and Guy knew this was because he was a working man. Esmond would assume his politics were left of centre. He could assume whatever he liked so long as he kept talking, Guy thought. Jessica talked as if a gag had been removed, relieved and excited to share everything they had done in the last weeks. She described their journey from the start, how they had gone to Paris only to find that the attaché they needed to give her a visa for Spain had returned to London, which meant they had to follow him.

'You went back to London?'

'Yes. We had to go via Dieppe – that's when we found Muv's letter, so I was able to reply.'

'Which meant they believed you were where you said you were for that much longer.'

She nodded shyly. 'I know it was wrong. I didn't want them to worry too much. But I knew I was safe and they wouldn't have let me go. I had no choice.'

Guy neither conceded nor disagreed with this.

The visa had finally come through when they got to Bayonne, and from there they had taken a cargo ship to Bilbao, an uncomfortable and rough journey that took three days across the Bay of Biscay.

'How did you get the visas?' asked Guy. 'I hear they've got tougher now, trying to keep out the volunteers.'

'Esmond has work for the *News Chronicle*, reporting on the war, and I'm to be his secretary.'

'You mean it, then? You intend to go back?'

The two of them had looked at each other then, a love-struck pact. Guy didn't need to hear an answer.

'Are you married?'

'Not legally, no,' said Esmond. 'We're minors in the eyes of the law, which is absurd but there's nothing we can do about that. We have to have our parents' permission. But we'll do it, as soon as we can.'

Guy took in this information, avoiding any comment on the matter. It was not for him to pass judgement; he simply wanted to conclude the case satisfactorily. They were two young people in love and on an adventure. The fact that they had frightened both their families and had him and Louisa searching for them – not to mention hordes of reporters and the considerable efforts of the Foreign Office and several consuls, attachés and an ambassador combing France and war-torn Spain to find them and bring them home – had not seemed to occur to them. Or if it had, it didn't bother them. It didn't seem particularly thoughtful – or particularly socialist.

'I think you'll have to come back to London to get the necessary permission,' was all he said.

'We won't do that.' Esmond's tone was firm. 'If they don't give us permission, we'll simply carry on as we are.' He took Jessica's hand. 'We don't care what they think.'

'I see.' Guy thought for a moment. 'I will have to return, and I need to report back on your whereabouts and your safety. You understand – that was the job I was entrusted with and it's important to me that I know I've done the very best I can.'

'Feel free, old man. You can say that.'

A touch grandiose from an eighteen-year-old, but Guy let it drop.

'Where will you stay tonight?'

For the first time, Jessica's face crumpled. 'I don't know. We have hardly any money. Just nine shillings.'

'Your Running Away money . . . ?'

'All gone,' said Jessica. 'As well as the money Muv and Farve gave me before I left. Esmond had an advance for his articles, but we've spent that too. We've been careful. There was hardly anything to spend it on in Spain, but . . . '

There was another uncomfortable silence. Jessica broke it by standing up with a scrape of her chair. 'Excuse me, I'll be back in a moment. I'm just going to powder my nose.'

The two of them watched her as she walked to the back of the café.

'I say,' said Esmond, 'could you lend us five pounds?'

'Lend?'

'Well, I mean, you could put it on your expenses, couldn't you? Her father will pay it.'

'Isn't that taking money from the Nazi baron?' Guy couldn't help himself.

Esmond shifted uncomfortably. 'You don't have to,' he muttered.

'It's fine, I will.' Guy pulled his wallet out, and in doing so felt Louisa's letter in his pocket. 'You can do me a favour in return.' He took out the photograph of Bernard Plum. 'Do you know this man at all? An Englishman – he works for an insurance company but has gone missing recently. My wife's looking for him in connection with another case she's working on. There's a sliver of a chance that he is in France or Spain, because he went to the war last year. I wondered if he might have been another volunteer, someone you may have come across.'

Esmond took the picture and stared at it closely. 'Hard to say. I met a lot of men out there and not always in the most comfortable of circumstances, if you get my meaning. Most of us were covered in mud or dust, or running for cover. He doesn't look completely unfamiliar in some way, but I can't tell if that's because I've met him or because he looks rather like several men I did meet.'

'I understand,' said Guy, tucking the photograph away again. 'If you could bear it in mind, perhaps ask around.'

'I'm in touch with other men from the International Brigades – other survivors. Bernard Plum, you say? What else do you know about him?'

Guy told him the details he had, and Esmond appeared to listen hard. He was sharp-witted, that was clear. He passed his hand over his chin, a mannerism that seemed too old for a youth his age. 'Hmm. I'm sorry I can't help you. But I'll ask.'

'What were you two talking about?' asked Jessica lightly as she sat back down.

'Some cove called Bernard Plum.'

'Who's he?'

'It's another case we're on,' answered Guy. 'I don't have many details, but he's gone missing from London and his wife has reason to believe he might have come to France, or gone to Spain.'

'To fight?'

'Is there another reason to go to Spain?' Esmond's tone was abrupt. Jessica flushed. To ease the tension, Guy pulled out the photograph again and pushed it across the table to her. Guy noticed Esmond react to this but said nothing.

'Do you recognise him?' asked Guy.

Jessica picked it up. 'I think I do.'

CHAPTER FORTY-SEVEN

Esmond snatched the photograph out of Jessica's hand. 'You don't.' He held it out to Guy, who was obliged to take it and put it back in his jacket pocket.

'What's going on?' said Jessica. 'I thought he looked like that girl Belinda's—'

Esmond pushed back his chair. 'We'd better go. We've got to find somewhere to stay and work out how we're going to get back to Spain, now that your family have botched our plans.' He shook Guy's hand briefly and went to the front of the café, to where he had stashed their cases by the front door.

Jessica stood, too. There was no question that she would do anything other than Esmond's bidding. She put out her hand. 'Goodbye, Mr Sullivan. Please send my love to Louisa, will you? I'm sorry for the goose chase. We honestly didn't mean for anyone to worry, not seriously.'

Guy shook her hand. 'I'll be staying another night at the hotel. If you do remember anything about that man, will you tell me? It could be important.'

'Jessica!' Esmond was calling from the door.

'I've got to go. Sorry.'

With the heaviness a parent feels for any missing child, Guy understood that she wouldn't be returning home. As far as she was concerned, she had left her previous life and she had no plans to return.

All that was left to do was to rest and bathe before beginning the journey back. When he returned to the hotel, Guy found a note for him from Nancy that said she and Peter would be leaving for London the next morning and he was welcome to join them for a drink before supper, at half past six in the bar next door. This prompted the thought that he did not want to share the long journey back with them; Nancy's company he might have enjoyed. Peter's, he would not. He telephoned to Rutland Gate and spoke briefly to Tom there, explaining that he had seen Jessica and Esmond, as had Mr and Mrs Rodd, but that they would not be returning to London with him.

'I'm sorry,' said Guy. 'There didn't seem to be any way to persuade them.'

'No. There wouldn't be. My sisters are not the type to go back on their word, for better or worse. Thank you for trying. I'm sorry it's been something of a wasted journey for you.'

When he had hung up, Guy realised that that was exactly the reason for the weight that sat in his chest. He didn't want to have come so far, for so long, away from his wife and daughter, only to return having achieved nothing. There had to be something he could do.

Guy pulled out Louisa's letter again. Jessica had mentioned a Belinda, and Esmond had been quick to silence her. Did she know something? And why would Esmond hide it? There were several other people in St Jean de Luz and Bayonne who had been to Spain, who might recognise the man in the photograph. Guy wasn't going to give up and go home just yet.

CHAPTER FORTY-EIGHT

~~~

G uy ran back to the café and stood outside it. He tried to
remember which direction he had seen Esmond and
Jessica walking off, and set off along the road. What he needed
was a cheap-looking hotel.

At the first two Guy called into, the receptionists shook their
head and shrugged apologetically. Guy saw a few men walking
around but there didn't appear to be many couples – it was not
the season for people to be there on a holiday – so he was hopeful that Esmond and Jessica might be easily remembered. The
third hotel said a young couple had been in to ask for a room
but that the hotel was full, so they had gone on their way. Back
out on the street, Guy looked about: there were three directions
he could go in. And then he saw it: rue Gambetta. It was the
street name Jessica had used as her false address in Dieppe. If
there was a hotel there, he knew it would tickle her: it would be
a joke she couldn't resist.

He was right.

Halfway up the narrow street was a sign for a *chambre d'hôte* but, before he had reached it, he saw Jessica and Esmond walking out, turning in the opposite direction. Guy called out and saw Esmond look around but, instead of stopping, he clutched Jessica's arm and propelled them faster up the road. Guy ran after them, without calling, and drew up alongside Jessica. 'Please,' he said, a little out of breath. 'I need to talk to you.'

Esmond kept on walking fast. 'We've said all we need to say. We're not going back to England. I'm sorry if it's made things difficult for you, but that's our final decision.'

Jessica mouthed 'sorry' but didn't stop either. Guy ran ahead and stood in front of them, blocking their way on the narrow pavement. 'It's not about going back. It's about Bernard Plum.'

'I told you, I don't know the man,' said Esmond, turning sideways, as if to push past Guy.

'Miss Jessica, you mentioned a Belinda. Is there something you know?'

'Well, I—' She looked at Esmond, as if for permission.

'You wouldn't understand,' Esmond said to Guy.

'Try me.'

'Look, all sorts of men have gone out there – each one has a story of his own. You don't always know why they're there. It's lawless at times, chaotic. I got shot at by our own side. The point is, no one is interested in anyone's past; it's about protecting the present and our future. We're there to defend principles, to stand against fascism. If a man doesn't want to be found, it's not for me to ask him why or to give him up.' He stopped, took a breath. 'God knows, I've relied on people to do the same for me.'

An elderly woman squeezed past them with a tiny white dog on a long leash, muttering something in French.

'We don't need to find this man because his wife is worried,' said Guy. 'It's because there's a woman missing. It's possible that her disappearance is connected to him. At the very least, he needs to be eliminated from our search. If we can find him, we can ask.'

'Let me see that photograph again.' Jessica held out her hand. She caught Esmond's eye, but there was a steeliness in hers that told him to back down. She looked carefully. 'I didn't meet him, but I'm pretty sure this was the photograph that Belinda showed me. She was a war nurse over there but she's English. I met her one night and she showed it to me – we were talking about our men.' She looked shyly at Esmond as she said this.

'Where did you meet her?'

'In Bilbao. I couldn't tell you exactly where. It was a makeshift café. They only served one kind of bean stew and revolting black bread. She and I were sitting next to each other, and we talked. She told me she'd been there for a while and had met him there. I don't think she said his surname was Plum, though.'

'He might have told her a different name.'

'Yes, perhaps. She didn't talk about him a lot. It was only because we were – well, we were being girls. I'd told her about Esmond, you see. From what I can remember, she said he had been in a battle near Albacete. He'd been injured or was sick in some way, and he had to return to London. That would fit, wouldn't it?'

'Do you know when that might have been?'

'Not exactly. Earlier this year but not by much.'

'Did Belinda know he had a wife?'

'No – or at least, she didn't mention that. But she was quite bohemian, she might not have minded either way.'

'That's such a snobbish thing to say,' said Esmond disparagingly.

'Sorry Es, but try as I might, I was brought up by snobbish wolves. I can't help it. I *am* trying.'

Esmond softened at this, and raised Jessica's hand to his lips and kissed it. 'I know. I shouldn't have snapped. I just wish everyone would leave us alone.'

'I will,' said Guy, though he was losing his patience at this young man's self-indulgence. 'Did you have a surname for Belinda? Or do you know anything about where she might be now?'

'Carter? Something like that. I think she was going to try and find another hospital to work in, wherever the battle lines were being drawn.'

Esmond was tugging at Jessica's hand.

'One more thing, that's all. Can you tell me what she looked like?'

'Yes, she was rather striking. Very dark hair and eyes, about my height but strong, somehow. She had visible muscles in her arms, I remember that. I'd say she was about twenty-five, twenty-six. Sorry, that's all I can think of.'

'No, that's very helpful. Thank you. I'll let you go now, and won't bother you again.'

They turned and walked away. Guy thought about calling out to Jessica to be careful, but he knew there was no point. They would do whatever they wanted to do.

PART TWO

CHAPTER FORTY-NINE

I n the Cannon & Sullivan office, as spring carried its blossom on the warm breeze, there was a steady ebb and flow to Guy and Louisa's working rhythm. In the month since the newspaper article in the *Daily News* which had mentioned that Guy and Louisa's detective agency had been hired by the Mitfords, a stream of business had come to their door. At first, Louisa had been shocked by the sheer variety of base behaviours: blackmail, suspected affairs, fraud by co-workers, theft by family members, counterfeit jewels sold to a dealer, a regular flasher in Holland Park (every Tuesday at two o'clock in the afternoon) and a forged painting bought at auction. The things people were prepared to do, the lies and the cover-ups, seemed more exhausting in their execution than any benefits the perpetrators could gain. But the bad guys provided work for Louisa and Guy. Louisa still felt a jolt of anticipation every time the telephone rang: would the person at the other end give them a much-needed clue or new business?

In spite of the newspapers running stories about Jessica and Esmond having been found, there were still a number of false sightings being reported everywhere from Dundee – where they were spotted ordering a steak and kidney pie – to Barcelona. However, the case, so far as the Sullivans and the Mitfords were concerned, was now closed: the young couple had not been able to get back into Spain but were, for the moment, living in Bayonne, refusing to return to England. Lady Redesdale planned to go out to visit them in the next few weeks, and it was likely that either Guy or Louisa would be asked to accompany her.

More pressing on their time were the four cases they had open. Bernard Plum was still missing, as was Petunia Attwood, but any further information had dried up. The police had opened an investigation to identify the body, wrongly identified as Petunia, as well as a murder enquiry. Bernard Plum was, naturally, a suspect, but since they had no resources in France and Spain, Louisa and Guy felt they were unlikely to find him if he was there. But Louisa was despondent about the police's efforts in any case: Guy had explained to her that if the police thought the dead woman was a prostitute killed by a client or pimp, they wouldn't be in a great rush to find the culprit. 'I'm sorry,' he had said, as if he should feel the guilt of an institution he no longer worked for, 'but I know what they're like. A woman who has died, with no one coming forward to claim her as a relative . . . there's not the incentive. And they won't think it likely that they'll find whoever did it.'

'Even with a named suspect?'

Guy had shrugged sadly. 'Even then.'

Julia Attwood telephoned the office once a week to ask if there was any news, and Louisa always found it hard to tell her there had been nothing. Louisa had sent two notes to Mrs Plum, assuring her that she had not stopped the investigation and asking her to be in touch if she heard anything. There had been no reply. Presumably the police would have been round to tell her that her husband was a suspect, which would have been a shock. Louisa half-wondered if she should go to see Mrs Plum, to check if she was all right after hearing the news, but they weren't exactly friends. If Louisa went there, it had to be because she was still trying to find either Petunia or Bernard, not to comfort her. Besides, Mrs Plum was almost certainly relieved that her husband had disappeared.

The burning question – how did the deceased woman come to be wearing Petunia's coat and have her engraved compact in the pocket? – remained unanswered. No matter which way Louisa turned it around in her mind, she couldn't work it out.

'Perhaps she donated it to a charity shop and didn't empty the pockets,' suggested Guy. In the end, that seemed the likeliest answer. If Petunia had deliberately vanished, she could easily have got rid of her coat, along with other things. Bernard's card could have been something she'd had once that had fallen through the hole in the pocket; it didn't definitely tie him to the crime.

In short, there were more questions than answers.

Nor had Louisa been able to find out anything further about Belinda Carter: there were three in the phone book, but none of them fitted the profile. Until something turned up, it was a dead end.

In the meantime, Guy was tracing the origins of a forged painting as far as he could while Louisa was checking out the qualifications of two applicants to a bank. Standard work that kept them ticking along.

Louisa had come to realise – as Guy had warned her at the

start – that a large amount of their time was spent simply verifying facts, or watching and waiting. But although this might have lacked an element of excitement and surprise, Louisa found she did not mind. Her brain was being used – that was the main thing. And when she returned home to Maisie, she was only ever completely happy to see her daughter. She tended to finish earlier than Guy, and often met up with Mary Moon, both of them pushing their babies on the swings at the park before stopping off at the grocer's on the way home to pick up some bits and bobs for supper. Mary sometimes talked about joining the agency when her children were older; she couldn't return to the police force as a married woman. As the days grew longer and the sunshine warmer, Louisa felt there was nothing more she could ask of her life.

Guy had made their second cups of tea of the morning, and Louisa was idly wondering which café they might go to for luncheon, when the telephone rang. It sat on Guy's desk but close to the edge, easily within her reach. They had an unspoken rule that they took it in turns to answer. Louisa picked it up.

'Good morning, Louisa Cannon speaking. Who is calling, please?'

'It's Mr Cornish, from Lee Worth. I think you had better come in.'

Louisa looked at the clock on the wall. It was ten past eleven. She had planned to finish at three o'clock today and there were still a few items on her neat 'to do' list, but perhaps she could fit it all in.

'Can you tell me why?'

'It's Bernard Plum. He's been here.'

'Is he still there?'

'No. But he took some files.'

'I'll be there as soon as I can. Thank you, Mr Cornish.'

Louisa put the handset down. Guy looked at her with raised eyebrows.

'It's Bernard Plum,' she said. 'He's been back to his office. He's not there now, but I think I'd better—'

'Yes, get there quickly. He could still be in London.'

'Should we telephone DI Morgan? Let him know?'

Guy's mouth twitched. 'I'll telephone him, but you get to the office first. I know it's not strictly correct, but . . . it was our case first.'

'You'll have to have lunch alone.'

'I'll survive.' Guy grinned. 'Go on. No time to waste.'

Louisa grabbed her bag and put on her Mackintosh, not even bothering to button it before she flew out the door.

CHAPTER FIFTY

A t the offices of Lee Worth, Louisa was shown quickly to Mr Cornish's office.

Mr Cornish ushered Louisa in before him and closed the door. 'Please, sit down,' he said, taking his own chair behind the desk. 'Can I offer you any tea or . . . '

'No, thank you.' Louisa saw Miss Piper sitting by the desk, looking as stout as before, but her face was rather pale today. Louisa greeted her. 'I take it you saw Bernard Plum, too?'

'Yes, well, it was rather extraordinary,' said Mr Cornish before Miss Piper could reply. 'He hasn't been seen, as you know, since he was suspended, pending the enquiry into the allegations made by Miss Attwood. The firm has made its investigation, in case you were wondering.'

Louisa wondered why people without any legal qualifications always lapsed into such formal language. She didn't remark on this, of course, but pulled out her notebook as she sat down.

'Did you talk to Mr Plum yourself, Mr Cornish?'

'Ah, no. I did not.'

'In that case, I'd like to direct my questions to Miss Piper as well as to you.'

'Of course, of course,' said Mr Cornish, sitting down and leaning his elbows on the desk.

Miss Piper turned towards Louisa. She looked composed, but Louisa thought she detected a tremor of nervousness in her eyes.

'He was last in the office on the 2nd February, I believe?' Louisa asked.

'Yes.' Miss Piper looked at her manager for confirmation, and he nodded.

'And you haven't heard from him at all until . . .'

'Yesterday – that is, last night.'

'Did you have any prior warning of his arrival here?'

It was stuffy in the office, with a stale smell of cigarettes.

'None whatsoever,' confirmed Mr Cornish.

'I want to get the facts absolutely right,' said Louisa. 'You suspended Mr Plum. This was due to last a month, while investigations were made – is that right?'

'Yes.'

'And have conclusions been made about whether Miss Attwood's claims were correct?'

'That's confidential information, Miss Cannon. I'm afraid I can't share that with you.'

'You can't tell me whether or not you found Mr Plum guilty of fraud, or you won't?'

Mr Cornish shook his head. The movement reminded her of Maisie refusing to eat her cabbage, lips pressed shut. 'I can't comment.'

Guilty, then.

'What about the other matter?' said Miss Piper, looking at Mr Cornish again.

'What other matter?' asked Louisa.

'He was off sick for a number of weeks last year,' Miss Piper answered, watching her boss for his reaction. 'But Miss Attwood discovered that he had been to Spain in that time. Fighting in the war, for the fascists.'

'On the *fascist* side? Are you sure?'

'Quite sure,' said Miss Piper.

If this was true, then Mrs Plum's hunch that he had gone to Spain and France was right, and it made Jessica's assertion that Belinda Carter, the nurse, had shown her his photograph correct too.

'Do you know how she discovered that?'

'She overheard him boasting. When she also suspected him of fraud, she told him she'd get him on one thing or the other. I told her not to do it.' Miss Piper was visibly distressed. 'But she said he had to be made to pay.'

Mr Cornish looked alarmed. 'You didn't tell me this.'

Miss Piper shook her head. 'I couldn't. I'm sorry. I promised Miss Attwood I'd keep it to myself.'

'Do you know what happened when she confronted him?' asked Louisa.

'No,' said Miss Piper. She had gone very still. 'That is, she wouldn't tell me what happened. Afterwards she said that she would talk to the managers.'

'Do you think she was frightened by him?'

Miss Piper looked at Mr Cornish, as if daring him to challenge her. 'Yes, I do.'

Louisa stared at her notebook. She had barely written in it.

'Did Miss Attwood tell you about this, Mr Cornish?'

He shifted in his seat. 'She told me she suspected his sick leave was a cover for a foreign trip but no more than that.'

'And was he questioned about his fraudulent sick leave?'

'I'm not entirely certain. There are people senior to me – they may have said something. He's worked here for a number of years. I expect he was given a warning, but no more than that.'

'I see. Do you happen to know whether anyone from the office has spoken to his wife since last night?'

'Not so far as I'm aware.'

Louisa gave what she hoped was a professional nod. 'I will be getting in touch with her after this. She has asked me to find him.'

That is, she wanted him found but not returned.

'I assumed as much.'

'Miss Piper, can you tell me what happened last night?'

'Yes. It was at a quarter to eight—'

'That's late to be in the office, isn't it? What time does everyone generally go home?'

'Half past five is the end of our day. Usually. But I was working late. I had some reports that I wanted to finish typing up and I prefer it when it's quiet here.'

Louisa thought she might start to feel nauseous soon if Mr Cornish didn't open that window. 'So it's likely that Mr Plum wasn't expecting anyone to be here?'

'I wouldn't have thought so.'

'There's no watchman?'

'Not as such,' said Mr Cornish. 'There's a caretaker. He comes and switches all the lights off, locks the doors after the last person has left. He lives nearby. The last person to leave telephones him, but he doesn't rush around if he's eating his supper. He opens the office early in the morning. We don't keep any money on the premises.'

'Right.' Louisa wanted to get her questions in the right order. 'What alerted you, Miss Piper?'

'I heard a noise in his office. It's next door to the one I work in, so I went to look. He was in his office, putting files into a bag.'

'Did he see you?'

'I was afraid of what he would do if he saw me, so I tried to back away, but I didn't manage it.'

'What happened then?'

'He didn't stop what he was doing. I told him that I would call the police if he didn't drop the bag, but he just laughed. He said there was nothing I could do, that he was taking what was rightfully his and I could stuff my . . . I'd rather not repeat it, Miss Cannon.'

'I understand.'

'He said I could tell the bosses that he'd resigned and we wouldn't be seeing him again. He'd decided to move to France. And he started to try to leave the room, but I grabbed his jacket and held him, briefly. I asked him where Petunia was.'

'That was brave of you. What was his reaction?'

'He pushed my hand away. He was angry. He said he didn't know where she was or why I was asking, and he hoped she'd taken a running jump into the Thames. I'm sure he didn't mean it, Miss Cannon. We were both shouting and rather shocked – it's hard to remember exactly how it all happened.'

'You've done well. I just need a little more. Why did he say there was nothing you could do when it came to calling the

232

police? Why was he so certain he could take the files without you stopping him?'

Mr Cornish looked down at his lap before replying. 'Because he knew Miss Piper wasn't likely to be alone. He told her that if she said anything, he'd report us for . . . That is, he'd known for some time that . . . '

'The two of you?'

'We can't have anyone know. I'm a married man, and Miss Piper would lose her job without references.'

'I won't tell anyone. But if Mr Plum knew this, why did you suspend him?'

'I resisted for a long time, but Miss Attwood continued with her allegations until too many people knew what she was saying. It would have been too damaging for the company.'

'Does this mean his suspension was paid leave?'

'Yes.' Mr Cornish splayed his hands on the desk in front of him. 'I'm not proud of what happened. But there you have it.'

'Yes, I suppose I do.' Louisa stood. 'Thank you for telling me. I need to think about whether any of this may be connected to Petunia Attwood's disappearance. But perhaps Mr Plum's wife will be relieved to hear that he intends to move to France. I don't think she'll be joining him.'

'Will you tell her? You understand that there's no one else we can talk to about this incident.'

Louisa nodded and left the room, grateful to get outside and into the fresh air.

CHAPTER FIFTY-ONE

❦

As Louisa did not want to leave Maisie, they decided that Guy would travel with Lady Redesdale to Bayonne to see Jessica and Esmond. Lord Redesdale had insisted upon this.

'He's worried,' explained Nancy, when she came to their office to make the request. 'This whole saga has had the most dreadful effect on them both. He simply wants someone to protect his wife, help her with the luggage and so on. It's rather touching, actually.'

'Of course we can discuss it,' said Louisa. 'Why not one of you girls, or Tom?'

'There's simply no point. Esmond sees all of us as Nazis and we'll make matters worse. Mr Sullivan, you saw their reaction, didn't you?'

Guy agreed.

'And I think they did talk to you a bit. At least, you're not seen as part of the ruling classes or whatever nonsense Esmond has come up with. It's tiresome. Not to mention dangerous. Why must a man drive a girl away from her family? We're all being separated now. Unity in Germany, Diana with Sir Ogre, and now Decca. Pamela is the only sane one, but she's been spirited away by her husband, too. Thank heavens Peter is much too sensible for that.'

Sensible being the *mot juste*, thought Louisa, but kept her thoughts to herself. She still found it puzzling that Nancy had ended up with a man who seemed so dull to the rest of them, but maybe that was the very reason she found him attractive. After all, Nancy had created enough drama during her early years to last several lifetimes.

After Nancy left, Louisa and Guy talked it over. He wasn't particularly thrilled at the prospect of a long train journey with Lady Redesdale, but Louisa had another idea. 'I think we should try again at the Petunia Attwood case.'

'How?'

'Something about it is niggling at me. I've written to Mrs Plum. I haven't heard anything back, but I assume that her husband went back to the house, even if only to collect things before he returned to France. She may yet reply. But I can't help feeling there's a connection between him and Petunia. It's too coincidental otherwise. Petunia accused Mr Plum of fraud, and they both disappeared at the same time. If he's returned to France, we should consider the possibility that he's in Bayonne, on his way to Spain. There was the Belinda Carter that you said Decca had met. She might still be there, too. It's an opportunity to investigate, at no cost to us.'

Guy pushed his glasses up his nose. It was a tic, and Louisa had grown used to seeing it when he was nervous. But he wasn't nervous now, she knew. He was thoughtful.

'You're right,' he said. 'We shouldn't give up on it just yet.

Perhaps we should look again at the letters that came to the office from women who think their sons or sweethearts might have gone to Spain. I can ask around about those names, at the very least.'

'You'll have time. Lady Redesdale will need to talk to Decca; she won't rush back. You'll have a few days. It sounds as if they only want someone to accompany Lady Redesdale on the journey there and back.'

'Agreed. I'll do it. I'll miss you, but I'll do it.'

'You won't,' said Louisa, laughing. 'You'll love every minute of it. Freedom and French cheese, and no being woken in the night by a small person.'

Guy said nothing, but put his hands on his wife's waist and pulled her towards him.

A few days later, Guy and Lady Redesdale disembarked from the train at Bayonne. It was hot now, a Continental heat that rose from the pavement and slicked his body with sweat by the time he had carried the bags the length of the platform and up the stairs. The journey had been pleasant enough – uneventful, which was the best that he could hope for. Lady Redesdale was less peremptory than she had been before Decca had gone missing, a touch slower and kinder in her instructions. Guy had done the journey in second class, while she was in first class, which meant that they did not have to address the difficulty of making conversation while travelling. Now that they had arrived at Bayonne, Guy sensed her nervousness. She talked constantly from the train to the station exit: had he checked where the hotel was, did he have a map, would Decca be there to meet her, would Esmond stay away, had they got their return tickets yet, would the porter be irritated not to earn a tip . . . Guy made the right noises at the right times, but the walk seemed a long one. It was a relief when they turned the final corner to see Decca waiting for them by the hotel door.

Decca ran forward, her eyes wet, arms out. Without speaking, she embraced her mother in a tight hug, the sort Maisie would give Louisa: arms around the neck, her head tucked in. Lady Redesdale stiffened at first, looking about her as if the people on the street would disapprove, but she was soon overcome. She had Decca back at last. With a brief low sound that came from deep within her, she wept in her daughter's arms.

CHAPTER FIFTY-TWO

With a few days to himself, Guy decided to return to the Hôtel le Pont Neuf to see if he could find Ivo Fernandez. He didn't hold out much hope. It had been weeks since he had last seen him, but it was the best place he could think of starting.

So it was with a pleasant sense of surprise that he spotted Ivo in the hotel's small courtyard. With the warmer weather, tables and chairs had been put out there. It was shabby but cool in the shade, and although the hotel's guests were still undeniably refugees, without their heavy coats and grey pallor, they seemed altogether more hopeful. Ivo looked thinner and had the kind of tan that was only gained from being outside for all daylight hours. When he saw Guy, he brightened with a grin and a friendly wave.

'Hey, *amigo*,' he called out. 'What brings you back here?'

'Good to see you, Ivo. Can I take this chair?'

'But of course, of course.'

Guy sat down and called a waiter over, then ordered fresh lemonade for the two of them. 'Is it too late for breakfast?'

The waiter shrugged in that particular way that could mean yes but could also mean no.

'Any pastries you have left, please bring them. I think we'll manage to eat them.'

Another shrug, even more half-hearted this time, and the waiter slouched off.

'I thought you were going to try to get to England,' said Guy. 'What happened?'

'I got sick. I'm better now, but I was in bed for a long time.'

'That must have been hard. Was there anyone looking after you?'

Ivo gave a wry smile. 'We are a band of brothers here. They were kind and brought me what they could spare. But it was not much.'

'Are you well now?'

'Well enough to eat.' He laughed as the waiter set down their drinks with a basket of croissants that didn't look too stale. 'Tell me, please, what I can do for you.'

Guy laughed too. 'You've got me right. I do need a favour. I'm here for a day or two.'

'Did you find the people you were looking for? The young man and woman?'

'Yes, they've been found. They were in Spain, in Bilbao, but they've come back here. I've accompanied the woman's mother here for a visit. She's hoping to persuade the couple back to London, but I doubt she'll be successful.'

'They have the bug for an adventure, yes?'

'Yes,' said Guy. 'But I'm looking for someone else now. A woman has gone missing – Petunia Attwood. And at the same time, a man she worked for disappeared. Bernard Plum. We believe he was in Spain last year and that he may be trying to get back there now. I've got photographs.'

Guy pulled out the picture he had of Bernard, as well as one of Petunia. 'We don't think he called himself Bernard Plum – he probably used a different surname. And he had a girlfriend, we think. Belinda Carter. I don't have a picture of her, though. We don't know much about her other than she possibly worked as a nurse on the frontlines.'

Ivo put down his second croissant and wiped the crumbs from his lips and fingers before reaching out for the photographs.

'I don't know anything about the women you mention. But this man. Hmm.'

'Do you recognise him?'

'Maybe. It's hard to say, you know. Men in the middle of a civil war do not look like this, with their combed hair and clean shave. They have beards and dirt in their fingernails. There is maybe something I recognise, but it is more the name Bernard. I have heard stories about him, I am sure.'

'What kind of stories?'

'Before I say more, you have to remember that this situation I am in is like a cooking pot for legends. Right now, there are a lot of us sitting around all day with not much to do and any story we hear is given many details and embellishments – is that the word?'

Guy nodded.

'Yes, so you have to be careful what you believe. You take it all with a great handful of salt. But I think I have heard of this Bernard as a brave man.'

'A brave man?' This wasn't the detail Guy was expecting.

'I could be wrong. It could be someone else,' cautioned Ivo.

'But if it is him, then I heard he was captured by a gang of men who said they were fighting for the government. They made him dig his own grave but when they put him in it, to bury him alive, he pulled one of them down with him, punched him out cold, attacked another man in the same way. The others ran off and he buried the two men who were left behind.'

'That is an extraordinary story,' said Guy.

'That's not all. He killed a pig with his bare hands and fed it to his brigade of men, who were starving. I think there are more.'

'Where did you hear all this?'

Ivo sat back, sated after four croissants and two glasses of lemonade. 'I don't know exactly. We don't have a camp fire to sit around, but it's the same sort of thing. We entertain each other. Like I said, take it with salt.'

'I will. Nevertheless, it's quite something to create such a legend. I suppose there may be a grain of truth in there some-where. Do you know where he's supposed to be now?'

'No idea, sorry, *amigo*. But we can ask around. Let us take a walk. We can ask about the women you say you are looking for, too.'

Guy settled the bill and the two of them headed outside into the midday sun. The sky above was cloudless and bluer than Maisie's eyes when she was born. At a slow pace, they walked towards the nearest square, where men, women and children sat in ragtag groups. They were not home, they had no home to travel back to or towards, they could not work or go to school, they would not beg. The children played games with sticks or chalk, skipped with makeshift ropes; the babies had long since learned to stop crying. Guy was deeply moved by the sight, though he did not know what to do with the uncomfortable feeling in his chest when he looked at them. He didn't even know what to call it: guilt? Frustration? They moved through the people, Ivo talking to those he knew, showing the photographs, repeating 'Bernard Plum', 'Petunia Attwood' and 'Belinda Carter', anomalous names clunking in the midst of their fast Spanish. Guy watched them shake their heads apologetically. *No, no, nada, perdón.*

Guy wondered if Keith, whom he had met outside the British consul, would know anything, but without his surname Guy had no idea how to find him. He kicked himself for sloppy detective work. The lowest ranked policeman knew you always took down the full name of any potential witness.

After they had gone around the square, Ivo told Guy that a few others had repeated the same stories that he had told earlier about Bernard.

'Has anyone seen any of this? Or met him?' Guy asked.

'No,' said Ivo.

'Did anyone know anything about his wife? Or girlfriend?'

'Someone said they had heard he had many lovers. That is all.'

'Part of the mystique of the man, I suppose, that he should have many lovers.'

'It is the Spanish way.' Ivo grinned, easing the tension.

'Ha.' Guy put the photographs away. 'I'm staying at the Hôtel de Fleurie. Could you keep asking for me? If you hear anything, anything at all, please come and find me there.' He pressed some money into Ivo's hand. 'Don't refuse this.'

'*Gracias.*' Ivo put it in his pocket. 'I will ask. I will do my best for you.'

CHAPTER FIFTY-THREE

⁓

B ack at the hotel, Guy ordered a simple luncheon and settled down for a peaceful hour. It wasn't to last. Before he had finished his onion soup, with its salty cheese and great hunks of bread, something he was savouring with a rare pleasure, Jessica and Esmond came over to his table. They brought with them an atmosphere he was beginning to recognise as familiar to their combined energy: a cauldron of fury and young love.

'Mr Sullivan,' Jessica announced as she sat down, 'we've been looking for you. Do you mind if we join you? We're starving.'

'Not starving,' Esmond corrected. 'There are people who starve for days in a landscape of abject poverty. We are merely hungry.'

'Yes, of course my love, only a figure of speech.' Jessica reached out and squeezed Esmond's hand briefly.

'Are you not joining your mother for luncheon?' asked Guy.

'No, she's got a migraine. She's lying down. It's not surprising, after such a long journey. She needn't have come – there was nothing to worry about. Everyone knows where we are, don't they?'

Their apparent maturity, thought Guy, only stretched so far. He decided not to answer her rhetorical question.

Esmond called the waitress over and they ordered some food – presumably put on Lady Redesdale's room bill. There was some general talk about what they had done in Bayonne since Guy had last seen them. Esmond had got a job with Reuters, translating and sending stories reported from both sides on the Spanish war that he listened to on the radio. 'It's not strictly legitimate, if you ask me, reporting at second hand, but they seem quite pleased with what we're sending them and it's two pounds a week – money we can't afford not to earn. It's the exact cost of our bed and board at the hotel.'

Their biggest complaint was that they couldn't get their Spanish visas renewed, and it seemed that they were doomed to stay in France.

'It's not England,' said Esmond, 'it's got that going for it. But socialism is not Communism, whatever the likes of Decca's father thinks.'

'I wouldn't know,' said Guy.

'You're not interested in politics?' Esmond was appalled, Guy could see that. Had he pinned his hopes on Guy being his true working-class socialist friend?

'No, sorry. I vote, and I'm glad women can vote, but I'm afraid I'm not your man when it comes to arguments of any kind.'

This wasn't strictly true – at least, not lately – but he didn't feel like getting into it with Esmond. There was a mildly uncomfortable pause while Guy finished his soup.

'There *was* something we wanted to talk to you about,' said Jessica in an appeasing tone.

'Oh, yes?'

'That man you said you were looking for – Bernard. I realised I got the name of his girlfriend slightly wrong. She's Belinda Cartwright, not Carter.'

'That could be helpful,' said Guy. 'How did you find that out?'

'Esmond bumped into someone he had been in the war with last year.'

'Oh?' Guy turned to Esmond.

'Yes, Max MacIver, he was one of the few men in the International Brigades that survived alongside me. A Scot. Tough as old boots.'

'Did you ask him if he knew Bernard Plum?'

'No. I'd put it out of my mind, to be perfectly honest. But he talked about being nursed back to health by this angel, Belinda Cartwright. That rang a bell.'

'Did he get to know her at all?'

'A little. She said she'd had a sweetheart but he'd left her, gone back to England. She was going to follow him there, though he didn't know it yet. I think Max was trying to distract her from that particular pursuit.'

'Where is Max now?'

'I don't know. Probably wedged in a tiny gap at the bottom of a cargo ship getting himself stowed back to Spain. He's that sort of man.' Esmond pulled out his leather pouch of tobacco. 'I'd be that kind of man too, but I've got Decca to think of now.'

That sort of remark buzzed in Guy's brain. He couldn't decide if he liked this chap or not.

'Well, it's a little more to go on. We tried to find a Belinda Carter that fitted the profile with no luck, so that may explain it. Thank you for telling me.'

Their food had arrived, along with a carafe of wine, which

Guy declined to share in. 'I'd better push off,' he said, 'check on Lady Redesdale, see if she needs anything.'

'She won't,' Jessica said airily. 'We'll see you later on, I hope.'

A couple of hours later, Guy received a message from Lady Redesdale to say she'd like him to come to her rooms. When he knocked and entered, he found her lying on a sofa, a thin blanket over her legs, the curtains almost drawn, letting only an inch or two of the bright sunshine in. On a low table beside her was a jug of iced water and an empty glass. Guy closed the door and stood close by, holding his hat. She didn't seem to have noticed him come in, although she had called out in response to his knock.

'Good afternoon, m'lady,' he said.

'Hello, Mr Sullivan.' Her voice was low, lacking her usual energetic authority. 'I do apologise for my state, but I've had a dreadful migraine and it hasn't yet quite gone away.'

'I'm sorry to hear that.'

'Don't be, there's nothing you can do. I have to wait for the good body to heal itself. I need to talk to you, because it's become apparent that I'm going to have to set about making arrangements for Jessica's wedding.'

'Beg pardon, m'lady?'

'I know it seems sudden, but that's just the way it is.'

She's pregnant, thought Guy.

'Of course. What can I do to help?'

'You're free to return to London. I shall stay here for a few weeks more. I'll ask Deborah to send me some more clothes. And we shall have to somehow put together a trousseau for Jessica. Oh dear.' She broke off. Guy had the awful feeling she was crying – something she wouldn't want to do in front of him; something he didn't want to witness.

'He's a coward. Not even to ask Lord Redesdale for her hand in marriage first. Of course, it's exactly what one would expect from a Communist, but it's very disappointing. I've told him as much.'

That must have gone down well.

Guy felt the need to say something reassuring. 'They seem very much in love, m'lady.'

'I'm sure they believe so. Unfortunately, it's not enough for a successful marriage. But there it is.'

'Yes,' said Guy, without any confidence he'd struck the right note. 'I'll look into trains. I expect there will be one tonight to Paris.'

'Thank you, Mr Sullivan. You've been so kind.'

'Is there anything I can do for you before I leave?'

'No.' Lady Redesdale had hardly looked at him during this conversation, but now she turned her head very gently towards him. 'I wish there was. Goodbye, Mr Sullivan.'

CHAPTER FIFTY-FOUR

Louisa was with Nancy at Rutland Gate, sitting in the library downstairs, when they heard a sudden noise from above. Louisa thought it sounded as if a large, heavy object had been thrown onto the floor. This was followed by repeated thumps – his lordship's feet stamping, it transpired – and a colourful invective of shouts. Nancy said someone had probably forgotten to put ice in the ice bucket, but as it went on they realised it must be something even more serious. Nancy went upstairs alone to investigate. When she came back down, she was two shades paler.

'Muv telephoned. The judge has given permission for them to marry within weeks, in France.'

'The judge?'

'If you remember, Farve had Decca made a ward of court after she ran off, through the family solicitors. It was meant to protect her from this happening, but it seems she wrote a letter of appeal to the judge and he's agreed with her.'

'Which can only mean one thing.'

'Yes.' Nancy sat down and put her head in her hands. 'Stupid, stupid girl. She simply doesn't realise what this means. She's thrown it all away.'

'Thrown what away?'

'You wouldn't quite understand. It's not the same for you – *lucky* you – but society will have nothing more to do with her, not ever again.'

'Perhaps she doesn't mind that.' Louisa had long since learned to rise above insinuations that her class had no moral compass. It simply wasn't an argument worth having with Nancy, or any of the Mitfords.

'No, it's not that. The bit she doesn't understand is that society means her family, too. She's chosen a way of life that will divorce her from us. Esmond hates us all, I know that. And in supporting him, she has to hate us too. But she's making it impossible for any reconciliation to come from us.'

'Right. You do have to explain that to me.'

'We have to think of the others. Deborah is yet to marry. She has already had her deb season compromised by these news stories.'

'You don't think that Diana and Sir Oswald's affair, or Unity's friendship with Hitler, is more damaging?'

'Those things are not pleasant, but they are not enough to cut one off from society.'

Louisa wasn't sure what to say to this. She had a long connection with the Mitfords, particularly Nancy; she had known them for almost half her life. She owed so much of who she was to them. And yet there were always these deep trenches of unassailable mores that lay between them.

She decided to change the subject.

'I hate to ask, but was there any mention of Guy?'

Nancy leaned back in her chair, as if flattened by the very atmosphere. 'Sorry, yes, there was. He will be on his way home shortly. Muv is insisting on staying out there to make arrangements, but I think she'll be persuaded to return sooner rather than later. There's hardly any point in her being there when neither of them are talking to her properly.'

'Then wouldn't you rather Guy held on, just in case?'

'Yes, you're probably right. None of us is thinking clearly.'

'If I may, I'll use your telephone here and call him at the hotel.'

Nancy nodded and waved towards the hall, where there was a telephone.

Fortunately, Guy was in his room, packing, when Louisa called, so he was easily found and brought to the telephone. Louisa explained that she had been there when the news had hit.

'"Hit" being the operative word, I imagine,' said Guy.

'I've never heard his lordship use such language.' Louisa giggled, keeping her voice as low as possible.

'I assume it means she's pregnant.'

'Yes, I think it must. Nancy is livid too – says everyone will cut them off, even the family.'

'Well, they're a funny lot.'

There was a pause. They didn't usually get time to talk at length on the telephone, especially not a foreign call. There were no pips here, but it would still cost a lot of money.

'I know you're probably getting ready to come back, but Nancy thinks Lady Redesdale might be persuaded to return home sooner, rather than stay out there.'

'I see.'

'In which case, it would be better if you were still there, to bring her back.'

'Yes. I'll do that then. If you think that's best.'

'I do.' Louisa clutched the telephone a little harder, as if Guy might feel her touch. 'We miss you, Maisie and I. It's not that I don't want you home.'

'I know. I miss you too.'

'Any news on Bernard?'

'A little. I've asked around, and it seems that a few people have heard of him. There are stories attached to him about extraordinary courage.'

'Oh. I can't say I was quite expecting that.'

'No. But I haven't met anyone who has actually met him, or seen him do any of these things. So I'm not any closer to the man himself.'

'How do they know what he looks like, then?'

'That's just it. They don't. It's more that he's an Englishman called Bernard. What if we've been barking up the wrong tree altogether?'

'No one has seen him recently?'

'No, but I'll ask around again if I'm going to stay at least one more night in Bayonne. One other thing. It's Belinda Cartwright, not Carter. In case that helps.'

'I'll look her up, try the phone book again. Why the name change?'

'Esmond bumped into a man he was in the International Brigade with last year, and this chap mentioned he'd been nursed back to health by Belinda Cartwright.'

'Which means she's a nurse for the Republican side. I wonder how she met Bernard, when he's a fascist.'

'So far as we know.'

'That's true. He could have lied to her. His wife said he was only political when it suited him – he'd choose the winning side, not the right side.'

'Charming.'

'Yes, quite. Darling, I'd better go. I'll kiss Maisie for you.'

'Yes, please. And ask Maisie to kiss you for me, too.'

Louisa laughed and they hung up. Belinda Cartwright, she thought. Another gossamer thread in this case that was too delicate to catch, somehow. And yet two people had vanished. If they were lovers or friends, or even co-conspirators fighting in a war, wouldn't someone have heard of them, known where they were? Wouldn't they be openly sitting somewhere, laughing in the sunshine, reassuring friends that they were alive and no one was to worry? Gossamer threads, perhaps, but strong enough to pull at Louisa and wonder what clue she was missing.

CHAPTER FIFTY-FIVE

When Louisa looked in the phone book, she saw there were dozens of Cartwrights. Her heart sank. There were about five or six 'B. Cartwright' entries, but it occurred to her that if this woman was young and had been living in Spain, it was unlikely that she was a homeowner. The chances were higher that she still lived with her parents when in London. If she was even from London. She could be from Liverpool or Leeds – or anywhere, quite frankly. Once Louisa knew where Belinda was from, she might be able to establish a connection with Petunia, if there was one.

She needed another route.

Donald Oliver.

She would telephone him, but she already knew that he didn't like to say anything on the telephone in case he was being over-heard or recorded. 'Just because you're paranoid, doesn't mean they're not out to get you,' he'd once said. To all other intents and purposes he seemed a reasonable and calm man; she'd liked him. But perhaps he was right: after all, the mere questioning of ideological beliefs was enough to threaten war. It was less about land grabs – though that was certainly still a part of it – than a desire to own the minds of the people who lived there. News was filtering through about the treatment of the Jewish people in Germany, and Louisa knew that there had been protests in Britain and America, but no real action taken. It was happening 'over there'; so long as it wasn't at home, it was easy to forget. It wasn't that Louisa didn't understand or even admire the stance that Jessica was taking; she just wished that it was possible to discuss it without it leading to aggressive divides. Esmond's belief that all the Mitfords were Nazis prevented him from hearing the more nuanced truth. Or maybe she was wrong. Perhaps there was no nuance when it came to fascism or Communism. You're either in or you're out.

Soho. She liked its atmosphere of unpredictability in the daytime. It was undeniably seedy, but it also lacked pretension: there were no genteel women walking tiny dogs at the end of long leashes, just to show off their newest hats. Instead, there were men in jaunty silk scarves and women who looked as if they hadn't slept for three nights but were laughing in spite of it. In Donald's shop the books were still stacked everywhere, higgledy-piggledy, and the customers still looked as if they hadn't eaten for a week. Donald was sitting by the till and happened to look up as she came towards him.

'Mrs Sullivan,' he said. 'What a delight.' He cocked his head to the side and put on an exaggerated quizzical expression. 'It will be a delight, won't it? I'm not to be hounded for withholding further information?'

Louisa laughed. 'No. Good to see you, Mr Oliver.'

'Did you find the rapscallion you were looking for?'

'You probably know that I did.'

Donald put his finger to his lips.

'I'm looking for someone else now,' said Louisa.

'Are you expecting to find them in here?'

'No. But I don't know where to start and I thought this would be as good a place as any.'

'That's a review for me to cut out and keep.' Donald stood and stretched his legs. 'Shall I fetch you a cup of tea?'

'Yes, please. Milk, no sugar.'

He disappeared through a doorway and Louisa browsed through the shelves for a minute or two. Perhaps she'd find 'Bernard Plum' inscribed in one of the books she picked up. No such luck.

'So to what do I owe this pleasure?' asked Donald, settling himself back on his stool after he'd found another for Louisa.

'It's another case. Not connected, but not entirely unconnected either.'

'More Communists on the run?'

'Possibly. It's a man. Bernard Plum.' She watched to see if his face changed on hearing the name, but it didn't. 'He disappeared at the same time as a woman, Petunia Attwood.'

'Have they run off together?'

'It's not something we've ruled out. But he has a wife. She's in London and she doesn't seem terribly keen on his return.'

'My theory seems quite likely, then.'

'It would be, except that Miss Attwood accused Mr Plum of fraud at the insurance company where they both worked. He was suspended while there was an investigation. In that time, they both vanished. A body was found with a personal item of

Petunia's and a business card belonging to Mr Plum. However, we've since discovered that the deceased was someone else. It begs a question or two, as you can imagine.'

'Ah.' Donald crossed his legs, and she saw that the hem of his trousers was coming loose.

'Meanwhile, my husband has been in France and he has asked around about this Bernard Plum.'

'Why?'

'His wife suspected that he might have gone there. They had spent quite a bit of time in France and Spain in the past, and he described himself as an adventurer.'

'The type of buccaneer who thinks a civil war sounds like a fun thing to get involved with?'

'Yes.' Louisa shifted on the stool; it was a little too small. 'Do you know many of those?'

'I've met a few. They're soon put right if they do get out there. The reports we're reading . . . frankly, it sounds apocalyptic.'

'Yes, Guy has told me. He's seen a lot of the refugees in Bayonne and says they're in a pretty desperate state.'

'Did he hear anything about this mysterious Plum?'

'Don't. You make it sound comical, and I really don't think he is.'

'Sorry. Bad habit. Go on.'

Louisa admonished him with what Guy called her Strict Teacher's Look. 'A few people seem to have heard of him, and there are stories of him being very courageous, but we haven't found anyone who has actually met him or witnessed any of these accounts.'

'Which could mean they've been invented.'

'Exactly. And there's a girlfriend of sorts, a Belinda Cartwright. She was working as a nurse—'

'Belinda Cartwright?'

'Yes. Have you heard of her?'

Donald put his mug down. 'I think so. There aren't all that many women who come in here, or who are known to have gone to Spain to the war, but she is one of them, if I'm thinking of the right person.'

'You've met her? Do you know where she is now?'

'Hold your stallions. She was working in the café opposite – although, come to think of it, it's been a while since I've seen her there.'

'How long?'

'I couldn't really say, but I don't think I've seen her since before Christmas.'

'And you talked to her?'

'Yes. I like to go there, as you know. We got chatting, and she was interested in the shop. I recommended a few books to her and she read them. We discussed them, that sort of thing.'

'Was it ...' Louisa tried to convey what she meant without words.

'What?'

'Was there a relationship between you?'

'Oh! Ha, no.' Donald put his mug down and gave an awkward cough. 'But we did get on very well. She's a firecracker. Too good for waitressing. I'm glad that she has had an adventure, though I'm not sure a war is the best place to go and find it. And you think she might have got mixed up with this Plum fellow, do you?'

'That's the theory. Do you have any kind of address for her? Do you know where her parents live, for example?'

'Yes, yes, I do. I sent her a couple of books in the post once.

She had 'flu and couldn't come in to work for a few weeks. Hang on a mo.' He rummaged around in the papers and notebooks that were stashed under his till, and triumphantly pulled out a scrap a moment later. 'Here you are! Number six Shrubland Road. It's in the East End. I've got an A–Z here – I'll look it up for you.'

'Thank you.' She took the paper and the instructions he wrote down. 'I'm going to go there straightaway. I can leave a note if no one's in. In the meantime, could you please ask at the café when they last heard from her and let me know what they say? You can write if it's easiest. I gave you my card before, I think? The address is on there.'

Donald opened the till and found her card, tucked beneath a solitary pound note. 'You see? I was paying attention.'

She smiled. It was always good to find an ally.

CHAPTER FIFTY-SIX

Having thought that, by now, he would be on his way home, Guy was feeling frustrated and homesick to be sitting in Bayonne. Lady Redesdale had finally recovered from her migraine, or pretended to, and persuaded her daughter to have supper with her alone. So when Guy went downstairs to the hotel bar, he wasn't too surprised to see Esmond sitting there. But he was surprised when Esmond suggested that the two of them go out into the town to find supper.

'I could do with a few beers, and I bet you haven't had a night off in a while.'

Guy put his hands in his pockets. He had a feeling that the beers would be on him. But Esmond was right. It had been a long time since he'd gone out, what with Maisie and his work. He wasn't a big drinker, but everyone needed to let loose once in a while, didn't they?

Not that he'd be going wild. Guy was conscious that Esmond was eighteen – not yet of age. For all that he had achieved – a remarkable amount, it had to be said – Guy sensed a reckless streak in Esmond that might have to be monitored.

'There's someone I know,' said Guy, 'a Spanish refugee, Ivo Fernandez. You might enjoy meeting him and he would like a beer too, I expect.'

'That sounds grand. Show me the way, old boy.'

'Not too much of the "old", thank you.'

Esmond gave Guy a playful punch on the arm. The ice had been broken. They set off to find Ivo.

Two hours and three beers later, Guy was sitting, feeling pleasantly light-headed, at a pavement café with Esmond and Ivo, who had been talking almost non-stop since they had met. Esmond had been full of questions for Ivo about how he saw the situation in Spain, his upbringing, his plans for the future. This had then mutated into a passionate argument on Communism and socialism, none of which Guy understood, and the appalling threat of fascism, which he did, albeit in a limited fashion. Ivo's accent became thicker with every beer he drank. Guy was footing the bill, which he didn't mind. Everything cost next to nothing out here, and in the heavy warmth of the evening, with the sea breeze gently coming in and the hubbub of the diners around them, it was worth every franc. At some point they ordered three steaks with potatoes, and it tasted like the best supper Guy had ever eaten. After that, someone had the bright idea to go on to a bar, several winding streets away from the square, and order absinthe. It was then that things became somewhat murky.

Guy remembered Esmond asking him what he and Louisa were doing working for Nazis. When Guy protested, Esmond started to lay it out in stark detail: he had seen Nancy and Peter at a Blackshirts meeting in Olympia a few years before, a meeting that had turned nasty and violent almost from the start; Unity, Diana and Tom had all been to Munich and dined with Hitler; Pamela's husband was a fascist sympathiser; Lord and Lady Redesdale had met Hitler, too, and attended dinners of the Anglo-German Fellowship, which claimed to seek peace with the Nazis. 'And everyone knows there's no point, when Hitler wants war.'

Guy, hampered by the absinthe – the one glass had been enough – and his thick head, asked how he could be so sure. 'Why shouldn't we try hard to negotiate for peace? No one wants war.'

'Hitler wants war!' was Esmond's response, soon joined by Ivo. There was a threat that the entire bar would start joining in, and Guy felt that this would not be conducive to international relations generally. He felt confused and uneasy. Unlike these young men, he remembered the Great War and, though he may not have fought in it, he had seen the devastation it had wrought upon the families and countries of those involved. Esmond's passion felt authentic, yet also misplaced. In determining that Hitler wanted war, he seemed to be saying that Britain had no choice but to go to war against Germany again, and Guy could not bring himself to say that. Not yet. Not ever, if he could help it.

Guy staggered outside into the fresh air, which hit the back of his throat and threatened nausea. He leaned against the building, breathing heavily, and almost didn't notice the man who had followed him out. It was dark in the back street; there was no moonlight and no streetlamp. Guy could not make out his face, but his accent was English.

'Are you the man who's been asking about Bernard Plum?'

Unable to think straight, still concentrating on his breathing, Guy nodded. 'Yes, that's me. Do you know him?'

'This is a warning. Stop looking for him.'

Sobriety cut through Guy like a knife.

'What did you—'

But he got no further. A fast blow landed on his stomach, forcing him to double over. This was followed by a kick to his knees. Guy sank to the ground. Instinctively he covered his face – and only just in time: he seemed to hear the crack of a boot against the side of his skull almost before he felt it. Winded, in pain and afraid, Guy was paralysed as he heard the man say into his ear, 'Fuck off out of it. I know where your wife lives. If I get the slightest . . .' Guy felt another kick, this time in the middle of his spine. He cried out with pain. 'The *slightest* word that you are still looking for me, then little Louisa had better start running fast. I've done it before, I'll do it again.'

The last thing Guy heard was the thud of heavy footsteps receding into the distance, then everything went black.

CHAPTER FIFTY-SEVEN

S hrubland Road took some time to arrive at and find, as it
was one of a maze of streets in Dalston, the East End of
London – not a part that Louisa knew at all well. She had grown
up in Chelsea, on an estate close to the river, a working-class
encampment almost, in the middle of artists and the rich people
for whom her parents had worked as a chimney sweep and
laundress (Mr Black and Mrs White, her friends called them).
Dalston was not quite another world; there was plenty for her to
recognise – men in their caps, the rag-and-bone cart plying its
trade, children playing in the street – but a few things spoke of
local flavours: the eel and pie shops, the tailors' workshops, the
smoking chimneys of breweries. Louisa knew there were slums
here, too: a poverty that was less than five miles from the riches
of Bond Street but might as well have been at the other end of
the earth.

The home of Belinda Cartwright's parents was a neat two-
storey terraced house with white net curtains in the window
and a shiny front door. It was a wide, busy road, with men and

women walking to or from work, or pushing prams. Louisa liked the busy atmosphere, noted the people that called out to each other in a friendly way, the children that were industriously skipping together. She got one or two questioning looks from those she passed, a stranger in these parts, or perhaps she looked like a snob in her neat cloche hat and Mackintosh. Her coat wasn't out of place in Hammersmith or even Kensington, which felt very far away now. She hoped that either Mr or Mrs Cartwright was at home, because she didn't fancy having to make this journey again soon.

Her first knock didn't yield a response, nor did the second a minute or two later. But as she was about to try a third time, with no hope in her heart, a woman leaned out of the front window of the house next door. 'You after the Cartwrights?'

'Yes,' Louisa called back.

'He's at work but she's in the garden, pegging out the washing. She won't hear you. Hang on a mo and I'll shout over the garden fence. Shall I say who's at the door?'

Louisa hesitated but, before she had made up her mind what to say, the neighbour had started talking again. 'Are you here about their daughter?'

Again, Louisa was stupefied in the face of the woman's loud questions.

'No one's seen her fer months.'

Louisa gathered herself. 'If you could let Mrs Cartwright know that I'm here?'

'Right you are.' The head bobbed back into the window. It wasn't long before the front door before Louisa opened. Ignoring the neighbour, who had also opened her door and was eyeing Louisa up and down, Louisa introduced herself and explained briefly that she was here to ask about Mrs Cartwright's daughter, and could she come inside? She indicated with her head the watchful neighbour and Mrs Cartwright let her in quickly.

Before the door had even closed behind her, she heard a sob catch in the woman's throat. 'Do you know where she is?'

Louisa felt as if the woman's grief had landed in her own chest with the weight of a heavy stone. 'I'm so sorry, Mrs Cartwright, I don't.'

'Then who are you? Why are you here?'

'Can we sit down? I'll tell you as much as I know. It isn't much, but perhaps I'll be able to help you.'

Mrs Cartwright took Louisa into the front room, which didn't look much used. Kept as best for important visitors, probably. There were neatly lined up cushions on the settee. Three mallards flew across the wall, their ceramic feathers glossy. Mrs Cartwright was just as neat, her greying hair tied back, her housecoat spotless.

'How did you find me? Are you from the police? They said they couldn't do anything but ... ' She stopped and took a breath. 'Please, tell me what you know.'

'I will, Mrs Cartwright. First of all, I'm not from the police. I'm a private detective. I've been looking for a woman called Petunia Attwood, who went missing around the beginning of February, we think. She worked with a man called Bernard Plum, whom she accused of fraud. He was suspended from work and it appears that he too went missing. It was at the same time as Petunia.'

'I don't understand – I don't know any of these names. What've they got to do with my daughter?'

'I'm sorry, I'm coming to it – this was just to explain the

background. We think Mr Plum may have gone to Spain, to fight in the civil war, and I met someone who thinks he may have met your daughter out there. Did she go to Spain?'

Mrs Cartwright closed her eyes. When she opened them, Louisa saw her confusion. 'She may have done. We'd argued enough about the Commies. She was always threatening to run off, but I didn't think she'd have the courage to do it.'

'She worked in a café, didn't she? In Soho.'

'Yes. I've been down there, but they didn't know anything. She stopped work there months ago. That's what they said.'

'The café is opposite a Communist bookshop, and I believe she got to know the owner, Donald Oliver. They talked about politics and books.'

Mrs Cartwright nodded. 'I saw those. She was sick last year, and he sent some. It was very kind of him. She's always been a reader. I don't know where she gets it from.' She raised a wan smile.

'Mr Oliver thinks it's likely that she would have gone to Spain. We've spoken to someone who thought she might have worked as a nurse on the frontline there. You didn't know about that?'

'No – well, you see, she's always been a difficult one, my Belinda. Different to us. She's clever, always did well at school – when she wasn't arguing with the teachers. But she was always restless, you couldn't get her to settle down to a thing. Her father and I, we've always had to work all the hours God sends, though I've retired now. The worry was getting too much and I've got arthritis in my hands, it's too painful. I worked as a seamstress. I made every stitch I'm wearing.' She said it with pride. 'There were a lot of rows at home around Christmas and she said she was going to go and stay with a friend in Margate, try and find some work there.'

'Did she say who that friend was?'

'No, I don't think she did. She didn't leave a forwarding address. She said she wanted to clear her head and she'd be back home. But we've not heard a word.'

'Did she take her passport with her?'

'She must have done, if she had one. She left her room bare. I don't think she had any notion of coming back. But it breaks her father's heart not to know where she is.' She lunged forward and grabbed Louisa's hand. 'Will you find her for us?'

Louisa squeezed her hand in return. 'I can't promise anything, Mrs Cartwright. I'll do my very best, though.'

Mrs Cartwright took her hand back, seeming embarrassed by her outburst.

'Do you have a photograph of your daughter?'

'Yes.' She left the room and came back with a small silver-framed photograph of a young, pretty woman with dark hair that fell in blousy curls around her heart-shaped chin. 'It's from when she was twenty-one.'

'How old is she now?'

'Twenty-six. It was her birthday on the seventeenth of March. When we didn't hear from her then, I started to worry. Wherever she was, she would always write to us, let us know she was well.'

'Can I just confirm that you haven't heard the name Bernard Plum before?'

'No.'

'Did Belinda ever mention having any kind of sweetheart?'

'She never talked about anything like that to us. We wanted her settled and married. She should have a baby or two by now. But every time we mentioned it she'd flare up like a Catherine wheel, so we stopped.'

'It's not too late, Mrs Cartwright,' said Louisa, feeling that if there was anything she could reassure her about, it was this. But she didn't respond.

'Would it be possible for me to take this photograph? Unless you have another?'

'You can take that one. I have others, but please don't lose it.'

'I won't. This is my card, with my name and address on it. If you hear anything from Belinda, please will you let me know straightaway? And I'll do the same for you.'

They said goodbye and Louisa was back out into the street again. Everyone was walking up and down as before, the noise of traffic and children the same as before. All that was different was the knowledge that was chasing around her mind: two women and one man had vanished, and she had no clues about where any of them might be.

CHAPTER FIFTY-EIGHT

Louisa had sent a couple of notes to Mrs Plum following the discovery that Bernard had returned to Lee Worth's offices, but had received no response. Now, with Belinda Cartwright also missing, she decided she had better return to the house in Rowditch Lane.

At first sight, nothing looked too different from Louisa's first visit to the Plum household. The front garden had a few daffodils pushing up through a narrow flowerbed to one side. An empty milk bottle stood on the step. The brass letterbox was dull, but there was nothing untoward. Louisa knocked. When she saw the front-room curtain twitch, she leaned back and smiled, gave a friendly wave. The bolts were drawn and Mrs Plum opened the door halfway, standing with most of her body hidden behind the door.

'Hello,' said Louisa, 'it's me. Can I come in?'

'It's not a good time.'

'Has your husband returned? Is he at home?'

'He's not here.' Someone in the street walked past. Mrs Plum flinched. 'You'd better come in, but quickly.'

Louisa stepped inside and Mrs Plum closed the door behind her. The air in the house was stale, somehow lifeless, as if Mrs Plum had been sitting in one chair for weeks. The two of them went through to the front room, where again there was nothing significantly different. But Louisa could see that the dusting hadn't been done for some time, the cushions were flattened, there was a plate on the side with crumbs on it, a mug with the dregs of cold tea.

Louisa sat down and Mrs Plum, after a moment, did the same. 'How have you been?'

'Fine.'

In the silence that ensued, Louisa realised that Mrs Plum was not going to be forthcoming about whatever she had been through in the last few weeks. 'I wrote you a note – did you get it?'

'Yes. I'm afraid I had nothing to say in response, which is why you had no reply. I've never been a good letter-writer.'

'That's absolutely fine. I'm here because there have been some developments. I was called by your husband's manager at Lee Worth. Mr Cornish. He told me that your husband returned to the office briefly, after hours, to retrieve some files. They believe he may have taken files relevant to the complaint that Miss Attwood made against him.'

'I see.'

'Did he return home at that time?'

'Yes.'

Louisa looked at Mrs Plum. Her skin was sallow, and she seemed to have lost some weight. The cuffs on her shirt were dirty – Louisa was sure she had pulled the sleeves down to cover bruises. 'I thought you were going to let me know if he came back?'

'I'm sorry, but you're not officially police, are you? I didn't see that I was obliged.'

'No, you weren't, of course. How long did he come back for?'

Mrs Plum stared at the window, though the limited view beyond was blurred by the net curtains. 'I don't know. Two or three nights, I suppose.'

'Did he tell you where he had been?'

Mrs Plum stood up. 'I'm going to have to ask you to leave. I would be willing to help, but my husband has done nothing wrong. He won't be returning to his job and if he has done anything criminal then they will have to ask the police to arrest him. Until then, I'd thank you to keep your nose out of our business.'

Louisa stood too. She could see that Mrs Plum wouldn't change her mind.

'I understand, and I'll leave now. Just one thing. Miss Petunia Attwood is still missing, and now there's another woman who we have reason to believe knew your husband in Spain. She, too, is missing. Her name is Belinda Cartwright.'

Louisa watched Mrs Plum carefully as she said this, to try to read something in her expression. Did she recognise the name? Was there a tiny tremor in the corner of her eyelid? Louisa couldn't be certain.

'I'm sorry to hear about that but I don't know anything of it, and unless you can prove my husband had anything to do with it—'

'Yes, I know. I'll stay away. I'll leave now.' Louisa walked to the front door and opened it. Before she stepped out, she turned back to Mrs Plum. 'I know a frightened woman when I see one. It doesn't have to be that way. I can help you be free of him, if you want.'

Mrs Plum kept her voice steady. 'Goodbye, miss. I'll thank you not to come back here again. Please, leave now.'

With regret at her powerlessness Louisa acquiesced and pulled the door behind her, hearing the locks turn and the bolts draw as soon as it was shut.

CHAPTER FIFTY-NINE

Back at home that evening, Louisa put all thoughts of Bernard Plum and the missing women from her mind. She wanted nothing more than to be with her baby daughter, who seemed to be learning something new and different each day. The latest delight was her attempt to talk: a mishmash of gurgles and laughter with animated sounds that accompanied every activity, whether she was kissing her favourite soft dolls or bashing the floor with a wooden spoon. At times like these, Louisa missed Guy strongly, but she and Maisie whiled away a few hours contentedly, Louisa cooking them a simple supper and reading Maisie the same favourite book several times.

At last, Louisa put Maisie to bed and came downstairs, ready for a cup of cocoa and a programme or two on the radio. Lost in thought while she stirred the milk, Louisa didn't hear the latch on the front door open, nor did she hear the door close again. When at last she realised she wasn't alone, it was sudden and shocking: without thinking, she picked up the saucepan of hot milk and threw it at the intruder who had come into the kitchen. Too late, she realised her mistake.

'Guy!'

'What the hell?' He stood stupefied until Louisa grabbed him by the hand and pulled him to the sink, where she quickly rinsed him off with a tea towel drenched in cold water. In the confusion and apologies on both sides, it was a minute or two before she saw that Guy had a nasty graze on the side of his face and there were faint purple bags beneath his eyes.

'What happened to you?'

'It was nothing, really,' said Guy, batting the cloth away. 'My suit is soaked. Let me go and change.'

'I can boil a kettle if you want a bath?'

But Guy had already left the room and was heading up the stairs. It took him a while to make it back down again. In the meantime, Louisa managed to pull together a supper of fried eggs and potatoes, relieved she had something in the cupboard. She remembered a bottle of cider left over from a Sunday lunch with Guy's mother a few weeks before, poured out two glasses and set them before the fire in the hearth. The room was simple – everything they owned had been either given or found – but the colours were pretty and it was comfortable. Happy that her husband was home, if confused by his sudden arrival, Louisa waited for him, keeping their food warm in the oven.

The minutes ticked past. Louisa fidgeted. She didn't want to put the radio on in case he came down at that moment. She wanted him to see that she was waiting for his company. Why was he taking so long?

Eventually, after half an hour, she heard him come down. He seemed to be walking awkwardly, judging from the sound of his footsteps: only one foot seemed to tread heavily. When he came in, dressed in flannel pyjamas and dressing-gown, there was an attempt at a smile on his face, but he was pale. He accepted her offer to sit and be served supper and a drink, but Louisa felt conscious of fussing more than usual. When he had eaten, she broke the uncomfortable silence, determined to find out what was going on. Why had Guy come home so suddenly?

'Lady Redesdale planned to stay on for the wedding but was persuaded by Decca to come home first. I had to wait for her and then it was all rather sudden. I had no chance to let you know and I had thought it would be a nice surprise ...'

'I'm not saying I'm not pleased to see you—'

'Good.'

Louisa jerked her head back. 'What is all this behaviour? It's not like you, Guy. And please tell me why you've got those marks on your face.'

'A refugee asked me for money, I refused and he got nasty. He hit me. If you must know, it was humiliating. I wasn't able to defend myself.' He stared into his lap. 'I don't like you to think of me like that.'

'Oh, darling.' Louisa got up and sat on the arm of his chair, wrapping his arm in hers to give him a kiss on the cheek. 'Nothing you do could change my view of you. Don't you think I know who you are by now?'

Guy kissed her back. 'Like I know you?'

'Exactly. I'm sorry you went through that. It sounds horrible.'

'It was. It's tough out there.'

The mood thawed, Guy told her about his time with Decca and Esmond. 'I'm not unsympathetic to them,' he concluded.

'They just seem very young, so casual and unaware of the upset they have caused.'

'That is the Mitford way,' said Louisa. 'I've had an interesting time of it myself.'

'With them? Or lately?'

'Lately. I went to see Mrs Plum today.' As Louisa said this, she felt Guy's body stiffen. 'Something is going on, though it's hard to pinpoint what. The house was dirty, but whether that was because she hadn't been there or because she'd been deliberately neglecting to clean it, I don't know. She seemed frightened of something, but if it was of her husband coming back, I'd have thought she'd have cleaned. The house was spotless before – too spotless.' As she said that, she caught sight of the dust on her own narrow mantelpiece. Some people were not natural housekeepers.

'I don't want you going back there,' said Guy.

'What?' Louisa ignored him, wanting to tell him more. 'I think there's something sinister. She seemed neglected, too. Thinner, and I'm sure she had bruises on her wrists. She pulled her sleeves down more than once.'

Guy picked up the poker and started prodding the fire.

'She told me her husband had come back home for a few nights—'

'What? When?'

'She wouldn't say exactly. I told her that he had been seen in his office at Lee Worth, taking files, and—'

'But that's—' Guy had put the poker back. He stood and picked up his empty plate, then took it into the kitchen.

'That's what?' she said to his retreating back. 'Anyway, she was very defensive. She said I wasn't officially police so she didn't have to tell me anything, and she practically pushed me out of the door. I'm worried about her. She has all the signs of being a woman whose husband beats her.'

'She's not the only one. We can't help all of them.' She could hear Guy put his dish in the sink. He'd leave it in there, without running a tap over it.

'I'm not suggesting we try to do that. I'm just talking about her.' She was in danger of snapping, she knew, but this particular subject always made her feel touchy. It wasn't her own history; her parents had been kind to each other, if not especially affectionate. But on the Peabody estate where she grew up, she had too often heard women explain away a black eye as having walked into a door. Everyone knew the truth, but no one ever did anything about it. If the police were called, which was rare, they would invariably say that it was a private matter between husband and wife. And then the wife would be left to suffer the consequences of her cry for help. If Mrs Plum didn't want to say anything, who could blame her?

'There was one other thing – so small I can hardly say it.'

'Perhaps you had better dismiss the thought.' Guy came back in but didn't sit. 'I'm tired, Louisa. I think I'll go up to bed now.'

'It's just, I said Belinda Cartwright's name and I think she reacted to it. That's all. It seemed like she recognised it and it was the final straw, the thing that made her push me out of the house.'

'We're not police, Louisa. We don't have the right to bring her in for questioning. If she doesn't want to talk to us, there's not a lot we can do about it.'

'Perhaps we should call your old colleagues?'

'And say what?' Guy rubbed his face and gave a sigh. 'Petunia

Attwood is missing, but she's a grown woman who could have left of her own accord, chucked in her job and run off with a lover. There are all sorts of reasons she wouldn't want to tell her sister or her boss what she was planning. Belinda Cartwright had a difficult relationship with her parents and didn't tell them much anyway, by the sounds of it. She could be somewhere in France. And Bernard Plum could be anywhere. You have to give this up, Louisa. There are no bodies, nothing to definitively tie these three people together other than circumstance and suspicion.'

'I just can't help feeling—'

'I know. And I don't dismiss your intuition. But feelings don't solve cases; evidence does. And evidence is how we get paid. Aren't there other cases we could be looking into? Didn't you say people have been writing and telephoning the office? Let's go in tomorrow and review them, see if there's anything else to pick up on. We need to earn some money. That's the other thing: who will pay us to find Belinda Cartwright or Bernard Plum? It was easy enough to do when I was travelling to France for Lord Redesdale, but not any more. Just drop it.'

'Yes.' What else could she do but agree?

Guy gave her a light kiss. 'Goodnight.'

CHAPTER SIXTY

A few days later, Louisa thought she would like to see Nancy and Lady Redesdale, if for no other reason than to tie up the last of the loose ends of their work and the remaining expenses that needed to be paid. She sent a note to Nancy suggesting a meeting and received a quick reply: they would give her tea tomorrow and she was welcome to bring Maisie with her.

With Maisie in her prettiest dress, a Liberty print with puffed sleeves that made her arms look even more delightfully chubby, the two of them arrived on the dot of four o'clock. Louisa heaved the pram up the front steps. Travelling there by two buses had been somewhat challenging: she was feeling rather frazzled and sweaty, but nonetheless she looked forward to introducing Maisie to the Mitfords. Her daughter was symbolic of how far she had come since she'd arrived at their door as a wrung-out, frightened young woman, and she was proud of her.

Annie answered the front door and helped her park the pram in the hall. 'Mrs Rodd is upstairs in the drawing room,' she said.

'Is Lady Redesdale there?' Louisa wouldn't usually ask this question, but she felt she'd got to know Annie a little.

'No, miss. I believe she's gone to Harrods.'

'Lord Redesdale?' He wouldn't think much of Maisie; after six daughters of his own, Louisa knew he felt he'd seen more baby girls than he'd ever wanted to in his lifetime. When Debo, the youngest, was born, no one even looked at her for three months. But still . . .

Another shake of the head. 'No, he's at his club.'

'So it's only Mrs Rodd up there?'

Annie nodded.

Why couldn't she have met Nancy at her house, then? Nancy only lived one short bus ride away from Louisa's home in Hammersmith. It was typical that Nancy wouldn't have thought about how difficult it would be for Louisa to bring Maisie all the way to Kensington. All too quickly, her pride and excitement had dissembled into a familiar frustration. Taking a deep breath – she was here now, she might as well make the most of it – Louisa asked Annie to lead the way and announce their arrival. At the very least, she would make sure that she and her daughter were treated like rightful and proper guests in this household.

Of course, Nancy's charm and warm enthusiasm for Maisie immediately dispelled Louisa's crossness.

'Oh, just look at the gorgeous thing!' exclaimed Nancy. 'She's grown so much since I last saw her. She'll have a beau asking for her hand in marriage any moment now.'

'Or be collecting her science degree from university,' said Louisa, then regretted it. She hadn't meant to sound so chippy.

'Absolutely. Nothing this girl can't do, I'm sure.' Nancy pulled funny faces as she bounced Maisie on her knee. Maisie obliged her perfectly with a gummy smile.

They settled down and Annie brought in a tray of tea things, though Louisa eyed the porcelain cups with nervousness at their close proximity to Maisie. She was at the stage of testing anything she could grab by bashing it on the floor. Hopefully she would be appeased with a slice of fruit cake.

'I've got a few last pieces of paperwork, receipts and so on from our expenses,' said Louisa. 'I can leave them here for Lord Redesdale?'

'Yes, of course. I'll make sure he sees them. Thank you again for everything you did. I'm sorry it was such a wild goose chase.'

'What's the latest news?'

Nancy handed Maisie back to Louisa and started to pour the tea. 'Esmond has written a nasty letter to say that the two of them may not get married after all and even if they do, they will bar Muv from the ceremony.'

'What? Why?'

Nancy shrugged. 'Do you still take milk?'

'Yes, please.'

'Here you are. I don't know. He's determined to drive not just a wedge but several large planks between Decca and her family, which seems very controlling and dangerous if you ask me. He's convinced himself and Decca that we're all Nazis, and that they want nothing to do with any of us. Muv is in pieces, and you know that is quite hard to achieve. I don't think I've ever made her cry.'

'Do you think they really won't marry?'

'I don't know. If it happens, it won't be until May. It's the Royal Coronation on 25th April, and the Old Humans have to be there in all their ermine. Muv will go to Bayonne after that. The naughty children have said that if they do grant us the dubious pleasure of their marriage at all, it will happen in France. They refuse to return to England under any circumstances. It means that none of the rest of us can attend, even if they wanted us there. But they've proved that they don't.'

'I'm so sorry, Nancy. It must be very upsetting for everyone.'

'Yes, it is. Debo is particularly upset. Decca was her nursery companion and she looked up to her tremendously. The only good thing that's come out of it is that Debo has sued the *Daily Mirror* for libel, and it looks as if she'll be awarded a vast sum. I expect Esmond will think they ought to have some of the money, seeing as, if it hadn't been for them running off, she wouldn't have had a case.'

'You don't think much of him, do you?'

'I don't, I'm afraid. I'm sure he's a very impressive young man, and he's certainly clever. But I don't see why they had to do everything in such a nasty and upsetting way. They've burned every bridge and won't be able to come back here even if they want to do so.'

'They'll be staying in Bayonne then, I take it?' Maisie had finished her cake. Louisa wiped her sticky hands with a handkerchief in her pocket. She'd first learned to keep one on her at all times when working as the Mitford girls' nursery maid.

'Yes. Esmond has work of some sort. At least Decca speaks French. I suppose she'll be able to pick something up to earn extra pennies. But she won't be of much use for long.'

A funny way to put it, thought Louisa. 'Would you mind if I got in touch with them?'

'No, not at all. But why?'

'Miss Jessica told me that she'd met someone I'm looking for – a woman called Belinda Cartwright. I'd like to ask if she's seen her again or heard anything from her. Guy wants me to drop the case, but I can't. It keeps niggling at me.'

'They're staying at the Hôtel des Basques. Here, I'll write it down for you. There's a telephone number, too, though it only goes through to the front desk, not to their room. It's the cheapest lodgings they could find, by the sound of it.'

'Thank you.' Louisa tucked the piece of paper into her pocket. 'Now, please tell me what you're doing. What are you writing?'

'Oh, I'm editing a book of Victorian letters, for my sins. I can't quite seem to pin down an idea for a novel. Perhaps I should write about Decca's escapades?'

And they talked gently on like the old friends they were.

CHAPTER SIXTY-ONE

L ouisa wrote to Julia Attwood to say that she was very sorry but there seemed no further place to look for her sister, Petunia, without police assistance.

Julia replied by return of post to say that she understood, even if she was unhappy. 'I will hold out hope for as long as I can that she is alive somewhere. At least, until I see any evidence with my own eyes to prove otherwise.' She had been forced to give Petunia's landlord notice and would be going there before the month was up to collect her sister's belongings; the rent was overdue and Julia couldn't afford to pay it. She wondered if Louisa might like to join her there, in case there was a clue that had been missed. She added that there was no need for Louisa to reply; she would be in touch nearer the time when she knew what date she was going to be there.

Louisa had only written the note to appease Guy. As his wife, she couldn't deny that he had adopted the more sensible business approach to the situation. He was now reviewing a number of potential jobs still coming through to their door thanks to the publicity generated by their involvement in the search for Decca and Esmond. But as a private detective, these missing women had got under her skin.

Louisa also wrote to Decca in Bayonne. She felt that there was some sympathy between the two of them and, from what Guy had told her of his most recent trip, it seemed that Esmond considered her husband to be a friend. More than he viewed any of the Mitfords, at any rate. If anyone was going to be a conduit between Mr Romilly and the Mitfords, it was Guy. All she asked of Decca was that she keep her ears open for any snippet of news or a sighting of either Belinda Cartwright or Bernard Plum, possibly also of Petunia Attwood.

When she sat down and really thought about it, though, it was depressing. Two women were missing; the chance that Bernard Plum had run off with both of them was very small. The options were: one, he had run off with one of them and he had no connection with the other beyond the coincidence. But, given that they both had links to him, the chance of that seemed fairly small too. Or, two, he had run off with one of them and the two of them had in some way disposed of the third. Or he had killed them both.

None of it was very pleasant to think about. Nor was it logical. As Guy had pointed out, there was no evidence, and the only body had no more than a tenuous link to Bernard Plum. There was no reason for the women not to be among the hundreds of people who deliberately went missing every year. They might have been escaping a husband that beat them, or a father that treated them badly, or they might have fallen in love with someone their family disapproved of, or simply fancied starting over somewhere where nobody knew them. Men and women went to fight in the Spanish civil war because they wanted to be brave and adventurous – or that was how they saw it; the reality was more likely dangerous and foolhardy. Esmond had told Guy that when he was in the International Brigades it had been so chaotic, men died after being shot by their own side. And yet the abundance of this stupidity was clear. Guy and Louisa had received several letters from wives, mothers and girlfriends who believed their men had gone to Spain to fight. What made it difficult to find them was that many men were forging their identification details in order to get a visa to Spain, now that the Spanish government had strengthened the border. Subterfuge was everywhere.

Louisa was in the office as she thought all this, absent-mindedly doodling on a piece of notepaper.

If Bernard Plum wanted to get away, to disappear, then he could do that in Spain. Under another name. And if he had made Petunia and Belinda disappear too, he would need to. Unless they had disappeared with him. Whichever way it had happened, he needed someone who could forge him a new identity.

Louisa added a PS to her letter to Decca: Did Esmond know of any forger who helped people to cross the border with false passports? Or of any other underhand means of getting to Spain from France? She reminded her that two women with associations to Bernard Plum were missing and she needed some kind of clue that would tell her if these women were alive or dead.

CHAPTER SIXTY-TWO

The next thing Louisa needed to do was to see Mrs Plum again. She couldn't shake off the worry she felt for her, and thought at least she could offer protection or support.

As soon as Louisa approached the gate to the Plums' modest front garden, she knew something was wrong. There were new, clear signs of neglect that had appeared in the week or so since she had last been there: dropped litter that hadn't been cleared away, weeds sprouting more fulsomely than the daffodils, a dull patina on the brass letterbox. The curtains were drawn; the nets looked grey. There was no milk on the doorstep – but, with only herself to look after, Janice might have cancelled deliveries.

Louisa knocked on the door and waited. After a minute or two, she knocked again. Then she opened the letterbox and looked inside: the hall was empty, there was no movement within. She stepped back and looked up at the house, but there were no further clues. There was no twitching curtain, no sign at all that someone was in there. Her heart began to hammer.

She went to the next house along and banged the brass knocker loudly.

No response.

There was no one in the house on the other side either, only a cat curled up by the window, enjoying the sun while its owners were out.

She scanned the houses over the road and thought she saw movement in one window. She ran across and thumped on the door. A man opened it. He had a friendly face and wore a shirt buttoned up with no tie.

'I'm sorry to bother you, but I'm looking for Mrs Plum – she lives over there. Have you seen her lately?'

The man put his hands in his pockets, rocked back on his heels. 'Hmm, I'm not sure that I have, now you mention it. I don't know that I ever saw her often, you know. I haven't noticed anything odd but . . .' He thought again. 'No, I can't remember when I last said hello. She's a quiet one, wouldn't say boo to a goose.'

'No,' said Louisa. She'd run out of ideas. 'Did you ever hear or see anything strange at her house?'

'Who are you, miss? If you don't mind me asking. Only, you have to be careful.'

'Yes, yes, of course. I'm Louisa Cannon. I'm a private detective. I've been looking for her husband, Mr Plum. That is, he came back a few weeks ago, I think. But possibly he went away again. And—' She stopped. What could she say? *Mrs Plum asked me to stay out of her business and not to look for him any more? She wouldn't tell me that her husband had come back?* That she suspected Mr Plum of beating his wife, of silencing her in some way, that his wife was frightened and unable to speak to anyone, that she had no family, she had nowhere to turn? Only she, Louisa, had guessed at this, but she had done nothing about it and now . . . Mrs Plum had gone.

If there was blood, it would be on her hands, too.

With a brief apology to the neighbour, Louisa stepped away. She knew she needed to get into the house, but she didn't want to do so if it meant she was acting against the law. It would compromise any discovery she made there. There had to be some proof that Janice Plum was away from her house against her will. Or Louisa needed proof that Bernard Plum was linked to the missing Petunia Attwood and Belinda Cartwright, then the police would search his house for any evidence as to what had happened.

There were no bodies, there were no notes. There was only a distressed sister and bewildered parents. There was no one to whom Janice was tied, so far as Louisa knew. Even her closest neighbours barely seemed to know her. How had she filled her days? To whom had she spoken? It must have been a lonely, hard life. In spite of what she had been through, her prettiness had still been visible, like a pressed flower beneath tracing paper, and from what she had said about the early days of her marriage, she must have had a sense of adventure once. She seemed like a survivor, but this situation was looking increasingly hopeless. Louisa knew there were 'bolters', women who fled in the night from their marriage and children, written off as selfish when they may have had no other option. Divorce was still hard to obtain: women might be able to claim it on the grounds of their husband's adultery, but this had to be proved. Sometimes it was easier to leave. Louisa wanted to believe that this was what Janice had done, but why? If Bernard wasn't there, if he had returned to France as he'd told Miss Piper he was planning to do, then surely Janice was better off staying in her house? It was a roof over her head, at least. Money must have been scarce if he wasn't giving her any. Perhaps the house wasn't abandoned or deathly empty; perhaps Janice had gone to work. Or simply gone away for a while.

There had to be a way to find out.

CHAPTER SIXTY-THREE

There was a gate in the side return, a narrow gap that presumably led to the garden and, hopefully, a back door. Checking that the man over the road had gone back inside, Louisa went through the gate and into the scrubby patch behind the house. There was little sign of tended flowers.

The windows were closed – everything looked as shuttered and abandoned as it did at the front. Then Louisa tried the handle of the back door. It turned.

Perhaps, she reasoned to herself, if it was open then it wouldn't be breaking and entering to go into the house.

Slowly, Louisa moved through the rooms on the ground floor. The kitchen was tidy, but for a plate and some cutlery left to dry by the sink. In the front room, where Louisa had sat with Janice, drawn curtains kept it dark and cool. It looked neither abandoned nor neatly tidied but somewhere in between. A novel by Ronald Knox was on the table by the settee, the ashtray was empty, there were no flowers in the vase.

Back in the hall, two coats hung on their pegs and a pair of walking boots sat beneath. A thin layer of dust could be seen on a low table with an address book on it. Tentatively, Louisa went up the stairs. Now, she felt illicit. If Janice suddenly came home, this would be hard to explain. Yet she knew that she wouldn't.

At the top of the stairs, there were three doors. Louisa guessed which one was the bathroom and took a quick glance in there: empty, clean, toothbrushes standing in their mugs, a tin of toothpaste on the shelf. She decided to go into the back bedroom first – most likely, the spare room. The bedroom was empty, but it was messier than elsewhere. She'd guess it was Bernard's space more than his wife's. There was a small day bed in the corner, made up with sheets and a blanket. Stacked on it were newspapers, a few books and some papers. She looked briefly but couldn't see much beyond household bills. There was a desk with drawers and an assorted jumble of office items on it, some of which looked as if they'd been pilfered from Lee Worth: an ink blotter, stamps, headed notepaper. In a drawer was a length of rubber tubing and a syringe – for drugs? She didn't have time to speculate, and closed it.

Moving quickly, Louisa went into the bedroom that over-looked the front garden. The room was compact, with plain blue wallpaper, a wooden wardrobe that had two or three frocks and a suit hanging in it, a dressing table with a hairbrush and a hand mirror. No pictures hung on the wall. The bed was made. Again, nothing was obviously missing but nothing looked as if it had been used in some time either.

Louisa looked under the bed and saw a brown suitcase there. She pulled it out, put it on the bed and snapped it open. Inside, thrown in loosely, was what at first sight appeared to be an assort-ment of women's clothes: two pairs of shoes, different sizes; two blouses, one blue, one white; two skirts in tweed and dark grey wool; two pairs of rayon stockings, two brassieres; a wristwatch; a silver necklace with a cross hanging from it; a battered leather handbag in dark burgundy.

Tucked into a side pocket, Louisa found what she had dreaded: a driving licence in the name of Belinda Cartwright and a gold necklace with a heart on it.

CHAPTER SIXTY-FOUR

ow it was a police matter. Louisa left the case on the bed and ran down the stairs and though the back door. She'd passed a police station on the way to the house, and now she ran there. At the front desk was a young female constable. Louisa spilled out as much as she could, trying to remain coherent.

'It sounds as if you were trespassing,' said the constable. 'I ought to arrest you.'

'You can if you like,' said Louisa. 'I don't care. I know I did the right thing. I know my hunch was right. Something has happened to those women and now you, the police, can help find them. None of us could persuade the police before, because they were adults who could have willingly left their lives. It happens. But this—' She stopped, overwhelmed by the emotion flooding through her. All these weeks of wondering what had happened to Petunia, knowing that something was wrong, unable to do anything. Knowing, too, that it wasn't right that Belinda had gone. And Janice. Where was she? Had Plum done something to her, his own wife?

Louisa waited at the station while the officer – whose name

she now knew to be PC Smiley – disappeared to find her superiors and ask for a search warrant. Louisa watched the clock on the wall – a mistake, because time dragged as slowly as treacle sliding down a wall. After a thousand years had passed, PC Smiley came out and asked Louisa to come with her to an interview room. Inside was a man sitting behind a table, looking serious.

'Good afternoon, Mrs Sullivan. I'm DI Bird. I understand that you're a private detective and you've been trying to trace the whereabouts of two women and a man, and now you believe there's a third woman missing?'

Relieved, Louisa sat down. 'Yes, I—'

'Do you realise that your interference and trespassing may have destroyed our chances of using this evidence that you suppose you have found?'

Louisa was blindsided.

'How are we to know that you didn't plant evidence in the case that you say is on the bed in the house?'

'Because it's my word.'

'Your word means nothing.' DI Bird sat back and folded his arms. He was roughly the same age as Guy, she guessed, but with a deeper receding hairline and a paunch that jutted over his trousers.

Louisa took a steadying breath, reminding herself that she was on the side of right. 'I opened the case, I found the women's clothes in there and the identification. I've replaced the case. You can check it for fingerprints, surely? It will be that either someone else's prints are on there, or only mine, which will mean whoever last handled the case wiped it clean.'

'Quite the little detective, aren't you?' he sneered.

Louisa had had enough. 'As a matter of fact, my husband was

a detective inspector for the Metropolitan Police, so I am familiar enough with procedure. I know that what I did was wrong, and I am prepared to take the consequences. What I am not prepared for is for you to waste valuable time giving me a ticking-off when you could be out there looking for these women.' She stopped and calmed herself before carrying on. 'You might also like to talk to your colleagues at Latchmere Road station. They are, supposedly, investigating the murder of a woman found dead on Duffield Street on the fourth of March. She was presumed at first to be Petunia Attwood, because she appeared to be wearing a coat of hers – she had a powder compact belonging to Petunia in her pocket. There was also a business card with Bernard Plum's name on it found inside the coat's lining. But it has since been proven that the body is not that of Miss Attwood.'

'Couldn't a relative identify her?'

'Her face was too badly disfigured when the body was found. It's possible that this murder is connected to our investigation too. The long and the short of it is: three women are missing and they all have a connection to Bernard Plum. Are we going to find him, or are we going to let him get away? I should warn you that my husband still has friends in high places and they may not look kindly upon your focusing on me rather than on the urgency of finding the missing victims and perpetrator.'

'Is that a threat?' But his voice was less certain now.

'No. I am simply asking that you return to the house and gather the evidence and get moving. Please, DI Bird.' Louisa changed her tone, urging sympathy. 'I know that these women are missing for a reason. I don't believe they willingly walked out of their lives. If Plum's wife is still alive – and I hope to God she is – then she will be in danger. We need to find out what happened to Miss Cartwright and Miss Attwood, we need to find Mrs Plum. Most of all, we need to find the man who's behind it all. But it has to be done *now*.'

DI Bird put his hands on the table and stood up. She regarded him, trembling from the anger and desire for retribution that was coursing through her every vein.

'Right, then,' he said, 'what are you waiting for?'

CHAPTER SIXTY-FIVE

With the Metropolitan Police now on the case, things moved at a different speed. Louisa had to acknowledge the need for their technical expertise. Back at the house, she showed PC Smiley and DI Bird the route she had taken through the rooms – including telling them which door handles she had touched – and led them to the suitcase, left on the bed.

'We'll take the case back to the station and check it for fingerprints and traces of blood,' said DI Bird. 'We'll need your fingerprints, too.'

'Of course.'

'I need PC Smiley to take a statement from you with regards to the investigation you've made so far.'

'Will you get in touch with Belinda Cartwright's parents, and Petunia Attwood's sister?'

'There's nothing definite for us to tell them yet,' said DI Bird. 'It doesn't look good, I'll say that. But until there's a body, there's a chance they could be alive.'

'Are you going to keep them hoping? That seems almost cruel.'

'I'm not trying to be either kind or cruel, Mrs Sullivan. I'm trying to be a policeman. I'm sticking to the facts and I'd advise you to do the same if you want any success in your profession.'

Stung, Louisa did not reply, but turned around to go back down the stairs. She felt humiliated, but pushed this to one side. What mattered was finding Belinda, Petunia and Janice.

That night, Louisa told Guy everything that had happened. His reaction was a shock to her.

'What the hell were you doing there? I told you to stop work on that case.'

'Those women are missing, Guy,' said Louisa. 'And now his wife has gone too. What if she's in danger? I can't sit by and do nothing. I'm surprised you feel you can.'

'You are putting yourself in danger!' shouted Guy. 'How can you do that to Maisie? To me?'

'I'm not doing it to Maisie – how can you say that? I would never risk myself in that way.'

'You just did! You did it today! I told you not to and you—'

'What? *Disobeyed* you? You don't get to tell me what to do.'

'I'm not – that's not what I meant. I'm trying to keep you safe. You're frightening me, Louisa.' He stopped and sat down, looking upset. 'I know what the risks are. I've worked in policing – I've seen things you can't imagine, I know what people are capable of. You haven't been up against danger like I have—'

'I have. I'm not some innocent, you know that. I'm a grown woman. I know what I'm doing. And I have to catch this man. Or *we* have to catch him.'

'No, Louisa. I mean it. Hand it over to the police. Please, I'm begging you, don't look for him any more. I couldn't bear it if something happened to you and it was my fault.'

'How could it be your fault?'

'Just . . . don't look for him any more. Promise me.'

'No, I can't make that promise. I won't.'

The following morning the two of them took Maisie for a walk to the park, hoping that it would distract them from their argument the night before. Louisa could not stop thinking about the details, riven by guilt. If she had done something sooner, Janice would not be missing too. As they sat on a bench, Maisie between them, cooing at the pigeons, Louisa risked bringing the subject up again.

'Now that we know they're all connected, perhaps there's a clue we missed at the start, before we realised,' said Louisa, cautiously, dipping her toes back into the icy waters.

'Does this mean you really are going to ignore everything I said to you last night?' said Guy.

'Not exactly. I am listening to you. I love you, and I would never put myself deliberately in harm's way. But I can't simply walk away from these women. If I can find them, or find him and bring him to justice – well, isn't that what we do, Guy? Isn't that why we set up the agency? Because we believe we are able to put right the wrongs of others, better than the police can? Because we are not corrupt, but driven by the right motives?'

Guy nodded miserably. 'Yes.'

'I will be careful, just as you are.' She took his hand and held it, felt the dry smoothness of his palm. His physical strength always calmed her.

'I'm going to get in touch with Julia Attwood,' said Louisa. 'I think she deserves to know what happened yesterday. She said she's got to pack up Petunia's flat. Perhaps there will be something there that we missed before. A letter from Bernard, or a neighbour who heard something.'

'You can't start interfering with DI Bird's—'

'I don't care too much what he thinks. I'm the one who has lived with this case for several weeks. I think she needs to know. And anything I find out, I'll tell him. Of course I will.'

'Fine,' said Guy, defeated. 'But I'm coming with you.'

Julia had given Louisa the address of her work, in case she needed to be found urgently, and it was there that the two of them headed after dropping Maisie off at Mrs Sullivan's. Julia worked for a gallery on Duke Street, which was only a few stops away on the Piccadilly line. Since it wasn't rush hour, the journey was relatively quick and easy. Louisa felt both afraid and relieved. To be physically moving made her feel as if she was taking some kind of action, which was good. But she worried it was futile, that they were moving in the wrong direction. Where was Janice, and where was Bernard? Every moment now felt a moment too long – another movement in time that could further endanger Janice. She felt sick to her stomach that it may be too late for Petunia and Belinda.

The gallery, Mountiman's Fine Art, had two large oil landscapes on easels in the window. The door was closed, but a small sign indicated that visitors should ring the bell. Julia came to the door. Her face visibly blanched when she saw Louisa.

'Come in,' she said. 'There's no one here.'

Inside there was the silence peculiar to galleries: a muffled hush that muted the outside world and permitted no voice to be raised louder than a whisper. The hung paintings were of English fields and country scenes in ornate gold frames, and Julia wore an outfit that was severely black.

They followed her to the back of the gallery, where she indicated two chairs on one side of a pretty table. She sat in the only chair on the other side. On the table were a few papers, a telephone, an art magazine.

'What's happened?'

Louisa was grateful to have Guy there with her. She'd never had to deliver news like this before. She imagined it didn't get easier, even with practice.

'There is news, Miss Attwood, but I want to say first that we don't know for certain yet what it signifies. But I'm afraid it doesn't look good.'

Julia was holding herself absolutely erect, her back straight, her hands on her lap. She bowed her head a little. 'Please, just tell me.'

'I went to Bernard Plum's house yesterday. I'd been trying to get in touch with his wife, Janice, and I was concerned because I hadn't heard from her. She wasn't there; the house was empty. It wasn't the right thing – the legal thing – to do, but I went inside. Upstairs, under the bed, I found a suitcase. There were two sets of women's clothes in there . . . and a gold necklace with a heart on it.'

'Oh!' Julia's hands flew to her mouth, and a sob burst out.

'The police have got the case now. They're looking at it for fingerprints. I wanted to tell you that I also found a driving licence in the name of Belinda Cartwright.'

Julia wiped her face with the back of her hand. 'Who is that?'

'She's from London, too, but she was a nurse in the war in

Spain. We think she knew Bernard Plum, too. She has been missing for some weeks. Her parents don't know where she is.'

'You think he had something to do with this other woman too?'

'Yes. And the house had clearly been empty for some time. We don't know where his wife has gone.'

'Oh, God.' Julia started to cry again. She pulled open a drawer, took out a tissue and blew her nose.

Guy spoke, in a low, gentle voice. 'Miss Attwood, you must try not to assume the worst yet.'

'How can I possibly do otherwise?' she said. 'I've been through this once before. I can hardly stand to do it again.'

'Have you packed up her flat?' asked Louisa.

'No. I had every intention of doing so, as you know, but the landlord wrote to say he had arranged for a new tenant and he would pack Petunia's belongings into boxes himself. She didn't own many of the larger pieces of furniture.' She burst into fresh sobs. 'She never could earn good enough money. She was paid a pittance – far less than she deserved – but because she had no dependants they would never agree to pay her more.'

'Where are the boxes?'

'They're here, because I don't have room for them at home. It's not much more than a bedsit, like Petunia's place. I was going to tell you. I just couldn't face looking through them yet. It seemed so final and now you've come here ...' She trailed off miserably.

'May we look inside? There may be something that we missed, something that could help us understand what happened.' Louisa watched her intently.

'Yes, I'll take you down there. They're in the basement.'

CHAPTER SIXTY-SIX

Julia took Louisa and Guy down into the basement of the gallery. There was only one bare lightbulb to give light down there, but there wasn't much to see. Some paintings wrapped in brown paper were stacked against one wall, and various boxes nearby were labelled *Tax Returns 1933*, *Invoices 1935*, and so on. Along one side were several boxes all labelled *Attwood*, plus an assortment of loose household items: a floor lamp, a rolled-up rug, an umbrella stand. The sight was poignant: that one person's entire life should be reduced to this.

'It all came in one van-load,' said Julia. 'I didn't even look at it all when it arrived, as I was with someone upstairs. As I said, I haven't been able to face sorting through it all and my boss doesn't mind it being here. I know I'll have to do it eventually but I feel that so long as there's a chance that Petunia might come back, I need to hold on to it.'

'Of course,' said Louisa. 'I understand. Do we have your permission to look in the boxes now? It's an outside chance, but we might find something that could help us.'

'Yes. Take as long as you like. I'll bring you both a cup of tea.'

Guy kept a penknife in his pocket, and they got to work. 'It's that new sticky stuff,' said Guy. 'I prefer string myself. What do they call it again?'

'Sellotape.' The shiny strips bound down the lids of the boxes, but the knife swiftly released them.

The first boxes yielded nothing beyond the familiar objects they expected to find: kitchen crockery (just two of everything); toothbrush, face creams. A couple of boxes of clothes, modest in their range. Books, a few framed prints of flower pictures. The most surprising find was a gramophone player and several records of popular big-band songs, though this too moved Louisa: it hinted at a woman who would have liked to go out dancing, to dress up and be swept away. It hinted at a longing for romance.

When they only had a couple of unopened boxes left, they found what looked like things Petunia had kept beside her bed. An alarm clock, a few paperback books (detective stories by Georgette Heyer and G. K. Chesterton), a cotton nightdress, a face cream and old correspondence. Some were loose, cards sent to her by her sister for her birthday and Christmas; some, which looked to be several years old, from her parents. The occasional thank you note from other friends: 'we mustn't leave it so long until next time' frequently expressed by different names, who didn't seem to have written to Petunia again. Louisa flicked through these, eliminating them fast from the investigation so that she could concentrate fully on what had caught her eye. Already she knew it would be of the most interest: a thick bundle of letters held together by a green ribbon.

The first thing they noticed was that some of the letters were addressed to Petunia at her home address and others to the office of Lee Worth, but they all seemed to have been written by the same hand, in blue ink. The paper was not particularly thick or expensive-looking; it was everyday notepaper in cheap envelopes. Louisa opened the envelope at the top of the pile. It was dated 13th November 1936. It wasn't a long letter and it was written in block capitals.

YOU KNOW WHAT I WANT. I WON'T STOP
UNTIL I GET IT.

There was no name anywhere, no address, no date, no signature. Guy opened the next letter, which was postmarked the very next day. Again, the note was chillingly brief, the sentiment almost exactly the same.

They went through the pile and realised that a note had been sent almost daily until 31st January.

The messages were unvarying in their menace. Occasionally there were spelling mistakes and the writer had made aggressive marks with the pen, scratching the paper.

Louisa got her notebook out and flipped back several pages. 'The last letter was sent only a few days before she disappeared.'

'Which means that whoever sent these notes knew she wouldn't be in the office. They knew enough not to send any more in case anyone else saw them,' said Guy.

This was the clue they had been looking for – and dreading. Once again, the terrible conflict of wanting to solve a crime came up against the harsh reality of what that crime had truly involved for the victim.

'Why didn't Julia find these letters before?'

'I don't know. Perhaps Petunia hid them? We could ask the

landlord where they were found. We can assume they were in the bedroom.'

'It was a bedsit – I don't think there was a separate room.'

'Well, then, somewhere near her bed,' said Guy. 'She might have kept them under the mattress.'

'Why would she do that?'

'In case whoever wrote them came to her flat and tried to get them back. Even without a signature, these are still incriminating. We need to know whose handwriting this is.'

'You know who we suspect.' Louisa's hands were trembling, the shock of what she had seen still reverberating through her. For someone who lived alone, receiving these letters must have been terrifying.

'Bernard Plum.'

'But why post them? Why not simply leave them on her desk? He seems confident that Petunia would know who had written them.'

'Someone else might have seen him near the desk. Or he did it to throw any potential investigation off his scent. We need to find samples of his handwriting, to see if they match.'

'We can't ask Janice,' said Louisa, 'but they must have papers at Lee Worth?'

'Right,' said Guy. 'I'll go to Lee Worth. You go to the police, the DI Bird you talked to yesterday, and let him know what you've found. I only need two or three letters for handwriting samples. You take the rest.

Solemnly they closed the boxes as best they could and stacked them into piles again. The action of doing this made Louisa determined that these few belongings should not define the life of Petunia Attwood.

CHAPTER SIXTY-SEVEN

When Louisa arrived at the police station, PC Smiley was at the front desk. She didn't greet Louisa but only said: 'They're not pleased with you.'

'What? Why?'

She held up a newspaper. 'Why did you do it?'

Louisa was thoroughly flummoxed. 'Do what?'

'Tell the newspapers.'

'I haven't said anything to the newspapers.'

DI Bird came out as she was saying this, and threw up his hands. 'Come on, Mrs Sullivan. Don't make this any harder than it needs to be.'

'I mean it. I don't know what you're talking about.'

PC Smiley held up the paper, turned to an inside page and folded over so Louisa could see the headline: three women missing. Louisa snatched the paper and read it. It wasn't a long story – whoever the journalist was hadn't managed to get a lot of details – but it named Belinda, Petunia and Janice. It said they were missing, that police were looking for them, that no one knew if they were dead or alive, but that Bernard Plum was closely connected to their disappearance. It urged anyone with information to come forward.

'This could wreck our investigation,' said DI Bird. His tie was loosened, and he didn't look as if he'd had much sleep.

'I haven't said anything! I don't know who could have, but why will it wreck the investigation? It might mean that someone comes forward with useful information.'

'If Bernard Plum is on the run, he'll know that we're on to him.'

'Of course he's on the run – he has been for some time. He's got to have been looking over his shoulder for weeks or he would have stayed at home when he came back to London.'

A dejected calm had fallen on them all.

'I don't like it,' said Bird. 'Someone has leaked it without my knowledge. Why would they do that?'

Louisa shrugged. 'Because they think people ought to know? Because they think it will prompt someone to remember something?'

'Who else have you spoken to about this case?' asked PC Smiley.

'First of all, until yesterday, it wasn't your case, it was mine. We've been looking for Petunia Attwood and Belinda Cartwright for some weeks. We've spoken to several people.' She stopped and handed back the newspaper. 'I've come here because I've got something important to show you. Can we go somewhere more private?'

DI Bird turned and walked away without saying anything, but PC Smiley gestured that they should follow. She whispered to Louisa that she wasn't to worry. 'He wants to find out what happened, that's all.'

'So do I,' said Louisa.

In an interview room, Louisa laid out the letters she and Guy had found. Silently, Bird looked through them. 'We assume that Bernard Plum sent these, I suppose?'

'Yes – my husband has gone to Lee Worth to see if they have any documents there with his handwriting on. We might be able to find a match.'

'It won't be easy. Whoever this is has written in block capitals. That disguises their natural hand, to a degree. And he worked at Lee Worth, yet these were all posted?'

'There are various reasons why he might have done that,' said Louisa.

'Yes, yes, I know. But it's not a *definite* link. Not yet.'

'It shows that Miss Attwood was being threatened by some-one, almost daily.'

'Would you call these threats?' Bird pushed the letters back to Louisa. 'Could have been a jilted lover. Or a jealous friend. Someone she'd annoyed. They're only letters.'

'I think if you got one of these every day, it would make you feel very threatened. And I think there is a link: the letters stopped and a few days later she went missing.'

'Hmm.' He didn't look convinced. 'I'll look through these again, if it'll make you any happier. In other news, we've been through the house with a fine-tooth comb but we haven't found anything else to give us reason to suspect that those women are dead. There are no murder weapons, no signs of a struggle.'

'You think Mrs Plum just left?'

'What do you want me to say, Mrs Sullivan? I agree with you that something fishy is going on here. But I couldn't tell you what that is exactly. As far as I'm concerned, *you* could be the missing link.' He gave her a meaningful stare, but she refused to be cowed. 'We've taken fingerprints off the suitcases and eliminated yours. There seems to be just one other set present, but we don't know whose they are. There's no sign of any blood on the clothes.'

'There's another way of looking at this,' said Louisa. 'What about what you *can't* find? Where are the passports? Has the piggy bank been emptied? Does it look as if Mrs Plum might have packed some clothes or taken a suitcase?'

'As useless as you clearly think we are, we've already done that.'

'And?'

'Mrs Plum's purse, with coins in it, was still there, in a coat pocket. There are two large empty suitcases in the cupboard under the stairs. No passports – but then again, not many people have those. Not the people that live around here, any rate.'

Louisa listened to all this and took her time before replying. 'Detective Inspector, will you pursue a case for these women? Miss Belinda Cartwright, Miss Petunia Attwood and Mrs Janice Plum. All of them have vanished. Their families and workplaces don't know where they are. We have found a suitcase with what appears to be two sets of women's clothing, Miss Cartwright's driving licence and a necklace that we believe was Miss Attwood's, in a house where Bernard Plum lived, and we know there's a connection between those women and him. There was a body found not far from here, wearing a coat that appeared to be Miss Attwood's, with her compact in the pocket and Bernard Plum's business card. The body, we know, is not Petunia's, but there has to be some sort of link, given everything else. We know that Miss Attwood received a series of threatening letters, and I have good reason to believe that Mrs Plum was intimidated, if not worse, by her husband.'

DI Bird pushed his chair back and stood up. 'I will be in touch with Miss Cartwright's parents to let them know. You can see yourself out, can't you?'

Louisa had been summarily dismissed.

CHAPTER SIXTY-EIGHT

~~~~~

Louisa departed the police station quickly. She left the letters with PC Smiley, who was sympathetic. 'I'd try to say something, but I'm afraid he would never listen to me. I'm only a constable – and a woman, at that.'

Louisa took herself home, collecting Maisie on the way, prepared to do nothing but wait for Guy to return, hoping that he might have got some kind of lead from Lee Worth that would mean she could persuade DI Bird to treat this as a murder investigation. But on the doormat she found a surprise waiting.

She immediately recognised it as an airmail envelope, with its thin, almost translucent blue paper. Hurriedly, she went into the kitchen and grabbed a knife to slit it open. The letter was from Decca. She got to the point quite quickly: the wedding was almost upon them and Lady Redesdale would be arriving soon. She was, apparently, quite insistent on being there. Decca hoped that Louisa could come too, because 'I feel there's a need for a buffer between E and Muv. I love him terribly, but I do so want this day to go as smoothly as possible and I think if you were there to stop Muv interfering too greatly, it would help enormously.'

Louisa was flattered. But there was more.

'And I hope it's not weak of me to say I'd like you here because there are times when I've felt unsafe, and it's nothing to do with the war. I don't want to worry Es, he'll make me go home. Please come out, so I can talk to you about it.'

Why couldn't she say it in the letter? Louisa was maddened. Was there a connection with Belinda Cartwright? She couldn't discount it but nor could she go to Bayonne on the strength of a *possible* lead. Then again, she could go if Lady Redesdale agreed to hire her as a travelling companion; Nancy might help to persuade her. Guy had been the one to go to Bayonne on the last two trips, and she was intrigued to see the place for herself after everything he had told her.

When Guy got home, he brought news – but not of the type she had been expecting.

'I was given fairly short shrift there,' he said. 'I don't think they are at all keen on any of this getting out. And the fact that one of their employees has been named as missing in the papers has rattled their cage.'

'You saw the article, too?'

'Yes, Miss Piper showed it to me. Who leaked that story? There wasn't a by-line.'

'I don't know,' admitted Louisa, 'and the DI gave me hell for it, too. He thought it had to be me, didn't want to contemplate the idea that it might have been one of his men.'

'It's not such a bad thing,' said Guy. 'It might bring someone forward with information.'

'That's what I said. He was concerned that it would wreck his investigation, but then he doesn't seem to be doing much of an investigation anyway. He said it's a missing persons enquiry and no more. My visit seemed to do more harm than good.'

'Don't worry.' Guy took Maisie from Louisa and put her on his lap, bouncing her until she started to laugh. 'He's being defensive because you know more than him.'

'Tell me your news from Lee Worth.'

'There's no match on the handwriting.'

'What? It's not Bernard Plum's?'

'It's not definitively *not* his penmanship, but we can't say either way for sure. The only examples of his handwriting they had were his signatures, and that's not enough to match it to the block capitals. The only documents that might have contained more of his writing in the files that he took that night.'

'Well, that's a strong connection, isn't it?'

'Not necessarily. It's far more likely that the files were taken because they would have revealed the truth about him stealing the money from claims.' He had Maisie resting her head on his shoulder, her eyes open, perfectly peaceful. 'Nonetheless, it's worth noting. I wasn't able to speak to Mr Cornish because he was in a board meeting, but Miss Piper was as helpful as she could be.'

'Did she say anything new?'

'It's hard to say. She was chatty, which was something I wasn't quite expecting somehow. And I could be wrong, but I felt as if she was trying to give me information in such a way that I wouldn't think she was trying to give it to me. Does that make sense?'

'Not entirely.'

'I mean, she told me twice that Miss Attwood had a

fascination with the Spanish civil war but when I asked her if she meant that she thought Miss Attwood would have gone there, she wouldn't answer the question. She changed the subject and started wittering on about how they had always gone for lovely walks in the park together or how she missed her friend and hoped she was all right.'

'Did you ask her whether she knew about the letters before?'

'She seemed genuinely shocked by them, but she thought they explained Miss Attwood's low moods. She had attributed her sunnier outlook on weekends to the fact that she had two days off from working in close proximity to Mr Plum, but now she wondered whether it was more to do with her not receiving letters when she was at home.'

'Or a combination of the two,' remarked Louisa. 'None of those letters, so far as we could see, made any definite threat to her, but it must have created a constant feeling of menace and being watched. I still say they have to have come from Bernard Plum because she had no other known enemies. Not to mention the fact that they both disappeared at the same time.'

'I agree with you, for what it's worth,' said Guy. 'I just don't know what we can do to take it further unless the police do.'

'And they're not right now.' Louisa started to fiddle with the cushions on the sofa, putting off what she needed to do next. 'I had a letter from Decca.'

'Oh? Saying what?'

'They're in Bayonne still, and their wedding is happening soon. Lady Redesdale is going there for it, much to everyone's surprise, and Decca would like me to be there too, to act as a buffer between the groom and the mother of the bride.'

'Ah,' said Guy. He kissed Maisie, avoiding looking at Louisa.

'I know you won't be keen on the idea, but I'd like to go.'

'Why?'

It was a reasonable question, of course. Was there a reasonable answer?

'Apart from anything else, I would like to see Bayonne, after what you told me about it.'

'It's not a beautiful place.'

'No, I didn't mean its beauty, but the effects of the civil war. I don't mean to gawp. It's more that I want to understand more of what Decca and Esmond believe they are fighting for. These huge events are happening and we seem to be unaware of them in Britain. It seems unwise, somehow.'

'It's not pleasant.'

'And I'm fond of Decca. She's asking me for her help, to make her wedding day a better one, and I would like to help, if I can.'

Guy sat heavily on the sofa. 'You know that I don't want you to go.'

'I don't want to go without your blessing, but—'

'You will if you have to.'

Louisa nodded.

'Then you have to promise me that you won't leave Miss Mitford or Lady Redesdale. That you will never walk alone down a street, especially after dark.'

'I won't do anything stupid. But is there really cause for you to be so afraid? Is there something you're not telling me?'

'No,' said Guy. 'But promise me.'

'Of course. I promise. And I'll be fine.'

CHAPTER SIXTY-NINE

Things moved quickly for Louisa. Nancy lobbied Lady Redesdale – for once in agreement with Decca – for Louisa to join their mother as a paid companion on the trip to France. (But Louisa had to promise Nancy that she would give her 'the real story on what happens out there' in return.) Lady Redesdale was booked to depart on a train in two days' time, which gave Louisa just about enough time to make arrangements for Maisie, buy food for Guy, and pull together all the notes she had made about the missing women and Bernard Plum. Guy arranged to meet DI Bird to hand it all over.

The two men met in a café close to Battersea police station. Guy was relieved to find that, in spite of what Louisa had been through with him, DI Bird seemed amenable to reviewing the case with Guy.

'You were in the Met, too, I understand?' said Bird, as plates of fried egg and bacon were put down before them.

'Yes, for several years. It was hard work but I had good people around me, for the most part.'

'Why did you leave, then?' Bird was understandably curious, but Guy didn't want to get into it – and the case in hand was more important.

'It's complicated. I'll tell you when we've got beers in front of us.'

Bird, his mouth full, gave a chuckle. 'Gotcha.'

'Have you got any further with Bernard Plum? Finding out more about his previous and so on.'

'The newspaper article has, predictably, brought forward several people claiming to have seen the missing women and Bernard Plum. We'll be doing our best to eliminate those from our enquiries.'

'You are making enquiries, then?' asked Guy.

There was a mildly uncomfortable silence before DI Bird cleared his throat. 'Yes. We've been reviewing the information we have to hand and we think that would be the correct step to take. There was one message in particular that has helped us to make this decision. I thought you would like to know. It's unorthodox, but given you are a former policeman . . . '

Guy acknowledged the compliment.

'It was from Mrs Plum's father, Mr Wood.'

Guy had read Louisa's notes before handing them over. 'I thought Mrs Plum didn't have any family,' he said. 'In Louisa's notes, it says her parents died a long time ago.'

'In a manner of speaking, she may have felt that was the case. Mr Wood told us – and he was able to verify certain facts about her, so I'm happy that we *were* talking to her father – that her husband had forced her to cut off her family. They were aware, he said, that Bernard Plum was an intimidating and frightening man, but Janice was impervious to their pleas to leave him.

He said there had been some distressing scenes at the start of the marriage, when she had attempted to introduce Bernard to them. They didn't know where she was living, or they would have tried to get in touch with her in London.'

'Where do they live?'

'A village not far from York. I got the impression that they were a world away from their daughter – in several senses of the phrase. They also told us that Bernard Plum has previous form. It wasn't known to us because the details were kept by a different force, but we've been in touch since and it's been confirmed.'

'What was the previous?'

'It was complicated by the fact that Bernard was a minor at the time – seventeen years old. He spent a short spell in a delinquency unit before going to prison, but he was released on good behaviour after only four years.'

'*Only* four years?'

'It was a sentence for serious assault – of a girl of fifteen. A brutal one, by all accounts, but his defence said that the girl was his sweetheart and she had told him that day that she was leaving him for someone else. It was a crime of passion by a youth. A one-off, not something the judge thought should ruin his prospects after rehabilitation.

'Did Janice know about this? Did her father tell her?' asked Guy. He thought of Maisie and the pain this poor man must have been through on realising to whom his daughter was married.

'No. The father discovered it too late. He said he was suspicious when he questioned Bernard about his years as a young man and kept receiving conflicting information. He happened to have a friend in the police service who did some digging around for him, but by the time he found out about it, Janice had cut them off.'

Guy put his knife and fork down. The memory of the sharp blows that had landed so squarely on his back had hardly faded. He was a strong man and he had been able to take them – just. The thought of that force landing on a woman made his chest feel tight. 'Have you managed to find out any more about him?'

'We've been trying to look through some other records but, as you know, it's a tricky job. Forces don't share information easily and you don't always know what to look for. We did have one bit of success, though.'

'Oh?'

'Looks as if he was arrested in the Cable Street riots last year. Not what you would have thought, however. He wasn't one of the anti-fascists, which made up most of the arrests. No, he was one of Mosley's unlovely lot. He was caught with a nasty weapon – a chair leg wrapped in barbed wire. They didn't catch him in the act, but there was blood on the wire.'

'Grim.'

'Quite.' Bird mopped up the broken yolk of his egg with buttered bread. He was a sloppy eater, not too pleasant to watch. 'They got him for possession of it, but he wasn't charged. A group of them were rounded up, I think.'

'He's a man with history,' said Guy.

'Yes. I'm afraid it doesn't look good for any of those women.'

'Have you found anything else in the house?'

'No. I can't see that his wife packed up to go – there's a suitcase, her purse. The fact that the back door was unlocked puzzles me.'

Bird and Guy sat in silence for a few minutes. Both plates were empty. The waitress stopped by and refilled their cups with tea.

'Hang on,' said Guy. 'I know this sounds strange, but hear me out. I'm thinking out loud here. We've got what looks like the evidence of two women having been killed: their clothes and pieces of identification packed in a case, hidden under a bed.'

'Not very well hidden.'

'Exactly. As if it was meant to be found quickly. Why would a killer do that? And then another woman apparently taken, but she's left behind everything in her house that you would expect her to have on her person if she was going to go anywhere.'

'Go on,' said Bird slowly. The cogs were clearly turning for him, too.

'And the back door was left unlocked. Surely, if someone was leaving behind evidence that he had killed two women, he'd lock the door behind him? Make it harder to get in and find?'

'Yes, so you're saying they wanted us – or someone – to get in there, and find that it was empty. Find that suitcase.'

'Exactly. So if the suitcase is a deliberate red herring, then the opposite must be true.'

'The women are alive?'

'Yes.' Guy exhaled, feeling shivers go all down his legs. That feeling he got when he knew he was on to something. The thing that he had been looking for all this time, the *click* that felt right. 'What if it's Bernard Plum's body we should be looking for?'

'What? You don't believe he's done something to those women?'

'No. That is, I do. I know he's a nasty piece of work.' Guy hesitated before he spoke again, unsure whether or not to reveal something he had kept secret. 'I came across him in France. He threatened me, told me to stop looking for him or he'd attack Louisa.'

DI Bird stared at Guy, disbelieving. 'When was this?'

'A few weeks ago. Shortly before he made an appearance back at the offices of Lee Worth. I haven't told Louisa yet.' Shame burned through him. 'I almost didn't realise it was him – he pretended to be someone else, a heavy acting on his behalf. I remembered the man as saying 'Stop looking for him.' But when my memory came back, I realised he'd said "Stop looking for *me*." What if something happened when he came back? He was on the run – what if he was on the run from being killed, not from the police?'

Bird pulled out some money and put it on the table. 'We need to get back to the station. Come with me, Mr Sullivan. I think we need you with us.'

CHAPTER SEVENTY

At the police station DI Bird introduced Guy to a number of his colleagues, then pulled up a list of the morgues. 'Do we have a proper description of Bernard Plum?' he asked.

'Yes, sir,' said PC Smiley, pulling out her notebook. 'Mrs Sullivan gave it to me, along with a photograph. He's forty-two years old, average height, around five foot ten, slim build, weight eleven stone or thereabouts, dark brown hair, brown eyes. Clean-shaven. He has a scar that runs from his collarbone to his left shoulder.'

'That's an identifying mark if ever there was one,' said Bird. 'This is my thinking. We need to call the hospitals and morgues, see if they have any unidentified male bodies that have been admitted in the last few weeks.' He turned to Guy. 'Your wife said there was a report from Lee Worth that Bernard Plum had gone to the offices to steal files. When was that?'

Guy checked his notebook. 'Not long ago – 30th March.'

'Right. We'll ask about any male bodies admitted after that date. While we're at it, we can ask about the women. If we're right, the one body we're not going to find is Mrs Plum's.'

'But if she's alive, where is she?' asked PC Smiley. 'She didn't take anything with her. She doesn't have much money, as far as we know.'

'She could have saved housekeeping money – plenty of women do,' said Bird. 'Squirrelled it away in a box under the floorboards.'

Guy had been polishing his glasses. The mindless action helped him think. 'Her family,' he said. 'If she knows she's safe to talk to them again, if her husband truly isn't in the picture any more, wouldn't she re-establish contact with them?'

Bird snapped his fingers. 'You're right. Smiley, who do you partner with?'

'PC Macduff, sir.'

'Then the two of you need to get on a train to York, go and find the family. Talk to them. See if they've heard anything. With luck, you'll find her there.'

'Yes, sir.' Trying to keep a grin off her face – Guy remembered the feeling well, and felt a pang of nostalgia for that moment of excitement when a case tipped in your favour – PC Smiley exited the room at speed.

When she had gone, Guy and Bird picked up a telephone each and started the first of their calls.

CHAPTER SEVENTY-ONE

~~~~~

A few days later, Louisa, Lady Redesdale and four suitcases arrived at Bayonne. The air was hot and humid, the sea breeze non-existent, and their mood was less jubilant than conciliatory. Louisa thought of Maisie and what her own wedding day would be like: she could only hope that it would be a great deal happier.

All the same, the young couple looked very in love, Louisa could see that. Decca and Esmond came to meet them at the station, Decca running ahead to kiss her mother. Esmond maintained his usual gruff demeanour but couldn't hide his pleasure at the plans that lay ahead.

'Goodness, Muv, what have you got here?' huffed Decca, lugging one of the cases. Esmond carried two more, while Louisa had her own modest cardboard suitcase. Lady Redesdale carried her handbag and a hat box.

'Presents from your sisters, and a few things for your trousseau that I thought might be useful.'

Decca gave her mother a wide smile. 'I want for nothing now I have Es, but it's very kind of you.'

Back at the Hôtel des Basques, where Esmond and Decca were living, the four of them recovered in the dining room with glasses of cold lemonade, bitter and refreshing. The hotel was undeniably run-down, with faded wallpaper and a threadbare carpet, but at least it was cooler inside. They talked about their journey from London, Decca asked after Maisie, and Esmond told them all that his mother, Nellie, would be joining them for the wedding. Lady Redesdale blanched slightly but said only, 'How marvellous.'

'So, Little D, what are the plans?' she asked. Louisa knew what it cost her to drum up even that much enthusiasm. For her other daughters, she would be involved in all the delightful minutiae of the wedding, from booking the church to finding the dress, ordering the cake and inviting the guests. Diana had had eleven bridesmaids at her wedding to Bryan Guinness.

'We're marrying at the British consulate—' Decca began.

'Not in church?'

Decca and Esmond exchanged the sort of intimate glance that young couples are inclined to do, which only serve to infuriate others around them. 'No, we believe in science, not God.' She turned to Esmond. 'Did I tell you about my burning desire to be a scientist when I was a girl? I even went to see the local grammar school because they had a laboratory that I was desperate to get inside. They said if I passed a test, I could go, but you can guess what happened, can't you?'

'Your father said no.'

'Actually, I was the one to say no,' said Lady Redesdale, 'although your father would never have allowed it, it's true. You had excellent governesses that you chose not to learn from.' She sighed, as though the last of her puff had gone out of her.

'Must we drag all this up again? Tell me more about your wedding plans.'

Decca poured another round of lemonade for everyone. 'There aren't any more plans. We go to the consul, we get married, that's it.'

'Haven't you any friends to ask? People you met in the ...' She trailed off.

'None. You and Esmond's mother will be our witnesses – we don't need anyone else there.'

'What about a dress?'

'I hadn't thought about that. We could look for something here? I must admit ...' She put her hand on her stomach and smiled. 'Most of my things will soon get a little tight.'

Lady Redesdale gave a sad nod. 'Yes, of course. We'll go shopping this afternoon. Louisa, perhaps you'd like to join us?'

'I'd like that.' Louisa could see she was the rather thin rope that was keeping the peace bound together.

'In that case, I'll see to Mother,' said Esmond. 'I think she's arriving in a few hours, and I haven't booked her a room yet.'

The shops of Bayonne were not exactly the boutiques of Paris. Queues of refugees could be seen outside cheap cafés, and when they walked through the park, Louisa's heart was wrenched by the sight of families sitting on the grass, their faces doleful. They weren't there for a picnic. Nor was she; Louisa was desperate to know what Decca was going to tell her, as indicated in her letter, but she couldn't ask her while Lady Redesdale was around.

Fortunately, she didn't have to wait much longer. Decca took them to a shop she said she'd like to try, but when they went inside and saw the rails of ready-to-wear cotton dresses, Lady

Redesdale said, 'It doesn't look as if they do anything that could pass as a wedding dress in here.'

'I don't want a wedding dress, Muv. A summer frock will do, something I can wear again.'

Once more, Lady Redesdale withheld her disappointment. 'Very good,' she said encouragingly. 'You know I'll never disagree with thriftiness. I'll ask the salesgirl to help us. If I can find one.'

She walked off in search of someone. As soon as her back was turned, Decca grabbed Louisa's arm. 'Something's happened,' she whispered fiercely.

'What is it?' Louisa was alarmed.

'Someone has been following me, I'm sure of it.' She released her grip on Louisa but continued to keep an eye on her mother, who was talking to a rather bored-looking sales assistant.

'I didn't want to say anything in front of Muv, because she'll only fuss and try to make me come back to London.'

'Does Esmond know?'

'Yes. No. I don't think he believes me – or he does, but he thinks I'm reading too much into it.'

'Didn't he think he was being followed at one time?'

Decca looked surprised, but there was no time to ask Louisa how she knew this. 'Yes, but it stopped some weeks ago – it was only a feeling, I think. Nothing happened. Perhaps that's why he's not inclined to believe it's true this time either.'

'What's making you think you're being followed?'

Decca put her hands on her hips and hung her head briefly. 'It's a hunch more than anything. I know how stupid that sounds.'

'It doesn't sound stupid at all. But can you name any incidents?'

'Walking down a side street and hearing someone behind me, but when I turn around there's nobody there – as if they've quickly slipped out of view. That's happened a couple of times. And I get the sensation of being watched when I'm in a café. It's not threatening, exactly, more unsettling.'

'Can you think of anyone who would follow you? Any reason at all?'

'No, and it's definitely me they're following because it's only happened when I'm not with Esmond. I almost feel as if—' She stopped and shook her head, as if disagreeing with herself. Then she caught sight of her mother and the saleswoman walking towards them. 'I feel as if they're trying to summon the courage to talk to me more than anything sinister. But that's not the oddest part.'

'What's the oddest part?'

'I don't think it's a man. I think it's a woman.'

CHAPTER SEVENTY-TWO

It wasn't, Guy knew, entirely unheard of for a private detective to assist the police. He knew, too, that Bird would have looked into Guy's resignation from the force, to check it had been for reasons that had nothing to do with misconduct, that he hadn't jumped before he was pushed, as it were. Even so, he was conscious that it was perhaps not strictly within the realms of procedure for him to be on a desk within the Metropolitan Police, making enquiries into a case that was no longer his own. Guy looked across at Bird – who sat with his tie loosened, his jacket undone – and saw that, of the two of them, he was the only one worrying, so he should just get on with the job.

They had divided up the list of hospitals and morgues in London between them, over a hundred altogether, and were steadily working their way through the list. It was taking some time. While reaching a hospital was fairly straightforward, getting through to the correct department was not. The right person then had to be found, who would take down the details of the body the police were looking for, before that person could go to look through the records. Not all of them were inclined to do so on the spot. In fact, hardly any were. Like most police work, it was tedious and frustrating, a process more of elimination than positive wins.

But they needed the body, and quickly. If Janice Plum had gone to York, they would have no reason to apprehend her without it. Furthermore, the body would further decompose, making the job of identification even harder. It might already be too late to match any fingerprints found on the suitcase that contained the women's clothing . . .

Having a body meant knowing how it had died, and that meant finding your suspect. Everyone knew how simple it was.

After making around twenty calls, Guy pushed his chair back from the desk and stood for a stretch. He would go in search of a glass of water or, even better, a cup of tea. Bird caught his eye; he was on the telephone listening to someone, gave a thumbs-down. Nothing yet.

Guy stepped away but, before he was out of earshot, he heard his telephone ring. Someone was calling back. With a *tsk* of impatience – it would only be someone to say there was no body 'of that description' here – he strode back and lifted the handset.

'Oh, good,' said the female voice at the other end. 'I was about to hang up. Is that Mr Sullivan?'

'Yes,' said Guy.

'I'm Miss Sturgess – we spoke earlier. I'm the registrar of the morgue at Deptford Hospital. You're looking for any unidentified males on our records that have been admitted since 30th March.'

'That's correct.'

'We don't have anything that matches your description.'

'Right,' said Guy, wondering how much more of his time would be wasted today.

'However, something you said about the scar rang a bell with me. So I went back to have another look.'

'Yes?'

'There is a male. The body is quite badly decomposed, but I'm sure of the scar. It runs from the collarbone to the left shoulder – it's very distinct. I'd say it was something he got in a knife fight. It's in an unusual place for any kind of medical procedure.'

'I don't know how he got the scar,' said Guy. 'It doesn't matter too much. But the rest of the description, does that fit?'

'Yes, I think it does. Average height and build, brown eyes. As I say, the body is quite badly decomposed, because it had been undiscovered for so long before it was brought in to us. The body was found in a shipping container that had been unloaded at Dover then put on a lorry. It was unpacked at a depot close to here, which is when the body was discovered. There were no personal items on the body that could identify it, although we could see a faint mark where a watch might have been.'

'Has there been an autopsy?' Guy was listening very intently, very respectfully.

'We compiled a report on the body. Given the circumstances in which it was found, it's almost certain that the man was trapped in the crate alive. It's unlikely to have been accidental.'

'How do you know that?'

'Because he was inside with no food or water. I don't think he was a stowaway. Also, the containers have to be closed and locked from the outside. If he had been shouting or trying to get out, the person who locked the container would have known.'

'I see. But you said you didn't have any bodies matching our dates, so how—'

'The body was brought in in the last week, but it was registered as having died at least a month before, which is why it didn't initially match the dates you gave me. I don't know if it fits with the person you are looking for.'

If this body was Bernard Plum, then he must have been dead when he was apparently seen taking files from Lee Worth – and before Mrs Plum went missing. Perhaps it wasn't him. Disappointment sank in Guy's stomach like a heavy stone.

'Just one more question, Miss Sturgess. The ship that carried the crate – you said it arrived in Dover, but where did it set sail from?'

'Let me check.' There was the faintest rustle while she looked through the report. 'Ah, yes. Here it is. Bayonne. Not sure I've pronounced it correctly, but does that mean anything to you?'

Yes. It certainly did.

CHAPTER SEVENTY-THREE

⁓

G uy hung up, almost stupefied by the final revelation. That Bernard Plum had been in Bayonne he knew, of course. But if he had been killed there, then that meant he hadn't been at Lee Worth stealing the files – so who could that have been? Perhaps that was a mistake that could be easily explained away – it might have been dark, Miss Piper might have been confused or leapt to conclusions – but why had Mrs Plum told Louisa that her husband had been home for a few days? And why warn Louisa so clearly against looking for her husband?

Before Guy could straighten this out in his mind, DI Bird had come up to the desk. 'Guy, something's come up and I think you should join me. We haven't got long. Grab your coat and I'll explain as we go.'

Hastily, Guy took his jacket from the back of his chair and put his hat on, half-running as DI Bird weaved his way out of the office. They emerged into the bright sunlight, blinking like baby birds. Guy had forgotten what it felt like to spend hours inside the back offices of a police station, buried deep in files.

Out on the street, they continued at a fast pace along the roads of Battersea until they reached the police station at Latchmere Road. Along the way, DI Bird explained briefly that the colleague he had been in touch with about the deceased woman mistaken for Petunia Attwood had telephoned that morning and invited him to question a man they'd recently brought in.

'They know we're looking for the three missing women and Bernard Plum,' said Bird, 'and apparently this gentleman is going to shed some light on it for us.'

In return, Guy explained what he had heard from Miss Sturgess: that there was every indication that Bernard Plum was dead, and had been dead for a month, trapped in a packing crate on a cargo ship that had sailed from Bayonne.

As for how this was all going to connect, neither of them could yet surmise.

At Latchmere Road station, Bird and Guy were met by a DI Vallings and shown into one of the anonymous rooms used for questioning witnesses, victims and suspects. Sitting at the table was a man who, it was immediately clear, had been shown the dirty side of life and gone back for more.

'This is Frank Ash and duty solicitor Mr Langton,' said Vallings, as the three of them took chairs on the other side of the table. Frank Ash was smoking a cigarette, his fingers stained yellow from nicotine. He twitched visibly as the men regarded him.

'We arrested Frank a few weeks ago for murder,' said Vallings. 'A young girl the same age as my granddaughter, not yet twenty. So far as we can gather, she'd been under Frank's thumb for some time, working the streets. That got us thinking about one or two other unsolved murders on our books.'

'The unidentified woman I've been asking you about, for example,' said Bird. No one took their eyes off Frank, but his gaze was darting about the room. The solicitor, who appeared to be as newly qualified as Vallings was ready for retirement, said nothing but straightened his pen and notepad several times.

'Right, Frank,' said Vallings. 'As we agreed. Tell DI Bird what you told me, and we'll see about lessening that sentence of yours. If you're lucky, it won't be the noose.'

Frank stubbed out his cigarette and gave Bird a cold stare. 'What do you want to know, then?'

'Did you murder the woman whose body was found—' Bird turned to Guy. 'Can you remind me of the details?'

Hurriedly, Guy flipped through his notebook. 'Found on Duffield Street on the fourth of March.'

'Yeah, that was me.'

'Can you tell us who the deceased was?'

Frank shrugged and his upper lip curled. 'I don't know her real name. She was a slut.'

Vallings leaned over the table and grabbed Frank by the shirt. Mr Langton pretended to inspect his pen.

'You tell them what you told me,' he growled, then let him go.

Frank didn't look cowed by this. Nonetheless, he started to talk. 'Christine, that's all I knew. She worked for me for a couple of years, but she was a stroppy bitch. I always warned her but she wouldn't listen. No one to blame but herself.'

'She didn't smash her face in with a hammer,' said Vallings. 'You did that.'

Guy felt the heat rise in his face. He whispered to Bird, 'Mind if I ask a question or two?'

'Go ahead.'

'Christine was found wearing a navy-blue coat with an engraved powder compact in the pocket belonging to a Miss Petunia Attwood. Can you explain that?' asked Guy.

'What was that?' Frank turned his stare on Guy.

Guy repeated the question, self-conscious, feeling manipulated.

'I don't know anything about that,' said Frank. 'She wasn't wearing any kind of coat when I dealt with her. She'd come running out the flat, the stupid cow. Shouting and screaming about how she wouldn't do it. She was on the job so she wasn't wearing much, if you get me.'

'Where did you leave the body?' asked Bird.

'Behind the bins.'

'What time was it?'

'The boozer had shut, so had to be after eleven. I don't wear a watch.'

'Weren't you concerned you'd be seen?'

Frank gave a wheezy laugh, showing his small grey teeth. 'Your lot have never been too concerned about what happens on Duffield. Plenty of you come down and use them girls yourself. Matter of fact ...' He gave Vallings another look. 'Didn't I see you round that way once or twice?'

'No, you did not,' said Vallings calmly. He turned to Bird and Guy. 'Have you got what you needed?'

'Not yet,' said Guy. 'I'd like to check if the name Bernard Plum means anything to you?'

Frank sat back and repeated the name a few times. 'No,' he said at last. 'That means nothing to me.'

*

338

After the interview, Bird and Guy went across the road for a cup of tea to review what they knew.

'The body was found the next morning,' said Guy. 'That means there were at least a few hours between when she was killed and when she was discovered. Is it possible that someone found her body and put their coat on her? Or a coat they'd found?'

'They might have done. It seems strange, but if the poor woman wasn't wearing much, maybe they thought it would do her some good.'

'Or they were trying to frame Bernard Plum.'

'Bit handy, isn't it? Finding a body they could use to frame him. It's not as if you can rely on that happening, whatever that low-life said about the policing round that way.'

'I know what you mean,' said Guy, 'but if someone had been looking for a way to frame him, perhaps they seized the opportunity. Most crimes happen by chance, as you know. What if Petunia herself put her coat over that woman?'

Bird raised his eyebrows. 'Only one person can tell us the answer to that question. But she's missing, isn't she?'

'I think I'll find her in Bayonne,' said Guy. He felt the hairs stand up on the back of his neck. That's what happened when he knew he had finally solved a puzzle. If he had fought back when Bernard was threatening him – if he had even told anyone what had happened – Bernard might still be alive today. Guy had been given a chance to make amends, and he was going to seize it.

CHAPTER SEVENTY-FOUR

A s Decca finished speaking, Lady Redesdale bore down on them with the salesgirl. They took Decca off to look at the summer dresses on offer. Louisa picked through some of the frocks hanging on the rails while she waited, thinking over what she had just been told. Why would a woman be following Decca? There was always the possibility it was a fan of some kind, a crazed personality who found the Mitfords fascinating. Louisa knew from Nancy that the occasional extraordinary letter would arrive at Rutland Gate, usually written in green ink, professing either undying love or hate. But these were rare, and it would take some motivation to drive a person all the way from England to Bayonne. Louisa decided against that option for the moment.

Decca and Esmond had admitted to making few friends, if any, on their travels. Partly, Louisa supposed, because they had been constantly on the move and because the atmosphere of war and strife was not a time in which to forge friendships. In any case, a friend would hardly be following Decca; she would make herself known, say hello. Could Decca have made an enemy along the way? That was entirely possible, Louisa supposed, if hard to gauge exactly what kind of an enemy – and why. What with their brand-new love for each other and their determination to be independent, it was difficult to imagine that they had engaged in any kind of row with an individual. Not enough to merit a stalking, at any rate.

The third possibility, a strong one, was that Decca had imagined it; she and her sisters shared a feverish imagination.

But this answer bothered Louisa. Decca was more serious than the rest of them – or rather, not so much serious, because she had a good sense of fun, too, but her intentions were worthy. She did not seek drama in the way that Nancy did, and she hadn't been a fibber, even as a little girl. If she was caught out doing something she shouldn't, she tended to admit it immediately. More usually, Decca would simply do whatever it was she had decided to do, even if everyone disapproved or found it odd, such as taking her pet lamb Miranda everywhere she went.

Louisa needed to find out whether it was true that a woman was following Decca, and she had an idea.

Louisa looked up at the back of the shop, where the dressing rooms were. Picking up a yellow cotton dress at random, she walked over to Lady Redesdale.

'I thought perhaps this might be worth considering? It's rather pretty.' She held it up briefly.

'Oh yes,' said Lady Redesdale uncertainly.

'I'll take it to Decca, so she can try it on.' Without waiting for an answer, Louisa went to the dressing room and knocked on the door. 'Decca, it's me. I need to talk to you.'

Decca pulled it open. 'I'm decent, don't worry.' Dresses lay in a heap in the corner. 'I don't know why Muv's doing all this. All I want is a plain frock. What's that you've got?'

'Here.' Louisa handed it over. 'I need to swap some clothes with you.'

'What?'

'If you're being followed, I'm going to walk around Bayonne looking like you – or as best I can. I don't know if it will do the trick, but it might.'

'Goodness, how thrilling.'

It might be dangerous, thought Louisa, but she wasn't going to press that particular point. There was a chance that the scheme might work. They were of similar height and build. If she wore a hat, Louisa was sure it would be difficult for someone to tell the difference. They swapped skirts, jackets and hats.

'Will Lady Redesdale notice?' asked Louisa.

'I doubt it,' said Decca. 'But I'll ask to wear one of the dresses we buy to go home. I'm sure she'll get me two as I'm determined to choose the cheapest. That way she won't realise I've got your clothes in a bag.'

'Thank you,' said Louisa. 'I'll see you back at the hotel later. Was there anywhere particular in the town that you felt you were being watched or noticed?'

Decca thought for a moment. 'Yes – in the main square, near the bridges and the Hôtel le Pont Neuf.'

'Perfect,' said Louisa. She turned to go, but Decca grabbed her hand. 'You will be careful, won't you? I don't know who it was, and if it was a woman then it's not so worrying, but . . .'

'Don't make me say any famous last words,' said Louisa. 'But yes, of course I will be careful.'

CHAPTER SEVENTY-FIVE

B efore setting off, Louisa decided to return to the hotel and
pick up some money and change into more comfortable
walking shoes.

'There's a message for you, Mrs Sullivan,' said the receptionist
when Louisa asked for her room key. 'Your husband called, but
he said not to call him at the office. He left a telephone number
and a name – it's not a direct line.'

Louisa took the note and arranged to make the call from the
hotel telephone. The number was a London one, but unfamiliar.
When the operator connected her, she was a little surprised to
hear the person answering say that she had reached Battersea
police station, and where would she like her call directed?

'My husband, Guy Sullivan, left me a message to call him
here. I believe he's working with DI Bird?'

'Connecting you now,' said the telephonist.

In moments, she was talking to Guy. 'What's happened?'

'There's been a development, but not one we were expecting.
We've found a body.'

'Oh God. Is it Petunia Attwood?'

'No, it's not female. It's Bernard Plum.'

Louisa was shocked into silence for a moment. 'Are you sure?'

'As sure as we can be. The scar is there and the height and weight are right. The body is quite badly decomposed because it was locked in a packing crate for some time.'

'Do they know how long?'

'Not exactly. But a few weeks, they think. The thing is, the body arrived at the morgue on 9th March. That's *before* Miss Piper says she saw Plum in the office at Lee Worth.'

'So was she lying about seeing him? Or she saw someone else and thought it was him? But the files were taken, weren't they?'

'She has been brought in for questioning, but she's adamant it was him that she saw. Everything she said before, she said again. None of it makes sense.'

Louisa tried to think quickly. She knew she couldn't talk for much longer on the telephone, or Lady Redesdale would question the bill. 'What was the cause of death?'

'They're not certain. They didn't do a toxicology report when the body arrived, but I believe that Bird has asked for one. It will take a while for the results, though – several weeks, possibly. There are no signs of strangulation, so far as they can tell. But his death was not accidental: he must have been deliberately left in there, as those crates can only be shut from the outside.'

'Do his fingerprints match the ones on the suitcase?'

'They don't know. They can't take fingerprints from him because of the decomposition.'

'There are more questions than answers, in other words.'

'Yes,' said Guy.

'Is there any sign of Janice Plum, his wife?'

Louisa could hear Guy breathing, as if he was by her ear, not hundreds of miles away.

'No. Two constables were sent to her father's house in case she showed up there. But he hasn't heard from her.'

'Four missing people, and the only body is Bernard Plum's,' said Louisa, thinking out loud.

'There's something else,' said Guy. He told her about the man who had confessed to killing the woman found on Duffield Street, and that there was no apparent connection between him and Petunia Attwood or Bernard Plum. Even more peculiarly, he said, the woman, Christine, had not been wearing a coat when he had left her.

'So someone else put Petunia's coat on her?'

'Looks like it,' said Guy.

'What if Bernard Plum's card was put in the coat to frame him?' asked Louisa.

'Great minds,' replied her husband. 'There's something else I haven't told you, but when I tell you, I want you to be careful, Louisa.'

'What?'

'Do you promise? That you won't go rushing headlong into danger?'

'Yes, I promise. What is it?'

'The packing crate was unloaded from a ship that had sailed from Bayonne.'

Louisa was silent. She was not sure she could keep her promise.

CHAPTER SEVENTY-SIX

DI Bird decided that he and PC Smiley would go to France. Even without a full forensic report on the cause of Bernard Plum's death, this was an investigation into the murder of a British citizen on foreign soil. Guy made his case to go with them: he knew Bayonne, and some of the people there, too. Not to mention that Louisa was already on the spot and he was afraid for her. In spite of his warning, he knew she would not stop trying to find – well, who exactly? Bernard had been locked in that crate some weeks ago, and they had no idea who had put him there. All they knew was that Janice Plum, Petunia Attwood and Belinda Cartwright had not yet appeared back in London, and the suitcase containing their missing clothes had been too easily found. Even with Bernard dead, Guy didn't know enough about these women. If they were capable of killing a man, who knew what else they might do to protect their secret?

Fortunately, before she left, Louisa had made arrangements for Maisie to stay with Mary and Harry, rather than leave Guy to look after her alone. Guy telephoned to let them know that it might be a few more days before he or Louisa could collect their daughter, and was relieved to hear Mary's reassurances that Maisie was perfectly content, enjoying the company of the other children, eating and sleeping well. All that remained was for him to pack a small bag and meet Bird and Smiley at Victoria station. They would take the overnight train and ferry to Paris, then on to Bayonne. Thankfully there were faster trains from Paris than from Dieppe, so it wouldn't take too long.

When they changed trains in Paris, Guy found the time to telephone the Hôtel le Pont Neuf in Bayonne. He left a message for Ivo to say that he would be arriving soon and would need his help to find three missing British women. He also telephoned the hotel Louisa was staying in to let her know he would be there soon.

Why the women would still be in Bayonne and how he hoped to find them this time, when they had evaded him and Louisa for so long, Guy couldn't say.

On the train, the three of them went over everything they knew. Bernard Plum's previous form marked him out as a nasty, dangerous man with the potential to kill. But had the three women somehow colluded to bring him to justice? And if so, why at that time and in that way?

Theories and suppositions maddened them, and they each yearned for the moment when they would arrive in Bayonne to start their search. With their pooled resources, and the help they hoped to get from the French police, Guy was more optimistic than before. So long as Louisa didn't find the women first and endanger herself . . .

CHAPTER SEVENTY-SEVEN

D ressed in unfamiliar clothes, Louisa found herself walking differently, like an actor in a costume. The hat was a touch too small on her head, so she jammed it down as much as she could, pulling the wide brim low. It was a straw hat with a pretty pale blue ribbon around it. Her skirt was straight, dark green, and made of a heavy cotton, almost military in style. Perhaps that had been the intention. The jacket had only three buttons and was the colour of a flapjack. None of it was terribly flattering, but at least it was quite distinctive to anyone trying to follow Decca. Louisa felt peculiarly British among the swarms of French and Spanish people around her. Surely, if someone was looking for her, they would find her quite quickly. It gave Louisa a funny feeling to look like a Mitford – or, rather, to look like someone that others would watch. Usually she preferred to blend into the crowd.

She wasn't entirely sure of her bearings yet, but she knew the square that Decca had mentioned, and she knew it lay due east of the shop, so she struck out in that direction. She had a pocket map of the town in her bag but felt that, since Decca had been staying there for so long, she wouldn't be looking at it. Dressed as Decca, she had better look as if she knew where she was going.

All the while, her conversation with Guy ran around her mind on repeat, like a needle stuck on a gramophone player.

The sun was beating down with full force, but a small breeze came off the sea. Louisa walked along streets that were wide and fairly empty, with only a few cars motoring past and some people walking. She avoided going down back alleys for the moment, although they were tempting for their shade, and kept heading towards the square, always looking ahead and resisting the temptation to check behind her. After ten minutes, Louisa was fairly certain that she could feel someone watching her. The question was, how could she know for certain?

The town wasn't big – it probably only took thirty minutes to walk from one end to the other – and Louisa had almost reached the square when she saw a sign for *Les Jardins Botaniques*.

The idea of a garden full of beautiful flowers of all colours and the cool shade of trees would have been temptation enough at any other time but, if she was being followed, the quiet would make it easier to hear another set of footsteps. Louisa headed through the gates.

Inside the gardens it was noticeably quieter, the few street noises hushed by the flat lawns and trees that were in full May ardour, their leaves as bright and green as they would ever be. Louisa saw a woman ahead, pushing a pram, but her path was otherwise completely clear.

It wasn't long before Louisa heard the tap of heels on the path. They were keeping time almost exactly with her own steps. She stopped, bending down to smell a bright pink flower, and gave a sly look behind her. A woman had stopped and was looking inside her handbag. She was small, with dark hair, but Louisa couldn't see her face.

Louisa continued walking, straight down the path. There was nowhere else to go and no one else in sight. The footsteps behind her started up again, faint but definitely there. One set of footsteps or two? She couldn't be sure, and she didn't want to stop and look again in case it alerted her follower. Her heart beating faster than her walking pace merited, she tried to think what to do. Should she stop and confront them? But she didn't know who the woman was, and now she was frightened.

She was cursing herself for being such an idiot – turning off into a quiet place instead of staying on the main streets – when a hand was clamped over her mouth and another grabbed her arm, pulling her abruptly off the path and behind a tree before she could scream.

CHAPTER SEVENTY-EIGHT

L ouisa was wrestled to the grass, struggling and gasping, where she lay, face up, her hands pinned down. She would have shouted, but she soon saw there was no reason to be afraid.

Her hair was longer than it had been in the photograph her mother had given Louisa, and her face more tanned, with freckles from the sun. But it was definitely her.

'Belinda Cartwright?'

Belinda looked startled. 'Who are you? How do you know my name?'

'I'm not Jessica Mitford,' said Louisa.

'No.' Belinda's hold relaxed slightly as she took this in, then tightened again. 'How did you know I was looking for her?'

'We knew someone had been following her, and I wondered if it might be you. You see, I know Donald Oliver.'

'He's not looking for me.'

'No, but your parents are. I mean to say, I'm a friend, not a foe. Let go of me, would you? I'm not going to run away. I want to talk to you.'

Belinda let go and sank down to the ground, while Louisa pushed herself up to sitting. They sat beside each other, dishevelled, catching their breath.

'Why were you following Miss Mitford?'

Belinda closed her eyes briefly. 'I've been trying to talk to her alone, without Esmond Romilly there. I don't know why I grabbed her – you – like that. I panicked. Who are you?'

It wasn't comfortable sitting on the ground. Louisa also felt the need to take control of the situation. She stood and offered Belinda her hand. 'Let's go and talk this through properly.'

On a bench in the shade, the two women sat. Louisa realised that Belinda would have no idea that she knew about Bernard Plum. The body had not been identified when it was discovered, and had lain in the morgue for weeks. She needed to draw a confession from her, to find out if her – and Guy's – suspicions were right.

'My name is Louisa Cannon. I'm a private detective, and I was hired to find Miss Mitford, and then to find a Miss Petunia Attwood. I believe you know her too, don't you?'

Belinda's averted eyes told Louisa all she needed to know. 'Yes. I may as well tell you that I have heard of you.'

'And you know that I have been trying to find you?'

Belinda nodded.

'Do you know Janice Plum?'

'Yes, I do.'

'Is she all right? Do you know where she is?'

'Yes, she's fine – better than she's ever been, I think.' Belinda smiled, unable to keep the secret any longer. 'She's here.'

'Here? In Bayonne?'

'Yes. Miss Cannon, she feels badly for what you've been put through, and she wants to explain. We all do.'

'All?' At some point, Louisa would have to stop asking so many questions, but her head was full of them.

'Petunia Attwood is here too.'

'I see.' Louisa tried to take this in. 'You know her sister is in considerable distress, not knowing where she is? As are your parents.'

'I know. We all know, but there was no other way. We will explain. There's a lot to tell you, although I'm not sure where to begin.'

'Why did you want to talk to Miss Mitford?'

'We need her help.'

Louisa was taken aback. 'Why would Miss Mitford help you? I'm not saying that she wouldn't, but—'

'We believe we saved Mr Romilly's life.'

CHAPTER SEVENTY-NINE

B elinda dropped Louisa off at a bar that was cool and dark, with only two or three local men sitting inside, nursing glasses of pastis. She promised to return within the hour with the others. When Belinda had gone, Louisa borrowed the telephone at the bar and rang the hotel. She left a message for Decca, asking her to come as soon as possible.

Half an hour later, Decca arrived. She rushed over to the table as soon as she spotted Louisa. 'What's going on? Are you all right?'

'I'm fine.' Louisa explained what had happened. 'Miss Cartwright has gone to fetch the others. She knows you'll be here. I thought you should be with me to hear their story. They believe they saved Esmond's life.'

'What? My Es? When? How?'

'I don't know. There's a lot they need to tell us.'

'I'll say.' Decca laughed suddenly. 'I can't believe I spent all those weeks in the middle of a war zone, and our greatest danger was in a sleepy French coastal town.'

'Hopefully not any more.'

'I'll have to rely on you for that,' said Decca. She ordered them drinks and they sat waiting, unable to think what to say in the meantime.

Fortunately, they didn't have to wait too long. Louisa kept her eyes fixed on the door but, when Janice arrived, Louisa barely recognised her as the lonely housewife she had seen only weeks before. She wore a pretty rose-coloured cotton dress with espadrilles, and her hair had been cut short and was blonder from the sun, her skin lightly tanned. A quiet air of confidence had settled about her. Not that she skipped into the bar; there was a hesitation in all three of them as they came in and looked for Louisa.

Janice was followed by the woman Louisa knew must be Petunia Attwood. She was older than the others. There was a heaviness about her manner, and her skin was sallow, perhaps only to be expected given her illness and the trials she had been through. But her eyes were blue and steady, and she wore a summer dress that looked new. Belinda, the last to pull up a chair, was hard to forget once seen, with dark hair and eyes that she could have passed off as Mediterranean heritage.

The five of them regarded each other seriously and somewhat nervously. Louisa decided to talk first.

'I've brought Miss Mitford with me, as Belinda mentioned something that I thought she ought to hear.'

The three women exchanged glances. Belinda spoke, and Louisa could see immediately that she was the unofficial leader of the trio.

'We want to tell you what we did – we want you to understand. There was no other option, no other way.'

'We will listen,' said Louisa. 'But you need to know that Bernard Plum's body has been found and identified.'

The three women's faces paled. 'How?'

'My husband and the police were looking for him. They took an educated guess that you were alive, that the suitcase of clothes and identification found in his house was a red herring.'

'But how?' Janice's cool demeanour had vanished.

'Because the case was too easy to find. It looked too much like evidence someone wanted the police to discover. And then there was the woman's body – obviously, it wasn't Petunia Attwood. We knew that already, learned that a while ago, but the man who killed that poor woman turned up. He said he knew nothing about a Bernard Plum. The evidence had been planted on her. Tell me, how did that happen?'

'It was me,' said Petunia quietly. 'I had to vanish. The street where she was killed wasn't far from where I lived. I knew what went on there because I helped those women sometimes, in small ways. Gave them a bit of money so they wouldn't have to work for a night, or I'd take them to a café for a decent meal.'

'Why did you do it?' asked Decca.

'I don't – or I didn't – have much in my life. It was something useful I could do. I had a good job and a flat I paid for, but I was often lonely. I knew what it felt like to be an outsider, to be treated as if my loneliness was a disease that people might catch. When I got my diagnosis, that is—'

'I know about that,' Louisa said gently.

'You do?'

'Yes – your doctor told us, me and your sister. It was how we knew the body wasn't you.'

Petunia nodded slowly. 'Poor Julia. I never wanted her to

know. I was so ashamed. But it also helped me focus. I wanted to do good, to make changes in the time I had left.'

'To do good?' asked Louisa.

'All right, yes. I wanted to get revenge. I had nothing to lose. I saw that poor woman and I knew all I had to do was put my coat on her and it would get me out of my life, and frame Bernard. It was wrong, I know that. But it seemed like the answer to everything in that moment. It was so easy to do, I thought it must be right.'

Belinda leaned forward. 'How do you know about Bernard?'

'We knew about his scar,' said Louisa. 'Because I asked Janice for his details when I first came to see her.'

'It ran from his collarbone to his left shoulder,' said Janice. 'He got it in a fight, a long time ago. I didn't know what would happen when I spoke to you – you can see that, can't you? At that point, we had no intention of—' She broke off, unable to say it out loud.

'The body was found in the packing crate, but it had no identification, obviously,' said Louisa. 'It lay in the morgue for some time. But when Guy – my husband – rang around all the morgues to see if they had an unidentified body that fitted Plum's description, one woman told him that her morgue had a body with the scar he'd mentioned. Once Guy realised the ship Plum was found on had set sail from Bayonne . . .'

'Do you mean they're looking for us? The police?' Janice's frailty had returned. Louisa could see her trembling, though the air around them was warm and sultry.

'I don't know,' said Louisa. 'But Guy has warned me not to talk to you if I find you. He's afraid.'

'You're not in any danger from us,' said Belinda.

'Aren't I?' asked Louisa. 'I know what you did. What's to stop me from turning you in to the police?'

'Because you're a woman.' This was Janice. 'You're our friend. We had to do what we did. He would have gone on and on, hurting more people.'

'And because Miss Mitford owes us. Please, you have to help us,' said Petunia.

'I think,' said Louisa, 'that you're going to have to explain. But we don't have long.'

'Why not?'

'If I know my husband, he's on his way here. And he won't be alone.'

CHAPTER EIGHTY

I vo was at the Hôtel le Pont Neuf to greet Guy, Bird and Smiley. DI Bird was sweating uncomfortably in the Mediterranean heat in his full English suit. PC Smiley looked no less awkward in her uniform with its heavy wool skirt and jacket, as out of place on the Continental seafront as a penguin in the Sahara. Their journey had been long and intense, and now they were here, Guy wasn't sure how they would get started. The omens weren't good when Ivo told them there was no room at the inn; the Hôtel le Pont Neuf was fully booked. It hadn't even occurred to Guy that it might be.

'We had better find Louisa, then,' he said, taking charge. 'We'll walk across to her hotel – it's not far from there.'

'Can we leave our bags behind?' implored Smiley. 'I don't think I can carry mine in this heat.'

They made the arrangements and stepped out into the street. Guy was struck anew by the sight of refugees all over the town. They looked even more desperate than before. There was the occasional recovering soldier in sight too – men who looked as

359

if they were far from home and had little idea as to how they would leave this town.

As they walked, Guy explained the situation to Ivo. 'We believe that whoever killed Bernard Plum may still be here. It's a long shot, but it's one we have to investigate.'

Ivo had been listening carefully. 'So there are three women you are looking for now?'

'Maybe.'

'They're all English?'

'Yes, though one of them, Belinda Cartwright, has spent quite a lot of time out here, working as a nurse in the war. She might speak Spanish or French, I suppose.'

'OK,' said Ivo. 'I think I know where to ask. It's a small town, and three Englishwomen together will stand out like thumbs.'

'I need to find Louisa first. She's staying in the Hôtel des Basques – let's walk down there.'

'I'll meet you there in an hour,' said Ivo. 'There's someone I want to ask questions of first.'

With a nod goodbye, the four of them parted.

CHAPTER EIGHTY-ONE

'I'm not promising anything,' said Louisa, 'but I do want to listen. I'll try to do so without judgement.'

Decca nodded in agreement. She had been hastily fetched after a telephone call to the hotel.

Petunia began. 'He came to work at Lee Worth a few years ago,' she began, with no need to say who 'he' was. 'He always charmed everyone – even me, for a bit. Even though he was only a claims clerk, he managed to get his own office, and he was friendly with the most senior men there, which was unusual for a man in his position. But I found out that when he had been claiming to be off sick last summer, he had in fact gone to Spain. On top of which, he had taken money off some of our oldest customers – perhaps to fund the trip. I knew if I reported him I'd have to have evidence, and I didn't.'

'Why not?' asked Louisa.

'I'd overheard him talking on the telephone. It would have been my word against his. Instead, I challenged him, and his reaction was very ... He frightened me.' She explained that her fear made her even more determined to do something. 'I knew he'd gone to the marches in Cable Street, on the fascist side, and that outraged me. People think women like me, secretaries, see nothing and hear nothing, but they're wrong.'

'I know,' said Decca. Her voice was warm and sympathetic, and Louisa could see the women relax a little.

'I thought if I went to his home I'd find out more. I knew he was married, but we'd never seen his wife. I knew – sorry, Janice.'

'It's all right.'

'I knew he was unfaithful to her, because of the gossip in the office. So I went to see her.'

'That's when my life was changed forever,' said Janice. 'And I'll always be grateful for that, no matter what happens next.'

Behind the bar stood a bored-looking waiter, polishing glasses and staring out of the door, where a scruffy dog lay, flicking its tail at flies. In spite of the stillness around her, Louisa's heart was beating fast, as if she had been running for miles and finally stopped to catch her breath. After all this time, there was clarity, a pattern visible in the kaleidoscope.

'Over the next several weeks, Janice and I became friends. When I knew he wasn't there, I would go and see her,' Petunia continued. 'I saw that she was being very badly treated by him. He beat her, but that wasn't the worst of it. He prevented her from leaving the house except to go to the shops to buy food, he was jealous of her talking to anyone else, he would become inflamed with anger if any object was out of place in the house or his clothes weren't folded the way he wanted—'

She had started to tremble with remembered fury. Janice interrupted.

'I can say it. Louisa, when she found me, I don't think I even knew who I was any more. There was no one I could turn to for help, or to tell me that this wasn't normal. He had forced me to cut off my family a long time ago, to the extent that it was easier for me to tell people they were dead. Over the months, when Petunia came to see me, we just talked. Just having someone to turn to helped me enormously – helped me to survive. And then we met Belinda.'

Belinda had met Bernard Plum in Spain when he was admitted to her hospital with a knife wound.

'I'm afraid he got on the right side of me very quickly. I was soon supplying him with morphine that I stole from the medicine cupboard. I'd been away from home for a while, and I suppose I was a little lonely, even among comrades.' Belinda looked apologetically at Janice. 'I'm so sorry.'

'I've told you, there's no need to apologise. I know who he was.' Janice folded her hands in her lap. 'Please, we need to tell her everything.'

'Yes.' Belinda held Louisa's gaze again. 'I suspected his injury – the one with which he was admitted to the hospital – was self-inflicted. I won't bore you with the details but after a while, even as a fairly untrained nurse, you get used to seeing terrible wounds and you quickly learn how they are caused and how to dress them. His was too neat. And his stories, though they were full of bravado – they just didn't ring true. But I didn't want to question him. I had already fallen for him. I'm embarrassed to admit it.' She gave Janice another sorrowful glance. 'Then he told me that he was trying to find a man called Esmond Romilly. The name meant nothing to me. But Bernard explained that he was a traitor to the cause and deserved to die. I assumed he meant to the Republican cause. It was only later that I discovered the truth.'

'Hang on, let me get this right,' said Louisa. 'He *pretended* to fight for the Republican side?'

'Yes,' said Belinda. 'He got himself admitted to the hospital and then, I believe, he was using me to help him find Mr Romilly. He didn't explain to me exactly how Mr Romilly was a traitor; I just took his word for it. All he told me was that they had come across each other when fighting for the International Brigades at the end of last year.'

'They'd met?' asked Louisa, incredulous.

'Not exactly. They would have been on opposite sides in battle, I know now. But people knew that Mr Romilly was Churchill's nephew. I think that might have been what set him off. When Bernard talked about him, he became so angry. I was afraid he meant to kill him. But you have to understand: death was all around us at that point. Lives don't become cheap, but when you have seen what the other side is capable of, you swear you will do anything you can to exact revenge. People talked a lot about how the Great War damaged soldiers, but in Spain the war is killing ordinary men and women, destroying their families and their livelihoods. It's impossible to escape unscathed or changed in some fundamental way. War makes you capable of committing acts you would never have so much as imagined before.'

Louisa could see that this speech had drained Belinda. She hadn't felt those feelings personally, but she had met enough men who had been broken by their experiences on the frontline to know that she spoke the truth.

One morning, Belinda went on, she came into the hospital to discover that Bernard had gone. Distraught, she quit her position and began the journey to Bayonne to see if he might be there, even though she knew how hard it would be and how long it would take. 'That's when I met you.' She looked at Decca. 'It wasn't quite by chance. Everywhere I went, where there were English volunteers and journalists, I asked around. I thought if Esmond was there, Bernard would be close by.'

Decca paled. 'Were you planning—'

'Yes,' Belinda interrupted her. 'I would never have harmed Esmond, but I would have told Bernard where he was. I thought it would make him love me. But when I met you and talked to you, I realised that you were both committed Communists, in spite of your posh backgrounds. I could tell that it was real.'

'Did you realise the truth about Bernard then?'

'I don't know. I felt confused more than anything. I didn't know where he was, so I couldn't confront him about it. I wrote to Donald—'

'Donald Oliver?' Louisa was startled, though she realised she should have joined those dots. 'So he knew where you were?'

'Not exactly, but I told him what had happened. He wrote and confirmed that Mr Romilly and Miss Mitford were to be trusted. And he told me that Mr Romilly thought he was being followed and was afraid.'

'So Donald knew where you were?'

'Yes. He feels bad about lying to you. He tried to help you as much as he could, but he thought you were part of the Establishment. He was protecting Esmond. All kinds of weird people were trying to get to him. You might have been one of them.'

A thought struck Louisa. 'Was he the one giving stories to the papers?'

'Yes. There was one reporter, Tony Little.'

'I remember him,' said Louisa.

'Donald earned some money selling titbits to him, then Tony got a taste for it. All sorts of people were coming out of the woodwork. And it was useful to us. We needed people to believe that we were missing, probably dead, probably killed by Bernard. And we needed people to believe that he was alive.'

'That's why the suitcase was under the bed, with your clothes and things in it.'

'Yes – we had to hold on to our passports but we were able to leave those things behind. I was hoping my sister could have my gold necklace.'

'What about when Plum went back to the office and took the files?'

'He didn't. Miss Piper agreed to lie for us. She's the only one who knows. She'll never tell anyone.'

Louisa took it all in. 'It's all very clever. But why did you do it? If you have ...' – she whispered, conscious of the men in the bar – 'killed a man, that's ... you know what that is. Why did you do it?'

'Petunia and I did it together. With a drug used for anaesthesia that I had taken from the hospital. I arranged to meet him at the docks. We knew where the crates were held, and I pretended that I would go in one with him to ...' Belinda said this, but not easily. Louisa felt afraid, even though the danger had long passed.

'When he got in one, I gave him an injection and he passed out, which meant I could empty his pockets. Then we nailed the crate shut.'

'Did anyone see you do it?'

'No. We'd paid one of the dockers to give us access. I expect he assumed we were smuggling something.'

'When Belinda came to my door, looking for him, not expecting to find me there,' said Janice, 'he was there. We had a terrible row. He beat me then, worse than he ever had before. And Belinda heard it.'

'I was on the pavement outside,' Belinda whispered.

Louisa knew that their plan had been forged in the heat of their united terror; she knew they felt they had no choice. She knew the police did little, or nothing, when called to a fight between a man and his wife. Even so, it was hard to condone what they had done.

CHAPTER EIGHTY-TWO

'What happens next?' asked Decca.

Louisa was grateful she had asked the question. What *were* these three women to do? They had killed a man and left behind their families and work. She couldn't see how they could return to England. If they did, was there any possibility that they could persuade a judge that they felt they had no choice but to murder Bernard Plum, to protect themselves and others from the harm that he could do?

Louisa knew the answer to that, and so did they.

'We're going to go to America,' said Belinda. The three of them exchanged a look of hope. 'We'll start again. It's a chance for us all to have new lives, somewhere no one knows us.'

'But how? Your names are known by the police. If they're spotted on any passenger lists, which they might easily be, there will be an extradition notice served on you. You'll be on the run, looking over your shoulder for the rest of your lives.'

'We're going to have new identities,' said Janice. 'That's why we're still here. We had to wait for the forger to do the work we needed. New passports, new birth certificates, new driving licences.'

'That's why I had to find Decca, to explain to her what had happened,' said Belinda, turning to Decca. 'Do you understand now that we saved Esmond's life?'

Decca nodded slowly. 'Yes, I think I do.' She looked wary, as well she might. Was she going to have to pay for this unexpected favour that had been granted her?

'We need money to pay the forger. We don't have much. We've spent all that we had surviving for the last few weeks, and we've had to put some aside for our fares.'

'But I don't have a penny,' exclaimed Decca. 'Esmond and I are surviving on peanuts ourselves. I'm terribly grateful to you, if that's the right word. I mean, of course I want Esmond alive. But I can't pay you for it. I didn't contract you to do this awful deed.' She was visibly shaken. 'I don't know what to do. I simply can't give you money.'

There was silence for a few moments.

'I thought your father was a lord,' said Petunia.

'Yes, he is, but that doesn't mean we have a lot of money. I mean, we do have more than most, of course we do. But he's not talking to me, and he wouldn't give me anything. My mother is here but she's awfully frugal. I couldn't ask her for cash. I've been telling her that I don't want it, in any case. Es and I are trying to be independent. It would be impossible to explain what I needed the money for.'

'How much do you need?' asked Louisa.

'Eighty pounds,' said Janice. 'And we need it now. We're meeting him this afternoon.'

'How will you get to America?' asked Decca.

'Cargo boats go from here to Southampton daily. We can get passage on one of those quite easily, and then take the *Queen Mary* to New York. She's setting sail in a few days.'

'Miss Mitford, would you come with me for a moment?' Louisa stood and beckoned to Decca. 'We'll be back shortly,' she said to the three women.

She and Decca stepped outside. Heat rose from the pavement and there was a strong smell of frying garlic and onions coming from someone's kitchen window. Both reminded Louisa that she was far from home. Decca stood beside her, looking rather lost. Louisa couldn't blame her: a lot of startling confessions had been made, and Decca probably hadn't the faintest idea what to do with all this new and troubling information. First, they needed to let it sink in.

'Let's sit out here for a bit,' said Louisa. 'They've told us everything, they won't go anywhere. They can't, without our help.' She spotted a couple of upturned orange crates on the pavement and picked them up. 'We'll use these.'

They sat, side by side, in the shade of the building. People walked past, hurrying along in their daily lives, baguettes poking out of shopping bags, groomed dogs on the end of long leashes. After a few minutes, Louisa had decided what she needed to say.

'Miss Mitford, I know this is difficult, but I think we have to find that money for them.'

'How can I—'

'Hear me out,' said Louisa quickly. 'I have money saved, but not enough. I can put in half of what they say they need. Can you ask your mother for the other half?'

'Es wouldn't like it.'

'Es wouldn't be alive to have an opinion one way or another if it wasn't for them.'

'I know,' said Decca miserably. 'But it makes me very uneasy. They have . . . I can't bring myself to say the word. But they've done *that* to a man. They didn't do it just for Es, did they?'

'No,' agreed Louisa. 'I think they were desperate. It wasn't done in cold blood; they were terrified. We can see that they thought they had no choice. It happened, and now they can't go back to England. You and I know that they would never be heard sympathetically in the courts.'

Decca started to reply, but Louisa didn't hear what she said. She had seen Guy, DI Bird and PC Smiley walking along the road. In a few seconds, if she didn't move, they would see her, too.

CHAPTER EIGHTY-THREE

'Quick,' said Louisa. 'Go into the bar, warn them to stay in there. I'll go and meet Guy now and see you at the hotel in half an hour.'

Decca dived into the bar and Louisa started to walk down the road, still across the street from Guy but knowing that he would see her. She pretended not to see him until he called out and rushed over. 'Louisa,' he said with relief. 'I've been wondering where you are.'

'I didn't realise you'd get here so soon.'

'We were lucky with the trains and made fast connections.' PC Smiley and DI Bird had crossed the road and greeted Louisa.

Bird caught sight of the bar that Louisa and the women had been in. 'Can we go for a quick drink in there? I could do with it.' It was true: his face was quite an unnatural red.

'No,' said Louisa, avoiding her husband's eyes, for fear he'd see that she had something to hide. 'I'd really rather we went back to the hotel. I ought to look for Miss Mitford. I'd only come out on a quick errand, you see. Where are you all staying?'

'We haven't booked anywhere yet. We've left our bags at the Hôtel le Pont Neuf but they have no room there.'

'Then we can ask if you can get rooms. And you can get drinks in the bar there – it's not far.' Before they could reply, Louisa started walking away fast, forcing them to catch up with her.

At the hotel, she had another shock. Standing in the lobby, checking in, was Donald Oliver.

'What are you doing here?' exclaimed Louisa.

'It's a real pleasure to see you too.' Donald smiled.

'I'm sorry, it's just – I wasn't expecting to see you.'

'Esmond asked me over for the wedding. I couldn't resist taking the opportunity. So many of our Communist compatriots are here too, and it seemed like a good chance to come and meet them. Always willing to help the cause, as you know.'

Guy stepped forward. 'Good to see you, Mr Oliver. Let me introduce DI Bird, PC Smiley.'

Everyone shook hands.

'And what is the British constabulary doing out here? An exercise in foreign relations?' Donald joshed, but Louisa was sure she could detect an undertone of nervousness.

'We're looking for—' Guy began.

Louisa cut him off. 'Really, this isn't the place to discuss it, and Mr Oliver hasn't so much as unpacked his bags. Guy, why don't you take DI Bird and PC Smiley through to the bar for a drink? I'm sure they must want one. I'll ask about rooms here. I'll see you in a few minutes.' Smiling, aware that Guy was bemused by her behaviour, she waved them off. At last they walked out of the hotel foyer to the bar.

'What's going on?' asked Donald.

373

'I'd like to ask you that,' said Louisa. 'What's all this about you selling stories to the newspapers about my investigations?'

'Not *selling*, my dear . . .' He stopped. 'How did you find out?'

She checked over her shoulder. 'I've just been in a bar with all three women. Belinda told me you knew where she was when I was looking for her. How could you do that?' she whispered.

'I'm sorry, but I had to protect Esmond. He asked it of me. He gave me the stories, told me what he wanted the press to print. It's us against the Establishment, that's how it is.'

'I'm not the Establishment.'

Donald gave a rueful smile. 'When you're employed by the Mitfords, you are.'

'How did you know that Janice Plum was missing?'

'I was in touch with Belinda's parents, and the police had told them. Tell me, how is she? Belinda?'

'She's fine but it's a complicated situation, as you can imagine. They're leaving for America as soon as they can.'

'I see. I take it the bobbies that came through here with your husband don't realise they are here.'

'No. They suspect that Janice is here, but they don't know I *know*. They're not even completely sure whether Belinda and Petunia are alive.'

'And you, Louisa. Are you against the Establishment?'

She thought about this. There was a long answer to this, she knew. One that took in her own childhood, torn between her poor, hard-working parents and her criminal uncle, her complex feelings around her work as a servant for the Mitfords, the case she had been involved in only a few years ago that had cost her her faith in the British government. 'Not in the same way as you, I don't think. But I am *for* protecting people who cannot protect themselves. That's what this is about for me.'

'Then I will help you,' said Donald. 'Tell me what you need.'

CHAPTER EIGHTY-FOUR

G uy knew his wife. There was something she wasn't telling him. Hurrying him, Bird, Smiley and Ivo out of the foyer so she could talk to Donald – what was she talking to him about? He trusted her, and knew that, whatever she was doing, she was doing it because she felt it was right. But what if they disagreed on what 'right' was?

In the bar, Guy settled the other three at a table and said he would find someone to get them a drink. He wanted to use the opportunity to edge around the corner and try to hear the conversation between Donald and Louisa. But when he got there, Donald had gone and Louisa was talking to the receptionist about available rooms in the hotel.

He felt ashamed. He'd got it wrong.

Louisa turned to him. 'Oh, there you are. There are two single rooms – shall we book them for DI Bird and PC Smiley? You'll be with me, of course. A porter will fetch the bags from Hôtel le Pont Neuf for you.'

'Thank you,' said Guy. 'Where did Mr Oliver go?'

'To his room, I think. Did you get everyone a drink?'

'I said I'd find a waiter, but I haven't yet.'

'I'll do that for you, but then I'm afraid I need to go and find Miss Mitford. There are all sorts of wedding preparations going on. I'm sorry.'

Guy thanked her again and returned to the bar, unable to shake the feeling that she was keeping something from him. Why wasn't she more curious about what the police were doing there with him? He couldn't believe that helping with the final details of Decca's wedding was more important to her than catching Janice Plum, and possibly Belinda Cartwright and Petunia Attwood. If his hunch was right, this could be one of the most significant arrests of his career.

Ten minutes later, having had a refreshing drink of lemonade, Guy suggested that Bird and Smiley go to their rooms to unpack. They would meet in an hour. In the meantime, though he didn't tell them this, he and Ivo would get to work.

CHAPTER EIGHTY-FIVE

H aving sent Donald to find Esmond, Louisa dashed to her room to fetch her traveller's cheques and cashed forty pounds at the front desk. It was all she had, written only for emergency use.

Well, what was this if not an emergency?

She ran out onto the road, hoping to catch Decca before she realised that the half hour was up: Decca must be back in her room. Just as Louisa turned to go back in, she caught sight of Guy on the other side of the street, talking to a young, dark-haired man. A Spaniard, by the looks of it. Who could that be? But she had no time to stop.

Back in the hotel, Louisa knocked on Decca's door. Decca opened it and pulled her inside. The room was small and untidy, with clothes thrown over various chairs and a sofa. The bed was unmade. A desk was covered with papers. A large radio sat to one side – presumably the one Esmond listened to for his news reports to Reuters. On the bed, side by side, sat Donald and Esmond, both leaning forward, elbows on knees. They stood when Louisa came into the room.

'I've been explaining everything to them,' said Decca.

Esmond put his hand out and shook Louisa's awkwardly. 'I feel rather ashamed,' he said. 'I want to say sorry.'

'What for?'

'For not trusting you, I suppose. But you see, a man in my position has to be careful—'

'I accept your apology,' said Louisa. She didn't have the patience for his youthful angst. 'But we need to get on.' She turned to Decca. 'How did you leave it with them?'

'I explained that the police were here, which frightened them terribly. They said they would get the next ship out. But they have to meet the forger with their papers, so they need the money.'

'Do you know when the ship is, or where it's leaving from?'

'Yes – five o'clock, from quay number six.'

'That's just over an hour. Have you asked your mother for the money?'

'What?' said Esmond. 'What money?'

Louisa explained.

'I'll have to tell Muv it's for us,' said Decca.

'No. I won't have her thinking I'm taking a penny from her or your father for our marriage.'

Donald laid his hand on Esmond's arm. 'I think, old chap, you're going to have to set aside your pride for this. After all, these women—'

'Yes, yes. I know. I didn't ask them to do it. But all right. It's what has to be done.'

'Thank you,' said Louisa. 'Lady Redesdale will have to cash traveller's cheques if she doesn't have the cash to hand. You could say you need it so quickly for a down payment for your hotel room? Or to surprise Esmond with a honeymoon trip?'

Decca's shoulders slumped. 'Yes, I'll do it. I'll meet you at the quay before five.'

'I'd like Mr Romilly and Mr Oliver to accompany you there,' said Louisa. She turned to them. 'There's a way for you both to make amends.'

CHAPTER EIGHTY-SIX

At a quarter to five, the air was heavy with heat and a head-ache had started to form at the base of Louisa's skull. It felt as if a storm was coming. As she walked towards the docks, she could feel the cool breeze coming in off the sea. She was trembling, afraid for what she was about to do, yet certain that it was the right thing. She only wished that it didn't mean keeping a secret from Guy. After what had happened on the ship with Unity a few years ago, she had sworn never to keep anything from him again. And yet, here she was . . .

As she walked, Louisa observed the people around her, looking out all the time for potential danger. Of course, there was none. People were going about their daily lives in the usual ways: carrying their shopping home; sitting at tables at pavement cafés, drinking aperitifs; chatting to friends; walking wearily home from work, a briefcase knocking against their leg. She felt conscious of her foreignness: the fact that the cooking smells, with their garlic and herbs, were unfamiliar; the chatter was incomprehensible to her. Yet she needed to navigate her way through the next hour with confidence and serenity. Could she do it?

As Louisa rounded the corner towards the docks, she started to breathe a little more easily. Nearly there. She looked for dock number six. The quays were mostly thrown into shade by the enormous cargo ships docked alongside, and everywhere were stacked giant towers of packing crates. Dockers were moving nimbly around, their tanned, tattooed forearms sweating as they lifted boxes, moved chains and yelled to each other. A barked instruction often elicited a quick riposte, with both parties laughing and shouting some more. Louisa hadn't realised there would be so many people about, but perhaps that was a good thing. There might be enough distraction for nobody else to notice the women. The noise explained why Bernard Plum's shouts, if there had been any, had gone unheard.

Almost by chance, it seemed, she saw a sign for Dock 6. She followed the direction of the arrow, picking up the pace, keeping her hand in her pocket, wrapped around the cash. As she turned a corner, around more packing crates, another stretch of the quayside opened up before her and a hundred yards away she spotted Belinda, Janice and Petunia, small cases on the ground beside them. None of them were talking, and even from that distance Louisa could see that each looked afraid. But that wasn't what took her breath away. There was a man there. A man whose figure she recognised even from behind: Guy.

Louisa started to run towards them, but before she could reach them she saw Decca, Esmond and Donald arrive from the other side.

Decca saw Louisa first and came towards her. Guy turned and saw Louisa too, but he didn't move. He stood and watched her run to Decca.

'I've got the money,' said Decca, handing it to Louisa. 'Why is Guy here?'

'I don't know.' Louisa was panicking. Guy had caught her deceiving him. She ran the last short distance to him. He had turned away from her. This time, of course, deliberately.

'Guy,' she called, feeling her voice break. 'Guy, please.' She reached him and touched him on the arm.

'Why didn't you tell me?' He didn't need to tell her that he felt betrayed: she could see it, she could feel it.

'I had to—' She stopped. 'Wait.'

Silently, she handed the money to Belinda. The three women stepped back slightly. She saw them say something to each other, but she couldn't watch or listen.

'Are you here to arrest them?'

'Yes.'

'How did you know they were here?'

'I had a man here. He had heard about English women looking for someone to forge papers, passports. There had been rumours of a man getting trapped in a cargo ship – the dockers had been talking.'

'You did good work,' said Louisa. Her heart banged in her chest like a tin drum rolling down a hill.

'No. I didn't. Not when I should have been able to ask my own wife where the women were. How could you keep that from me?'

'I had to, Guy. I've heard their story—'

'A story that convinced you they deserve to escape arrest for murder?'

'No! That is … yes, in a way. It wasn't murder; it was self-defence.'

'However you frame it, he was intentionally killed, Louisa. Most likely drugged.'

'Yes, yes, I know. But he was a horrible man, Guy. You know that as well as I do. Starting with what he did to that young girl.'

Decca bravely came towards them. 'I don't want to interfere—'

'Then don't,' snapped Guy.

'Louisa has done the right thing, Mr Sullivan. If they hadn't killed him, he would have gone on to kill someone himself.'

'An eye for an eye?'

'No,' pleaded Decca. 'It was more than that. He was a bully, he beat his wife, he lied and betrayed her. He stole at work, he was a fraud.'

'Then he should have been given up to the police. Justice would have prevailed.'

'No,' said Louisa. 'It wouldn't have. Women don't win cases like that. You know it's true, Guy.'

'It's too late, anyway. DI Bird and PC Smiley are on their way. I sent Ivo to fetch them.'

Louisa looked to her left. The women were standing there, hardly knowing what to do. She went over to them. 'Is your ship here? Do you know where to get on?'

'Yes,' said Belinda, her face white beneath her tan, 'but what about … he said there's a policeman coming. A British one.'

'That means they know what we did. We've got no way out,' said Janice.

'Where is the man you were meeting? With the papers?'

'Just down there,' said Belinda. 'I hope. The ship leaves in ten minutes. We were supposed to meet him fifteen minutes ago. I don't know if he's waited for us.'

'Just go.'

'Won't your husband come after us?'

'I'll make sure that he doesn't. *Go!*'

Belinda ran.

As she went, Louisa saw a young, dark-haired man arrive and walk towards Guy. He looked confused to see so many people standing there. She heard him say that the police were coming.

There was no time to lose. Louisa returned to her husband. 'Guy. Please. You know I'm on the side of right. I wouldn't have done this if I didn't have to. We have to let the women go.'

She saw him soften, slightly.

'But they're on their way.'

Louisa knew what to do. She went over to Donald and Esmond. 'I need you to stop the police from coming here. Whatever you need to do. Do it.'

'But which direction are they coming from?' Donald had gauged the situation, and he was right: there were two possible avenues.

Guy came up to them. 'Ivo will show you. But that's all he can do.'

'Thank you, Guy.'

He shook his head. 'Don't. I don't know how we'll explain it, but we'll worry about that later.'

Ivo ran off, Donald and Esmond behind him. They had only just gone out of view when Louisa heard shouts, English voices rising in anger.

Belinda returned, carrying the papers she needed. The ship's horn sounded, and she jumped. Moving fast, Janice and

Petunia picked up the bags. Belinda waved them over and the three of them started to run. Decca, Louisa and Guy were just behind him.

'It's leaving now!' shouted Janice. Louisa saw that tears were pouring down her face. On the other side of a stack of crates, they saw a narrow gangplank leading onto the ship. A sailor stood on the quayside, untying a rope.

'Wait!' shouted Decca, catching up with him. She talked to him in fast French. Louisa saw him hesitating, pausing long enough for the women to reach the gangplank. All three of them ran on, across to the ship. It wasn't far, yet it was enough to take them to a new life, a place where the horrors of the past might never be forgotten, but at least they would fade into no more than the occasional bad dream.

The sailor gathered the rope and went onto the ship, drawing the gangplank up behind him. Guy put his arm around Louisa's shoulders.

'I did the right thing,' she said.

'I know.'

It was all she needed to hear.

CHAPTER EIGHTY-SEVEN

A day or so later, Louisa sat beside Guy in the British consul at Bayonne on an uncomfortable wooden chair. Donald was on Guy's other side. Beside them were Lady Redesdale and Mrs Romilly, the latter fanning herself in an exaggerated manner with her hand. Above, a wooden fan whirred, dispensing no cool, merely moving the warm air around. The room was dark in spite of the bright sunshine outside, the windows high and small, the oak panelling and gloomy oil portraits better suited to a country house in Wales than this sunny corner of France.

Before them, side by side, stood Decca in a pale pink cotton dress and Esmond in a cream linen suit. Their backs were turned to their small audience as they faced the British consul, a man with a round stomach and a thin moustache. He wore not a priest's cassock but a suit, a gold tie pin glinting in the ray of sunshine that fell across him. He spoke briefly, Decca and Esmond replied, and within minutes they were husband and wife.

'Thank God that's over,' Esmond's mother said loudly. Lady Redesdale's face pinched in response to this, but she stretched out her arms to embrace her daughter and congratulate her. Esmond stood a little back, allowing the party to move out of the room.

'Congratulations, Mrs Romilly,' whispered Louisa to Decca. The bride smiled. She looked exceptionally pretty today, full of happiness and hope.

'Thank you. I know it's only a piece of paper, but it does feel a bit different, doesn't it?'

'It does,' agreed Louisa. She knew it was true: though she had committed herself to Guy long before their wedding, on the first night of their marriage, she had lain in bed with him and felt as if a glass bubble had been drawn over them both, a protective cover that would be with them always.

Afterwards there was a small, but gay, lunch for the newly-weds, and Decca unwrapped a few presents. A set of hairbrushes from her mother with *J. L. R.* on the back, a portable gramophone player from Deborah, a pearl and amethyst necklace with matching earrings from Diana – Decca put them on immediately; their richness was quite at odds with her simple frock – and some books. She was already wearing a ruby and diamond ring on her wedding finger, which she kept sneaking looks at, smiling each time.

When the last of the champagne had been drunk, Mr and Mrs Romilly caught a train to Paris, where they planned to enjoy the nightclubs, they said, and see some friends. Their married life had begun, and they would be a family soon.

Louisa and Guy stood on the platform to wave them off and looked ahead to the train track, heat shimmering above the dark metal. It stretched ahead, its lines laid across Europe, through fields of sunflowers and towns they did not know the names of.

The train would take the bride and groom ever further from those they had always known. Overhead, the sky was blue and cloudless but for a single aeroplane, flying low, a white trail fading in its wake.

POSTSCRIPT

On 20th December 1937, Decca and Esmond's baby was born: a girl, Julia Decca Romilly. At the time, they were living in Rotherhithe, in the East End of London. When Julia was four months old, a measles epidemic broke out in the area. Decca was concerned, but when a nurse at a local clinic told her that a breast-fed baby would be immune, she took her baby home, only for both of them to be struck down by the virus a few days later. Desperate, Esmond hired two nurses to look after them around the clock. Decca recovered, but Julia died of pneumonia on 28th May.

The grieving couple – 'like people battered into semi-consciousness in a vicious street fight,' wrote Decca – fled to Corsica the day after the funeral, and thereafter to America. There they rebuilt their lives and lived happily, working in New York and then in a bar in Miami. When war broke out in Europe, they followed the news closely. When Neville Chamberlain resigned as prime minister in October 1940, Esmond and Decca felt certain that Britain would no longer try to appease the Nazi government in Germany. At that point, Esmond signed up to volunteer for the Royal Canadian Air Force, in the knowledge that he would be engaging in a war against fascism.

On 9th February 1941 their second daughter was born – a healthy baby, Constancia, known to all as Dinky. Decca and Esmond had been separated while he trained in Canada, and they were even further apart when, as a pilot officer, he flew nightly raids over Europe while his wife and child remained in Washington, where they had moved from Miami. Decca nearly flew back to England with the baby to see him in the summer of 1941, but the plan was put on hold when she miscarried her third pregnancy. Finally, on 1st December, after they hadn't seen each other for six months, Decca cabled her husband to tell him that she and Dinky would be leaving in a few days to sail to England: *Leaving Friday so terrifically excited darling.*

On 2nd December, Decca received a telegram herself, but it was not the reply from Esmond that she had been expecting. It was from the War Office: *Mrs E. M. Romilly . . . Regret to inform . . . that your husband pilot officer Esmond Mark David Romilly missing on active service 30 November stop letter follows.*

An anguished Decca was desperate to believe that Esmond had been captured as a prisoner of war. It was another two weeks before she received the fatal blow, from Decca's cousin and Esmond's uncle, Winston Churchill. As prime minister, he investigated the incident personally. Churchill told Decca that Esmond's aeroplane had left the base at 4.45 p.m., one of nine planes on a raid of Hamburg. His last bearings were confirmed to be about 110 miles east of the Yorkshire coast, over the North Sea, after he had sent a message to say he had low oil pressure in the port engine and was heading home. He had sent an SOS signal, but contact with him could not be made.

The following morning, thick fog prevented any search until noon, when three air-sea rescue aircraft set off to search in the remaining daylight hours in a sea that was cold and choppy. There was more fog in the days that followed, forcing the rescue operation to be abandoned.

Esmond's body was never recovered. His plane had vanished.

WHO'S WHO IN 1937

The parents: Lord and Lady Redesdale (David and Sydney Mitford)

Their daughters, in order of age:

Nancy Mitford (b.1904) (Mrs Peter Rodd)
Pamela Mitford (b.1907) (Mrs Derek Jackson)
Tom Mitford (b.1909)
Diana Mitford (b.1910) (Mrs Bryan Guinness then, after 1936, Lady Mosley, but her marriage to Sir Oswald Mosley remained a secret until 1938)
Unity Mitford (b.1914)
Jessica Mitford (b.1917), known as Decca
Deborah Mitford (b.1920), known as Debo

Also of note in the family:

Lord Redesdale's aunt on his father's side was Lady Blanche Hozier, known as Aunt Natty. She had three children: a daughter, Clementine, who married Winston Churchill; a second daughter, Nellie, who was the mother of Esmond and Giles Romilly; and a son, Bill, who died by suicide in 1921.

HISTORICAL NOTES

WARNING: CONTAINS SPOILERS!

In some ways, it's a strange task to put together this combination of fact and fiction, and never have I felt it more strongly than with this book. Jessica Mitford was an accomplished writer, and wrote a memoir of her own childhood and marriage to Esmond, *Hons and Rebels*. If you would like to read her version of her history – her sisters did not agree with all parts of it – it is a funny and entertaining book, moving in parts. I recommend it.

So why did I write this?

I think there is value in attracting people to history with an enticing charm, as it were. Nothing makes me happier than when readers tell me that these novels have sent them diving off into the history books 'to find out more'. I believe that we need the lessons of the past to help us steer our futures, especially now, when the parallels between our 21st-century world and the between-the-wars era are so acute. In putting the Mitfords into fictional situations and seeing how they might have reacted, we can indulge in an exercise of testing our own mettle: how might we have fared in the same circumstances? Because those circumstances may well yet appear again.

I try to pin as much as possible on genuine historical events, but remind the reader here that all conversations are figments of my imagination, as are several of the characters, including Bernard Plum – there was no attempt made on Esmond's life, nor did he and Decca aid the escape of three women.

A few facts follow, simply because I think it is interesting to see which elements of the novel are rooted in history: quite often, it's the more unexpected elements of the story.

Decca and Esmond did indeed meet at the house of 'Aunt Dorothy', Mrs Allhusen – Havering House near Marlborough. Esmond had been told by his brother, Giles, that Decca had been enquiring after him and that she wished to go to Spain to fight. Jessica Mitford has written that, even before she met her cousin, she was 'half in love' with him. Esmond suggested to Dorothy that Decca might make an interesting houseguest. Mrs Allhusen had unofficially adopted Esmond after his mother had told a court that she could not control him, and there was a threat of his being sent to a remand home; Dorothy had offered to be his guardian.

During the aforementioned weekend, Decca and Esmond fell in love; their love was enough to make her risk losing her entire family for him. But as Mary Lovell says in *The Mitford Girls*, running away from home with Esmond Romilly was all Decca's dreams come true.

Decca could not have known it at the time, but when her father, Lord Redesdale, came to the station on 7th February 1937 to wave her off and wish her an enjoyable holiday, it was the last time she would ever see him. The two were never reconciled. Twenty years later, he cut her out of his will. And yet, Laura Thompson wrote in *The Six* that, a few years after she left, Unity asked him 'in her direct way whom her father would most like to see walk into the room, he answered instantly: "Decca".'

The battle of Cable Street happened on Sunday 4th October 1936. It was a rally of the British Union of Fascists, led by Sir Oswald Mosley. He was dressed, as were several of the leading members of the party, in black shirts, military-style jackets and Sam Browne belts; many people felt they were emulating the look of SS officers in the Nazi party. The march of men and women, somewhere between two and three thousand of them, was held in the East End of London, where there was a large Jewish population. Anti-fascist protestors gathered – some say as many as twenty thousand. Six thousand police officers were deployed to protect the BUF march. The anti-fascists built road blocks, using a lorry to cordon off the end of Cable Street. The fascists retreated, and a bloody battle ensued between the anti-fascist protestors and the police. It led, ultimately, to the Public Order Act of 1936, which banned the use of military-style uniforms in such gatherings.

It is also widely understood that many people were there that day, particularly the anti-fascist supporters, who were compelled to volunteer to fight in the Spanish civil war. Around two thousand British citizens signed up to serve with the Republican army, the government that was defending itself against Nationalist forces led by army generals including Franco. The Nationalists were supported and given military aid by Hitler and Mussolini, while the British and French governments, supported by the League of

Nations, held a 'non-interventionist' policy. This meant that the Republican government found it difficult to buy arms, finding some only in limited supply from Russia and Mexico.

The British citizens who signed up to fight with the International Brigades included some notable literary figures: W. H. Auden, George Orwell and Stephen Spender. The American writer Ernest Hemingway famously joined them, too. The organisation 'British Medical Aid' was founded, which raised funds and opened two frontline hospitals in Spain; British doctors and nurses went to work in them, though they were notoriously hard places. Many other volunteers went to drive lorries and ambulances.

A handful of British fascists also went to Spain, along with others from France, Russia and Ireland. Numbering around a thousand altogether, they were reportedly not particularly welcomed by General Franco.

The Spanish civil war was long and bloody. It lasted from 17th July 1936 to 1st April 1939 and was seen by many as a precursor to the world war that was looming on the horizon. It is difficult to calculate the death toll because of the numbers of unregistered volunteers who went to fight, as well as the civilians who were caught in the cross-fire and buried in shallow graves, but it was certainly in the hundreds of thousands. Four thousand refugee children were evacuated to Britain. Most were returned to Spain by 1938, but others were dispersed to around a hundred children's homes in Britain.

The character of Donald Oliver was inspired by the real-life David Archer, who ran a bookshop at 4 Parton Street in Soho. It had portrait sketches on the ceiling and stocks of Communist literature. The shop also had its own printing press, and was Dylan Thomas's first publisher. The business was run on a philanthropic basis by David, also a former Wellingtonian, who struck up a friendship with Esmond after the young man visited his bookshop in his school holidays, having arranged to meet a Communist correspondent there.

The News Chronicle was a British daily newspaper that closed in 1960 when it was absorbed into the *Daily Mail*. It gave Esmond Romilly an advance of £10 to return to Spain in 1937 and be their war correspondent; the job offer was to enable him to get a visa. With Jessica acting as his 'secretary', she was able to get a visa too.

Diana and Sir Oswald Mosley were married on 6th October 1936 in the drawing room of Joseph Goebbels, the Nazi propaganda chief, with Adolf Hitler in attendance. The marriage was kept secret until the birth of their first child in 1938. This meant that Diana's family, and the world at large, believed she was 'living in sin' with Sir Oswald; the younger members of the family were forbidden to see her.

The history of domestic violence is long in anecdotal evidence, short in law. The term 'domestic violence' does not even appear in British legal phraseology until the mid-1970s. There are, however, some connections with divorce law. The Matrimonial Causes Act 1923 allowed either a husband or wife to petition for divorce on the basis of their spouse's adultery. Previously, a woman had to prove both adultery and cruelty. A further act in 1937 offered additional grounds for divorce: cruelty, desertion and incurable insanity.

But proving it was another matter. Police did not get involved in disputes between husbands and wives unless the threat of physical violence was imminent or actual; even then it was widely assumed by the general public for it to be near impossible for a wife to prosecute her husband. Until very recently, convicting someone of domestic violence meant charging them under common assault laws: controlling, coercive behaviour – whether emotional, psychological or physical – was only recognised by law in the UK in 2015.

Before records and databases were computerised, police forces did not share information easily. Someone who committed a crime in one part of the country would not easily be found out in another. It is only very recently – and partly down the efforts of eminent criminologist Clive Emsley – that there has been any kind of central record that shows where historical archives are held.

Tracking and monitoring the behaviour of someone who consistently demonstrates violence against women is still notoriously difficult, although there are signs that this is changing in policing. I took information about the pattern of common behaviours shown by a man exercising coercion that leads to homicide from *In Control* by Jane Monckton-Smith, who campaigns for more transparency and legal changes to enable such pattern tracking in policing. Her methodology is not without its detractors, but in a world where a quarter of women in all age groups suffer violence at the hands of an intimate partner,* we need to address changes – and solutions – without delay.

---

* The World Health Organization report studied data published between 2000 and 2018 in 161 countries.

ACKNOWLEDGEMENTS

With the greatest of thanks, as always, to the amazing team at Sphere: Ed Wood, Andy Hine, Stephanie Melrose, Laura Vile, Kate Hibbert, Helena Doree, Thalia Proctor, and of course Catherine Burke and Charlie King of Little, Brown. The UK team are well supported by Minotaur of St Martin's Press, especially Catherine Richards, Sarah Melnyk, Allison Ziegler and Nettie Finn.

Thank you to all the international publishing houses that have backed and supported this series, not least for generating readers, bloggers, Instagrammers and vocal fans. I love it when I hear from them.

Thank you to George Seatter for providing technical advice in this book.

Thank you to Federico Chiara of *Vogue Italia*, whose commissions for my short stories have allowed me to boldly trespass in creative directions I might not have otherwise dared to go.

I'm grateful to authors Laura Thompson (*The Six*), Max Arthur (*The Real Band of Brothers: First-hand accounts from the last British survivors of the Spanish Civil War*), Peter Sussman (editor of *Decca: The letters of Jessica Mitford*), Meredith Whitford (*Jessica Mitford: Churchill's rebel*) and Jane Monckton-Smith (*In Control: Dangerous relationships and how they end in murder*). Their books provided inspiration and knowledge. Any mistakes contained in this book are, of course, my own.

Finally, thank you to my family – Simon, Beatrix, Louis and George – who give me love, encouragement and lunch, just when I need it (on the understanding that the dogs get theirs first).

SELECT BIBLIOGRAPHY

The Real Band of Brothers: First-hand accounts from the last British survivors of the Spanish Civil War by Max Arthur (Collins, 2009)

The Mitford Girls by Mary S. Lovell (Little, Brown, 2002)

Hons and Rebels by Jessica Mitford (Phoenix, 1999)

In Control: Dangerous relationships and how they end in murder by Jane Monckton-Smith (Bloomsbury, 2021)

Decca: The letters of Jessica Mitford edited by Peter Y. Sussman (Weidenfeld & Nicolson, 2006)

The Six by Laura Thompson (Picador, 2017)

Jessica Mitford: Churchill's rebel by Meredith Whitford (Endeavour Press, 2013)

Turn the page for a sneak peek at
Jessica Fellowes's new novel

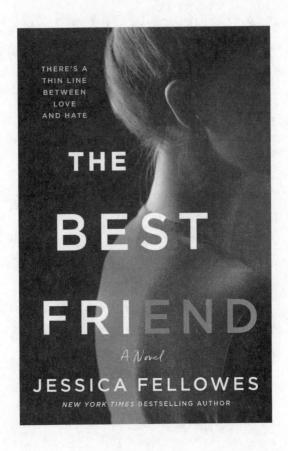

Available Now

Prologue

In her mother's studio, as the sun faded gently, Georgie rifled through the assortment of abandoned papers weighted down by a painted stone: old bills, postcards from long-forgotten friends, affectionate notes from her late stepfather. She stopped and read one or two old letters, put some things straight in the bin, others to the side to deal with later. But she stilled when she reached the photograph. The paper was curling at the edges, its shine and stiffness long gone. There was a white border and the image itself was lightly bleached, perhaps at one point it was in a frame and too much sun got to it. The picture was of two women standing close together, smiling, and though she couldn't see it, Georgie thought she could tell from their proximity, the angle of their bodies, that they were holding hands. They were of almost the same height, one slimmer than the other with dark hair, the other fair. The dark-haired woman was a touch blurred at the edges, as if she was laughing, unable to stay still long enough for the shutter of the old-fashioned camera. There was no one else in the picture, though someone had to be there taking it.

There was no indication that the women were interested in the photographer, though they were looking directly into the lens. Whatever was making them smile, even laugh, was only known to them.

Georgie stared at the photo for some time until she realized who it was.

History is black and white, she thought, but the past is all color.

Kate and Bella.

Bella and Kate.

Bella / Kate.

AGE SIX

Bella. *Bella.*

Yes?

What are you doing?

Drawing.

What are you drawing?

A rainbow.

Bella?

Yes?

Are you my best friend?

Yes.

Am I your best friend?

Yes.

Forever and ever?

Yes, Katie. Ever and ever.

AGE NINE

I will be the queen, and you can be the handsome prince.

No, Kate. I don't want to be a boy.

All right, then. You be my servant.

Yes, a norphan.

What's a norphan?

You know, somebody whose mummy and daddy has died.

That's An Orphan, not a "norphan." Silly.

Don't call me silly.

Are you an orphan, Bella?

No. My mummy is alive but she is very ill and special people have to look after her. My daddy went to heaven when I was in my mummy's tummy.

You never met him? You never even saw him?

No. Can we play the game now?

Yes, call me Queen Katherine.

All right, but I don't want to be Bella in the game. Call me Penny.

Penny?

Yes.

Penny, fetch me my crown—we are going to go and find me a handsome prince.

What about one for me too?

But you're a servant.

Yes, but I'm a norphan too. My dead mummy and daddy were a king and queen. I deserve a handsome prince too.

Penny, fetch me my crown—we are going to go and find *two* handsome princes.

OK.

I never heard a fairy tale with *two* handsome princes.

This is *our* fairy tale.

Sarah Weal

JESSICA FELLOWES is an author, journalist, and public speaker, best known for her official *New York Times* bestselling companion books to the *Downton Abbey* TV series. Former deputy editor of *Country Life* and columnist for *The Mail on Sunday*, she has written for *The Daily Telegraph*, *The Guardian*, *The Sunday Times*, and *The Lady*. Jessica has spoken at events across the United Kingdom and United States and has made numerous appearances on radio and television. She lives in Oxfordshire with her family.

Read all of the
MITFORD MURDERS SERIES
BY JESSICA FELLOWES

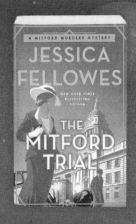

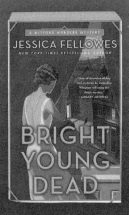

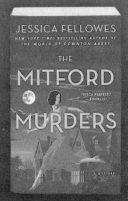

"A must-read series."
—Susan Hill, author of *The Woman in Black*